THE SWEET SCENT OF BLOOD

"The fast pace of the plot and the fascinating cast of characters will give you a happy little vacation between two covers."

—Charlaine Harris, #1 *New York Times* bestselling author of *Dead Reckoning*

"I loved it to pieces . . . a splendid first novel. Fast and furious, funny and fae, the first Spellcrackers book is a cracker of a read . . . damned good."

—Simon R. Green, *New York Times* bestselling author of *A Hard Day's Knight*

"I really loved *The Sweet Scent of Blood*. The interactions among the magical cast are beautifully handled, and Genny's narrative voice is perfect . . . all in all, a great read, and a great world which I'm looking forward to revisiting."

—Mike Carey, author of the Felix Castor novels

"This is a world where supernaturals . . . mingle freely with humans . . . Things get nicely atmospheric with touches of humor in the middle of massive misdirection, threats and bloodletting, with a sexy overlay of corsets, a satyr colleague, bondage and even a little girl-on-girl action . . . a fun read . . . This first novel [is] a standout."   —*Locus*

"A darkly comic spook show . . . This is funny, frothy and expertly set up."   —*Death Ray*

"McLeod does a fabulous job of detailing the setting and the supernatural characters that populate each scene. *The Sweet Scent of Blood* is intriguing and intense at times, with fast-paced action and dark discoveries around every turn."   —*Darque Reviews*

"Surprisingly assured and pleasingly engaging. Good fun . . . and nice to read a British-style Dresden or perhaps a Rachel Caine."   —sffworld.com

"From the opening passage, [McLeod's] characters jumped off the page and took the reader by the hand through a London that blended myth and legend with the modern world . . . a tale that will stay with the reader long after the final page is turned . . . The undead and the fae face off in a no-holds-barred tale. Definitely an author to watch."   —*Falcata Times*

Ace Books by Suzanne McLeod

THE SWEET SCENT OF BLOOD
THE COLD KISS OF DEATH

THE COLD KISS
OF DEATH

SUZANNE McLEOD

ACE BOOKS, NEW YORK

THE BERKLEY PUBLISHING GROUP
Published by the Penguin Group
Penguin Group (USA) Inc.
375 Hudson Street, New York, New York 10014, USA
Penguin Group (Canada), 90 Eglinton Avenue East, Suite 700, Toronto, Ontario M4P 2Y3, Canada
(a division of Pearson Penguin Canada Inc.)
Penguin Books Ltd., 80 Strand, London WC2R 0RL, England
Penguin Group Ireland, 25 St. Stephen's Green, Dublin 2, Ireland (a division of Penguin Books Ltd.)
Penguin Group (Australia), 250 Camberwell Road, Camberwell, Victoria 3124, Australia
(a division of Pearson Australia Group Pty. Ltd.)
Penguin Books India Pvt. Ltd., 11 Community Centre, Panchsheel Park, New Delhi—110 017, India
Penguin Group (NZ), 67 Apollo Drive, Rosedale, Auckland 0632, New Zealand
(a division of Pearson New Zealand Ltd.)
Penguin Books (South Africa) (Pty.) Ltd., 24 Sturdee Avenue, Rosebank, Johannesburg 2196,
South Africa

Penguin Books Ltd., Registered Offices: 80 Strand, London WC2R 0RL, England

This is a work of fiction. Names, characters, places, and incidents either are the product of the author's imagination or are used fictitiously, and any resemblance to actual persons, living or dead, business establishments, events, or locales is entirely coincidental. The publisher does not have any control over and does not assume any responsibility for author or third-party websites or their content.

THE COLD KISS OF DEATH

An Ace Book / published by arrangement with The Orion Publishing Group

PRINTING HISTORY
Gollancz hardcover edition / July 2009
Ace mass-market edition / May 2011

Copyright © 2009 by Suzanne McLeod.
Cover portrait photography by www.sorted.tv.
Cover design by www.nickcastledesign.com.
Interior text design by Kristin del Rosario.

For information, address: Gollancz,
an imprint of The Orion Publishing Group,
Orion House, 5 Upper St. Martin's Lane,
London WC2H 9EA, United Kingdom.

ISBN: 978-0-441-02039-3

ACE
Ace Books are published by The Berkley Publishing Group,
a division of Penguin Group (USA) Inc.,
375 Hudson Street, New York, New York 10014.
Ace and the "A" design are trademarks of Penguin Group (USA) Inc.

PRINTED IN THE UNITED STATES OF AMERICA

10 9 8 7 6 5 4 3 2 1

For Josh, Harry and Lillie
with love

Chapter One

The child stood barefoot and ignored in the cold, sheeting rain; her long dark hair was tossed by the fractious wind and her ragged clothes hung off her undernourished body. She was no more than eight or nine years old. She waited, staring at me from dark angry eyes. My heart beat faster at the sight of her, fingers of fear scraping down my spine and setting my teeth on edge. All around her people hurried across the wide expanse of cobbles towards the warm lights of Covent Garden, heading for the shelter of the glass-covered market with its shops, cafés, street entertainers and busy stalls. The late-October storm raging through London meant the witches were doing a roaring trade with their Body-Brolly spells, Dri-Feet Patches and Wind-Remedy Hairpins: twenty-first-century commerce at its most expedient. And none of the late-afternoon punters stopped to help the child. No one even noticed her, other than me.

But then the girl was a ghost.

Not many humans have the ability to see ghosts.

I'm sidhe fae. Seeing ghosts isn't a problem for me – at least not the seeing bit – but having a ghost decide to haunt me? Well, that had definitely become a dilemma ever since

Cosette had appeared a couple of weeks ago. I told myself again it was stupid to be afraid of ghosts – not when they couldn't physically hurt the living – and forced myself to ignore the irrational need to turn and run. Taking a deep breath, I continued jogging steadily towards her. As I neared, she held her hands out in supplication and opened her mouth wide, and the storm-winds shrieked and wailed as a surrogate for her silent scream.

I stopped in front of her and suppressed a shudder. 'Cosette, we really need to find a way to communicate,' I said, frustration almost edging out my fear. 'I want to help, but I can't if I don't know what's wrong.'

She grasped her shift and ripped it open. The three interlacing crescents carved, red raw and bleeding, into her thin chest didn't look any better than the last dozen times I'd seen them. The wounds weren't lethal – they weren't even recent; Cosette had been dead for at least a hundred and fifty years, judging by her clothes – but my gut twisted with anger that someone would do that to a child. The triple crescents were something to do with the moon goddess, but what they meant to Cosette, her death, or why she was haunting me, I was having trouble finding out. I'd asked around, done the in-depth internet trawl, spent a fruitless day in the witches' section at the British Library, hired a medium – and hadn't that been a waste of time and money – and got nowhere, so even Cosette's name was one I'd given her and not her true one. Next stop in my ghost-appeasing hunt might have to be a necromancer. And finding one of those wasn't going to be easy. Necros aren't the sort to advertise their services, not when commanding the dead – as opposed to just talking to them – is illegal . . . but both Cosette and I needed the break.

'I see it.' I stared at the bloody symbol and shivered as my wet hair dripped cold down the back of my neck. 'But I still don't know what you want me to do about it.'

Dropping her hands to her sides, she stamped a foot in silent annoyance. Then, as usual, she moved to peer around me as if she'd seen someone, flickered, and disappeared like a light popping out.

Nerves twitched down my spine as I thought that this time there would be someone – or some*thing* – creeping up behind me. I turned to check. The façade of St Paul's Church loomed blankly over me, a candle-like glow shining through its tall arched windows, the tall brass plaque on its false entranceway a dark rectangle against the sandstone. Goosebumps pricked my skin, the chill from my rain-soaked running shorts and vest adding fuel to my anxiety. Three Soulers – Protectors of the Soul – huddled together under the church's high over-hanging roof, the reproduction lantern above them throwing the red Crusader crosses on their long grey tabards into sharp relief. Briefly I wondered why the rain hadn't driven them to decamp into the Underground, their usual MO when faced with bad weather; no point trying to Protect Souls from the vamps, witches and anything magical – which included me and the rest of London's fae – when those souls weren't around to be preached at.

I put them out of my mind and scanned the church for any-thing that might have spooked Cosette. The gates to either side of the building gaped wide, leading into the shadowed garden beyond. I peered at a darker patch nearest to me and stretched out my inner senses—

'Well, if it isn't the sidhe sucker-slut,' a familiar voice sneered behind me. 'Bet she's waiting for her vampire pimp.'

I turned slowly, giving the woman a cool stare as I faced her. She stood smirking at me from under a huge black umbrella, her brown curly hair frizzing in the damp, the navy security uniform she was wearing bulging around her more than ample body, making her look like the Michelin Man. Ex-Police Constable Janet Sims. The 'ex' bit was her own fault – she'd had a crush on a colleague, a friend of mine, and her jealousy had led her to ignore procedure – and me, when I'd needed help – which was her choice, but of course, I was the one she blamed. Just my bad luck that after she'd been sacked, she'd got herself a job working for Covent Garden Security, and now she just happened to 'bump into me' on a daily basis.

'Nah, she's waiting for the paparazzi, aren't you?' Janet's blonde-bitch sidekick lifted her hands to camera-frame me with her fingers. 'Over here, Msssss Taylor,' she yelled, then pulled a mocking 'poor you' face. 'Only the paps have stopped coming round, *Genevieve*. You're yesterday's news now, and no one wants a sidhe sucker-slut round here, so why don't you take your orange catty eyes and run off to Sucker Town where you belong.'

Mentally I sighed; getting my picture on the front page with London's big-cheese vamp – now thankfully deceased – was causing me more problems than I could've imagined. Still, Janet and her sidekick were a small – if, thanks to that enormous brolly, annoyingly dry – problem, even if they now amused themselves by hunting for my metaphorical blood with almost more zeal than a vampire. So far I'd kept my patience, and practised turning a deaf ear, but . . .

'Well, I can't stand here chatting all evening.' I pushed my wet hair back from my face and added sweetly, 'I've got a hot date with a satyr to get ready for.' Sadly, the satyr was my boss and the hot date was work, but hey, you go with whatever you've got when faced with a pair of wannabe harpies. I smiled at them, enjoying the green-monster glow that leapt into their eyes, then turned and walked away, not listening as they muttered snidely behind me.

As I got to the corner, I glanced back and *focused* that part of me that can see the magic. Just as I'd suspected, an Eye-of-the-Storm spell cast a greasy slime over Janet's huge black umbrella and dripped fat globules down around the two women. For a moment I hesitated. All I had to do was cup my hand and *call* the spell; the wind would strip the huge monster of a brolly from Janet's grip and leave the pair of them screeching and scrambling like a pair of proverbial drowned rats in the storm. I curled my fingers into a tight fist and told myself not to crawl down to their level. Their jibes weren't worth it, nothing more than sticks and stones and all that. Of course, the bit about words not hurting was fine until the words came with magic attached to them – but Janet and her sidekick weren't witches, just witches' daughters. Their fathers had been human, not sidhe, and the two women might live in a world of magic, they might even catch glimpses of it, but they'd never able to use it. They'd had to buy the Eye-of-the-Storm spell, and any spell worth its salt wasn't cheap, as I knew only too well.

I laughed; a short mirthless snort. I might be sidhe, made of magic, but that didn't mean I could do much with it. Oh, I could *see* the stuff, even *call* or *crack* or *absorb* a spell, but no matter what I tried, my own spell-casting abilities had proved to be about as good as those of a witch's daughter. I didn't know why; just one of the magic's little ironies. Still, that particular magical difficulty was an old one; I had others much higher up the list, including whatever it was Cosette the ghost wanted.

I jogged towards my flat, wondering where the hell I was going to find a necro – other than, maybe, literally in hell?

Five minutes later and I was home and in the dry, or at least in the communal hallway; I still had five flights of stairs to climb. I placed my palm on the front door and the cobalt-blue of the Protection Ward shimmered up like a neon-fuelled heatwave in the dimness, then disappeared back into the framework as it activated. Taking my hand away, I breathed in the familiar scent of beeswax polish mixed with the more recent – and much less welcoming – additions of musty damp earth and garlic.

'Damn witches,' I muttered, wrinkling my nose at the smell.

I flicked the switch but as usual nothing happened; the bulbs in the light fitting hanging from the high Edwardian ceiling were still missing. The landlord, Mr Travers, was going through his shy phase. It didn't matter to my witch neighbours; they could all *conjure* bright-spheres. But while I've got orange 'catty eyes' – although personally I prefer to call them amber – my night vision isn't much better than my spell-casting abilities, so I had to rely on the streetlight filtering in through the stained-glass transom window above the front door. And it did nothing to relieve the deep shadows creeping up the stairs or to illuminate the tall, dark, unmoving shape on the first-floor landing above me.

My pulse hitching, I peered into the darkness, then sighed with jittery relief as I finally made out the thick handle and bound birch twigs of a defensive spell-broom. Damn witches again! Not only were they laying the garlic on a bit thick, but they also insisted on cluttering up the stairs. Still, at least it wasn't another ghost. I shuddered and grabbed the towel I'd stashed before my run and rubbed it over my damp face and hair. Toeing off my running shoes – Eligius, the goblin cleaner, isn't the type to appreciate wet footprints on his highly scrubbed black and white tiled floor – I pulled a dry sweatshirt over my head and felt the chill start to recede.

'Genny.' A deep bass voice made me jump. 'If I might have a word, please?'

Heart sinking, I pasted a smile on my face and turned to face my landlord. 'Of course, Mr Travers.' *So long as that word isn't eviction*, I added silently, looking up at the nearly eight-foot-tall mountain troll.

He was still doing his impression of the Incredible Hulk, except where the Hulk was green, Mr Travers was various shades of brown. A voluminous camel-coloured velvet sack-thing covered him from neck to ankle, leaving his lumpy brown and beige arms bare. The pale beige was his natural colour; the brown, misshapen lumps were baked-on earth that hadn't yet flaked away. He'd been happily stratifying in the basement – a counter-effort against the erosion from London's air pollution – when my neighbours had insisted he dig himself out to deal with their concerns. In other words, me.

'I'm sorry, but Witch Wilcox has complained again.' His forehead cracked into deep fissures as he frowned.

Witch Wilcox lived on the third floor, and was the most vociferous in her determination to have me evicted. Not only that, she was retired from the Witches' Council, so not someone who was easily ignored.

'I'm not sure I've done much to complain about,' I said, aiming for diplomacy.

'It's not about anything you've done as such, Genny,' he rumbled grumpily. 'Her granddaughter's come to stay with her for a while. Apparently the girl's just lost her job and her boyfriend both and is feeling a bit fragile. Witch Wilcox says she's not sure that having a sidhe fae living in the same building is a good idea in her granddaughter's current condition' – he leaned over and tapped the mailbox – 'particularly with all the mail the vampires keep sending you.'

What the—? Forget diplomacy! 'What does she think I'm going to do, drag her granddaughter off to a vamp club and force her into Getting Fanged just because the suckers are sending me a few letters?' I snorted. 'I mean, even if I did decide to do something so utterly stupid, her granddaughter's a witch, so no way would any licensed vamp premises let her past the door.'

'I know that, Genny, and so should she.' He scratched his arm furiously, causing little clods of dirt to fall onto the marble-tiled floor. 'I've tried reminding her about the old agreements, and that there isn't a vampire in Britain that would break them, but she doesn't want to listen.'

The agreements weren't just old but ancient, dating back to the fourteenth century, when the vamps and witches ended up in a mediaeval Mexican stand-off with a group of Church-sanctioned vigilante witch-hunters. The hunters' zero tolerance policy towards enchantments and sorcery didn't discriminate when it came to finding a likely perpetrator. Faced with a mutual enemy, the vamps and witches voted on survival and negotiated a live-and-let-live truce; one that's still in force today.

Of course, nowadays the witches like to forget who saved them from being tortured and crispy-fried at the stake, but the vamps have longer memories and longer lives – thanks to the Gift some of them had no doubt been there – as well as the whole my-word-is-my-honour thing going on. So witches, or anyone under their protection, which had included me until a couple of months ago, would be the last to end up as the wrong sort of guest at a vampire's dinner party. Unfortunately for me, it doesn't stop the witches being paranoid.

'I wanted to keep you informed, Genny.' Dust puffed from Mr Travers' head ridge in an anxious beige cloud. 'I really am sorry, you're a good tenant.' His brow ridges lowered in sympathy. 'But if she takes her complaints higher, well, it won't be up to me any more.'

'I know, it'll be up to the Witches' Council.' I patted his arm in a vague attempt to thank him, then wished I hadn't as I dislodged a large lump of dried mud, revealing a patch of raw, wet-looking skin beneath. The musty smell increased and I struggled not to cough. 'Let's hope the Council don't take her too seriously,' I added when I could.

'I'll be putting in a good word for you anyway, Genny.' He dug in the pocket of his sack dress and pulled out a paper bag, offering it to me in apology. 'Butter pebble?'

I took one, not wanting to be rude. 'Thanks.' I smiled, adding, 'I'll save it for later.' *Much* later, like never, seeing as I wasn't into breaking my teeth. 'And thanks for letting me know. I'll try and sort the mail problem.'

He briefly smiled back, his mouth splitting to show his own worn-down beige teeth. 'I've been thinking . . . um, actually, I was wanting to ask you something, Genny.' He paused and looked down, seeming embarrassed at the small pile of earth by his feet. 'Umm, that is if you don't mind?'

''Course not,' I said.

He nudged the earth with his slab-like toes. 'I was wondering about getting polished,' he rumbled quietly, his eyes flicking up to meet mine then back to the ground. 'I've heard a lot about it, but I wasn't sure if I was too old . . . but there's a party for Hallowe'en, and' – he held out his patchy arms – 'I can't go like this.'

'Er, I don't think—'

'I know the younger trolls do it,' he rushed on, his face cracking with worry, 'and some of the concrete ones, but I didn't want to look silly or anything. What do you think, is it a good thing or not? And I'm not sure if it will hurt; some of these new methods aren't always the best, are they?'

I blinked, not sure if I was qualified to give beauty tips to a troll; and I liked Mr Travers, no way did I want to give him the wrong advice. But the only troll I knew well was my friend, Hugh – Detective Sergeant Hugh Munro – and he was in the Cairngorms with his tribe, recuperating after being injured in the line of duty. Hugh was more of a traditionalist, but thinking of him . . . 'Well,' I said, frowning, 'I know a troll who's got himself polished, he works for the police, Constable Taegrin's his name.' And Constable Taegrin might possibly know where I could find a necro, so . . . . 'I could ring him and see if he'll talk to you about it, if you want?' I added.

'That would be great, thanks, Genny!' Mr Travers' face split in a relieved smile. 'I knew you were the best person to ask.' He held the bag out again. 'Another butter pebble?'

I accepted politely and he ambled almost silently away down the hall, mumbling about finding a dustpan and brush. Feeling slightly bemused, I tucked both sticky pebbles into a carrier bag, together with my wet shoes, then turned to contemplate the offending mailbox; my personal pigeon-hole was full as usual. No wonder Witch Wilcox was complaining.

The eerie theme tune from *Halloween* drifted tinnily through the hallway and it took me a second to realise it was my phone ringing. The ring-tone wasn't my choice, just an irritating consequence of my job working for Spellcrackers.com. I'd cleared out a gremlin crew from Tower Bridge and the critters had retaliated by springing a techno-hex on my phone. I'd been trying to *crack* the hex for over a week, never mind it was nearing All Hallows' Eve and sort of appropriate – having the phone run through a selection of horror film ring-tones was *so* not professional; it unsettled too many of the clients. I grabbed the phone from the back of my running shorts but my irritation turned to a grin as I checked the caller ID.

'Grace,' I said, then remembered why she was calling; my vamp-mail problem was worrying her, and while I loved her to bits for checking I was okay, neither of us needed the extra stress. I tried for a distraction. 'Don't suppose you know any necros, do you?'

'I'm a doctor, Genny, not an information service,' she said in her usual no-nonsense voice. 'Plus, I don't think a necro's going to help you if that medium didn't. I told you, wait until Hallowe'en; you'll be able to talk to your ghost then.'

Wrapping the towel round my shoulders, I shuddered. 'There is no way I'm spending *that* night in a churchyard. That'd be like asking you to stay in the same room as a spider.'

'Humph! Well as you keep telling me, spiders can't hurt anyone, and the same goes for ghosts. Plus it's a cheaper, quicker option than a necro,' she pointed out. 'Then again, HOPE is likely to be busy that night, so you might not have time to visit a churchyard.'

HOPE is the Human, Other and Preternatural Ethical Society's clinic. The clinic treats Vampire Venom and Virus infection, or 3V, to give it the more politically correct moniker, as well as anyone who falls foul of magic. Grace was one of the Speciality Registrars there – it was where we'd met and become friends – and she was right; Hallowe'en is always like half a dozen full moons wrapped up in one. All the loonies – human and Other – would be out, and HOPE would end up dealing with the fallout, in addition to more than its usual number of anxious humans wondering if Getting Fanged had been the *cool* choice after all.

'Don't tell me,' I said, hopping on one leg then the other as I pulled off my wet socks. 'I'm going to be asked to come in and work.'

'I don't think there's any asking involved,' she laughed. 'That new admin manager's got you and all the rest of the volunteers pencilled in on the rota.'

'That's because someone showed him the CCTV tape from last year.' I tucked the sodden socks into the carrier bag. 'The one where the Chelsea Witches' Coven are having hysterics 'cos their darling daughters thought it might be fun to go partying over in Sucker Town.'

Getting Fanged at one of the vamp celebrity clubs is safe enough – the only time the vamps go into the red is when it involves blood, not cold hard cash – so no one ends up with 3V from visiting them; just with the odd blood-loss hangover from overenthusiastic donating. But Sucker Town is a popular destination on All Hallows' Eve and the rules are different there. Vampires give trick or treat a whole new meaning.

'They were lucky the vamps gave them a wide berth and none of them got bitten, let alone infected,' Grace huffed. 'Stupid, irresponsible idiots. Let's hope the lecture they got about the downsides of 3V and G-Zav' – the venom-junkies' methadone – 'made an impression and we don't have a repeat this year.'

'Hope so,' I agreed wholeheartedly, having first-hand experience of those same 'downsides' myself since my fourteenth birthday – just over ten years ago now. Being dependent on G-Zav is *so* not a fun way to live but it beats the alternative of being some sucker's blood-slave.

Or at least I always thought it had.

Now I wasn't so sure.

'Anyway, apart from being rattled by your ghost,' Grace said cheerfully, interrupting my wavering thoughts, 'how's my favourite sidhe this wet and windy evening?'

I snorted. 'Given that I'm the only sidhe in London and the only one you know, your bedside manner sucks.'

'And talking of vampires?' Her voice rose with the question.

'None of the suckers jumped out at me, so I'm still here, still taking the tablets, and I've still got my requisite eight-plus pints of blood.'

'I can tell most of that by the fact you're on the phone,' she said drily.

I grinned. 'Your powers of deduction are second to none, Grace.'

'Now we've got past the rather excessive compliments,' she said with more than a touch of snark, 'let's get back to the vampires and how many invitations today.'

I poked at the invitations filling my mailbox and said, 'About the same,' hoping she would accept that. Trouble was, now that every vamp and their blood-pet knew about my 3V infection it made me an even more attractive meal ticket than before. So far, it was just invitations – ultra-polite requests for my company at various celebrity-studded functions, all sent in identical expensive cream envelopes – but the hard knot in my stomach told me it probably wouldn't be long before the vampires dispensed with the postal option and started delivering their 'invitations' in person. And didn't that give me something *fun* to look forward to.

'How many?' Grace asked, her voice as sharp as surgical steel.

Dogs and bones have nothing on Grace when she wants something, so I gave in. 'Hold on a min.' I slid the phone onto the mailbox and dug out the latest batch, squinting at them malevolently in the dim light. *Genevieve Taylor, Bean Sidhe*, was written across the top envelope in a bold, rust-red script. Holding the envelope to my nose, I sniffed, and the faint scent of liquorice and copper made my mouth water – the sender had mixed his or her blood into the ink – but then, the vampires don't miss a trick when it comes to self-promotion. Ignoring the annoying throb that the scent raised into life at the curve of my neck, I ran my finger over the envelope edges, counting, then picked up the phone. 'Nine today,' I said.

'Two more than yesterday!' I could hear the worried tap-tap of her pen in the background. 'That's not good.'

'Tell me about it,' I muttered. 'I feel like I've got this big sign round my neck: *Exclusive trophy sidhe ~ latest must-have accessory for those of the fanged persuasion* – next thing you know they'll be queuing round the block. That'd really make the witches throw their cauldrons out of their prams.'

Grace's sigh echoed down the phone. 'Talking of witches, have you heard yet if the Witches' Council are going to re-instate their protection?'

'I don't think I'm high on their list of priorities.' I dropped the invites on the top of the mailbox, thankful Grace couldn't see me cross my fingers at the evasion.

'But it's been ages, they should have been able—' I winced as she went on accusingly, 'You haven't asked them, have you? Why not, Genny? And please don't tell me it's some obscure faerie pride thing.'

'It's nothing to do with pride, Grace.' I picked at a loose thread on the towel, pulling it as it unravelled. 'There's just no point, that's all. You know the only reason the witches gave me back my job at Spellcrackers was because of the Mr Octo-ber murder fiasco. And it's not just the job, but my flat too.' No way could I live in Covent Garden without the Council's permission. 'I'd really be pushing my luck if I asked for any-thing more.' Never mind the witches were probably going to succeed in getting me evicted anyway at this rate . . . but I kept that to myself.

'I still think you should ask, Genny,' she said. 'It would put a stop to your stupid idea about coming to some sort of arrangement with that vampire—' The sound of her office phone ringing interrupted her and she said hurriedly, 'Gotta go, love you.'

Feeling guilty relief at not having to rehash the next part of the conversation, I tucked the phone away and pursed my lips at the pile of invitations. I turned the top envelope over; the red wax seal on the back was impressed with the shape of a clover leaf. That told me it was from Declan, master vam-pire of the Red Shamrock blood, one of London's four blood families. The conniving Irish bastard *so* didn't know when to quit. Quickly I checked the seals on all the rest, but the one I was half-dreading, half-hoping for, the one from the vampire I wanted to 'come to an arrangement' with, still wasn't there.

Malik al-Khan.

Nearly a month since he'd last put in an appearance.

I was beginning to wonder if he ever would.

And if he didn't, then all my 'conversations' with Grace about 'arranging' to solve my 3V problem the vampire way instead of the medical one would be for nothing. Malik was the only possibility; I didn't trust any of the others. Not that I really trusted Malik, but . . .

I ripped the envelopes in half, pulled open the junk mail bin under the mailboxes and shoved them in, then slammed the door shut.

My only wish was that I could dispose of the vamps themselves as easily.

I closed my eyes and massaged my temples, trying to ease my ever-present headache; popping G-Zav tablets like they were sweeties might be keeping a precarious lid on my venom cravings, but the side-effects were about as pleasant as being roasted alive over a dwarf's furnace. Sighing, I put the towel in the carrier bag with my socks and shoes, then headed for the stairs, the pervasive smell of garlic increasing as I climbed.

The real puzzle was why some enterprising vamp hadn't just gone straight for the caveman thing, knocking me over the head and dragging me off by my short sidhe hair. Of course, it's illegal for a vamp to use any form of coercion – physical or psychological – without their *victim's* consent (not that vamps have victims any more, now they're called *customers*, a.k.a. fang-fans). And the vamps are good at playing the law-abiding game, so the last time one of them won a one-way trip to the guillotine for unlicensed feeding was back in the early eighties.

But the humans don't think we fae need the same protection as humans, not when the vamps can't mind-lock us or trick us with their *mesma* unless they'd infected us, and not when we're often seen as more dangerous than the once-human vampires. Then there's the fact that we fae are even more of a minority than the blood-suckers; a minority that's not as politically aware and not always as pretty. So it's not surprising we get a less-than-fair hearing when it comes to human justice.

Or that we end up as fair game for the vamps.

What we really needed was a great public relations manager. Idly I wondered if the one that had kick-started the vamps' Gold-Plated Coffin promotion was still around. Not that I had the money to pay for a no-expenses-spared PR campaign. I could only just afford my rent, and that was *with* the subsidy I got from working for a witch company.

I stepped onto the third-floor landing and the garlic stench almost overpowered me. I stopped to cough, glaring at Witch Wilcox's door. Of course, I wouldn't need the subsidy if she succeeded in getting me evicted.

'Ow!' Something stung my bare calf. I hopped and slapped at my leg, then *looked* at her door.

Crap. It wasn't just the garlic she'd laid on a bit thick; she'd added to the Vamp Back-Off spell sprayed on her door and the magic now spread over the landing like an enormous sea anemone, its deep purple body fanning out into a multitude of paler violet-coloured fronds that rippled through the air and circled a dark hole that looked disturbingly like a gaping mouth.

'That's different,' I muttered in amazement. The thing looked more like a trap than a vamp deterrent, and my calf was throbbing like someone had branded it with a red-hot poker. Whatever the spell was, no way did I want to tangle with it.

Carefully, I inched my way along the landing, keeping my back tight against the wall. As I moved, the fronds shifted, questing towards me as if they'd caught my scent. I breathed in sharply as one whipped past my stomach and ducked as another narrowly missed slashing across my cheek, the eye-watering smell of garlic and bleach trailing behind it. Then as three more of the lethal fronds flailed after me, I turned and bolted for the stairs, carrier bag clutched under my arm. I jumped, yelping, as the spell stung the back of my neck, then as I almost missed the steps, I managed to grab for the banister and safety.

I sat down heavily on the stair, breathing shakily as I checked the welt on my calf; the skin wasn't broken, it was just swollen, red and painful. Gingerly, I touched the back of my neck. It felt the same. What the hell was the daft old witch doing, *casting* . . . whatever that anemone thing was? It seemed excessive, even with her paranoia about her beloved granddaughter – never mind the fact that even if a vamp managed to bypass the Ward on the building's main door, none of them could pass over her threshold; unless of course she was stupid enough to invite them in. I glowered down at the spell. The fronds were undulating lazily now, but I got the impression they were just watching and waiting.

'It would serve the old witch right if I *cracked* her spell,' I grumbled, rubbing my sore leg. Trouble was, true *spellcracking* blasted the magic back into the ether, which made for a quick clear-up – except the *cracking* also blasted apart whatever the spell happened to be attached to. Somehow I didn't think I'd get away with turning the witch's door into a pile of jagged splinters. I could always tease it apart, the safer, if more laborious, way of dismantling spells, but that would take more time than I was willing to spare. And she'd just replace it anyway.

Damn. I thought about saying something to Mr Travers, but the garlic meant the spell was somehow tagged for vampires – not that eating garlic will stop a vamp from getting the munchies; some of them actually like the added flavour. Mind you, smearing a bulb or two over the pulse points might make them think seriously about dining elsewhere, as would chilli: red swollen lips are bad for the image, never mind the pain. Of course, the garlic smearing only works if the vamp's brain is still engaged and they're not lost in bloodlust. Not much stops a vamp then.

I had no idea why the bleach was in there – maybe it just made a handy, albeit nasty base. But whatever the reason, the old witch's Anemone spell was the business.

And then there was my problem with actually complaining: how was I supposed to explain why magic aimed squarely at blood-suckers was taking its ire out on me? Somehow I doubted that my 3V condition would be enough, never mind it was easy to disprove. And letting everyone in on the real reason – my last secret – would mean not just eviction, but losing my job too. No, there was no way I could complain, not when it meant admitting my father was a three-hundred-year-old vampire.

My phone broke into my musings with something that sounded suspiciously like the theme from *A Nightmare on Elm Street*. Damn gremlins! I checked the display to see a message from Grace; she was coming round after her shift

ended. I texted her back to say I was working and to let herself
in, then as I caught sight of the time, everything, gremlins,
ghosts, witches and blood-sucking vampires, went out of my
mind. I had a job to go to; my 'hot date with a satyr' or rather,
my boss, Finn, and if I didn't hurry up I was going to be late.

Then my 'date' would be 'hot' for all the wrong reasons.

Chapter Two

My 'date' *was* hot; nothing to do with Finn, my boss, but entirely thanks to the gas-fired heaters in the underground tunnel. The air they blasted out was enough to raise the temperature to a level that only a fire-dragon would appreciate. But I could cope with the heat; it was the ghost part of the job that had sweat slicking down my spine.

The hairs on the back of my neck rose as another ghost shuffled into view, his bloated, blackened feet scuffing along the dirt floor, sending little puffs of dust into the still air. A deep cut marred his left cheek; the bone it revealed was white and glistening. His eyes stared blankly out of sunken sockets and the end of his nose was eaten away by a huge black sore. He headed straight towards us and I counted the seconds down – *three, two, one* – then winced, half in sympathy, half in teeth-gritted anxiety, as he hit the wall of the protective circle in which Finn and I sat. The ghost's lipless mouth flattened against the magic while his skeletal hands scrabbled for purchase not more than four feet in front of me. I suppressed a shudder, shifting nervously in my deckchair as he slid his way round the circle until he was back on route and shambling off on his way.

Sighing with relief, I touched my laptop keypad and entered the time against the ghost's name – Scarface – on the spreadsheet, then duplicated the info on my pad, just in case. The laptop might have an extra-strength Buffer spell in the crystal stuck to its case, but I wasn't taking any chances. All it needed was a stray bit of magic and I'd end up with one *cracked* crystal, one dead hard drive and an irretrievable ghost survey.

I tapped my pencil on my pad and wondered for about the hundredth time what I'd done to deserve a night sitting under London Bridge counting ghosts, especially after my frustrating run-in with Cosette. And not just any ghosts, but the ghosts of fourteenth-century plague victims. My phobia's bad enough when the dead look relatively normal, without adding in all the stomach-roiling stuff. Not to mention we were camped out deep in the bridge's foundations in the area known as the tombs – right on top of the plague victims' burial pits.

Could my night get any worse?

'That's the fifth time he's done that,' I said, drawing a little Edvard Munch face, mouth wide open in a scream. 'I was sort of hoping he'd catch on that there was something in his way by now.'

Finn looked up absently from the book he was reading – a history of London Bridge – and my heart did its usual stupid leap inside my chest. I gave it my standard lecture. Sure, Finn looked great; his handsome, clean-cut features always had plenty of females – and not a few males – drooling, never mind the broad shoulders and honed muscles that stretched his old navy T-shirt. Even his bracken-coloured horns that stood an inch or so above his hair and marked him as a satyr just added to him being a gorgeous hunk of male. But it was just a look. He was wearing his usual Glamour, one that made him appear more human, so even in his snug, washed-out jeans there was no hint of his sleek furred thighs, or the tail I knew he had. *It's just a look, nothing to get worked up about.* Yeah, and I didn't believe myself either. Not that his true form was any less gorgeous, just different – wilder, more feral. But his Glamour made things easier when dealing with humans. A bit of Otherness is tolerable, even sought after, but show too many differences between our species and monsters like prejudice and bigotry raise their ugly heads and the humans start reaching for their not-so-metaphorical pitchforks.

Damn, running into bitchy witches' daughters and tangling with paranoid neighbours was turning me into a pessimist.

'Who's done what?' Finn asked, a faint line creasing between his brows.

I sighed. Or maybe it was spending time with a hot satyr who didn't seem to notice me any more. Previously he'd asked me out often enough that I'd wished he'd stop. Oh, not that I hadn't wanted to say yes – maybe not for Happy Ever After, but I'd definitely wanted a chance at Happy for Now with him – but keeping my secrets meant I'd always said no. Then the Mr October thing happened. Finn had been determined to play the white knight, and in a desperate attempt to scare him off and end his sacrificial tendencies, I'd told him that saving me from the vamps was really a moot point seeing as my father was one, and my ending up back with the suckers was probably inevitable. He'd gone quiet at my confession, an expected but still painful rejection, then in the end we'd both sort of saved each other and ourselves. But afterwards, when I'd been sure I'd lose everything now he knew – my job, my home and most of my friends – he'd kept my secret, and done some smart talking for me with the Witches' Council. But as for any sort of relationship other than work, knowing about *that* half of my parentage seemed to have been the kiss of death. Not that I didn't understand why.

The old adage of being careful what you *wish* for was never so true.

Or so disheartening.

'Gen, who's done what?' Finn repeated the question, his moss-green eyes losing their vagueness.

'Scarface just passed by.' I pointed my pencil at the ghost disappearing into the distance down the tunnel nearest to Finn, one of a row that led off at right angles from the one we were in, areas between the foundation supports once used for storage, until they'd started to dig the place up and turn it into a tourist exhibition. We sat at one of the T-junctions facing each other, watching for ghosts from all directions. 'He bumped into the circle again,' I added, pleased my voice came out steady.

Finn cast a professional eye over the eight-foot circle. He'd *drawn* it – literally and magically – in the clearest part of the site, using salt for binding, shredded yew to keep out the dead and sage for clarity and protection. When I *looked* I could see it enclosing us like a huge bubble – not a comforting thought when bony fingers kept poking at it.

'Hell's thorns, Gen, the circle's fine,' he said, pushing a hand through his dark blond hair and scratching behind his left horn in faint exasperation. 'It'll take more than a couple of knocks from a ghost to break.'

'Yeah, I know.' I lifted up the laptop to give my jeans a chance to cool down and balanced it on the chair's frame. It wasn't just the circle, though; I felt like I wanted to warn Scarface or something, tell him to walk round the side.

Finn gave me a reassuring smile, teeth white against his tanned skin. 'I know you're worried, but just try and relax, okay?'

'Sure,' I agreed, and he went back to his reading.

Except relaxing wasn't an option, not with the sweat still itching down my spine. So instead I stared down the brightly lit tunnels, watching for the next ghostly spectre, telling myself yet again it was irrational to be scared. Scarface was just a soul-memory trapped by a traumatic death, stuck on replay like a faulty DVD, nothing more. If he'd ever felt anything like fear or panic, or wanted anything from the living, those feelings were long gone. I flashed back to Cosette waiting for me in the rain. Despite her wounds, she was angry, not frightened or distressed. Damn, I really needed to find out what she wanted. My phone call to Constable Taegrin had been a part success; he'd been happy to chat to Mr Travers about polishing tips, but his voice had turned disapproving when I'd mentioned my ghost problem and asked about necromancers. He'd not refused outright, but I wasn't pinning my hopes on him. I thought about asking Finn if he knew any necros, then decided against it. Cosette wasn't work, and Finn was snowed under seeing as he'd only recently taken over the franchise and become the boss for real. The laptop flipped over to the screensaver – **Spellcrackers.com** ~ *Making Magic Safe* – and, tired of balancing it on the chair, I leaned over to settle it on my backpack.

'Here, let me.' Finn reached out to help and his fingers

touched mine. Green and gold magic – his and mine – flashed where our skin met like excited sparklers going off.

I froze. The magic was doing its usual, urging us to get together like we were the last two fae in the world. And even though I knew it wasn't going to happen . . . a foolish hope still surfaced that this time he might say something, anything other than—

'Sorry,' he murmured, carefully removing his hands from mine and letting go of the laptop.

The magic fizzled away into nothing.

'No probs,' I said readily, making sure I kept the disappointment out of my voice and carefully placing the laptop on my backpack.

He settled back in his chair and concentrated on his book.

I tried to settle back in mine, and decided that focusing on the ghosts was marginally better than angsting over might-have-beens, so I checked out the spreadsheet for who was next. Posy. Right on time, the hairs on the back of my neck rose and Posy – a dirty bandage hiding most of her face, the hem of her skirt in rags – ambled by clutching a withered bunch of flowers. I marked her details on the pad and tapped them into the laptop, fingers trembling slightly. Something about this ghost job had me spooked – even without the bad pun – and not just because of my phobia. But when I'd mentioned my vague suspicions to Finn, he'd dismissed them.

Chewing the end of my pencil, I scanned the underground site again. Bare bulbs in their yellow hanging cages lit the place brighter than the midday sun, even though it was past midnight. The bright lights didn't make me feel any better: they cast weird shadows over the abandoned builders' tools, turning them into hiding places full of staring eyes, watching. Thick cobwebs stretched across the arched brick roof and damp stained the walls with algae-slimed patches. And it smelled old and musty, with an underlying whiff of putrefying flesh – a smell Finn had assured me existed only in my overactive imagination, not that his assurances made the smell go away. The place was creepy enough even without the steady stream of ghosts drifting by. Finally my gaze skittered over the more modern breezeblock wall blocking the River Thames end of the tunnel and landed on the cordoned-off area in one corner.

An avalanche of grey human bones spilled out over the floor. The very bones I'd been trying to ignore all night, especially as I had an odd notion that they kept whispering my name.

'Tell me why we're here again?' I asked, more to shut the whispers out than anything else.

Finn briefly looked up, a flash of irritation crossing his face. Hell, irritated was better than half-heard whispers, so I prodded a bit more. 'I mean, they're developing this as part of the tourist attraction and they want the ghosts to hang around to add to the spooky ambience, but apparently something is frightening them off.' I could sympathise with how they felt right now even if I didn't like them. 'What I don't understand is, why hire Spellcrackers? I mean, we find magic and break or neutralise spells, right? And ghosts are nothing to do with magic, so why doesn't Mr Developer just get a medium down here to check them out?'

'I told you, he doesn't want that, Gen,' Finn said, smoothing out a page. 'He's worried that any contact might disturb the ghosts even more. He just wants them watched, to see if we can discover why they're disappearing.'

Happy Head limped past, half his skull missing, a vacant smile on his face, his body transparent as a reflection in a glass window. Suppressing another shudder, I leaned over, tapped the laptop and keyed in his info. The ghosts were all following the same pattern, each one appearing so many minutes after the previous and almost at the same moment in every hour. So far all the ones we'd surveyed appeared to be turning up on cue. Of course, the place was as quiet as the proverbial grave just now.

'How does he know they're taking off for wherever anyway?' I dug the heels of my boots into the dirt. 'I mean, all the workers are human, aren't they? So they can't see ghosts.'

'He says the builders have noticed a difference – a change in the atmosphere, fewer of the usual chills that humans get when they're around ghosts.'

'Maybe it's the builders themselves who are causing all the problems.' I drew a hammer hitting the top of the Scream-face's head.

Finn mumbled something unintelligible and turned another page.

I subsided into silence, frowning at him from under my lashes. Definitely something not right, but what? I *looked*, but other than the circle – now faintly glimmering with green and gold – and a vague ash-like haze over the pile of old bones near the blocked-off wall, that wasn't so much magic as maybe the remnants of a ghost, there was nothing. I couldn't even see Finn's Glamour, but then he'd obviously worn it long enough it was part of him now. I doodled, plucking at my T-shirt where it was sticking to me with the heat, as I tried to pinpoint my unease.

Finn flicked his fingers and a bottle of water appeared in his hand. He held it out to me. 'Want some?'

'Thanks,' I said as I took it, careful not to let our fingers touch; the bottle was ice-cold, straight out of his fridge at home. Brownie magic's a wonderful thing, if you're able to use it, which unfortunately I'm not. I took a grateful, cooling drink as he flicked his fingers again to *call* another bottle for himself.

'Here comes another one,' he said, pointing with the bottle. 'Lamp Lady.'

Goosebumps pricking my skin, I watched from the corner of my eye as she came into view and slunk past, hugging the wall, her shawl pulled tight over her head, the full skirts of her blood-splattered gown dragging a wide swathe in the dusty floor. As she passed each hanging light, it flickered and hissed out, then sparked back to life as soon as she reached the next. It'd been the same routine every time she'd appeared.

I put the water down, and tapped away at the laptop, then backed up her details on the pad, frowning as my doubts about the job started to click together in my mind. I stared at the little figures I'd been drawing. A horned man on a horse – okay, so it looked more like a monkey riding a pot-bellied pig – but I finally realised what my subconscious was trying to tell me, where my *unease* was coming from. It wasn't so much the job, but Finn and his attitude. He was doing his usual white knight act again. Damn, I was usually quicker than this at catching on.

'Y'know,' I said thoughtfully once Lamp Lady was out of sight, 'I think this job is one of those wild goose chase things.'

Finn didn't look up, which sort of confirmed my suspicions. 'How do you work that one out?'

'Well, the ghosts have all been down here for so long, they're stuck. They're all following exactly the same pattern, right down to the exact second they appear, one after the other.' I tapped my pencil. 'They're used to the place being creepy, and even bumping into the circle, Scarface still keeps to his routine. So I don't see how there's anything that would disturb them.'

'Gen, we're being paid to do the job, and at night rates too.' He said that as if it should have been enough of an answer.

'Uh-huh. So why doesn't Developer Guy want anyone here during the day time?'

'Because he wants it all done on the quiet.' He turned another page. 'Doesn't want any bad publicity.'

'Bad publicity!' I snorted. 'A tale of ghosts disappearing wouldn't be bad publicity; it would be a whole lot of great free publicity.'

He didn't answer me, just unscrewed his water bottle and tipped it up. I waited until he'd finished, trying not to stare at the way his throat worked as he swallowed, then said, 'C'mon, Finn, what's this job really all about? Because no way does it look like any of the ghosts are dong the vanishing act.'

He sighed in resignation and closed his book. 'The job's as described, Gen. I even talked to a couple of the workers. It all sounds like a normal run-of-the-mill haunting. You know, chill spots, figures seen out of the corner of the eye, invisible touches, the odd smells—'

'Hah, putrefying flesh, right?' I gave him a told-you-so look.

'Yeah well' – he half smiled – 'the ghosts disappearing is probably just the builders getting used to them, sort of like white noise. And I told him that, suggested he didn't waste his money, but he insisted he wanted it all checked out.' He shrugged, aiming for nonchalance and not quite managing it. 'Once I give him the results, that'll be the end of it.'

'And that's it, nothing else?' I asked.

'I know you're nervous about the ghosts, Gen, but there's nothing to worry about, really.'

'Then why are you being evasive?'

'Leave it, Gen.' He gave me an unhappy look. 'It's not important, okay?'

'Fine, so I'll tell you then. Mr Developer asked for me to do the job. He probably got snippy when you said I couldn't do it on my own and offered to provide his own security or something. Probably even said he'd supervise it himself, didn't he?'

'Something like that,' Finn muttered, flicking his fingers and making his empty bottle disappear.

'Damn, I should've known. It's one of those pseudo-job things. The guy's got all curious about the sidhe sex myth, how we're all supposed to be gagging for it.' The jobs had got more frequent since the internet video of me kissing a vampire had surfaced; the girl-on-girl aspect of it seemed to be adding fuel to the fantasies. Of course, if any of those oh-so-curious humans had bothered to read up on the myth they might not be quite so enthusiastic. The myth had survived from back when the world was closer to nature. The fae held the fertility rites to replenish the land and encourage its fecundity. And yes, there was a lot of sex involved, but it was only on specific dates, not a free-for-all thing as most of them seemed to imagine.

'You should have told me, Finn,' I carried on. 'You can't keep doing your usual and trying to protect me. I can look after myself, you know. I've been doing it for long enough.'

'Gen, I'm your boss, and I wouldn't be a very good one if I let you walk into a situation where I knew you'd be at risk.' He leaned towards me, forearms resting on his thighs, earnest. 'All it needs is one human to get angry at being disappointed and then complain to the police that you tried to Glamour him. You'd end up being arrested and maybe even convicted. Is that what you want?'

Not when conviction meant the guillotine, fuck no! But— 'That's not what I mean, Finn. It's not that I don't appreciate the back-up, or the thought. But if I know a job's iffy, I can deal with it. It's you keeping me in the dark that gets me all annoyed.'

He snorted. 'Well that's the pot calling the kettle black, isn't it?'

'And what the hell is that supposed to mean?' I snapped.

'C'mon, Gen, the suckers are sending you sackloads of mail, one of your neighbours is trying to evict you. And now I've heard you've got a ghost a-haunting you. But whenever

I ask you if everything is okay, you nod and say yes, every-thing's fine.'

'That's because they're not work problems, Finn, they're my personal life.'

'Hell's thorns! What, so now I'm your boss I'm not sup-posed to care about what goes on in your life?' Angry emerald chips glinted in his eyes. 'I want to help you, only you won't let me!'

'Why, Finn?' I said, confused at his anger. 'Why do you want to help me?'

'Because we're friends, Gen, and that's what friends do.'

I dropped my pencil and slapped my hands round his; sparks exploded again as the magic reacted. 'If we're friends, Finn, why are you ignoring this, why are you pretending there's nothing going on between us? Until everything hap-pened you were keen enough to explore it—'

'This isn't about that, Gen.' He pulled his hands away, frustration and some other emotion I didn't recognise darken-ing his eyes. 'You need to stay away from the suckers, and the invitations need to stop. At least that way, there'll be less for the witches to complain about and the Council won't agree to the eviction request' – he paused, a muscle twitching along his jaw – 'or anything else.'

Ignoring the shiver of hurt that he'd brushed aside my ques-tions, I said slowly, 'Anything else means my job, doesn't it?'

'It took a lot to get the Witches' Council to let you come back and work for Spellcrackers, Gen, but your job's still under probation. If they think the vamp connection is getting too untenable, they'll go back to their original decision.' He rubbed his hands over his face. 'Gods, Gen, if it was just me, I wouldn't care, but I can't go against the Council, not if it means losing the franchise. The whole herd's got their money invested in Spellcrackers.'

A sick feeling settled in my stomach. Crap. That wasn't good. 'You should've told me,' I said quietly.

'Yeah, maybe,' he said tiredly. 'But it's been difficult with everything. It just wasn't the right time.'

I looked down, not sure what to say next, then, deciding things couldn't get any worse, I opened my mouth to—What?

Ask what I could do to help him? That was a no brainer really; if I could make my problems go away, then most of Finn's would too. Maybe I should ask how he could help *me*?

The hairs on my body sprang to attention and my head jerked up.

Scarface the ghost had bumped into the circle again. He stood there, arms outstretched, and for a second I thought I saw something in his sunken-eyed stare, then he started his usual slither around the outside of the circle. A whisper made me glance towards the pile of bones. There was nothing there. When I looked back the ghost was gone.

'Did you see that?' I said, pointing at where I'd last seen Scarface.

Finn gave me a puzzled look. 'See what?'

'Scarface, he bumped into the circle again, then disappeared.'

'Gen, he didn't disappear, look' – he pointed – 'he's shuffling on his way just as he usually does.'

I turned. Sure enough, the ghost was slowly making his way down the tunnel.

'You've been staring blankly at that corner over there for ages,' Finn added, his withdrawn boss expression back on his face. He stood, stretching his arms above his head. 'I think it's time we called it a night anyway; we've more than enough info on the ghosts. I don't trust the developer not to decide to visit us. You've got enough problems without that.'

Frowning, I entered Scarface's details into the laptop and closed it down. I glanced up at Finn. Should I try resurrecting our earlier conversation? Or maybe leave the talking until I'd had a chance to think everything through. I decided on the cop-out; it was late, or early, depending on which way you looked at it. I folded up my chair, clumsily catching my finger as I realised what I'd seen in Scarface's eyes. *Anger*. Only how could a ghost, one that was nowhere near sentient, suddenly become angry? It didn't make sense. Still, as Finn correctly pointed out, I had problems enough to deal with already, without adding another to my to-solve list. Then I remembered that Grace should've finished her shift by now and would be back at my flat. A heart-to-heart chat with her was just what I needed.

Chapter Three

There was a vampire in my flat. I stood on the landing out-side my door, mouth dry, tension coiling in my stomach. I didn't have a spy hole – not that looking through a spy hole the wrong way would do me much good, but I didn't need one. The vamp's presence hit my inner radar like a cold slap in the face.

There was only one vamp who could cross my thresh-old . . . Malik al-Khan. Looked like he'd finally decided to do the bad penny act and turn up.

Taking a calming breath, and thankful that Grace had got caught up in an emergency at HOPE and wasn't here yet, I raised my key—

The door swung open, making me start. A girl – rather, a woman – stood there. Thick black eyeliner shaped her amused brown eyes, her dark hair was pushed into an art-fully messy topknot, tiny ruby-eyed silver skulls hung from her ears and her full breasts were almost bursting out of the deep pumpkin-coloured bustier she wore over a black net skirt. Ignoring her, I looked over her shoulder at the vampire standing a few feet behind her.

He wasn't Malik.

My pulse leapt in my throat as fear slammed into me. How the hell had the vamp got in?

'Genevieve,' the woman said, standing back to usher me in.

To my own flat!

What the fuck were the pair of them doing here? Anger rolled over my fear, but anger wasn't going to help, or get my questions answered. I shoved it and the remnants of my fear far enough away that I hoped the vampire couldn't taste them – didn't want to get him excited – then eyed the woman with wary suspicion.

She arched one perfectly drawn-in black brow. 'Don't you think it might be better to come in instead of loitering out on the landing?'

I frowned again at her breasts and realised I recognised her: Hannah Ashby, human, top City accountant and self-certified vamp-flunky, a.k.a. *business manager*.

Except the master vamp she flunkied for was dead.

And I had no idea who she was working for now, but I did know it wasn't the vamp behind her. He was too young to be anything more than sharp-fanged muscle.

I walked past her and stopped just inside the door, quickly scanning the large room that doubled as my lounge and kitchen.

My computer was on the floor in the corner – its usual place – but its standby light glowed red. I always left it switched off. The huge amber and gold rug that covered most of the wooden floor hadn't been moved, but the pile of floor cushions and throws in the same bronzy colours were closer to the wall. The stack of glossies and newspapers on the low, wide windowsill had been tidied, and on the kitchen counter, the goldfish bowl – home to my new pets – was next to the sweet shop-sized jar of liquorice torpedoes as I'd left them – except both were on the wrong side of the sink. Whatever the pair had been looking for, they hadn't found it, otherwise they wouldn't still be here. And unless conducting an unobtrusive search wasn't one of Hannah's strengths – something I doubted – she wanted me to know she'd clawed her sharp, orange-painted fingernails through my belongings.

But why? It only served to make me angrier, as if invading

my flat with a muscle-vamp wasn't enough . . . an answer came in a memory, my father's calm, precise voice cautioning me: *those that cannot control their anger are subject to mistakes.* But controlling my anger didn't mean I had to be polite, not when being rude might gain me the upper hand.

'Trick or treat's not until the end of the week, Ms Ashby,' I said, eyeing her outfit with disdain. 'And aren't you supposed to be the one knocking on the door, instead of entering uninvited?'

'Please, call me Hannah.' Her black-lipsticked lips lifted in a gracious smile. 'As for *uninvited* – well, we have broken blood together, you and I, after all. Not wanting to embarrass you with your neighbours, we used the back way.' She gestured at the open bedroom door – I'd left it closed. The window in the bedroom led out onto a small, flat, gravelled roof I used as a mini-garden in summer . . . and to an old fire-escape ladder to the church's grounds below – the ladder I used as an alternative exit route all year round.

'How considerate of you,' I said sarcastically.

A chill draught barrelled through the open door and rattled the gold, copper and amber glass beads of my chandelier – my one extravagance when I'd moved in a year ago – and I looked at the vamp standing beneath them. Of course, Hannah, being human, would've had no problem using the window as an entry point; it's the only part of the building not protected by wards, something I was going to have to rectify. But the six-foot-plus vamp posing in the middle of my living room like he was expecting someone to take his picture *would* have needed an invitation – from someone whom the threshold recognised.

'I'm curious.' I flicked a hand in the vamp's direction, wishing the gesture would just make him disappear. 'How exactly did *he* get in uninvited?'

'Blood, of course. I offered you mine without constraint, and you accepted it in the same vein.' Her amused smile widened. 'It gives us a connection, and allows for some leeway in the usual proscriptions. So I invited him in on your behalf.'

Momentary panic flashed through the banked anger inside me. Crap! Did the fact I'd drunk her blood (in a desperate, weird moment of need I wasn't too keen on remembering) mean that she could invite any of her fang-pals into my home?

But then, she wasn't the type to worry about technicalities; if she thought she'd found a magical loophole, she'd use it. I *looked*, and only just managed to stop from gasping in surprise. Air was moving in a constant stream around her – where I imagined her aura would be if I could actually *see* peoples' auras – and it flowed out from her to the vamp and then back again in a swirling figure-of-eight. Then I realised it wasn't air. It was power; turbo-charged power that almost obliterated the small spells stored in the ruby eyes of the ear-rings she wore. Somehow she was using it to blank the vamp's presence in my flat, despite the fact she hit my radar as just plain human with no magical abilities. But then I'd always suspected she had a source of power from somewhere . . . and power this strong meant Hannah was a sorcerer.

She'd done a deal with a demon.

Demons outrank vamps in the bad news stakes. Although one good thing about demons, they only ever turn up this side of hell when invited, and not even the stupidest sorcerer would issue an invitation without taking the necessary precautions. Hannah Ashby didn't strike me as stupid, and a Consecrated Circle is kind of hard to miss.

Of course, some people's demons are other people's gods; it just depends on the religion, so that didn't necessarily make her bad. But a demon's power is like any tool, it's what you do with it – and how you pay for it – that matters. Demons, like necromancers, don't come cheap. And it's the currency a sorcerer chooses that makes them either grey, black, or just plain old evil.

And since my good luck was in short supply lately, I was betting Hannah was the evil type.

Suppressing another spike of fear, I walked over to the kitchen, pulled out the vodka from the fridge's icebox and a glass from the cupboard, placed them on the counter, and faced my unwanted visitors.

'If we were all friends' – I unscrewed the bottle – 'I'd offer you a drink. But we're not friends, so please, tell me whatever it is you've come to tell me, then take a not-so-subtle hint and vacate the premises. I'd appreciate it.'

'I'm sure we can offer you something you'd appreciate more, Genevieve.' Hannah executed an MC's flourish towards the vampire, the light catching the silver death's head ring with its emerald eyes on her ring finger. 'Can't we, Darius?'

Darius the vampire grinned at me, flashing all four of his fangs, and leisurely stripped out of the ankle-length black leather coat he wore. He swung it over his broad shoulder, leaving him standing there in nothing but his black calf-high boots and snug black Calvin Kleins. His grin widening, he rubbed his hand over his smooth-muscled pecs like he was adding more oil to his already glistening skin and then slowly walked his fingers down his six-pack, finally hitching his thumb into the low-slung waistband of his shorts. Decorating them was a wide-open diamanté mouth complete with red-beaded fangs that showcased his bulging package as it glittered provocatively in the overhead light. He tossed back his highlighted tawny-coloured hair as if to an unheard drum roll, then did a slow thrust and grind with his hips, finishing off by blowing me a kiss.

I sighed and gave him a *so what?* look. I'd seen it all before – there were plenty of acts like his down in Sucker Town in the blood-houses, performed by desperate, eager blood-pets. I'd also seen *him* before, when he'd still been human. Yep, the vamp doing his own version of a sucker lap-dance in my living room had not long graduated from being a blood-pet himself; he'd only had his fangs for just over a month. No wonder Hannah was able to lead him round like a bloodhound on a leash.

I pursed my lips at Hannah. 'If he's supposed to be auditioning for the Chippenfangs, you've come to the wrong place.'

She trailed her fingers over his well-defined bicep, her orange nails bright against his pale skin. 'The Chippenfangs don't even come close to Darius here.' She gave me a conspiratorial smirk. 'Believe me, I know.'

'Great! Well, I'm sure we could swap sexual conquest stories all night, Hannah, but to be honest, I find it all a bit uninspiring.' I looked pointedly at the grinning vampire, who was now flexing the burgeoning part of his anatomy so the diamanté mouth just covering it was yawning its own wide grin. 'So forget the show and get on with it.'

She chuckled, the sound low and husky. 'Uninspiring is not

a word I would use for Darius – satisfying, inventive, enduring, maybe, but—' She opened her eyes wide as if an idea had just popped into her head. 'Why don't I give you a taster? The proof is in the eating – or in Darius' case, in the *drinking*.'

Apprehension twisted like a sharp hook inside me. A drink sounded like exactly what I needed. Trouble was, alcohol wasn't going to slake that need, or going to be much help with what was coming next. I wanted to physically shove them out of my home, maybe even do something impossible, like stun the pair of them, or magic them far, far away. But my total lack of ability at *casting* spells meant it *so* wasn't going to happen. Instead, I carefully poured the vodka into the glass and, willing my hand not to shake, I lifted it in salute. 'Knock yourselves out, why don't you,' I said, and took a composed sip, the icy alcohol a welcome burn down my throat.

Hannah smiled like a sweet shop owner who knows the kid's got her nose pressed against the window and all she has to do is open the door. She stepped in front of Darius, then slowly shimmied back against him, sliding her hands behind to caress his hips. He dropped his coat, excitement dilating his pupils. Wrapping his arm round her waist he moulded her body to his, then pushed her head back to expose the length of her throat. I stared transfixed, my own cravings rising inside me, knowing they were deliberately taunting me, but unable to force myself to look away. They smiled, twin expressions of triumph. The vamp kept his eyes on mine as he licked a wet line along her bare shoulder and up the side of her neck to the lobe of her ear. He set her skull earring swinging with his tongue, then sucked it into his mouth. She sighed deeply and dug her nails into his thighs. His nostrils flared as he scented her and his eyes turned opaque with greed. With a quiet growl that had heat pooling in my own belly, he lowered his mouth to her pulse.

I held my breath, lust curdling like acid in my stomach, my grip on the bottle dissipating the chill, watching, waiting, for him to bite.

He struck, his fangs piercing her flesh, and she moaned and went limp in his arms. A trickle of blood leaked from between his lips where he fed. Mesmerised, I followed its course as it trailed over the ridge of her collar bone and snaked down between the mounds of her corseted breasts, which bloomed red with the heat of a venom-induced blood-flush. He lifted her up and held her dangling, fast little pants coming between her parted lips as his bite brought her trembling and shaking to orgasm.

Then she was walking towards me, an inviting smile on her black-painted lips, the venom-bite already swelling at her throat. I blinked, confused, but as she reached me the scent of liquorice and sweet copper invaded my senses and I could think of nothing other than what I wanted. My mouth watered and I swallowed painfully, hunger cramping my stomach, lust tightening my nipples and slicking damp wet heat between my legs. I licked my dry lips before I could stop myself.

'Such a long time, Genevieve, since you've had a taste.' She touched her fingers to the bite at her throat, gasping a little as she pressed the tender skin and clear fluid seeped from the pinprick fang marks. I swayed towards her, drawn by the sight. 'Why should you deny yourself when all you want is here for the taking?' she murmured.

My heart thudded in my chest, deep echoing beats that thundered in my ears. A distant part of me knew what she was doing, offering me what I craved, tempting me, but I didn't care. She was right. It had been too long.

She held her hand out to me, encouraging, enticing, her fingers so close to my mouth that all I needed to do was touch my tongue to the venom glistening on her fingertips—

I closed my eyes for a brief moment.

I was not going to do this.

I grabbed her wrist.

I was not going to give in to her, to it.

I held her hand where it was—

Was I?

I shoved her hand away. 'Not biting, Hannah,' I said and jerked my head at the scantily clad vamp grinning over her shoulder. 'So take your fang-pet and get the fuck out.'

She pursed her lips, then nodded as if coming to a decision. 'That's what I like about you, Genevieve, you don't allow what's in your blood to distract you from what's important.' She reached back and stroked her fingers down Darius' smooth, muscled chest. 'It's something else we share.'

I clenched my hands to stop from reaching for her, not sure if I wanted to smash my fist into her face, sink my teeth into her neck, or offer my own throat to her fang-pet. 'What. Do. You. Want?' I said, struggling to keep my voice even.

'To do you a favour of course.' She smiled. 'As a *friend*.'

'I told you, we are *not* friends. So why would you think I want another of your favours?'

'The last one worked out well enough, didn't it.' It was a statement, not a question. 'If not for me, you wouldn't be here, Genevieve. You would no longer be master of your own destiny. Instead, you would be blood-bonded to a vampire, your blood and your body and your magic his to use as he willed.'

Okaaay, now that was stretching things. A lot.

The Mr October mess might have ended up with the vamp whose blood-bond I'd taken dead, and nothing left but scattered ashes, but other than the 'drinking her blood' favour – and how much help that had actually been was still debatable – Hannah hadn't had much to do with it. Still, it wasn't worth the argument; she was just warming up her sales pitch, after all. We both knew that.

'Just get on with it,' I said, resigned. 'Then go.'

She leaned closer. 'You've got 3V, Genevieve. Everyone's talking about it – the vamps, the witches, the blood-pets – and those that didn't see you get bitten last month heard about it. And without a regular shot of venom—' She pulled a sympathetic face. 'There's the constant headache, the hot flushes followed by agonising stomach pains, the incessant need to scratch, the heavy labouring of your heart, the extreme fatigue . . .'

She sounded like one of the hard-hitting infomercials for HOPE.

'. . . and that's not even the worst, is it?' She pointed at my new pets swimming lazily in their goldfish bowl, her face screwing up in disgust. 'I mean, *ew!* Leeches! Then what's going to happen when the cravings get too much for you? When you suffer a stroke or a heart attack? You're sidhe, your body won't die, it'll recover eventually, but the cravings will shatter your mind and send you insane. Is that truly what you want?'

Did she *really* expect me to answer that?

'And these aren't the solution either.' She placed a packet of little black pills on the counter between us; no doubt pinched from my bathroom.

She was right, taking the G-Zav – the vamp-junkies' methadone – might work on humans, but my sidhe metabolism is too fast; the reason why I was popping the pills like they were going out of fashion.

'Of course,' she carried on, 'unlike everyone else, you and I know you've had 3V for, oh, ten years, isn't it now?' She tapped the tablets. 'And while you might be fooling them into thinking these are how you're coping, I recognised the spell-tattoo on your hip; we both know how you've been satisfying your needs.'

Ri-ight! She'd seen the tattoo when she'd done me the 'blood-drinking favour'. I'd bought an all-singing, all-dancing, all-blood-sucking Disguise spell from the Ancient One, a sorcerer who'd been around a lot longer than Hannah. Venom is so addictive that even vampires still need a regular fix, usually from other vamps – or secondhand from a convenient blood-pet – so using magic to give myself all the attributes of a vamp in order to hunt Sucker Town in safety had seemed like a good idea at the time. Trouble was, the spell might've been solving my venom-cravings for the last three years, but lately I'd discovered it had turned out to be not so much a disguise as a whole new body – one that already belonged to someone, a vampire called Rosa.

It was another problem on my to-sort-out list, after the vamps, my neighbours, Cosette – and now Hannah.

It was getting to be a long list.

'But here's the dilemma,' Hannah continued, lowering her voice. 'Now that Malik al-Khan has discovered you've been borrowing the body of his beloved Rosa, he's not going to let you continue with that little charade, no matter how closely yours and Rosa's bodies are entwined.'

She wasn't wrong. Malik *had* threatened to kill me over Rosa's body. But since he'd thrown away the opportunity when he'd had the chance, and had now done a vanishing act, Hannah's assessment of my problem was out of date, as was her knowledge. It also meant he hadn't sent her here in his place.

'Okay, Hannah,' I said drily. 'We've done the doom and gloom bit, so why don't you show me the light at the end of the tunnel.'

'Here's your light, Genevieve.' She reached up and cupped Darius' face. 'Young and handsome and so recently Gifted that he's both biddable and controllable. And he has no master, no one to tell tales to, so no one need ever know what you do with him.'

No master? I frowned at him. That wasn't possible, was it? Unless—? Well, maybe shacking up with an evil sorcerer had its compensations.

'Doesn't Darius have anything to say about it?'

She smiled up at him. 'Do you?'

'Yes.' He grinned, enthusiastically flashing his fangs.

Now I remembered: Darius was a man of few words and that was his favourite. If it wasn't for the predatory intelligence lurking in his eyes, I'd have thought him simple.

'Think about it,' she said softly. 'No need for tablets, no need to be at the mercy of any vamp that takes a fancy to you, no need to do any deals with them. Freedom, independence and control of your own life. And look at him, he's the icing on the cake.'

She could be reading my mind with her offer – in fact, I wasn't sure she wasn't – but even as I considered her little scenario, I knew it wouldn't work, not in the long run. Darius might not belong to a master vamp now, but as soon as one of them found out I was using him as a venom-pet that would change. Never mind that even contemplating the role reversal bit was giving me a queasy feeling in my stomach; I was anti being a blood-slave myself, so no way did I want to own one, however willing he appeared. Then there was the other, Hannah-sized, fly in the ointment: Darius might not have a master vamp calling his shots, but he did have her – a sorcerer. Whoever she was working for, herself or someone else, she wasn't here for my benefit.

'So how do you think this would work then?' I said slowly. 'Do we split the week between us and give him the seventh night off?'

'If that is what you want.' She smiled.

'I'm kind of more interested in what *you* want, Hannah.

Like, what you were looking for and didn't find when you searched my flat?'

She patted Darius' chest. 'Looks like we've been rumbled, my pet.' She glanced round before giving me a rueful smile. 'There wasn't much to search, though – oh, don't get me wrong, I like what you've done with the place, but wouldn't you like something more—Well, some place where Darius could pop by and no one would notice, somewhere that belonged to you that wasn't dependant on the charity of the Witches' Council?'

Now we were getting to the cherry on top. 'Okay, now I'm biting.'

Satisfaction flickered in her eyes. She leaned forward, eager to close the sale. 'You were given a present from the Earl' – London's big-cheese vamp, the vamp I'd given my blood-bond to, the vamp now thankfully waterlogged ashes – 'he gave you a Fabergé egg containing a sapphire pendant. It was one of the earliest, made in 1886 in Saint Petersburg as a gift from Tsar Alexander III to Tsarina Maria Fyodorovna, and is, according to records, now lost.' She held her hands out. 'All you need to do is sell it.'

My mouth almost dropped open. The Fabergé egg was some cherry!

I'd all but forgotten all about it – probably because I'd never wanted it in the first place, or ever considered it mine. The Earl *had* given it to me during the Mr October thing, not so much as a present, but more a sort of gem-studded blackmail note, an added inducement to get me to take his blood-bond. And while I'd realised it was *valuable* – it was Fabergé, after all – I'd sort of imagined it was a recent one, or an expensive copy, not a lost original.

And how the hell did Hannah even know about it?

'Oh and before you say you don't have it, Genny' – her smile hardened – 'just remember I used to look after the Earl's business activities. I know he gave you the Fabergé since I arranged its delivery to you myself. On his behalf, of course.'

I narrowed my eyes at her thoughtfully. There was something wrong with what she was saying, only I couldn't quite work it—

'I have contacts, Genevieve,' Hannah carried on, her voice brisk and businesslike. 'I can arrange for a quick sale at a good price; sixty per cent to you, forty to me, and the services of Darius here whenever you need them.' Her look turned sly and she touched a finger to the base of my throat. 'On his own, or, if you prefer, a ménage à trois?'

I didn't bother answering that one.

'Here are my details,' she added, holding out her hand palm up.

Darius produced a card from somewhere, reminding me of a well-trained magician's assistant. She placed it on the counter next to the G-Zav pills.

'Call me tomorrow and we'll set up a meeting to arrange the sale.' She smiled. 'I think this could be a very profitable and enjoyable relationship for both of us.'

I stood sipping my vodka and watched them leave, then turned on my computer.

'The egg's worth how much?' Grace spluttered coffee, her brown eyes widening with shock.

I snagged a clean dishcloth from under the sink, rinsed it under the tap and held it out to her. 'Ten to twelve million quid, if you believe Google,' I repeated, grinning at her wide-eyed amazement. 'It's a Fabergé, after all.'

'Goddess!' She blinked, then took the cloth and dabbed thoughtfully at her baggy jumper.

I studied her, worried about how tired she looked. The bruised circles under her eyes and the slight grey tinge to her latte-coloured skin made her look a good five years older than her actual twenty-nine, and her plump shoulders were on their 'been working too long' downward slump. I wished she'd take a break and not push herself so hard all the time, only *that* argument was older than all our more recent ones about me and the vamps. But since my place is nearer to HOPE than her house in Wimbledon, at least she'd agreed to crash with me if she was on back-to-back shifts, rather than camp out in her office at the clinic. Although tonight *that* plan wasn't working out too well. When she'd finally got away after her emergency, it was only to end up helping me in my cleaning frenzy as I tried to rid my flat of the nasty lingering *presence* of my uninvited visitors.

'It's a good job the egg wasn't still here then,' she said, throwing the cloth into the sink. 'People have killed for much less than that.'

I snorted. 'Tell me about it.'

Luckily, the egg was locked away in a bank vault rather than cluttering up my flat, otherwise I'd probably not have seen it again in this life – or much else, once Hannah and her lap-dancing fang-pet had disposed of me.

Fae might be hard to kill, we might live for centuries, but we're not immortal, and certainly not where *that* amount of money is involved.

Grace dried her hands and then shoved them into her short, curly hair and shook her head. 'Grrr, I hate it when things like this happen to you.' She dropped her hands and narrowed her eyes at me. 'So, what are you going to do about it, Genny?'

'I'm not sure yet,' I said, keeping my tone casual. 'I suppose try and find out who the egg really belongs to now the Earl's dead and take it from there.'

'Which means talking to that vampire, Malik, doesn't it?' She pressed her lips together and gave me her concerned look, the one that had disapproval skirting round its edges.

'Grace, I can't survive on these.' I poked at the G-Zav tablets sitting on the counter between us. 'You know what I was like before I bought the Disguise spell – some days I couldn't do much more than sit and shake, the cravings got so bad. And I can't use the spell any more, not now I know the truth about it.'

She gazed at me for a moment, indecision wavering on her face, then sighed. 'I know you can't, Genny. It's not morally right to use someone else's body like that, not even a vamp's.'

'And Hannah Ashby's little visit on top of all the invites from the vamps sort of means I can't stall any longer, however much you want me to,' I said quietly. 'I need to sort it all out and Malik appears to be the best way.'

'I'm not disagreeing, not now. It's just—Oh heck, Genny, you know what the vampires are like, better than I do,' she said, frustrated, then she threw her hands in the air in reluctant acceptance. 'What am I saying? Of course you know better than me, you were brought up with them, although Goddess knows what *that* must have been like.'

'I've told you!' I gave her a teasing smile, trying to lighten her mood. 'Not much different from any other child's whose father is still living according to eighteenth-century Russian aristocratic traditions, with nannies, private tutors, servants, learning how to dance, dressing for dinner . . .'

'Exactly.' She laughed, sounding slightly dismayed, and crossed her arms. 'There's just no way I could *ever* imagine dinner.'

'Okay, I admit it,' I said drily, 'I was the only one whose meals turned up on a plate instead of on two feet, but hey, I was a kid, I didn't know any different, so to me that was normal.'

And okay, occasionally someone would get too enthusiastic over their 'food', but accidents happen – as Matilde, my stepmother would say – and then the 'accidental meal' would continue to walk around – looking confused and a bit misty – even after the 'leftovers' had been 'disposed of' . . . but nearly everyone has phobias, don't they? Spiders are Grace's, mine just happens to be ghosts.

'And dinner was always *very* civilised.' I grinned, just to distract Grace a bit more. 'Wrists only, of course.' Which was true; anything else was behind closed doors. My father had strict rules about that. So I'd never seen anything like Hannah and Darius' vamped-up sex show until my first visit to Sucker Town. My father would have been horrified, same as Grace was when I'd told her about it, albeit for different reasons.

'Yes, it was so civilised that you ran away when you were fourteen,' Grace said, her voice still concerned, but with a thread of reproach for my teasing.

'Yeah, well,' I sighed, instantly apologetic, 'as I told you, it wasn't so much to do with my father as with a mistake he made.' Like arranging for me to marry another vampire, a future I was utterly happy with, until the vamp turned out to be a psychotic sadist.

'Are you sure that you're not making the same mistake with this Malik?' Her forehead creased with worry.

'I'm not planning on getting that close to him' – despite

the traitorous thoughts my libido occasionally had – no, I was
aiming to keep any future association between us at arm's
length. Literally. Malik coveted my blood, had done since I
was four; I needed his protection and his venom, so the wrist
was as good a meeting place as any. It was what I'd planned
to tell him when he next put in an appearance – only now it
looked like I'd have to go and find him. Which would give
him the upper hand – not such a great negotiating position.

'What about Finn?' Grace said, then as I started to speak she
added, 'And you know I'm not talking about your job, Genny.'

'Finn's not interested in anything else,' I said quietly.

'Rubbish! Of course he is – why else would he keep quiet
about your father and go up against the Witches' Council if he
wasn't interested? He's being careful and considerate, Genny,'
she said earnestly, reaching out to grasp my hands. 'You told
him this big, big secret, something that both you and he know
could cause a major upset in your life. Maybe he thinks if he
asked you out now, you'd think you had to say yes, just to keep
him sweet.'

Hope flickered inside me. *Was she right?* Had Finn decided
not to ask me out any more because he thought I'd only be
saying yes for the wrong reasons? And not because one half
of my parentage repulsed or terrified him? It sort of fit with
his usual white knight persona.

'Of course,' Grace carried on, 'with him backing off like
he has after hearing your secret, it means you've lost your
trust in him too. Which is probably why you blew up at him
earlier.' She squeezed my hands. 'You like him, Genny, a lot.
You should talk to him and sort it all out.'

She was right on both counts. I did like him, *a lot . . . and*
I didn't trust him. How could I when I wasn't sure what he
wanted? But maybe if I talked to him?

Then she lifted my left hand up between us in accusation;
half-faded bruises encircled my wrist. 'You've had *these* for
over a month, Genny, and with your sidhe metabolism, you
should've healed them in a couple of hours. I know its some
sort of *property mark*.' Her face screwed up in revulsion.
'How can you think of having anything to do with that vamp
after he did this to you?'

Because I've finally accepted, regardless of what I want, or you want, I don't have much choice. I need him, or some vamp anyway, and – not even trying to fool myself here – some part of me wants him. More importantly, once given, I know his word is his bond.

Only I didn't say it out loud; it wasn't what Grace wanted to hear. But if she didn't understand about Malik, she *was* right about talking to Finn. Oh, I wasn't holding out as much hope on the relationship side as she was – not when I was about to do a deal with a vampire – but maybe he could help with the rest of my non-vamp problems . . .

'You're right.' I smiled ruefully. 'I'll have a chat with Finn, okay? Later on today at work.'

'Good, now we're getting somewhere!' She wrapped her arms round me in a hug.

'Don't get too excited,' I said, hugging her back and breathing in her familiar floral perfume with its faint antiseptic tang. 'I'm not ruling the vamp option out yet. And talking about going somewhere—' I glanced up at the clock. Dawn was still a couple of hours away, but I was itching for my next G-Zav dose, and with the amount of amphetamine the pills contained, I wasn't going to be sleeping any time soon. 'I'm going for a run.'

'Run! It's wet and cold and dark and—' She gave a very un-doctor-like squeal of horror, but then, Grace is more a fair-weather type of girl, and she wouldn't be seen dead in running shorts. 'Well, if you're not using it, I'm going to bed. I got enough exercise to last me a week after walking up those five flights of stairs.'

'Exercise is good for you, Grace.' Grinning, I bounced on the balls of my feet. 'Isn't that what you doctors are always saying?'

She sniffed in disdain. 'Bring doughnuts back, that's all this doctor is saying.'

Chapter Four

It was snowing inside Tomas' Bakery, a blizzard of dust-fine flour that whirled and eddied like a maelstrom, making the interior a complete white-out. I stood outside, pushed my hands through my hair and groaned. Tomas' ex-girlfriend had sicced another of her malicious spells on him again. Now I was having visions of Tomas and whoever else might be inside slowly suffocating from a lungful of ground-up wheat. But even his ex couldn't be that stupid, could she? Still, she'd gone too far this time. Tomas was going to have to stop being so nice and forgiving and report this to the police; if he didn't, then I would. It wasn't as if he'd done anything to deserve her vindictiveness either; he'd only gone out with the witch a couple of times, not jilted her at the altar. But Tomas was six foot of blond Nordic muscle-bound weightlifter, and a lot of the market witches had their eye on him. And trust me, bunny-boilers have nothing on witches when it comes to acting out their jealous fantasies.

Damn. Just what I didn't need after the night I'd had.

Not that the night was officially over yet; there was still nearly an hour before sunrise. But an hour's hard running had worked off the amphetamine so I'd come for Grace's doughnuts. The bakery is down a side street crammed in between a secondhand book shop and a fancy florist's, and on my usual morning run route. When I'd sprinted past it earlier nothing out of the ordinary had snagged my attention, but now I realised what had been missing. There was no smell of baking bread. I should've noticed that; Tomas had asked me to sort out so many of his ex's nasty little spells over the last couple of weeks that I'd made a permanent date to pop in at the end of my run whether I wanted doughnuts or not. But the conversation with Grace, my other problems and what I was going to say to Finn when I saw him had been on constant replay in my mind as I'd been pounding the pavements . . . I blew out an annoyed breath at myself for missing something so obvious, and *focused* on the bakery.

The dizzying flour-storm shone with magic, as if each individual grain had been tagged with whatever spell was causing the blizzard. I needed to find the heart of the spell to *crack* it but the stuff glittered so much I couldn't *see* past it. I closed my eyes briefly and upped my concentration, but the centre of the spell was still too elusive; whatever magic animated the flour was hidden within it. I frowned, trying to think—

'You're that faerie, aren't you?' A lad around seventeen poked his spiky head of black hair out of the florist's. 'I saw you earlier when you ran past.'

I picked my way through the obstacle course of black-painted metal buckets and cardboard boxes packed with sweet-scented blooms to speak to him. 'Do you know if anyone's in there?' I pointed at the open bakery door.

'Tomas is. He waved at me when the boss dropped me off with the flowers.' The lad's tongue slipped out to taste the silver hoop piercing his bottom lip. 'Oh, and there was this woman, she went in just before all the flour started flying around.' He came out and stood next to me, thumbs hooked in the belt loops of his baggy cargo pants. 'Then I heard some shouting and yelling like they were fighting, then there was this big noise like someone falling over, then it went all quiet.' His tone was offhand, as if the whole thing bored him, or maybe he was just trying to be cool. 'Haven't seen neither of them since.'

I pressed my lips together. What if Tomas' ex really had done something stupid and he was lying in there hurt? Tomas was a friend; not only that, he was soft as faerie moss. No way would he defend himself against a woman, never mind that when magic's involved all the muscle in the world isn't going to help. I reached for my phone, then realised I'd left it at home. Damn gremlins and their hex.

'Ring the police,' I told the lad, 'and tell them just what you've told me. Tell them there's a witch involved, and to send the magic squad, you got that?'

He bent and snapped open a pocket near his knee and pulled out a tiny silver phone attached by a chain. 'Sure, if you say so.'

I gave him the number and he punched it in. 'You going in there?' he sniffed.

Was I? I had a moment's hesitation, then decided waiting outside wasn't for me, not if I could do something. 'Yeah, just tell whoever gets here first that I'm in there too, okay?'

'Sure.' He twisted his lip-hoop with a nail-bitten finger. 'Gotta sort the delivery until the boss gets back anyway.'

I pulled off my sweatshirt and dunked it in the water in one of his black flower buckets, then caught the lad staring intently at me, phone clamped to his ear. I ignored him–after all, I'd just stripped down to a black Lycra cropped top in front of him, and okay, I'm more the slender-verging-on-skinny type, nowhere near as endowed as a Page Three model, but hey, put any half-naked female in front of most teenage lads and staring's what happens.

I wrapped the sweatshirt round my head as a face-mask, shivering as cold water trickled over my shoulders. Breathing shallowly through the wet cotton, hands stretched out in front. I launched blindly into the flour-blizzard. The magic buzzed around me in a way that had my stomach roiling with nausea and I briefly wondered if the spell was doing more than animating a sack-load of flour. I walked slowly forward, going by memory, sliding my feet cautiously from side to side so as not to trip over any prone bodies. Half a dozen steps had me bumping into the counter. I felt my way along it, the flour-storm itching over my skin like tiny insistent insects trying to burrow beneath my flesh.

I gritted my teeth at the mental image and stifled the urge to scratch.

The end of the counter took me by surprise and I stumbled. I did the foot-slide-and-walk thing again, thankfully finding nothing, until I reached where my spatial memory told me the door to the bakery kitchen should be. I slapped my hands against it, feeling around for the handle, then shuffled back to pull the door open. The light filtering through my sweatshirt brightened. I stepped through the door and the sudden absence of the itching sensation had me hoping I'd left the flour-storm behind. I dragged the wet, flour-caked material from my head and dropped it. White-gold light hit my face and instinctively I squeezed my eyes shut. Then as I blinked away the negative afterimage, the bright-blurred edges of the kitchen gradually resolved themselves into something recognisable and my mind finally caught up with what my eyes where looking at.

Tomas lay flat on his back on the long stainless-steel table that he used for making the bread.

He was naked.

He was evidently very excited.

And just as evidently, very, very dead.

Chapter Five

Tomas lay on his back, his hips thrust upwards, arms out-stretched, head thrown back, mouth and eyes wide open, his pupils fashioned into gold-bright orbs by magic, a grotesque statue sculpted rigid at the ultimate high of sexual pleasure.

Shock had me staring with disbelief.

Tomas hadn't been killed by a jealous witch.

The French call the pleasure of orgasm *le petit mort*, the small death. Tomas' death hadn't been small – but then, humans are too fragile to survive the full force of faerie sex outside of the Fair Lands.

The white-gold light shimmered over his body, lining his pumped-up muscles with hard contours, and a detached part of me could see why the market witches had been battling over him with their broomsticks. Then sadness and anger washed away the shock and I moved towards him, an insane glimmer of hope telling me to touch him, that maybe he wasn't dead, maybe this wasn't real, maybe it was all just some elaborate illusion. I reached out and gently placed my forefinger to his forehead. Golden mist curled like rising smoke from his open mouth and spilled the scent of honeysuckle into the air.

Honeysuckle is the scent of my own Glamour, my own magic.

Horror rushed through me, raising the little hairs on my body. My heart thudded against my ribs. I took an involuntary step back, and another, then yelped, high-pitched, as the hot prickle of a Ward hit my shoulders. I turned and *looked*. The doorway was still open behind me, the flour-storm a swirling white curtain, but a Ward now vibrated up from the threshold like rising heat; a basic, bought-off-the-shelf Knock-back Ward, the sort that usually had big warning signs that read **Danger – Keep Out**. Someone wanted to make sure I was caught red-handed and still clutching the smoking gun when the police arrived.

'Fucking bastard!'

I shoved the questions of who and why and how away. There was nothing I could do for Tomas, however much I wished there was, but there was still his ex, or whoever the woman was, to find. I walked through the kitchen carefully. Glass-fronted ovens lined one wall, small blue-tinged flames dancing in their huge stainless-steel cavities. Two commercial-sized food mixers were bolted to the floor, flat paddles jacked up above their industrial-sized bowls. And half a dozen large metal flour barrels were stacked under a high rectangular window next to the bolted and padlocked back door. I eyed the barrels. They were big enough for someone to hide in, but my gut and the fact there were more Knock-back Wards vibrating on both the back door and the high window told me the woman was long gone.

Rats and traps came to mind.

And escaping wasn't going to be an easy option.

'Genevieve.' My name slid like sorrow and silk over my skin, making me shiver. *Mesma.* I recognised his voice with its not-quite-English accent and, heart thudding in my chest like a cornered cat's, I turned to look at him.

Malik stood just inside the kitchen, the flour-storm behind him dimmed by the shadows shifting round him. His black hair curled into the darkness of his long leather coat, and the coat itself merged into the blackness of the clothes he wore beneath. I'd seen him draw those same shadows into himself, using them to hide himself from sight. He studied me, his skin gleaming pale as the shadows dissipated, his obsidian eyes enigmatic; his part-Asian heritage obvious in their shape. Once I'd thought his face perfect, pretty even, but he'd played with my mind and my perceptions and now with only the edge of prettiness left, he was more beautiful, more male, and more frightening than my imagination had let me remember.

I frowned. Something wasn't right; not the fact that I was frightened – vamps are predators, and being wary of them is just common sense – but this feeling was . . . different. Then I realised that *thinking* about coming to some arrangement with him was nothing compared to contemplating it while he was standing in front of me like some dark angel. Damn. Maybe Grace was right yet again and I was just kidding myself that I could negotiate with him on my own terms when the 3V and my attraction to him meant I probably didn't have my own best interests at heart.

Mentally I shored up my resolve and said, 'Malik al-Khan,' grateful my voice came out dry as dust.

He inclined his head, an elegant movement that echoed the past. And going by the power I'd seen him wield he had a good five hundred years of past too, maybe more, for all that he appeared to be around my age, twenty-four. Like all vamps, he looked the same now as when he'd accepted the Gift. An unfelt breeze ruffled his hair and lifted the edges of his coat, dislodging the faint patina of white that covered him, and I glanced down at the flour still stuck to my own damp clothes and sighed.

Vamps get all the best magic tricks.

His eyes flicked to the body that lay on the baker's table between us. 'It was unwise of you to enter and not wait for the police.'

'Yeah well, I'd sort of come to that conclusion myself.' I grimaced. 'I don't suppose you can tell if there's a witch or anyone else hiding around here somewhere, can you?'

He closed his eyes and took a deep breath. 'There has been no witch here, in this part of the shop, for a day, possibly more, and no one now other than us and the dead man.'

Okay, so Tomas' ex wasn't around, and the barrels held only flour. Then another thought clicked. Malik had been following me; had he overheard the boy talking? 'The lad

outside said he'd seen a woman come in and heard some sort
of fight?' I narrowed my eyes in question.

'He lied.'

'Ri-ight.' I pursed my lips. Good old vamp super-senses,
better at spotting a fib at fifty paces than any polygraph
machine ever would be. 'He's part of the set-up then?'

'Not necessarily; there was some confusion in his mind.'
He pushed back the fall of dark hair from his forehead. 'As I
said, Genevieve, it was unwise of you to enter.'

Confusion? Caused by some sort of spell? Still, back to
being the trapped rat and now with a scary vampire in tow. So
not the way I wanted to start my day. Still, I looked sadly at
Tomas; his day had started a hell of a lot worse than mine, so
I really was the better off. Until the police got here, at least.

I frowned at Malik. Why *had* he followed me in? 'You do
realise that there are Wards stopping us getting out, and that
the police will be here any minute, don't you?'

'I informed the boy that the police would not be required.'
He turned his head as if listening, giving me the sculptured
line of his profile. 'He believes you will deal with any problems and has put it from his thoughts.'

My pulse sped up. He'd mind-locked the boy, given him
instructions. The vamp trick isn't illegal – just as any other
form of hypnotism isn't – so long as no crime results. It meant
there were no police rushing to arrest me. Or to rescue me.
One of those good news, bad news things. Still, at least it
bought me some time. Tomas was dead. Someone had used
him to frame me and – I clenched my fists – I was going to
find out who it was, and why. My eyes moved suspiciously
to the vampire standing like a beautiful statue not three feet
away.

'Is this anything to do with you?' I indicated the dead body.

He treated me to his usual impassive expression, then
started walking with graceful purpose around the body. I held
my place as he rounded the feet and closed on me, refusing
to allow him to intimidate me. Finally he stopped, his coat
brushing against my bare legs. Dark spice mixed with the
scent of leather curled through me, shimmering lust in my
belly. I ignored it; with the 3V in my blood, it was nothing
more than a chemical reaction to his nearness. *You just keep*

telling yourself that, whispered a mocking voice in my mind. I ignored that too.

'This looks more like your handiwork, Genevieve,' he murmured, looking down at me, his breath disturbing my hair.

'Yeah' – I lifted my chin to meet his eyes – 'like I couldn't work that one out, except of course I didn't kill him.'

'Which is always the standard response of both the innocent' – he wrapped cool fingers round my left wrist; the bruises there heated to his touch – 'and the guilty.'

'I'm fae, Malik.' I jerked out of his hold. 'The fae can't lie.'

'That is true.' His voice licked over me like hot flames. 'As far as the truth goes.'

'Fine!' I glared up at him. 'If we're doing the pedantic stuff; yes it's impossible for the fae to lie outright, but they' – I paused to correct myself; I was fae, after all, even if I hadn't been brought up amongst them – 'we fae can usually skirt around the edges of the truth and misdirect. And of course the same holds for vampires.'

He shifted away, so quickly that I almost swayed. Then he bent over Tomas' heavily muscled chest and, eyes closed, inhaled deeply.

I frowned in consternation. 'What the fuck are you doing?'

He lifted his eyes to mine; incandescent pinpricks of power flared red in his pupils. 'The scent could be yours.' His expression turned predatory. 'It is almost indistinguishable.'

Apprehension fluttered under my ribs at the intensity of his gaze and I forced myself to stand my ground. 'Yeah, he smells of honeysuckle, I know. But he's been dead at least a couple of hours, so truth or not, I've been with others all night.' Grace, then Hannah – okay, she and Darius weren't the most reliable of alibis, but hey, I had something she wanted. And before she turned up I'd been on the ghost job with Finn.

'No.' A fine line creased between Malik's brows as he stared down at the body. 'It is only recently that this human has been killed, maybe half an hour at the most.'

'But he's all stiff!' I had a sudden visual of just how stiff a particular part of Tomas' body was and stopped. The *double entendre* seemed wrong with him lying dead and unable to defend himself. I pushed the thoughts away and carried on.

'I thought rigor didn't set in until two to three hours after death?'

'The body has not reached the stage of rigor mortis yet.' He moved back a couple of paces to study the body. 'This is an example of cadaveric spasm: should death occur at a moment of high emotion and extreme exertion, the body's muscles seize in position. It can happen where the human has drowned or suffered a heart attack whilst fleeing, or as the result of an overload of sexual stimulation as here.'

I almost asked him if he'd taken a course or something, then thought better of it. Vampires don't just see a lot of death, they cause a lot of death, never mind the current bat-shit PR propaganda the public has swallowed bloody hook, line and sinker. Of course, vamps were considered dead themselves up until the court case back in the seventies; then a disinherited widow decided she'd be better off as a divorcée after her rich husband accepted the Gift and left his millions to his new master. She got her medical experts to prove that daytime vampires still produced brainwaves, ergo no clinical death there then. And wasn't it a handy coincidence that the judge's decision removed yet another nail from the coffin in which the vampire's *human* rights had been buried in?

'If you look here—' Malik crouched and pointed to where the body's back ribcage met the stainless-steel table; a faint bluish-red line discoloured the skin like a thin bruise. 'It is only now that the blood begins to settle. Death occurred within the last hour, probably not long before you entered the shop.'

I worked it out. Tomas had been killed while I was out running, a time I had no alibi for.

'And I would not have been able to sense the body,' Malik carried on calmly as he straightened up, 'if it had been less fresh.'

Nice image! 'So what,' I said, 'you just happened to be following me and decided to drop in and give me the benefit of your expertise in determining the time of death?'

He gave me another impassive look, like this time my question was so stupid that it wasn't worth answering.

'Didn't think so,' I said drily. 'And I suppose you've only been following me for my own protection?'

He inclined his head with a wry twitch of his mouth. 'If that's what you wish to believe.'

'More like you're concerned about losing what you consider to be your property,' I snorted, 'and just want to chase off any other vamps that might be getting ideas.'

'Genevieve.' A hint of impatience laced his voice. 'If you were my property there would be none that would risk my displeasure, save one. But after the last challenge meeting, in the eyes of all other vampires you do not belong to me, you belong to Rosa.'

Rosa! *Malik's beloved*, as Hannah had called her. Rosa was a touchy subject as Malik had been the one to give her the Gift, and at one point he'd been determined to rescind that same Gift rather than let another borrow her body – not one of my most cherished memories – until he'd discovered it was me doing the borrowing. Even so, I wasn't entirely sure where he stood on the Rosa/me issue now.

'Even if Rosa were in truth your master,' he carried on, 'instead of the puppet you have made of her body, she would not be strong enough to keep you from those that would seek to persuade you to their blood. It is a situation that must be dealt with before it escalates further.'

'And what exactly do you mean by that?' I said warily.

'It is not a matter for discussion now, Genevieve.' He brushed his hands together, then indicated the dead body. 'This is a more immediate predicament. Someone has gone to great efforts to ensure you appear guilty. Have you any ideas who might have done so?'

'Haven't a clue,' I said, *but I intend to find out.* 'The only other time I've been framed for a murder I didn't commit, it was your doing.'

Irritation flickered across his face. 'Unfortunately for you, my plan then did not succeed. If it had, you would not have become involved in all that followed, and I would not have the need to watch over you now.'

'Look, don't bother with the watching thing, or whatever it is you're doing. The last thing I need is a shadowy vampire stalker.'

Something dangerous surfaced in the dark pools of his eyes and I swallowed past the sudden fear constricting my throat. He reached out and grasped my left wrist again. My pulse beat fast and eager under his touch. 'I have laid my claim on you,' he said as he lifted my wrist until it was level with my face; the bruises there bloomed like red roses and blood trickled down from between his pale fingers. 'I will not let another usurp that claim.'

'I am not a thing to be claimed, Malik,' I snapped, trembling with both rage and the need that rushed through my body. 'And if you want my blood, then you're going to have to start negotiating to get it.'

He stilled, staring at me, emotions I couldn't read flickering across his face. Then he raised his other hand and cupped my cheek, brushing his thumb over my lips. They tingled with his touch and my anger washed away with the desire that leapt through my body – mine or his, or both, I couldn't tell. He leaned closer, the scent of him invading my senses, holding me captive. Sliding his hand around the nape of my neck and threading his fingers into my hair he tugged and without conscious thought I tilted my chin, offering my throat. He kissed his lips to the soft, vulnerable skin under my jaw, a gentle, almost reverent kiss.

'You think you will dictate terms to me? When and where and how much?' The words whispered against my pulse. 'But what if I do not wish to negotiate, Genevieve?' Sharp fangs drew a line of heat down my flesh. 'How will you stop me?'

My heart stuttered. The need to give him everything I was ached deep inside me. I placed my palm against his chest, spreading my fingers over the lean, hard muscle . . . and I pushed him back, forced my mouth to say the words my body didn't want to. 'Negotiation is all I'm willing to offer; without that, then I will kill you.'

'Then we will negotiate.' He smiled, but the shape of his mouth was sad. He released my wrist and drew away, putting space between us. I closed my eyes, resisting the urge to go to him, resisting the call in my blood. Damn vamp! *Negotiate* meant talking, not messing with my mind, but of course, he knew that. I breathed, concentrating on the faint scent of honeysuckle in the air, the vague sourness of gas from the ovens, the earthy smell of fermenting yeast. Opening my eyes, I looked down at my wrist. There was no blood and the bruises were once again just warmer imprints on my honey-coloured skin. It was just him using my own susceptibility against me. I clenched my fists, angry with myself that I'd let him do that so easily, and looked back at him.

He was staring up at the small high window. 'Dawn approaches.'

As soon as he spoke, it was all that I could feel, all that I could hear, almost like a shrill alarm getting louder and more insistent, driving all other thoughts from my consciousness. I shook physically with the feelings, then almost kicked him in annoyance. *Mesma.* Crap, he *was* still messing with my mind. Dawn wasn't going to harm me, but it would him. Vamps don't do sunlight, or even the gloomy October daylight that would be filtering through the small window in the next few minutes. But the particular vampire trapped in the kitchen with me didn't look too worried, but then he was old enough that he wouldn't have followed me into the trap if he'd thought he'd be in real danger, so he was still playing games. But why?

'Does being out at dawn mean you're going to burst into flames and collapse in a pile of ashes?' I asked, instilling vague interest into my voice.

'Your own father was a vampire.' He frowned. 'Yet you appear woefully ignorant of our species.'

I shrugged. 'I know staking doesn't always kill you, not without taking the head and the heart, but hey, seeing a vamp in daylight without some protection is a new one for me and I don't want to take anything for granted. I mean, up until I met you I thought that revenants were just a scary old myth.' He didn't even flinch at the dig – revenants are the scary skeletons in the vampires' closet, and he was the one who proved the myth was real. 'And I'm sure that wasn't the only part of my education my father neglected.'

'No,' he said, tucking his hands in his coat pockets. 'I will not burst into flames, nor would any vampire who has reached their autonomy. Those who still bow to their master's hand would be dependant on their master's goodwill to keep them alive. But the touch of the sun can bring much pain and a lingering disability; many would wish to choose a quick, final death to end their suffering.'

'So what's going to happen to you?'

'As I have told you before, Genevieve, I carry the true Gift.' His lips thinned to a grim line. 'So long as my remains are not scattered, I am able to heal any injury, even a day in direct sunlight . . . eventually.'

'What do you mean "eventually"?' I frowned.

'Some things take time.'

'How much time? Days, weeks, months?'

'The window faces north and the day is cloudy . . . a few weeks, maybe.'

Damn, that wasn't what I wanted to hear. No way did I want him out of action for all that time. A day in jail I could cope with, but weeks . . . I glanced at Tomas' body. I had a murderer to look for.

'If you get out now, can you get to somewhere safe in time?'

'Yes.' His expression turned thoughtful. 'But why would you be concerned for me?'

'Stop playing with me, Malik. When the police do finally turn up, I'm probably going to be arrested on suspicion of his death.' I waved a hand at the body. 'But you've been following me and I bet you know exactly where I've been every minute of last night.' I smiled, knowing it didn't reach my eyes. 'You're my Get Out Of Jail Free card.'

'You want me as your alibi?' he said, as if the idea hadn't occurred to him.

'I think you owe me one after the last time, don't you.' I made it a statement. 'And of course, there's the fact that you want something from me' – and I had a suspicion it wasn't just my blood – 'otherwise why follow me in here to *offer* your help.' I made that a statement too. 'So me sitting in prison while you recover isn't in either of our best interests, is it?'

He inclined his head in tacit agreement, then moved and touched his hand to the open doorway to the front shop. Magic sparked like a match flaring as his hand brushed the Ward. 'There is still our predicament, Genevieve.'

'No problem,' I said with a confidence I wasn't entirely sure I felt. I stood in front of the back door and *looked*. The black bars of the Knock-back Wards pulsed and as I studied the spell I realised long black cables of magic linked the three Wards – two on the doors and one on the window. I would need to remove all three to get Malik out. No way was there enough time to dismantle the spells, and the kitchen was too small to *crack* the magic – bits of wooden door or shattered glass raining down wasn't going to help anyone – which left only one option: I'd have to absorb the spells. Of course, that option had its own drawbacks.

'Just so you know—' I started, turning back to Malik, then blinked as I saw him texting on his phone. Why, or rather *who* was he texting? He'd always struck me as a loner, not like the rest of London's vamps, who could call on others of their blood-families. I shook my head and went on. 'When I remove the Wards, the magic might do something to me, but don't worry about it, okay?'

He looked up, curiosity in his gaze. 'What will it do?'

'Difficult to say, maybe knock me out for a second or two, or it might just make my hair stand on end, or maybe even nothing at all. The magic can be a bit capricious when it wants, but the effects wear off quickly enough. So just get out safe and come back at sunset with my alibi.'

'As you wish,' he said, and went back to his texting.

I gave Tomas one last look, not really wanting to leave him but knowing there was nothing I could do for him now other than find his killer. Then, I took a deep breath, held out my hands and *called* the Wards.

The magic hit me like a ton of bricks falling on top of me, smashing my bones and pulverising my flesh, filling my lungs with dust until I felt like I was inhaling razorblades. Somewhere in my mind I screamed as hot flames scorched through my body. Fire destroyed the edges of my vision. Hard hands circled my wrists, lifting me, jerking my shoulders from their sockets. Blood, thick and copper-sweet, filled my mouth; the reek of burning flesh was in my nose. And the bricks kept falling, and falling, burying me beneath a mound of magical rubble.

Chapter Six

'Genevieve, my dear, I would very much appreciate it if you woke up now.' The Earl sounded faintly bored, but as he was one very dead vampire, I decided I must be having a nightmare and went back to floating in the sparkling mist and golden sunlight he'd distracted me from.

'*Now*, my dear,' the Earl repeated, more insistently, and a sharp pain in my hand made my eyes snap open.

A blur of red and black and pink resolved itself and my startled reflection looked down at me from the large mirror on the ceiling. I blinked as I took in the details. I was lying on black satin sheets on a bed the size of a small football field. There was a surgical shunt taped to the back of my left hand, delivering clear fluid from a drip, and three heart monitor pads stuck to my chest, their wires trailing out of view. My honey-coloured skin was mottled yellow and green with bruises, except for some pink shiny patches that looked like newly healed burns.

I didn't look so good; to be honest, Frankenstein's monster probably looked better. Oddly, I was dressed in a slinky red satin negligée that clashed with what was left of my singed and frizzled amber hair. The red slinky number was also at least two sizes too big in the bust area: it gaped down the front, not leaving much to anyone's imagination. Around me the rest of the room's décor kept going ad nauseam with the red and black theme: carpet, walls, even the ornate curtains framing the French doors and the pre-dawn sky. Yep. Definitely dreaming; hospitals don't usually go for Bordello Tacky.

'Good morning, Genevieve.' The Earl sat on the bed next to me, blond hair flopping over his pale, aristocratic face, the blue of his Oxford shirt bringing out the azure colour of his eyes. The blue blazer and grey flannel trousers all contributed to his relaxed At Home in the Country look – but the look was an illusion; he was the top dog in London's vampire food chain . . . or at least he had been before I'd killed him. Damn. Why couldn't I have a normal nightmare, like running through an eerie forest being chased by something horrible and nameless, instead of a surreal dream about dead vampires in the middle of a weird hospital make-over show?

He smiled broadly, flashing his fangs. 'I was beginning to feel a tad concerned for you, my dear. I have been attempting to awaken you for quite some time now.'

'Go away,' I said, only it came out more *gawwwrr*.

'I knew you'd be delighted to see me.' He patted my red satin-covered thigh. 'And just to put your mind at rest, I am not a dream, nor some drug-induced hallucination' – he lifted my unresisting hand up from where it lay on the bed – 'in spite of the morphine in your body.' He flicked the shunt and the sharp pain came again.

'Grreeoffmee,' I slurred, wishing he would go *pop!* or whatever dead-dream vampires were supposed to do.

'I see that you are finding this hard to accept.' He released my hand and we both watched as it thudded onto the mattress and bounced. 'I must admit, I did myself at first, but I have become used to the idea that I am not truly dead.'

The pain in my hand receded and I tried to roll over in an effort to go back to the sparkling mist and end the nightmare. Or at least in my mind I did. My body stayed where it was. My own horrified eyes stared down at me as I realised I couldn't move, my heart thudded slow and heavy in my chest and fear crawled into me on shuddering, drug-muted claws. Maybe this wasn't a dream.

'Iwatchedgoblinsscatterashes.' My words still slurred, but I was getting a little more control now.

'Yes, so you did. That was rather an unpleasant surprise.' He smoothed a hand down his blazer lapel. 'It was a much more pleasant revelation when I realised I had not quite shuffled off this mortal coil' – he flashed fangs again – 'or, in my case, *immortal* coil.'

'Happywithyoudoingshufflingbit,' I muttered in disgust.

He sighed. 'The medication is stifling your thoughts, my dear. It is annoying; I particularly wished to converse with you. Allow me to remedy it.' He picked up my hand again and jerked out the shunt. I struggled in cotton wool-wrapped terror as he sniffed my inner wrist. 'Your blood is as deliciously sweet as ever, even with the drugs.' His two needle-thin venom fangs extended between his sharp canine teeth. Gripping my forearm tightly, he plunged all four fangs into my flesh.

Pain ripped through me and my arms and legs twitched like a dying fish as my brain's message to fight struggled to reach my muscles. I screamed, but he clamped his hand over my face, muffling the sound as he pressed my head back into the black satin pillows. Then the world turned hazy and silver as his venom flooded my blood and hit my heart like a sledgehammer, and the pain dissolved in the rush of promised pleasure. My heart beat faster and faster. Heat and lust suffused my body as the venom-induced adrenalin sensitised every inch of my skin.

He reared up his head and inhaled deeply. 'You know how this works, don't you, my dear? With so much of my venom in your blood, your body will continue to crave sexual release, but it will be unable to reach it other than through my feeding.' He leaned over and pushed aside the negligée, smiling as he pinched my left nipple. I arched into his hand, the pain/pleasure nearly destroying me. 'Of course, it would be quite crass of me to take advantage of you in this condition, when you are unable to defend yourself.' The Earl gave a satisfied sigh and licked a spot of my blood from his bottom lip. 'But it is edifying to know I haven't lost my touch, as it were.'

I swallowed back the urge to beg, trembling uncontrollably as my body tried to cope with the venom. It's like any other addictive substance: the more you get, the more you need – for vamps, it's a great way to ensure your food follows you around like little blood-bloated sheep: a quick hit of venom with every bite keeps the sheep happy and healthy, and unwisely trotting back for more.

The Earl had given me more than a quick hit. If I'd been human, I'd be halfway to a heart attack. And that's the bottom-line reason why fae blood is such a sought-after commodity by the vamps; it's not our magic, or that we taste sweeter than humans.

We just don't die so easily.

There's *so* much more fun to be had when your victims can survive whatever torture you choose to inflict. And leaving me primed and desperate was just another form of torture.

'Bastard,' I finally managed to gasp.

'Now, now, my dear.' He placed a warning hand on my stomach. Sharp need rippled through my body, forcing another desperate moan from my throat. 'I would prefer you to keep a civil tongue in your head; our time together will be so much more enjoyable if you do.'

I gasped a couple of breaths, willing myself to ignore the cravings itching through my veins. The venom had cleared the clouds of the drug from my mind and my body. If I moved fast enough, maybe I could escape—

I still couldn't move.

Fear blasted full-force into me.

The Earl could do anything he wanted with me.

Panic constricted my throat.

I couldn't stop him.

I gulped for air, *calm*, wanted to scream again, *stay calm*, tears pricked my eyes. I opened them wide, not wanting them to fall, not wanting to give him the satisfaction, but felt their wetness roll down the side of my cheek.

He watched me, his blue eyes cold, detached.

Another tear followed.

He leaned over me – his breath in my face was musty and stale – and pressed his index finger to the corner of my eye. He followed the path of the teardrop, stopping when he reached the terrified pulse under my jaw, which beat slow and weak against him. He inhaled, his nostrils flaring in satisfaction. 'Good. I see you finally understand the situation, my dear.'

'What do you want?' I whispered, hating the catch in my voice.

'I would like us to watch the news together.' He pinched my cheek, then lifted a remote control and pointed it at the wall in front of the bed. A soft hum filled the room and a large painting of an over-endowed nude male reclining on an uncomfortable-looking chaise longue smoothly gave way to a huge plasma screen.

'Ah, here is the delightful Inspector Crane,' the Earl said cheerfully. 'I believe she has been searching for you, my dear.'

I stared numbly at the screen as I slowly pulled myself back from the yawning chasm in my mind. After a time the patrician lines of Detective Inspector Helen Crane's face came into focus. I recognised her severe expression, her blonde hair pulled back into a tightly contained bun. She looked every inch the 'I'm in charge here' fortysomething poster woman for the modern police force, guaranteed to encourage ambitious new recruits everywhere. Factor in that she was a powerful witch, not to mention high up in the Witches' Council and she *so* wasn't someone to have as an enemy.

Trouble was, neither of us liked the other. We'd butted heads during the Mr October murder, and it wasn't just because she'd wanted me to stay out of the investigation. No, our main bone of contention was Finn, my boss. At some point in their past, DI Helen Crane and Finn had jumped the broom together, and even though he said it was over, anyone could see she wasn't of the same opinion. It didn't matter that my relationship with Finn was nebulous at best; if DI Crane had been here, her feelings towards me where anti enough that I had no doubt she'd be cheering the Earl on from the sidelines.

I was thankful she was just on the TV.

And as she headed up the Metropolitan Police's Magic Murder Squad, seeing her giving some sort of news conference outside the MMS headquarters, Old Scotland Yard, wasn't any sort of surprise. The Earl turned the volume up.

'—nothing more to report on the disappearance of Genevieve Taylor, the sidhe fae who is believed to have information about the tragic death of Tomas Eriksen, a local baker and businessman,' Inspector Helen was saying. 'Mr Eriksen was a much-liked and well-respected figure within the community of Covent Garden, and he will be sorely missed. Should anyone have information about the whereabouts of Genevieve Taylor, we ask them not to approach her for their own safety, but to call Old Scotland Yard immediately on the number now showing on the bottom of the screen. All calls will be treated as confidential.'

'Detective Inspector Crane,' someone shouted, 'is it true that the sidhe is a suspect in the murder of Tomas Eriksen?'

Flashbulbs popped. The inspector's three jade brooches and dangling garnet earrings glittered and for a moment I thought I could almost see the spells she'd stored in the gemstones. 'We want Ms Taylor to help us with our enquiries—'

'Inspector, Kim Jones for the *Daily Mail* here, what evidence do you have that the sidhe murdered Mr Eriksen?'

'If she's not the killer,' was shouted from the crowd, 'why are you saying she's dangerous?'

The inspector held up her hands, her collection of rings looking like expensive knuckledusters. 'It is believed Ms Taylor was injured when the bakery exploded, and is thus not fully cognisant of her surroundings; we don't think she would deliberately hurt—'

Shock sliced through me. 'The bakery exploded?' I blurted.

'How else did you think you were injured, my dear?' The Earl muted the sound. 'I understand there was a lot of loose flour around; the news bods have had an expert on to explain the chemistry, something about starch being easy to burn and dust catching fire at the slightest of sparks, and then, *boom!*' He threw his hands in the air to illustrate his point. 'The explosion looks quite extensive.'

Questions jumped into my head; I picked out the most important. 'Was anyone hurt?'

'Only yourself and Malik al-Khan, who is sadly much worse off and unlikely to be around in the near future to provide you with any aid.' He smiled happily and briefly squeezed my thigh, causing another wave of craving to wash painfully over my body, effectively silencing my other questions. 'Oh look, this is my favourite part,' he said, pointing the remote at the plasma again. Through lust-blurred vision I recognised the bakery. The CCTV recording showed the back of someone – *me* – dressed in running shorts and sweatshirt talking to the florist's lad. I glanced around, giving the camera a good look at my profile and then stripped off my sweatshirt . . . The date-time stamp on the picture flipped to around half an hour later when the front of the shop exploded outwards, spraying large amounts of broken bricks, debris and dust into the air. Bright orange flames started to flicker amongst the devastation. The TV screen switched back to a picture of a silent talking head.

'You do have a capacity for upsetting people.' The Earl brushed a speck from his knee. 'It really is rather careless of you, my dear.'

I stared at the TV, my mind sifting through everything. Was he right? Had I angered someone enough for them to kill poor Tomas just to set me up? Or was there some other reason? Whatever it was I wouldn't know until I – or the police – found his murderer. Trouble was, if I walked into Old Scotland Yard without an alibi, DI Crane would have me banged up faster than I could say *I'm innocent*. She'd already convicted me in her own mind, and very nearly to the world. No way was she going to be looking for anyone else, let alone another sidhe, to pin Tomas' death on – especially when I was the only sidhe in London. And then there was the fact that I *am* sidhe fae: unlike a human, there'd be no sitting in jail serving my time for me, just a quick one-way trip to the guillotine.

The Earl was gazing at me expectantly, and since he appeared to be offering me the carrot after effectively threatening me with his fang-tipped stick, I dutifully asked the question. 'What's the deal?'

'Direct and to the point as usual. It is one of the several aspects I cherish about you, my dear.' He licked his lips. 'But of course, business before pleasure.' He waved at the TV screen. 'I can make this problem go away.'

Surprise, surprise. 'How exactly?'

'Why, friends in high places.' He gave a quick frown. 'Or is it low?' Then he smiled as if I should get the joke. I didn't. 'Well, anyway,' he carried on, 'friends who have the same ideals that I do, and who are, very rightly, concerned about the current situation.'

It was my turn to frown. 'What situation?'

'Why, my tragic demise, of course.' He squeezed my thigh and a slither of lust made me gasp again. 'My passing has left a breach in London's vampire community. I fear the lack of true leadership will result in utter chaos. All my careful planning, my nurturing of our current status, will be destroyed by incompetence.'

'What the—?' I stopped at the Earl's admonishing look, conscious of his hand on my leg. 'I don't understand what you're talking about.'

His expression turned condescending. 'Allow me to explain, my dear. I have worked tirelessly this last eight hundred years to ensure vampires here in my country are both respected by and respectful of humankind.' He adjusted his cuffs. 'It is how we were able to successfully recover our human rights; it is why we have not been hunted almost to extinction as in the Russias and the East. It is why we do not have to barricade ourselves into our castles as they do in the rest of Europe.' He spread his arms wide as if to a larger audience. 'To ensure that continues, I conceived the idea of vampires contributing to the entertainment and media industries, and thus elevating ourselves from the common perception of blood-sucking parasites subservient to the Witches' Council to revered celebrities with the power to influence the human world as we so desire.'

Megalomaniac soap-box, much!

'With my presence gone and me no longer the dominant voice,' he carried on, 'I fear that the reactionary elements within our society will force a situation where we have to return to hiding our faces, to pretending that we are something we are not in an effort to live lives of precarious comfort.'

I narrowed my eyes. 'That still doesn't tell me what you want.'

'You are my blood-bond, Genevieve.' He beamed at me. 'You will be my avatar.'

'What?' I was still none the wiser.

'All will become clear, my dear.' The Earl waved a dismissive hand at the French doors. 'Sadly, though, our time together has run out. Dawn approaches, so I will leave you to rest until later.' He smiled his charming smile and then vanished.

Stunned, I stared at the empty air, not entirely sure if his fang-filled grin had remained like the Cheshire cat's.

Then I realised I could move.

I had to get out of here, wherever *here* was. I struggled to sit up, my hands slipping on the stupid satin sheets, my arms and legs feeling like they belonged to someone else, the numbers on the monitor at the side of the bed flashing ever faster as my heart beat a crescendo in my ears—

The bedroom door opened.

A man walked in carrying a large wooden tray, a worried frown on his fortysomething chalk-white face. He wore jeans and a rumpled T-shirt and white gauze bandages were wrapped thickly around his wrists and elbows. He stopped at the bottom of the bed and looked at me from eyes magnified like a startled owl's behind his wire-rimmed glasses. His hands were trembling enough that the contents on the tray chinked. Then the frown disappeared and he smiled, showing even white *human* teeth.

'Oh good, you're awake, Ms Taylor.' Little wooden legs clicked out under the tray as he placed it down on the bed. 'I was beginning to get concerned about you.'

Chapter Seven

I stared at the tray's contents: a chilled bottle of Cristall – my brand of vodka – sat next to two glasses, one empty, the other filled with orange juice; a small porcelain dish of liquorice torpedoes, and what looked like a BLT sandwich. Other than the red rose in a cut-glass bud vase, the tray held all my favourites – if it wasn't for the fact that he was a vamp's flunky, I'd be worried I'd picked up a stalker instead of a slightly worse-for-wear jailer.

'Who the hell are you?' I demanded.

Owl Eyes flinched as if I'd hit him. 'Doctor Joseph Wainwright. Joseph. Didn't Malik tell you—?' A high-pitched alarm cut him off and we both looked at the heart monitor. The little red numbers were flashing 302: 302 beats per minute. I pulled the electrodes off my chest, wincing as the skin ripped away with them. What the fuck were they stuck on with? Superglue? The red numbers blinked out, the heart graph flatlined and the monitor's alarm started squawking loudly. I slapped it quiet.

'Whose blood-pet are you?'

His eyes were wide with shock. 'You should be dead with a heart rate like that.'

Duh: not human. 'C'mon, Doctor Joseph Wainwright – *Joseph* – which vampire is your master?'

'Malik al-Khan, of course.' His frown returned.

'Not the Earl?'

'The Earl's dead—'

'The Earl was just here talking to me,' I snapped. 'He bit me—' I stuck out my wrist to show him, then jerked it back and peered at it. There were no fang holes.

'It's the morphine,' Joseph said in a conciliatory voice. 'It can cause—'

'Hallucinations, dreams, yes, I know.' I frowned as confusion filled me. It hadn't felt like a dream. 'He turned the TV on, showed me the news.'

Joseph glanced behind him at the muted screen. 'I've had it on the news channel while I've been watching you. You've probably just absorbed the information.'

Had the Earl just been a nightmare? Of course, if I was going to have nightmares, the Earl would certainly be up for a starring role. And DI Crane, she was an understudy nightmare star if ever there was one. With her on the telly, no wonder my brain was playing tricks on me. But what if it hadn't been a dream? What if the Earl *was* alive? No way was I waiting around for him to pop up again. My heart speeding, I slid over to the edge of the bed and swung my legs off. My feet sank into the soft plush red carpet and a sudden attack of vertigo made me sway. I clutched at the slippery sheets, bewildered. What was I doing? Oh yeah, getting out. Getting dressed, and getting away before they came back, him and the inspector . . .

'Ms Taylor, I really don't think you should get up.'

I frowned up at him – no not him, *them*: the two startled owls looking back at me.

'I've been looking after you,' they said, 'and so far your injuries from the explosion haven't been improving. I really don't think you should—'

I tuned him out and squinted at the mirrored wall of wardrobes instead. Wardrobes meant clothes. Only the expanse of red carpet I had to cross was rolling like the sea. Why the hell was the room so big? I squinted again and a figure peered back at me, glistening with sweat, chest, neck and arms as red

as the sea. All the red was making me hot and dizzy. I wiped
my face, and the red-faced girl wiped hers. I looked down at
my hand; it was damp with pink-tinged sweat. I had an instant
of clear thought: I was crashing into a mega blood-flush. A
sick feeling roiled in my stomach. If I didn't do something, I'd
end up having convulsions, maybe even a stroke, which meant
I'd be unconscious, helpless . . .

Panic bubbled up in my throat again. There was something—

A hand clasped my wrist.

Flinching, I jerked back.

'Just keep calm, Genevieve.' The words sounded firm, in
control, and I looked up at Joseph, who smiled confidently
back, his face slightly distorted behind a clear face-mask. I
frowned; the mask meant something, something good. The
panic started to recede and my mind started remembering
what needed to be done. I took a breath.

'That's it, Genevieve. Now I want you to kneel down on
the floor.' He pulled me gently and I slid to my knees. 'Good.'
He crouched and placed a green plastic bucket between us, his
expression grim. 'Now, I'm going to take some blood, nothing
to worry about, so just relax.' He held up another shunt, its
clear tube trailing down to an empty blood bag.

'S'not quick enough,' I slurred, 'need . . . knife.'

His eyes lost some of their confidence. The shunt disappeared, then he held a scalpel in front of me. The blade
glinted in the mirrors behind him.

I nodded, my heart pounding frantically under my ribs,
a fine tremble shivering under my skin. 'Do it.' I pushed my
arm into the bucket.

He touched the point of the scalpel to the red vein bulging down my inner arm. Watery pink sweat dripped off my
chin and splashed onto his gloved hand. I heard him gasp and
looked up, catching the nervous expression in his owl-like
hazel eyes.

'It's been a while since I've done this.' He swallowed, his
Adam's apple bobbing.

I grabbed the hand holding the knife, felt him start, then
I sliced deeply, scoring the vein from my elbow to my wrist.
Sharp pain flipped into pleasure that rushed like electricity

through my body. My blood welled, thick and viscous like molten tar, and the scent of liquorice and copper and honey filled the air. The urge to cut my skin again, to chase that pleasure, to see more of my blood sparkling bright along my skin was a seductive whisper, calling me, urging—

'For the love of God!' Joseph yanked his hand from mine, flinging the scalpel away. It clattered off the mirrors and landed noiselessly on the thick carpet.

Taking a deep breath, I sat back on my heels and closed my eyes, trying to ignore the warm, wet trickle of blood running down my arm. I listened to the faint splash as it fell into the bucket and the slightly fast cadence of his breathing as I waited for my heart to slow back to normal. Venom junkies had been known to die from blood loss once the desperate bliss of spilling their own blood short-circuited their minds.

After a while, I asked, 'What day is it?'

'Friday,' he said quietly.

Damn, last I remembered it was Tuesday morning. I'd lost three days. I opened my eyes. Blood the consistency of runny honey still slopped into the bucket, but it was slowing. I squeezed my arm just below my elbow, pulling the cut apart; the small pain rippled into a promise of pleasure that had me squirming.

Joseph frowned. 'Why are you doing that?'

'My blood's too thick' – an aspect of the venom – 'and if I don't do this, I won't lose enough and the venom will throw me back into another blood-flush.'

'Ah yes.' He looked down at the bucket, then up at me. 'You've been heading for a blood-flush since yesterday; you're hypertensive, and your red blood cell count is the highest I've ever seen. I was debating whether to bleed you or not before you regained consciousness, but your other injuries haven't been healing, so I wasn't sure if it would do more harm than good.' His frown deepened. 'I've never treated a sidhe before.'

I looked down at my patchy skin. 'This isn't bad for a couple of days.'

'That didn't happen in a couple of days. Malik gave you his blood as soon as he could. He carries the true Gift, so he healed you to this in about an hour. But there's been no change since then.'

It was my turn to frown. That didn't sound right. *No pain, no gain*; the words teased at the edge of my mind, nothing to do with exercise – wasn't there something about fae needing to feel some pain for the magic to kick in with the healing? Then I remembered I'd been floating somewhere golden and warm, riding along with the sunshine, until my subconscious mind reconstituted the Earl and dropped him into my nightmare. 'You had me stoked up on morphine, didn't you?' I asked slowly.

'Of course, you were in a lot of pain; I didn't want to see you suffer. Your metabolism works a lot faster than a human's. I had to up the dose quite a bit before it took effect.'

Was that why I hadn't healed? Too much morphine?

'I shouldn't worry about getting dependant or anything after this short period of use,' he added. 'When morphine's used for pain relief it doesn't appear to affect the addictive centres of the brain.'

I blinked. 'I've got 3V, Joseph. It negates the effects of any other chemical addictions and it kills off any diseases or infections.' If it wasn't for the obvious side-effects, 3V could keep humans as healthy as the proverbial horse. 'Or didn't they teach you that at doctor school?'

'Sorry, yes, I know.' He grimaced, staring down into the bucket for a long moment. 'The reassurance stuff is standard spiel; you end up saying it all the time. Everyone gets all concerned about morphine being derived from opium.' He shrugged tiredly. 'But 3V only contradicts other infections when in the host; they're still carried by the blood, and blood transference can still pass them on to someone who doesn't have 3V.' He tapped his face-mask. 'That's the reason for the get-up.'

'You haven't got 3V?' I stared, surprised. 'But you said Malik was your master?'

'I didn't, not exactly.' He smiled ruefully. 'You didn't look like you were ready for a long explanation. I do a lot of work in Sucker Town – I'm part of the Health Department's monitoring group – and I've seen the effects of 3V and I didn't want to be infected.' He indicated my arm dripping blood into the bucket. 'Malik and I are friends; he would no more go against my wishes than fly to the moon.'

Friends? Wounded vamps don't have friends, they have automatic survival responses. In other words, they mind-lock the nearest blood supply, sink fangs into it and the venom overdose turbo-charges the red blood cell production while making sure the victim doesn't get the chance to run away, usually because they're unconscious and paralysed by a stroke caused by the venom-induced hypertension. Great for the vamp, not much fun for any of his *friends*.

I looked at the bandages on Joseph's arms, assessing him. 'Malik can't be too hurt, not if you've been feeding him.' I pulled and squeezed my arm again. 'If he'd gone into blood-lust, you'd be just another blood-slave by now.' Or dead.

'Yes, Malik's explained all that to me.' He sighed. 'We've worked out a failsafe plan: a tranquilliser gun. If he's hurt in any way, I shoot first, then ask questions later, once he comes round. The tranquilliser is the same one they use on big cats, like lions and tigers. I've been keeping him under the last few days so he's safe enough to look after.'

Ri-ight! Well, that was certainly one way to deal with an injured vamp. I gave my arm another squeeze. It hurt, no ripples of anticipated pleasure this time. I checked my colour out in the mirror. The red splotches had gone, my skin was its usual warm honey – with the added pink and shiny bits – and my heart thudded a calm tattoo in my chest.

'I'm about done here,' I said. 'You got a spare bandage I can use?'

He didn't seem to hear, just stared thoughtfully at my blood plopping into the bucket.

'Joseph?'

His head shot up. 'There's just over a pint there.' Speculation lit his eyes. 'Do you think you could manage some more? I wouldn't ask but I've already transfused two pints of my own and Malik still needs more.' His hands trembled where he clutched the rim of the bucket. 'I didn't trust anyone else to help, not with your problems with the police.'

When he put it like that, how could I refuse?

'Sure.' I clenched, then unclenched my hand, having to pump the blood out now.

Two pints would probably take Joseph's body about six weeks to make the red cells up. 3V halved that timescale for a

human. With 3V turbo-charging my own fae metabolism, I'd
make the red cells up in around a week – yet another reason
the vamps are so hot for a fae to snack on. Fae really are their
ultimate fast food.

I looked into the bucket. That should do it. 'I'm done here,
Joe,' I said, and gave him a quick smile. Now to find out how
much of a jailer he intended to be. 'So how are you fixed for
lending me some clothes and letting me use the phone?'

'You're leaving?' His expression behind the mask turned
worried. 'But what about Malik?'

'I'm sure you can look after him better if I'm not here.'
As I stood I saw the wound on my arm was already scabbing
over. 'And anyway' – I gave him a rueful smile – 'I'm not the
nursemaid type.'

'Okay.' He pursed his lips. 'Clothes should be no problem,
but I'm afraid I can't let you use the phone.' His face creased
up in awkward embarrassment. 'It's not that I don't want to
help, but you'd be phoning your friends, and I don't want any
calls to get traced back to me or here. This is one of Malik's
safe houses.'

I frowned. 'Aren't you being just a tiny bit paranoid?'

'Maybe' – he shrugged – 'but you're wanted for murder,
and they can monitor phones, especially mobiles, if they
know the numbers. I saw it on that film, the one where the
spy who's lost his memory is on the run.' He gave me a sheep-
ish look. 'Of course, it could just be dramatic licence, but I'd
rather be paranoid than find out I'm right when the police are
knocking on my door.'

Fine, no point wasting my time arguing with him, not
when I'd been lying around comatose for three days. I had
enough other things I wanted: a shower, some food, scissors
to sort out my hair – and it was about time I started looking
for Tomas' murderer.

And I knew just where to start.

With the kelpie that lived in the River Thames.

Chapter Eight

The wind rippled the surface of the River Thames, pushing it into choppy grey ridges. I traipsed along Victoria Embankment, keeping close to the low stone wall that overlooked the river. Russet and brown hand-shaped leaves from the sycamore trees blew along the pavement, a smattering of cold raindrops hit my face and the river scent freshened the ever-present traffic fumes clogging the late-afternoon air. The constant line of cars, taxis and buses rumbled along, stopping and starting again with each quick change of the lights. I shuffled my way past camera-toting tourists, chattering school kids and an overweight jogger who was puffing and stopping as often as the traffic.

No one paid me any attention – but with the too-large parka I was wearing almost reaching my calves and the baseball cap hiding my tell-tale amber hair, I looked like any other homeless youngster wandering around aimlessly, even without the rolled-up jeans and old trainers stuffed with newspaper. Oddly enough, although Joseph's mirrored wardrobes had been full of women's outfits, it had all looked more appropriate for a night out at an S&M club than for wandering the streets of London incognito. Joseph had mumbled something about a friend and blushed red to the tips of his ears, then offered me some of his own clothes, but he still wouldn't let me use his phone. I'd phoned Grace from a public box and told her everything; it hadn't been an easy conversation, but in the end she'd agreed with my plans.

I slowed as I neared the RAF Monument. At the top of its granite column, the golden eagle gleamed in the grey afternoon light as it stared out across the river towards the slowly revolving Ferris-wheel of the London Eye. The waist-height gates on either side of the base were padlocked shut; behind them steps led down to a landing platform jutting into the river, then the steps turned and disappeared beneath the brownish murk of the water. It's not an obvious entrance to someone's home, but then, London's fae rarely advertise their presence, nor do they welcome unlooked-for visitors, let alone inquisitive humans. So most tourists stop, read the inscription about the Air Force's departed servicemen, cast an incurious look over the gates and then move on, none of them conscious of the subtle spell that gently urges them on their way.

I halted in front of the inscription and traced my fingers over the letters, wondering if Tavish, the kelpie I'd come to see, was home. Tavish is a techno-geek for hire – he's rumoured to freelance for the Ministry of Defence, one of the reasons he keeps his entrance at the Whitehall steps. (Of course, the other reason his home is here is that the River Thames from Lambeth Bridge and down to the sea is his feeding ground.)

Hacking into the news services or even the police files to get me a copy of the full CCTV footage of the bakery that was currently splashed across the country's TV screens would be as easy as diving for pennies on the riverbed – something else Tavish could do with his eyes closed. And if there were any clues in the recording, deciphering them wouldn't be much more difficult for him.

Nerves fluttered in my stomach as if I'd swallowed a flight of dragonflies.

Now I was here, I wasn't sure it was such a great idea . . .

Trouble was, Tavish and I had history – if you could call half a dozen casual dates history – but the possibility for more had always been there. Not that I'd wanted to end the fledgling relationship, but at the time my secrets were still just that – *secret* – and I'd been keeping my distance from other fae. I tapped my fingers indecisively on the top of the gate. I'd probably suffered more in the way of futile regrets and disappointment over the break-up than Tavish ever had, but dump any male – or female, for that matter – without a good explanation and their ego isn't going to be happy. Dump a centuries-old kelpie, one of the wylde fae, and it wasn't just his ego I needed to worry about.

But I had more important things to concern me than my past personal life, and the CCTV footage wasn't the only reason I'd come to see Tavish.

London has three gates that join it to the Fair Lands, and Tavish is one of the gates' guardians. If there was another sidhe in London, Tavish should know . . . which meant he should know something about Tomas' murderer. Even as I thought it, a shiver of awareness prickled my skin with goosebumps. He was home, and he knew I was here.

I took a guarded look round, checking no one was watching me too closely, and then clambered quickly over the gate on one side of the column. Magic clung to me as if I'd walked through a heavy mist. I jogged down the steps to the landing platform, then gripped the iron railing with one hand and crouched, peering into the water swirling a few inches below me. I could just see the top of the old archway, which had been bricked up in the late eighteen hundreds, when the Victoria Embankment had been built to hold back the river. Taking a deep breath, I reached down to touch the tail of the carved stone fish statue mounted on the centre of the arch, but before my fingers connected, I felt the hair rise on my body and I hesitated.

I stood up and turned to look back up at the road. Cosette the ghost was standing on the pavement, watching me from the other side of the gate, an odd, considering look on her childish face. Indecision wavered inside me; should I go up to see her? Then common sense took over; we still couldn't communicate, so the best thing I could do was sort this mess out first. I gave her a nod and a wave, then turned back to face the river.

I reached down again and wrapped my fingers around the fish statue's tail. The railing stayed hard beneath my other palm, but as the magic pressed solidly against me the traffic noise, the chill autumn wind and the ozone scent of the Thames disappeared. The world *shifted* around me, not as movement that could be felt, but something deeper, as if space itself was being reshaped. The magic took me out of the humans' world.

And into *Between*.

Below me, the river was gone, replaced by an abyss so deep and dark my head spun with vertigo. Slowly I straightened, still staring down, unwilling – almost unable – to take my gaze from the chasm. There was something seductive about it; I felt as if I could launch myself into it and find what I sought . . .

I forced myself to turn, to put my back to the emptiness. *Between* is the gap that links the humans' world and the Fair Lands. It's a dangerous place, the magic that fuels it is fierce and untamed, and persuasive enough that the legends about those who stray from the paths are full of wonder or terror or death.

Or nothing at all.

The sky, deepest blue and curved like a huge bowl overhead, brightened. A hot yellow sun blazed like a furnace and in seconds sweat slicked between my breasts and down my spine. Inside me, the Knock-back Wards I'd absorbed at the bakery flared, the magic lifting its nose like a dog snuffling around this new place. I dug inside the jacket pocket for a couple of liquorice torpedoes and stuffed them in my mouth. As soon as the sugar hit my system, I used the extra boost and willed the Knock-back Wards into quiet sleepiness. Mixing spells with the magic here, even those as basic as the Wards, could be a hit-and-miss affair: sometimes it worked, sometimes it was like putting a match to a touchpaper.

I scanned the area. Before me was a beach of golden sand that stretched further than I could see. On one side was a white cliff with a sand-coloured camouflage tent pitched at its base, shadowed by the overhang: Tavish's home, or at least its current façade. On the other side of the beach was a glittering, mirror-dark sea, but the water was still and silent, and probably as deep as the abyss.

Tavish was in the water – in his human shape – but still in the water.

Damn, that *so* wasn't a good start.

He was sitting at the water's edge, half-submerged, with his back to me. I could see his long legs stretched out in the shallows, his arms braced behind him on the sand as he raised his face to the sun. The bottle-green dreads that streamed down his back looked like seaweed hung out to dry, the silver-beaded tips glinting in the sunlight. He didn't acknowledge me. Ignoring the nerves still twisting in my stomach, I shrugged out of the jacket and sighed in relief as a cool breeze teased around me. I almost ditched the jeans too – the T-shirt Joseph had given me was long enough to pass as a baggy dress – but instead I just removed the baseball cap and ran my fingers through my shorter hair. I kicked off the old trainers and walked down the dozen steps to the beach. The sand was pleasantly warm beneath my feet, not as burning-hot as the fiery sun would suggest . . . but this was *Between*. And expecting *Between* to follow the rules of the humans' world was a recipe for disaster.

When I was close enough to see Tavish's delicate gills flare like black lace fans either side of his neck, but far enough away – from him and the water – that I almost felt safe, I stopped.

'Hello, Tavish.'

'Long time nae see, doll.' He turned to look at me over his shoulder, his face breaking into a welcoming smile, his sharp-pointed teeth white against the darkness of his skin – not black, but the deepest green found where the sunlight just penetrates the depths of the sea. 'But you took your ain sweet time getting here. I've been expecting you this last two days.'

I smiled back, couldn't help myself as my magic exalted at the sight of him and the nerves inside me settled. I sat where I was, crossing my legs Indian-style, and trailed my fingers through the soft sand. Tavish might be centuries old – he's cagey about how many – but like most fae he didn't look like he'd reached thirty yet. He's the most fae-looking of all those I know, and yet somehow he still easily passes for human without using a Glamour. His long, angular features, Roman-straight nose and almost pointed chin are a less delicate, more male face than my own, but with enough echoes of my own face that anyone can see the sidhe in his make-up. I'd often wondered if he wasn't a lot older than anyone guessed, maybe even born in the Shining Times, when the sidhe would procreate with any living thing that attracted their attention. Only Tavish doesn't have our cat-like pupils – or any pupils at all; his eyes are a brilliant silver with a rim of white, like the horse that is his other shape. He wasn't so much handsome as compelling, alluring . . .

I dragged my gaze from him, realising I was staring like a charm-struck human – one that would unwittingly follow the kelpie anywhere, even into the treacherous water – and made an effort to look at the rest of the scenery.

'The place looks different,' I said as an opener. 'More tropical than your last.'

'Aye, well, I fancied a wee change,' he said, his accent soft and warm. 'This time o' year the Highlands can be a wee bit blowy, for all the heather colours the hills with nature's own beauty.'

I waved back at the abyss. 'So what happened with that?'

'Hmph,' he snorted, ''twas nae in the plan, though you're in luck, for it had a hankering tae be this side of the steps, got itsel' all decked out with one of those rope and plank bridges. It took me a heck of a while tae convince the magic tae move it over there.'

Which is *Between* all over. It's malleable – unlike the humans' world or the Fair Lands – in fact, malleable enough that anyone with enough magical mojo can impose their will. But sometimes the magic comes up with its own quirky interpretation of what it's asked for. Tavish had forged his patch a couple of centuries ago, but even after moulding it to his own desires for all that time, it looked like the magic could still leave him living on a knife's edge – or rather, a cliff's edge . . .

'It wants something,' I murmured, frowning.

'Aye, doll, don't we all!' He laughed, the sound a soft snicker. 'Doesnae mean we're going tae get it, though.'

Disappointment slid inside me. I lifted a handful of sand, letting the grains fall through my fingers. Maybe he wasn't as welcoming as his smile had suggested. 'Does that mean you're not going to help me?'

'Nae, doll, it means I mayn't be having the answers you seek.' He rolled onto his front to face me, propping himself on his arms. The water surged over his wide shoulders and streamed down the muscled indentation of his spine, sparkling aqua and turquoise against his skin. 'But ask away.'

I blinked away the afterimage of the bright water, then said slowly, 'You know the CCTV recording they're all showing on the news? Is there any chance it's been tampered with, or that there's a clue that the police haven't shown or picked up on yet?'

'There's naught on the recording tae see, other than yoursel' going intae that shop.' His gills flared. 'And the explosion.'

'Really not what I was hoping to hear.' I pursed my lips.

'The wonder of it is why you chose tae go in anyway, doll.' He drew a wavy line in the sand and the breeze picked up, ruffling the sea behind him.

'No wondering about it, Tavish.' I frowned, trying to work out why he was asking. 'I've been in there nearly every morning for the last couple of weeks.'

'Why?' he persisted, scooping a deep sand-basin in front of him.

I drew my knees up and hugged them, not happy about his tone. 'The baker was having a few witch problems – milk turning sour, bread not rising, that sort of thing.'

'Sounds more like brownie problems, but' – water trickled into the sand-basin – 'you get where I'm going wi' this?' He looked at me enquiringly.

'Someone's set me up,' I stated, hoping he wasn't asking me anything else, like *was I guilty*. 'Yeah, I managed to work that one out for myself. Trouble is, while Tomas – the dead baker – told me it was a witch. I never actually met her.' I gave him a wry smile. 'Maybe you can see where I'm going too?'

'Aye, 'tis true: witch or sidhe, there's nae possibility of a human telling the difference betwixt them if the sidhe doesnae want them tae.' The small puddle in the sand overflowed in front of him. 'But then there's nae sidhe in London other than yoursel', doll. Hasnae been this last eighty-odd years.'

Which was when there'd been a falling-out between London's fae and one of the sidhe queens, and the queen had sealed the gates.

A hundred years past, the queen in question had fallen in love with a human and chosen to bear a son. Of course, her son had been human, as are all children born of sidhe and human, so she'd left him behind when she'd returned to the Fair Lands. But she loved him, and visited him as he grew up, and she charged London's fae to watch over him when she wasn't there. Then one day he fell in with a bad crowd, and he ended up being lured to his death by the vampires. The queen blamed London's fae and not only did she seal the gates, she also laid a *droch guidhe* – a curse – on them *that they should also know the grief in her heart.*

Which explains why so many of London's faelings – humans with lesser fae blood – end up victims of the fang-gangs in Sucker Town through no true fault of their own.

Of course, no one likes to air their dirty laundry in public, so the accepted reason for the sidhe not visiting London when they were known for putting in appearances elsewhere was that they preferred to live in the Fair Lands rather than have to deal with the hustle and technology of the capital city.

'Maybe one of the gates from the Fair Lands has been opened?' I said, resting my chin on my knees. 'If so, then another sidhe could've come through . . .' I trailed off and watched Tavish and the water in front of him from under my lashes. I built a small ridge of sand in front of me with my toes.

He snorted again, and waves crested far out in the dark sea. 'There's nae one o' us could open our gates wi'out the others knowing.'

I'd been hoping for a more informative answer than that, like whether the gates *had* actually been opened, but Tavish was wylde fae, and the wylde fae can be tricky. They can talk around things when they want, sometimes for no other reason than a bit of mischief.

I tried another tack. 'What if it was a sidhe who opened one of the gates? Would you know then?'

'There's naebody like the fae when it comes tae carrying ill will.' His smile had a hard edge to it. 'And lately the Ladies Meriel and Isabella have been refusing even tae treaty wi' the queen's ambassador.' He lowered his head, the silver beads tinkling as his dreads fell forward, and blew ripples across the overflowing pool in front of him. 'Should another sidhe take it intae their minds to visit, they'd find nae entry through. The gates are sealed from this side now.'

Damn: so the gates *were* a dead end. Still, the CCTV footage had to be worth a look. Warm water slipped past my little ridge and over my toes, swilling sugary sand about my feet. 'Can I watch the recording then?' I asked, inching back. 'I might be able to see something.'

''Course y'can, doll.' He smiled and slipped back beneath the water's surface. '*Come for a swim wi' me first.*' He whispered the words in my mind.

I pushed myself to my feet, moving as slowly as I dared, feeling the pull of his magic. 'Swimming with you isn't a good idea, Tavish.' The water swirled around my ankles, soaking my jeans. I looked towards the tent, knowing I should walk out onto dry land, but the water wanted me to stay, and there was something wistful in the way it crept like a curious fish around my knees. I gazed down at Tavish, floating under the water, a trail of turquoise and aqua bubbles rising from his gills. Fascinated, I watched as they flashed like shooting stars over the dark surface of the sea.

'*Come intae the depths wi' me, my lady.*' His eyes were glowing silver orbs. '*Death clings tae your heart.*' His voice turned soft, cajoling. '*Let me hold you close, sing tae you o' the everlasting rhythms of the sea, let me taste o' the darkness that stains your soul, steal those sweet breaths as they leave your soft lips.*' He reared out of the water, glorious and naked, his muscles lean and firm under the shining wetness of his green-black skin. 'There is kindness in the depths, and peace.' He offered me his hand and his pledge: *a pledge to lift the sorrow that fell about my shoulders, to pull away the heavy cloak of self-blame and grief and despair for those that I'd hurt, for those I'd lost . . . for those I'd killed.* He tossed his head, the magic cascading over him in rainbow hues that glittered and sparkled in the brightness of the sun.

And he took his other shape.

My pulse sped with wary excitement. He was still Tavish, but *not*. In his horse guise his nature ruled him, stripped away his civilised veneer, made him wild and feral and more like the magic itself.

The kelpie horse whickered softly, nostrils flaring, and stepped closer. He butted his nose against my chest, his whisky-peat breath warm against my T-shirt. I stroked the

softness of his muzzle, his chin whiskers tickling along my
arm, and reached up to trail gentle fingers over the black-lace
gills that fluttered under my touch.

'You're beautiful,' I whispered, the water sliding around
my thighs. 'Beautiful and beguiling— but you know that
already.' He whinnied, mocking, derisive, his two-toed hoof
pawing a groove in the sand. I ran my palm down his sea-
slick neck and moved to rest my hand on his forequarters. 'It's
tempting, to think of riding into the sea with you, to give you
what I feel, to let you take that from me . . .'

His head swung round, ears pricking expectantly forward,
tail flicking impatiently over his sleek, muscled rump. I leant
against his side, my heart pounding with anticipation. His
magic tugged at me like a strong current, urging me to go
with him, to let him take me into the sea's warm embrace. He
nudged my hip and I licked my lips, tasting not salt, but
peat and fresh-water sweetness. I tangled my fingers in the
knotted dreads of his mane, feeling my own magic rise to
join with his, and light more dazzling than the sun misted
from my skin, gilding his green-black coat with shimmering
golden dust.

I rubbed my cheek against his neck, placed my lips against
his warm skin. 'Yes, I'll swim with you, kelpie' – his ears
twitched back and I started to draw away – 'one day, but that
day hasn't—'

Green lightning arced around us, sizzling into steam as it
hit the water. The kelpie horse screamed with rage, rearing
up and lunging towards the beach. The turbulent wave that
spread out behind him knocked me off my feet and I sank
below the dark sea. I kicked out with my legs, reaching for
the surface above me. A hand wrapped around my ankle and
I kicked, panicked, until it loosened. I burst out into the air
above, heart pounding, gasping for breath. The shore was further away than I remembered – time and space and magic
conspire to deceive in *Between*. I started swimming, annoyance and fear fuelling me. *Damn kelpie!* And stupid me – I
knew better than to let myself get seduced with his magic.
Now I had to swim for my foolishness. Ahead of me the kelpie
cut through the water, a charging water-horse, and galloped
out of the crashing waves onto the shore. His angry screams

sliced the air. Another flash of green lightning hit the sand next to him and it exploded in a cloud around him, obscuring him from view.

Someone was throwing Stun spells around like they were firecrackers at a troll's New Moon party.

Panic hit me before I remembered no one could pass Tavish's entrance without his say-so. He *knew* whoever it was attacking. And he wouldn't have let them in if he didn't think he could deal with them . . . I just wished he'd remembered that he'd left me struggling in his rage-lashed sea. Arrogant bastard. I clamped my lips tight together and doggie-paddled towards the shore, doing my best not to drown. Within minutes my arms ached and the jeans were like lead weights around my legs, determined to drag me under. I trod water as I struggled with the zip and finally managed to push the jeans down over my hips – then promptly panicked again as I followed them under into the depths below.

Water choked my throat and burned down my nose as I struggled back up to the surface and then gulped for air like a stranded fish. Then trying to ignore the cramp stabbing into my left thigh, I pushed out again. But hard as I swam, the shore was still too far away, and I realised that *something* – either the kelpie or the magic – was holding me back. Anger filled me, giving me another burst of energy. No way were they going to keep me out here any longer. As soon as I thought it, the sea became calmer and easier to swim through, and the beach suddenly got a lot, lot closer.

The kelpie's screams grew louder in my ears, and other, deeper roars of anger and challenge slashed through them. As my hands and knees scraped against the sandy bottom, I lurched to my feet in the shallower water, then stared at the fight before me. The kelpie reared up, still screaming with rage, his forelegs thrashing through the air, then thudding down discordantly into the sand. A heavy-built silhouette of a satyr rose against the brilliant blue of the sky, horns curving sharp above his head, ready to charge. *Finn?* What the hell was he doing here? An angry wave crashed into me, taking my legs from under me, and I fell back. I scrambled forward out of the water again, struggling to get my breath, until I was beyond the tideline.

Then I watched, my heart in my mouth, as the satyr lunged between the kelpie's hammering forelegs, thrust up with his horns and gouged a bloody wound across the kelpie's chest. The kelpie's hooves struck down on the satyr's back, knocking him down, but as the kelpie reared up again, the satyr rolled out from under the hooves and came up into a crouch. The kelpie thudded back down onto four legs, his broad chest heaving, sweat and blood combining in a pink froth on the green-black of his coat.

The fight was awe-inspiring and terrifying, and I understood why their ancestors had been worshipped as gods or feared as demons. It was also fucking stupid, all the more so because I suspected they were fighting because of me – and by the looks of them, they weren't going to stop until one or both were unconscious. Being fae, that could take a long, long time, and I had better ways of spending mine than watching two idiot fae pound each other into the sand. Like looking for a murderer! Bad enough I'd let myself get enticed by Tavish's magic—

'Stop!' I yelled, but neither heard me.

Fuck. I was too far away. Frustration rose inside me and the Knock-back Wards shifted uneasily – giving me an idea: maybe I could use them in some way? And even as I questioned it, the magic answered and I felt the weird sensation of a heavy metal bar being dropped into my hand. Almost without thinking, I lifted the bar above my shoulder, holding it like a spear. With the magic vibrating through me like high-voltage electricity I concentrated my will and threw it, aiming for a point in the sand between the two fae.

I held my breath.

Where the spear struck a padlocked door materialised into existence. Buzzing over its surface were the black and grey stripes of a Knock-back Ward. The satyr was on one side, the kelpie on the other, and neither appeared to notice the door. They lowered their heads and charged—

—and as both crashed into the mirage of the door the release of magic exploded out, lifting me off my feet and knocking me back into the water. *Again.* I scrambled up again and looked towards the sudden stillness.

The fight had stalled. Both fae lay groaning on the sand, the door an incongruous barrier between them.

Smiling in grim satisfaction, I strode towards them, my nose flaring at the sharp, scorched smell that stung the air.

Finn lay on his side, crimson blood staining his horns, deep grazes and cuts marring the smooth tanned skin of his back and shoulders. More blood and sand clogged the usually sleek sable hair that covered his lower body and flanks, and his hooves were ragged and torn.

Tavish lay on his back, arms outstretched, in his human shape once again. His dreads were matted and tangled and bright crimson blood bubbled from the jagged wound across his chest.

'What the fuck do the pair of you think you're playing at?' I yelled. 'I came here for help, not to be half-drowned, and then end up refereeing a fucking fight!'

Neither spoke. They just glowered at each other, their expressions equally closed.

I kicked at the sand in frustration. 'Right. So if either of you is going to help me, then do it. If not, then you can just fuck off back into the water, or wherever the hell you came from. But. Stop. Wasting. My. Time.'

Turning my back on them, I stormed towards the camouflage tent. I knew how Tavish's computers worked; I didn't need him or anyone else for that. I lifted the fabric door and ducked under it— A wind as fierce as a hurricane blew against me, making me stumble. I grabbed hold of a wooden tent pole to keep from falling. My skin prickled with magic as hot air eddied round me, stripping the water from my dripping T-shirt and wet hair. I'd forgotten that Tavish had his threshold tagged with a Clean-Up spell. I waited until the magic cooled, telling me the spell was done, then stepped forward.

And *shifted* from *Between* and back into the humans' world.

And back to my problems.

Chapter Nine

Tavish's underground living area hadn't changed since my last visit. The walls were grey blocks of rough granite, much like the RAF monument above, and the floor was flagged with smooth dark-grey slabs. To one side of the high-ceilinged space was a low black suede sofa. A black granite slab sat solidly in front of it on a huge white long-haired skin rug belonging to some animal that had never roamed the humans' world. I'd never felt comfortable walking on the rug with shoes on, let alone with bare feet – something told me the granite slab wasn't just there as a convenient coffee-table – so I skirted round it and headed for Tavish's office. A glass wall divided it from the rest of the space.

The glass wasn't just a stylish break between his living and working areas. When I *looked*, the complicated Buffer spell that protected all his computers from getting zapped by magic lit the glass up like a sun-flare. And there was a lot of gear to protect: a three-high by five-wide bank of flat-screen computer monitors curved around a selection of keyboards and rollerball mice posed on flexi-stalks. It looked like a cross between a giant's electronic bouquet and a hacker's mega-expensive wet dream.

I pulled open the glass door; the low background hum of the electronics buzzed against my ears and I swallowed back the flat taste of the ionised, recycled air. Most of the monitors were playing sections of one large screensaver – a coral reef with darting shoals of tropical fish, and a pair of sharp-toothed sharks swimming lazily from one screen to another – but the monitor front and centre was paused on the CCTV footage showing 'me' standing in front of Tomas' bakery talking to the florist's boy.

My stomach did an anxious little jump at seeing it again. I hooked one leg under me and settled into the leather chair, reaching for the nearest keyboard—

'Tavish says to remember the bracelets and the gloves,' Finn said quietly from behind me.

I stopped, hand in mid-air. 'Thanks,' I said and snagged a pair of the extra-thick surgical gloves from the box under the desk. I snapped them on and pulled them up over my wrists, then gingerly picked up two silver cuffs from the tray next to the box. They were half an inch wide and peppered with industrial-grade diamond chips. I clasped them round my wrists on top of the gloves so the silver didn't burn my skin. The cuffs and gloves were probably overkill – seeing as each computer had its own individual Buffer spell glowing away – but I wasn't going to take the chance of frying their hard drives by not wearing the magical inhibitors. Tavish might like me, but not that much.

'Are you okay?' Finn's voice held concern.

'I'm fine,' I said, still simmering with annoyance over the fight between him and Tavish.

'You don't look fine, Gen.'

I glanced down at the baggy T-shirt that was all I was wearing – Joseph's boxers had been too large for me, and none of the fetish underwear in the mirrored wardrobes had appealed. Tavish's Clean-Up spell had dried and de-sanded the T-shirt, but that was it. I sighed. Okay, I didn't look so good, but hey, what did he expect after all I'd been through? Explosion and deep sea swimming anyone?

I turned to look at Finn. He was leaning against the wall next to the monitors, his arms loosely crossed. His horns had shortened to a couple of inches above his dark blond hair and his sharp feral features were Glamoured back to his more usual clean-cut human handsome. There were no signs of his recent fight; his black chinos and black dress shirt with its thin electric-blue stripes and – I checked – highly polished black boots looked like he'd just taken them from his wardrobe, which he probably had, using magic.

I shrugged. 'Not all of us have the ability to *call* fresh clothes whenever we want to.'

'I'm not talking about the clothes, Gen.' He came over to crouch by the side of my chair. 'I'm talking about this.' He gently touched a pink patch of skin on my forearm. A tingle slipped inside me before the cuffs glowed and shut it down. 'You've been injured.' Anxiety shaded the moss-green of his eyes.

'I'll heal good as new in a few days,' I said firmly, still furious that he hadn't thought to check I was okay before he'd started chucking Stun spells around. I narrowed my eyes. 'What are you doing here, anyway, besides your little spat with Tavish out there?'

'Hell's thorns, Gen,' he said, exasperated. 'What do you think I'm doing here? You've been missing since Tuesday morning; I've been worried about you.'

'And now I'm not missing any more.' I tilted my head enquiringly. 'Are you here to help, or is there some other reason?'

A puzzled line creased between his brows. 'Of course I'm here to help, why else?'

'Oh, maybe so you can tell Detective Inspector Helen Crane, your ex-witch wife, where I am so she can come and arrest me?' I said, not keeping the suspicion out of my voice.

'Helen's a police officer, Gen.' He straightened, his face closing up. 'She has to go by the evidence.'

'Yeah, right.' Disappointment twisted through me. Of course he'd take her side; it didn't seem to matter that she might be looking at the evidence through blinkered eyes gone green with jealousy. I turned back to the monitors, clicked on the play button and started the CCTV footage rolling. The monitor-me stuck her hands on her hips outside the bakery and looked around.

'She doesn't need to arrest me anyway,' I said after a moment. 'I've got an alibi, someone who can prove I wasn't with Tomas when he was killed.'

'Who?' Finn's reflection appeared in the screen. I blinked as another reflection, Cosette's, shadowed his. I swivelled the chair round to look and my knees bumped into Finn's legs he was so close, but she wasn't there. Damn, it was bad enough being haunted by a ghost without letting my imagination run away with me.

'Who's your alibi?' Finn asked again.

I frowned up at him, then opened my mouth to say Malik— Then I didn't as my mind hit a snag I hadn't considered before. Not only was Malik laid out with his injuries right now, but naming a vamp as my alibi was going to be like waving a bloody flag in the face of the Witches' Council. It was one of those 'damned if I do and damned if I don't' things. Shit.

'It's a sucker, isn't it?' Accusation sharpened Finn's voice. 'Gods, Gen, *why*?'

I sighed. 'I wasn't *with* him, Finn, he was following me. But it does mean he can vouch for my movements after I got home.'

He pushed his fingers through his hair, a worried line creasing between his brows. 'You weren't actually with him in person when the human was killed?'

'No,' I said, turning back to watch the screens. 'I was running.'

On the monitor the florist's boy came out of the shop and I picked my way past his flower buckets to talk to him.

'The problem, Gen,' Finn said, 'is that even if you'd been with this vampire, I'm not sure how it would work as an alibi now. There's been a lot of speculation in the newspapers, and quite a lot of the anti-fae prejudices have resurfaced.' He paused. 'Even the barrister I spoke to isn't hopeful. He said that because you're fae, he'd be happier if you'd been in a room with half a dozen goblins watching you, to testify you didn't use any magic. He thinks that all it would need is the prosecution to suggest you could kill like that without physically being there . . .' He trailed off.

On the recording I stripped off my sweatshirt and dunked it in a bucket, then disappeared inside the bakery – walking into the trap.

'So unless the real murderer puts in an appearance, I'm already tried, judged and convicted,' I finished for him. 'Looks like your ex has done a bang-up job,' I added bitterly.

'You disappearing didn't help, Gen,' he returned angrily.

'Finn,' I snapped, 'Helen's got it in for me because of you. You might think your relationship with her is over, but she doesn't, and I'm the one that's getting the short end of a very vindictive stick.' I clenched my fists, my fingers sweating inside the plastic gloves. 'You need to sort it out with her.'

He swung the chair round again and leaned down, dismay flickering in his eyes. 'It *is* over between Helen and me, Gen, but it's complicated. I didn't realise it would affect you as it has.' He dipped his head. 'My apologies, my Lady.'

I stared at him, incredulous. 'I don't know what game you're playing with all this "my Lady" crap, but you can forget it.' I turned back to watch the monitors. 'And just for the record, "complicated" is not an excuse, it's a way of life.'

The screen in front of me looked down on an empty, rain-blurred street. The stack of cardboard boxes outside the florist's was doing a precarious Tower of Pisa lean to one side. The door to the baker's stood open. The shop window was a blur of white. As I listened to Finn's quiet breathing behind me I watched the empty street, wishing something would appear on the screen that would solve everything – the murder, Finn, the vamps, and all the other problems screwing up my life – so my own life could stop being so damn complicated. I almost laughed out loud. No way was that ever going to happen! In reality my life had never been that normal anyway.

'No one could find you,' he said. I heard the question in his voice, but ignored it. The chair moved as he gripped the back of it. 'Helen even had a chapter of coven witches cast a Seek-and-Find spell. It came up negative.'

Strange . . . I tapped my fingers on the chair arm, thinking. On the monitor the florist's lad picked up a couple of boxes from the leaning stack and carried them into his shop. A Seek-and-Find spell, with the power of a coven chapter behind it— 'When did they cast it?'

'Not till late last night. Helen had to wait for a warrant, and budgetary approval.'

"Last night" I'd still been out of it, doped up on morphine under Joseph's medical care. Still, the spell should have found me; so why hadn't it?

'I watched the coven *cast*, Gen,' Finn said. 'When they

couldn't find you, that's when I realised you had to be in *Between*. The spell wouldn't be able to locate you if you were . . .'

Of course, *Between* was out of this world. Literally. Except I hadn't been—

'. . . here with Tavish.' Finn finished almost with a growl.

'What?' I said, irritated at his tone. 'Why the hell would you think I was here anyway?'

'I phoned the bastard and asked if he knew where you were,' he said tersely. 'He swore he didn't.'

'That's because he didn't.' I pinched the bridge of my nose; my 3V headache was making its reappearance. 'If he made you think otherwise, he was more likely doing his usual and yanking your—' I stopped; satyrs are touchy about their tails, for some weird reason. 'He was just doing his mischief-making thing,' I carried on. Finn had to know what Tavish could be like since he'd just waltzed straight into his home – even if it appeared the pair of them had some sort of jealous rivalry going on over me. Something I wasn't too impressed with! 'I got here not long before you turned up and decided to go all postal!' The florist's lad stuck his lip out, admiring his silver ring in the shop window, then turned to look behind him at the empty street. 'And why the hell were you lobbing Stun spells about anyway?'

'So where were you then?' Finn ignored my question.

I pursed my lips, still annoyed. 'Staying with a friend.'

'What's going on, Gen?' he demanded. 'Why'd you disappear like that without even a phone call?'

I snorted in disbelief. 'It's difficult to use the phone when you're unconscious.'

Finn jerked me round to face him. 'What do you mean, unconscious?'

'Un-con-scious,' I said sarcastically. 'It's what happens when you get blown up, or haven't you been watching the news?'

'But you didn't get blown up, Gen.' Confusion crossed his face. 'You were seen running away before the explosion—'

'What?' I grabbed his arms. 'Who by?'

'Him!' He pointed at the screen. 'The boy in the shop next door. His statement says you went in to sort things out with

the baker and left shortly after, and then the place exploded.
There's nothing on the recording to back him up, but he's so
adamant about it that Helen thinks you used some sort of
Compulsion or Memory-Altering spell on him.'

Crap! I hadn't – not to mention I couldn't afford any spell
that expensive – but Malik had – or at least, not a spell . . .
he'd mind-locked the boy when he'd stopped him phoning the
police as I'd asked.

'Yeah, well, I didn't,' I said, not sure if I was pissed off that
Finn thought I'd deliberately disappeared after the explosion
or mollified that he was now looking gutted that he hadn't
turned up at my sickbed laden with fruit and flowers.

Then remembering that Grace had advised me to talk to
him . . . I did just that.

I filled him in on most of what had happened, leaving out
certain things – like the blood-flush, and where *exactly* I'd
been, of course. 'So the first I really knew about anything was
when I came round earlier today,' I finally finished.

'Gods, Gen, I'm sorry. If I'd realised you'd been that
badly hurt' – he brushed a strand of hair away from my face,
remorse darkening his eyes – 'I wouldn't have been so angry,
or stupid. You know I'll help you all I can, don't you?'

A tense knot I hadn't known was there loosened inside me
and I realised now I wasn't feeling quite so scared, or alone.
And what about Helen? said a snide little voice in my head. *It's
pointless bringing her up again*, I thought, and silenced it.

'Thanks, Finn,' I said. 'I appreciate it. And I'm okay
now' – I gave a rueful smile – 'other than all this . . .' I waved
at the monitors. 'I'm hoping there's some clue to be found on
the recording.'

He hesitated, as if he was going to say something, then
smoothed his hands over my shoulders. 'Okay.' He straightened, lips quirking in a half-smile. 'I'll watch with you.'

'I didn't realise you and Tavish knew each other,' I said
absently as I turned back to the screens. 'You never mentioned it.'

'I've known Tavish since I was a kid.' Finn's voice was
quiet, thoughtful.

I leaned over and hit the rewind symbol on the monitor and
the recording zoomed backwards. Time to see if anyone got
to the bakery before me.

'Where is Tavish, anyway?'

'Probably playing with his food,' he muttered. 'There was a jumper two nights ago, off London Bridge. The body's not surfaced yet.'

The hand clutching at my ankle when I'd been in Tavish's sea came back to me. I frowned up at Finn. 'Tavish abides by River Lore; he only takes those who want to die. You know that.'

'Is that what he told you?' His mouth turned down with derision. 'Don't be naïve, Gen. River Lore is just a nicety for the humans, and all he truly agreed was not to actually charm them into the water. He's never given up his first claim on whoever he finds in the river. And anyway, he's a kelpie; it's part of who he is.'

'What?' I snorted. 'Like you're a fertility fae and I'm sidhe so it doesn't matter what we want or what we care about, we just succumb to the magic?'

'Of course not.'

'Then why should Tavish be any different?'

Finn shoved a hand through his hair. 'He's spent centuries being different, Gen. He can't change that.'

'Is that why you were throwing Stun spells at him? You thought you were saving me?' I huffed in exasperation. 'Will you stop doing your white knight thing, Finn – there's no way Tavish would hurt me!'

'Hell's thorns, Gen, River Lore says he can take someone if they've *killed*, doesn't matter whether they want to die or not. He won't make allowances for you; he's not going to care that it was a sucker and that you had no choice.'

'Of course I had a choice, Finn – I just didn't like the other option; being a vamp's blood-bond for eternity isn't my dream lifestyle.' At least not since I was fourteen, I added silently to myself. I swung back round to face the monitors. 'Anyway, it's not like I haven't been in the water with Tavish before . . . and that vampire wasn't the first I've killed,' I finished quietly.

He didn't say anything, just crossed his arms and withdrew into himself. I sighed, staring down at the diamond-chipped cuffs. Arguing with Finn wasn't getting either of us anywhere, and we couldn't seem to stop arguing either. The magic kept sparking between us, but something, Helen or my vampire parentage probably, was holding him back. Worse, I didn't know why I just couldn't resign myself to the fact there wasn't going to be anything more between us than me working for him at Spellcrackers. Though even that looked like it wasn't going to continue much longer. Snuffing out the little flicker of hope of something more I'd foolishly kept alive, I reached out, stopped the recording and set it playing forward again.

'I don't know what to say, Gen,' Finn said, his voice soft, uncertain.

'I'm not asking you to say anything, I was just telling you.' I swallowed past the constriction in my throat. 'It happened years ago, so it's not important now.' I'd been the stereotypical runaway, straight off the bus, and the vamp had been the clichéd predator, thinking he could use me as bait for a bigger prize, except, at the risk of another cliché, he discovered he'd bitten off more than he could safely swallow— Maybe we needed a change of subject. 'Why would you think I'd be here with Tavish, anyway?'

'What? Oh everyone knows that you and Tavish are . . . courting.'

'Tavish and I aren't courting,' I said, surprised, watching as I ran past the bakery, the florist's lad turning round to stare after me. 'We spent a bit of time together a while back, but I hadn't seen him for at least six months until now.'

'Gen, six months is nothing to a fae, and it doesn't take much for gossip to start. The witches're bad for tittle-tattle, but the fae are ten times worse. There's not that many of us in London: the dryads, the naiads in Lake Serpentine, my own herd and the few solitary fae that hang out at the dragon's eerie. They're all as interested in what goes on with each other as anyone. You're the only sidhe' – *yeah and look how that was turning out* – 'and you might not know any of them, but that doesn't mean they're going to ignore what you do.'

'Aye, that's true, doll.' Tavish's voice sounded behind me.

I glanced over my shoulder as he strolled towards me. The wound across his muscled chest had healed to no more than a faint shadow. He was dressed, sort of, in a long pair of orange silk harem pants, the beads in his hair coloured to match. He looked like he'd just walked off the set of *The Arabian Nights*.

'Why are folk talking about us courting,' I asked, wondering exactly what sort of mischief he'd been up to, 'when we're not and never have been?'

'Which is what I told the Lady Meriel yesterday' – he grinned – 'when she was asking after you and wondering whether I'd seen you recently.'

I stared disbelievingly at him. 'What's it got to do with her?'

'She's a might bothered about the human's death.' He took a pair of surgical gloves from the box and snapped them on. 'Understandable, really. She and her naiads are the easiest of London's fae tae find.'

I frowned, puzzled. 'What's us courting or otherwise got to do with the human's death?'

'Nary a thing, doll.' He leaned over me, his peat-whisky scent curling round me and causing my own magic to rise and heat to pool inside me. The diamond-chip cuffs flared, cutting it short. I squirmed slightly in my seat, wondering if he'd done it deliberately. He gave me an innocent look and I knew he had. Damn kelpie. I glared at him, but he just grinned, reminding me of the sharks swimming lazily through his screensavers. Then he punched a couple of keys on one of the keyboards; a monitor to the left switched to a local news programme. 'But take a wee watch o' this.'

The news showed a crowd held back by a row of human police in riot gear, some sort of protest. A group of Soulers, their long grey tabards emblazoned with red Crusader crosses, gathered to one side; the rest were mostly women, some with kids in tow, all jumping up and down, shouting and waving handmade placards.

The camera zoomed in on one placard: **HANDS OFF OUR MEN**, then panned along the rest: **GO HOME FAIRY FREAKS. SOUL STEALERS. MAKE BRITAIN A FAERIE FREE ZONE**.

Tavish pointed at the screen. 'Lake Serpentine. The humans started throwing salt, then pouring bleach and petrol intae the water and setting fire tae it, until yon police came along and stopped them. There were a few casualties on both sides, but it's mostly peaceful now.'

I leaned forward, hugging myself in disbelief. 'This is insane.'

'Aye, doll, insane it is. The newspapers sensationalised the

human's murder. It doesnae take much tae inflame a few big-
oted people and the rest all follow like sheep,' he muttered,
almost echoing my thoughts of a few days previously. He
pointed to another screen; it showed a load of naked men running into some water. 'This is the other side o' the coin: while
one crowd screams and shouts tae banish us, this lot are up for
partaking o' some faerie sex themselves.'

It was more than insane. I pressed my fingers to my temples –
my headache was beating against my skull now – and stared
at all the screens. The florist's boy came out and put out some
buckets, stuck his lip out again and peered at himself in the
shop window, then turned sharply to look down the empty
street. The Soulers and the women waved their placards.
Naked men splashed into the water. On another screen was a
fire engine in some sort of park.

'What's that about?' I pointed at the fire crew hosing down
some trees.

'A gang took a torch to the trees in Green Park,' Finn said,
and I looked over my shoulder at him. 'Luckily none of the
dryads were in residence.' His lips pressed together in a grim
line.

And something hovered at the edge of my mind—

'And you being nae around hasnae helped, doll,' Tavish
added, derailing my thoughts. 'Then the police-witch wouldnae hae been askin' everyone tae look for you.'

And now I was found.

I looked across at Finn. He frowned back at me, but didn't
say anything. If I gave myself up, would it stop all this? Or had
it already gained too much momentum? Even if giving myself
up did stop the unrest, who knew how long it would be before
Malik was well enough to testify? And while I was sitting in
jail – or worse – no one would be looking for the real murderer.

What if it wasn't all a set-up, but just a coincidence?

What if, despite Tavish's assurance no gate had been
opened, there was another sidhe in London?

Set-up or not, what if they killed again?

I waved at the screens. 'You're showing me this for a reason, aren't you?'

Tavish swivelled the chair round so I faced him, as Finn

had done. He braced his arms on the armrests and leaned over me, his eyes serious, his dreads swinging down over his shoulders. 'Aye, doll, you cannae hide away much longer. This needs tae be brought tae a close. There's the usual solution being proposed tae appease the human justice. You offer up an *Umaidh* tae take your place. Mayhap it'll mean a few years spent in the Fair Lands—'

'Seriously, that is not an option, Tavish,' I sniffed. 'No way am I sundering flesh, let alone part of my soul, to animate a temporary changeling just to get its head chopped off, and in case you haven't heard, I've got 3V, so I'd be out of my mind within six months, not to mention I've never even been to the Fair Lands.'

'Or,' Tavish carried on as if I hadn't interrupted him, 'you could stay in *Between*.'

I dropped my head back. 'Still the same problem, Tavish.'

'No, there's not, Gen,' Finn butted in. 'You're not the first fae to have *salaich sìol*; that's what I've been trying to tell you.'

'Dinna fash yersel' aboot that now, lad.' Tavish waved a dismissive hand at Finn, but kept his eyes on me. 'T'would only be a solution if you'd killed the human as they think you have. But there's nae human death darkening your soul.'

I looked at him suspiciously. 'What?'

He grinned, teeth sharp and white. 'Well, you dinna think I wanted tae swim just for my ain pleasure, did you?'

Crap. He'd been testing me. 'You could've asked,' I scowled.

'But there's nae joy in just askin', doll, not when I could have a wee taste o' your soul.'

'Fuck you.' I glared back at him.

'Any time, doll, I've told you. An-y time!'

Movement drew my attention back to Finn; he was staring at me, surprise on his face, and I realised he'd thought Tavish and I had been doing more than just courting. All around him the monitors reflected ghost screens in the glass . . . and the memory of the florist's boy admiring himself came back to me. I swung the chair back round, dislodging Tavish's hold, and reversed the CCTV film, starting it from where I was racing by on my run.

'Look,' I said, excitement sparking inside me, 'see how the

boy uses the window to check out his appearance? And then when I run by he sees my reflection and turns to watch.' I fast-forwarded on. 'Now look: he's admiring himself again, and then he turns round because he's seen someone, but there's no one there. The street's empty. See how his head whips back to check the reflection.' I paused the recording and squinted at the screen. 'There *is* someone else there, look.'

Tavish leaned over my shoulder. 'Aye, doll, seems so, and they're using magic tae hide, but whatever spell they've used, they've nae cast it correctly. They've nae remembered their mirror image.'

I smiled in triumph, pointing at the screen. 'Any chance you can zoom in on the reflection?'

'Maybe.' Tavish swung the chair back round and grasped my arm, pulling me onto my feet. 'I'll work at it.' He sat, staring intently at the screen, fingers flying over the keyboard. 'Only thing is, doll, it may not be enough tae clear your name.'

'Clearing my name can wait,' I said, determined. 'I'm more interested in finding the killer before they go on to their next victim, and that footage might tell us who it is.'

Chapter Ten

'If you do me a copy of the recording I'll take it into the police and get them to have a look at it,' Finn said, leaning over Tavish's shoulder.

'I doubt the police will do better than me, lad.'

'They won't,' Finn agreed, 'but if I show them where to start, they can compare it with the original. Then at least they won't think you've tampered with the evidence.'

'Aye, you're right.' Tavish nodded, reaching down to snag a new storage stick from the shelf below. 'T'would nae take much to falsify something, and the humans tell their own falsehoods too often to believe that others dinna follow suit.'

I leaned on the back of the chair and pointed at the florist's boy. 'It's not just what the recording shows; the boy must know something.' I turned to Finn. 'Do you think you can get Helen to interview him again and find out?'

'Yes, I'll ask her,' he said as he ran a hand through his hair and rubbed his left horn.

'Thanks.' I gave him a quick smile, then I mentally crossed my fingers. Time for the next part of my plan: the one that had been slowly forming in the back of my mind. I needed to summon the phouka and I wasn't sure how either of them would react. Or maybe they wouldn't, maybe I was just being paranoid. I decided to ease into it in bite-sized stages; though thinking of biting and the phouka at the same time wasn't necessarily healthy.

'Um, Finn,' I said, 'before you go, any chance you could *call* something from my flat for me?'

A line creased between his brows. 'It depends what it is. The magic only works if you can picture what you want and where it is exactly. I'm not sure I could do that with someone else's things.'

'Okay. I was hoping for some clothes.' I sighed, looking down at the T-shirt. 'But if not, the other thing I wanted was one of those shiny black pebbles I've got, the ones I keep in the white dish shaped like a leaf.' I tilted my head in question. 'Do you know the ones I'm talking about?'

'Yes, I remember them,' Finn said, thoughtfully. 'They're in your bedroom.'

'That's right,' I agreed, keeping my voice even. Finn had only been in my bedroom a couple of times, but the pebbles were on my bedside table and hard to miss. Next to me Tavish stopped hitting the keys and swung his chair round, an intent expression on his face. My heart missed a beat. This was going to be tougher than I thought.

'The ones you keep on *your* side of the bed,' Finn said with an edge of mischief to his smile.

'Both sides of the bed are *my* side, Finn,' I said drily. Did he really have to make it sound as though we were sleeping together, the bastard? Still, better they get distracted by jealousy than figure out the real reason I wanted the stones. Finn started flicking the fingers of his right hand and relief filled me; he'd had his bit of fun, now he was *calling* for them. Then he frowned. 'On the side nearest the door, right?'

'Yes,' I said, giving him a get-on-with-it look. Tavish gave a soft snort and Finn's gaze shifted to meet his eyes. Something passed between them and this time my heart sank. Crap. Then Finn looked back at me, his face lighting with some emotion I couldn't decipher, and his fingers stopped moving.

Crap. What had Tavish just told him?

'So, doll,' Tavish said quietly, 'what's so important aboot these stones?'

Briefly, I closed my eyes. 'A friend gave them to me. They're just something I think can help me, that's all.'

Tavish looked at Finn. 'What are they?'

'Haematite,' he said, frowning. 'But there're no spells on the stones, I checked.'

He'd checked? When? Not that it mattered; there'd never been any spells on the stones.

'Doesnae need tae be,' Tavish said, then pointed at me. 'The magic's in her. And if you're planning on summoning one o' the sidhe queen's ambassadors, doll' —Tavish leaned forward, his expression unusually serious— ''tis too dangerous. The Lady Meriel and the Lady Isabella willnae allow it, and I told you, I canna open the gate without their knowledge.'

Crap! I should know better than to try and fool a centuries-old kelpie.

'Look,' I said, turning to Finn, 'all I need is for you to *call* the stones for me.' I looked over my shoulder at Tavish. 'And I don't want you to stop him. You don't need to worry about the others; the phouka doesn't use the gates.'

'Aye, she wouldnae, meddling bitch that she is.' Tavish snorted in disgust.

'Ah,' Finn said, drawing my attention back to him, 'and Tavish didn't exactly stop me. The stones aren't there any more.' He held his hands out, giving me a rueful look. 'Or at least they're not on the bedside table, and if I don't know where they are, I can't *call* them. Ask me thrice if you want.'

I stared at him, wanting to do just that, but he wasn't trying to be evasive, so I knew he was telling the truth. Damn. 'But I never move them.' I pressed my lips together in frustration. 'So there's no other place for them to be . . .'

'The police have been in, Gen,' Finn said gently. 'They've searched through the flat.'

My stomach twisted. Shit. I pinched the bridge of my nose, hating the thought of strangers going through my things again, and trying to think what to do next.

'I'm sorry, Gen.' Finn rubbed a consoling hand over my shoulder. 'I didn't know until after.'

I clenched my fists in determination. If I couldn't get the pebbles, there was another way. I turned back to Tavish. 'Okay, here's what I need: a Glamour to change my appearance, clothes, a phone and some money. You can get me all that, can't you?'

Tavish's gills flared, then snapped back against the skin of his throat with an almost audible whisper that yelled trouble in the back of my mind. 'Aye, but it doesnae mean I will,' he said calmly.

'Just wait until after Tavish has looked at the recording, Gen,' Finn said. 'Don't forget you've been badly hurt.'

'I'm fine.' I stuck my hands on my hips and gave them both an annoyed look. 'So the pair of you can stop right now. I'm going to do this, with or without your help. Even if you get something off of the CCTV footage it still won't tell us where the sidhe is. The phouka might know something, or be able to track them—'

Tavish reached out and grabbed my arm, scattering my thoughts as he traced his fingers over the healing burns. 'What in the River's name happened tae you?' he asked.

I blinked at him, puzzled and vaguely confused, as if I'd forgotten something. Why was he asking about my injuries?

'I got blown up, Tavish, with the bakery – you must've seen it on the recording. Not to mention that I don't look any different from when you first saw me outside,' I said, still perplexed. 'You must've noticed then.'

'Ach, doll, my heart is full o' sorrow that I didnae.' His touch was light over my skin, soothing away my exasperation. 'I dinna always look at a body's shell; I like tae see the core of those around me, nae the deception they offer tae the rest. The fae are too easy wi' their Glamour, like the lad here' – he jerked his head at Finn, the orange beads on his dreads shifting to silver – 'fooling folk wi' his prettiness.'

Finn was standing at ease with his hands in his pockets. He didn't say anything, but the relaxed pose didn't hide the tension in his shoulders.

I frowned at Tavish. 'Finn works mostly with humans; the Glamour makes that easier.'

'Aye, so he says, but he dinna always wear it quite like that.'

'Times change, kelpie,' Finn answered quietly, but there was an edge to his tone. 'Something you seem to have forgotten.'

'Okay,' I said slowly, suspicion cutting through the odd fuzziness in my mind as I looked from one to the other. 'Just what is going on between you two?'

'Dinna fash yoursel' about us, doll.' Tavish smiled and tugged me closer so I stood within the V of his legs. His hands felt warm as they clasped the bare flesh of my arms. 'And then there's your own soul, Genevieve.' Iridescent turquoise swirled through the silver of his eyes, a whirlpool of colour that pulled me under and wanted to drown me in liquid desire. 'Your essence is like a fine river, streaming with golden currents that shine more dazzling than the sun and are a delight to the eyes, your waters so sweet and pure and warm that a soul would slip joyfully into your depths and yield up their life to the blissful pleasure of your embrace.'

I smiled happily down at him, then bent to brush my lips across his, tasting earthy orange sweetness. 'Tavish,' I whispered soft against his mouth as his hands tightened on my arms, and I was surprised in some distant part of me at the yearning that threaded through my voice. 'That's all very pretty, but my wrists are burning up,' I said just as softly, and without as much longing. 'So maybe you could leave off trying to sic me with your magic until later, otherwise I might just let mine go and then it's Goodbye Computer time.'

He looked down and horror filled his face, then he shoved the chair back and dropped my arms like they were radioactive – and maybe they were, since the diamond-chipped cuffs were glowing like small supernovas.

A muffled laugh behind me made me turn. Finn leant back against the glass wall, smiling in amused smugness. 'Doesn't look like the *bean sidhe* is going to fall for your watery charms, kelpie.'

What the hell was I? Some sort of bone for them to fight over?

'You're just as bad as him.' I strode over to him and jabbed him in the chest, my finger and the cuffs glowing at the same time. 'You used to try exactly the same thing on me. And never mind your little innuendoes just now; it didn't get *you* anywhere either.'

Finn lifted my chin with his finger, a wicked glint in his eyes. 'Want me to try again? I'm sure I could do better now.'

'No,' I said slowly, turning back to Tavish as my memory caught up with what was going on, 'all I want is what I asked for.' I turned to Tavish. 'And just in case you've forgotten after that little bit of trickery you pulled on me, that's a Glamour to change my appearance, clothes, a phone and some money.' I opened the glass door. 'And if you feel like trying anything again, just remember: I really will fry your computers next time.'

Chapter Eleven

I stood outside Tavish's tent and stared up at the tall sand-dune covered in pale pink heather rising before me. It blocked out any sight of the sea.

'So what happened there?' I asked, bemused.

'I think that was you, Gen,' Finn murmured quietly. 'Tavish mentioned something about you interfering with his magic. He didn't sound too impressed.'

'But I haven't done anything,' I said.

''Course you did, doll,' Tavish snorted. 'When you were digging your pretty toes intae my beach.' He gave my shoulders a quick squeeze. 'Seems the magic's taken a fancy tae you.'

I frowned, I knew *Between* was malleable, but this was Tavish's patch. I thought back to earlier, when I'd been watching him scooping out a sand-basin. I'd known he was doing magic, but I hadn't realised my wishful building of a small ridge of sand would result in anything like this – no wonder Tavish wasn't impressed, never mind I'd threatened his computers!

I looked down at myself. He'd already got his own back.

I'd asked for a Glamour to change my appearance. I'd been

hoping for something nondescript. What I'd got was a blonde-bimbo look with boobs so big that I could fall flat on my face and still be a foot away from the ground. Okay, maybe that was a slight exaggeration, but hey, Page Three was not going to be saying no to me any time soon. Of course Tavish had denied any ulterior motive, saying that it wasn't his fault; he'd based the spell on the white bikini-clad model advertising a luxury holiday resort in the same brochure his sandy beach came from. After that little magical *hiccough*, I'd insisted on real clothes so he'd emailed a local shopkeeper who owed him a favour, then *called* the shirt, jeans, leather jacket and train-ers I was now wearing. Mind you, I'd had to keep on the white bikini that had appeared with the Glamour plaited into my hair, since he'd *forgotten* the real underwear I'd also asked for. Still, the bikini was better than nothing, and he had *called* a brand new pay-as-you-go phone and an Oyster card, as well as giving me a thick wad of twenties.

'Come see your door, doll.' Tavish took my hand and pulled me across the sand.

The door that had materialised into being when I'd thrown the Knock-back Ward at Tavish and Finn still stood where the spear had landed. I walked a complete circle around it. It had changed. The bars and padlocks and chipped paint had given way to something that looked more like an office door, with frosted glass in the top half. Behind it I could see people-shaped shadows walking past. I reached out and grasped the handle—

—and stepped out of the end of a narrow alley and onto the wider street. Apart from one elderly woman who started, no one noticed me appear out of thin air, but then, they were all hurrying along, heads down against the driving rain. After an odd moment of disorientation, I realised I was on Clink Street and almost exactly where I wanted to be. I stuck my own head down and started dodging the puddles, grateful for the trainers. I dashed past a side road, catching a glimpse of the *Golden Hind*, the replica Tudor warship in which Sir Francis Drake sailed around the world, and briefly wondered if they'd managed to evict the selkie who'd been squatting in the captain's cabin for the last fortnight. I reached the Clink and almost slipped down the small flight of worn stone steps that led into the museum. I paid my admission and walked slowly through the exhibits towards the large back room.

A concrete troll sat at a big wooden table, rolling a crap-shoot of plastic dice back and forth between his large slab-like hands. He was old – or at least he'd had a hard life; his nose was missing a chunk and his age cracks had been filled with blue-coloured grout, making his pitted concrete skin look like it had a map of wriggling blue lines drawn on it. It reminded me of the blue oxygen-starved veins of a hungry vampire. The troll's name was Blue, unsurprisingly appropriate, and the info plaque in front of him stated that trolls had been used as jailers at the Clink as far back as the fifteenth century. Of course, being an interactive museum, Blue was dressed for the part in a shapeless woollen frock-coat, ragged knee-length trews and a thick dirty-cream woven shirt. Half a dozen roughly dressed humans hovered behind Blue; I wasn't sure if they were inter-active too, or just hanging around in the hope of a game.

The place has a reputation for gambling, which was why I was here. Only it wasn't money I was hoping to win.

Blue looked up as I sat down opposite him, his mouth split-ting into a thin crevice of a smile that didn't manage to hide his ill-fitting set of human dentures. ''Ello, miss, wot can I do yous for, then?'

I folded my hands together on the table, allowing the edge of a twenty to show. 'I want to cast the bones.'

'Can't say as casting bones is a game, miss.' He took a blue tea-towel-sized hanky from his pocket and dusted off his bald head. 'But yous can always 'ave a go at playing the dice if yous like.'

'I like,' I said.

Ignoring the plastic set he'd been throwing, he rummaged in his coat pocket and produced three pairs of dice. He laid down the first set; they were a mottled amber shot through with gold. 'Jawbone of a fire-dragon,' he rumbled softly. The second pair were black, the corners rounded smooth. 'Shoul-der blade of a mountain troll.' He handled them reverently, his forehead creasing so deeply that a thin sliver of blue grout popped out and powdered on the table. He set the last pair down, whispering, 'Hip of Phouka.' The dice glimmered faintly with silver light; their original owner was still alive.

'What's the game?' I asked calmly, my knuckles whitening with the effort it took not to just reach out and grab the last pair of dice and *call* to the magic in them.

Blue shook himself. 'Craps do yous?'

I nodded. 'Fine by me.'

The air flickered around Blue and in a couple of moments both he and the rough-looking men were surrounded by about twenty more, some more distinct than others. I shuddered. The place was *full* of ghosts. I'd forgotten the museum was a known hangout for them, and this group was way more sentient than the ones under London Bridge. I watched them warily from under my lashes, not wanting to attract their attention any more than I had to. They sported a motley collection of chains, shackles and hangman's nooses, and one clomped noisily round in a large metal boot. I doubted they were the real deal, just locals who liked the accessories.

'You calls an' I rolls, miss. Three correc' calls and yous wins.'

The ghosts pressed forward, merging through and past the living men as they gathered round the table to watch the proceedings.

I relaxed slightly. They were here for the game, nothing malevolent. 'Ready when you are,' I said.

'Place yous bets, ladies and gents,' Blue rumbled. 'Roller is Blue.' He laid his hanky carefully on the table on his right. 'An' caller is the pot.' An anaemic-looking man placed a small metal bowl to Blue's left.

I tossed my twenty into the bowl.

The crowd shuffled and muttered and a pile of translucent coins appeared on Blue's blue hanky. A few notes were stuffed into my pot, some solid and others less so. The betting system didn't make any sense to me, but most of the punters were ghosts, so who was I to complain?

'Wot dice do yous choose, miss?' Blue peered at me from his small blue-glass eyes.

'Hip of Phouka,' I murmured.

The others disappeared back into his pocket. Blue gently picked up the Hip of Phouka bone dice and held them out to me. 'Yous want to kiss 'em for luck, miss?'

My heart stuttered in indecision for a moment, then I

nodded. It was a tradition: if you called on a wylde fae for help, you needed to offer them a promise. The phouka's preference was for flesh. Bending forward, I kissed my lips to the dice. The phantom taste of raw, bloody meat made my stomach roil with nausea. I sat back, taking a deep breath and swallowing my horror.

The phouka was well known for liking her food überfresh.

Using a tall plastic beaker, Blue scooped the dice up and slapped one large hand over the cup. Shaking it vigorously, the dice rattling around inside like a hangman's skeleton, he said, 'Call.'

'Big Red,' I called.

The crowd murmured with approval.

Blue nodded sagely and rolled. The two bone dice tumbled out onto the table: a four and a three.

'Big Red it is.' He scooped and shook and rattled again. 'Call.'

'Midnight.'

The crowd muttered, sounding less encouraging this time.

Blue did the sage nodding thing and rolled again. The dice stopped precariously near the table edge, both showing a six. 'Midnight is it.'

A collective sigh hummed through the room.

'Last call,' Blue rumbled, a fine grey dust rising from the neatly drilled holes in his scalp as he rattled the dice.

'Snake Eyes,' my mouth said before I'd made the decision to speak.

The crowd stilled, suddenly silent. Snake Eyes was bad luck, a losing throw; I'd been planning on calling an ace and deuce. I clenched my hands, angry – stupid to have kissed the dice without *looking* first – but it was too late now, I'd called.

Blue rolled, and I watched with sick inevitability as the first die stopped with one dark pip showing, then the other bounced and landed with two pips uppermost.

'Ace and Deuce,' Blue rumbled, carefully pocketing the dice and then drawing the pot of money towards him. 'Sorry, miss, no winnin' this time, yous lost.'

Fuck. Playing the crapshoot was supposed to be just a formality if you weren't human. And the Glamour was on the surface only, it couldn't affect the outcome. Someone had tagged the dice with some sort of spell. I scanned the crowd – living and ghosts – but nobody's face registered any more interest than was normal.

I produced another twenty and forced a smile. 'Let's try again.'

'No can do, miss.' Blue shook his head sadly. 'If yous don't win first go-round, yous don't get no more chances 'til next sundown.'

I crumpled the twenty in my fist. Damn. No way did I want to wait until tomorrow night—

A chill hand wrapped its fingers around mine and tugged at my arm. I turned to stare into the big empty eyes of Cosette, the child-ghost who was haunting me. I froze, my heart pounding as I struggled with the urge to tear my hand from hers and jump up and run like the hounds of Hell were after me.

Cosette tugged again, more insistently this time. I got the message; she wanted me to go with her. With a reluctant look at the crap game, I let her pull me away and out to the museum entrance. As soon as I stepped outside, she pointed up to the street, and then flashed out of existence.

A female stood at the top of the entrance stairs. She stared arrogantly down at me from under the dark brim of her fedora hat, her tall, graceful body clad in a smart russet trouser-suit. Her eyes shone startlingly green, the colour of new leaves in spring, no whites, no pupils. Behind her stood a short, chunky male, his brown pinstripe suit at odds with his rain-wilted straw Panama. His eyes shone the same spring green as his companion's. Neither had any eyebrows, which made their pale faces look oddly unfinished, and both were obviously bald under their hats, but then, pruning the twigs off their scalps was a long-standing tradition. Shit. What had I done to deserve being waylaid by a pair of dryads?

'Ms Taylor?' The female tilted her head and her domed forehead lined in a slight frown. 'Ah yes, I see now,' she murmured. 'The Glamour is very good, Ms Taylor; no wonder the trees took some time to locate you.'

Damn tree spirits, they had their spies everywhere. All it took was a breath of air and info could pass from one side of London to the other faster than it took to ask, *'What's that rustling noise the leaves are making?'*

Fedora spoke again. 'I am Sylvia. My mother, the Lady Isabella, wishes to speak with you.'

'What about?'

Fedora's mouth thinned in disapproval at my blunt question, but she still answered. 'She is disturbed by the current unrest in London. It appears to be getting less comfortable for fae as the days and nights go by.'

'Tell Lady Isabella,' I said flatly, 'that I'm sorry for whatever problems she is having, but I'm not sure that my speaking to her right now is going to help.'

'I think you've misunderstood me, Ms Taylor. I am afraid this isn't a request, and if necessary' – she snapped her fingers, and Chunky in his limp Panama moved to stand at her side – 'I will have to use force.' Her smile was more a baring of her brown-stained teeth than anything friendly. 'Although of course it would be better if you accompanied us quietly.'

And of course, going quietly was only better for her, not me! I let my shoulders slump, briefly looking round to see how many more dryads were skulking round. I picked them out by their hats. A tall, slightly bent-over male in a black Stetson to the left, a pair of skinny saplings wearing knitted beanies – yellow and green – the other side of the road, and to the right . . . I couldn't see. The corner of the building had me in a blind spot.

Time to hustle.

I placed my foot on the first step. 'I really don't want any trouble, you know, Sylvia,' I said, keeping my voice soft and calm. 'But I would like to phone my boss. I don't want him to worry.' I took another step up, showing willing.

'You may contact your employer in the car, Ms Taylor.' She indicated a glossy green Rolls Royce a few yards along the road.

'Fair enough.' I pasted a resigned look on my face, looking up at her and Chunky, and made a show of patting my pockets. Which way to make a break for it, left or right? The car was left, all the easier to bundle me up and into if I went that way. Of course, they'd have to catch me first. So it looked like right was the preferred escape route, even with the blind spot. I exaggerated a frown, then held my hands out, empty. 'Damn! I'm sorry, Sylvia, but my phone's not in my jacket pockets.' It was in my jeans, so not a lie. I jerked my head back. 'Maybe it's in the museum?' I raised my voice in question.

Her pale face narrowed in annoyance, then she breathed sharply in through her nose. 'Malus, help Ms Taylor retrieve her phone. Quickly, please.'

Chunky nodded and started down the steps.

'Hey, I'm really sorry about this.' I smiled sheepishly, took another couple of steps up to meet him, then shot my arm up as if to catch him, saying loudly, 'Watch out, the steps are slippery from the rain.'

He started and looked down, hands reaching out instinctively as I'd hoped, and I grabbed his wrist and yanked. He overbalanced, teetering forward, then toppled, doing a diving belly-flop into the museum, hitting the ticket desk Panama-hatted-head first.

Fedora's mouth gaped open in surprise. I took the rest of the steps in a leap, bent forward and head-butted her hard in her stomach. She fell back, landing with a spine-cracking crunch on the pavement, a whoosh of air whistling from her open mouth. I jumped over her trouser-suited legs and ran.

I went right, racing past the shocked face of the two Beanies, and jinked to one side, only just evading the grappling arms of a giant oak-sized guy with a purple-patterned bandana tied low over his mahogany-skinned forehead. I picked up my pace and sprinted along Clink Street. The cobbles were still wet from the earlier rain, the air chill with moisture, and the early evening greyness was dissolving into streetlamp sodium that spilled halos of light onto the ground.

My heart was beating fast and adrenalin was pumping through my body as I wondered what the hell Lady Isabella was up to. Okay, so maybe her life was out of kilter with the anti-fae demos, but that was no reason to send her dryads out to kidnap me. Had she been the one to booby-trap the phouka's dice? I stretched my legs, sucked air into my lungs and felt my body settle into a familiar fast-run mode. One good thing about running regularly: a couple of days' forced bed-rest doped up on morphine hadn't dented my fitness much. I could keep this pace up for a good few miles, but I could hear the dull boom of feet behind me and the rhythm sounded as practised as mine. I was almost sure it was the guy in the bandana chasing me; the others had looked too stunned to react that quickly – and Bandana Guy had been the only one who'd tried to stop me. I didn't check behind; I was either faster than him or not and looking back wasn't going to change that.

The buildings on my left ended abruptly and the bulk of the *Golden Hind* filled the gap, its masts rising into the star-spiked sky. A crowd of City types heading for post-work drinks at the pub beside the boat spilled across the narrow street in front of me. I waved my arms, grinning like a lunatic, and shouted, 'Whoo hoo! Girl coming through,' and they laughed good-naturedly as I dodged between and past them.

A few seconds later I heard irate shouts of 'Watch it' and 'Hey, man!' and 'Getoutheway!' behind me: sounded like Bandana Guy hadn't managed to dodge quite as quickly. I raced on – but the trouble was, I could keep running, but I needed somewhere to run to, somewhere where a dryad couldn't go. Dryads were fae, so a threshold wasn't going to stop them like it would a vampire. A gust of wind blew past me, and in seconds rain started pelting me in the face like an ice-cold shower. Iron and steel would stop most fae, but the dryads were born in this world, their trees grew in the soil, drank whatever chemicals polluted the rain. My arms pumped and I could feel the wet blonde ponytail of my Glamour slapping against my leather jacket as I ran. Dryads had no problem with cars, but trains . . . they didn't like trains. None of them used the Tube. And there were no trees to spy me out; underground I'd be safe from the tell-tale whispers of the rustling leaves.

I reached the fork in the road: the left went round underneath London Bridge, but it took me further away from the nearest station and kept me out in the open. To the right was the quickest way to the Underground, but as I veered to go that way, I realised right wasn't an option: two tall, gangly men were racing towards me with long, ground-eating strides. Both wore turbans wrapped around their heads. Maybe if they hadn't been running, or if their faces hadn't glowed with an odd pale luminescence like freshly stripped wood, or if their leaf-rustling cries hadn't whistled past my ears, I might not have seen them – but seeing them wasn't going to make them disappear.

'Shit,' I breathed out as I changed direction, sprinting left. 'Pulling in reinforcements is *so* not fair, guys.'

The road curved in a deep bend and I took the straight quick line across pavement and grass and jumped a low-walled frontage. Rounding the corner I saw the quiet street stretching under the bridge and away into the distance. Three sets of echoes matched the pounding of my own feet. The driving rain stung my face and soaked cold into my shirt. Ahead I could see the green and blue flashes of the pavement lights under the bridge: straight on took me into the City, an area the dryads were uncomfortable in because of its lack of trees and multitude of hard surfaces, but it wasn't the smart option, not when I didn't know it well. But if I remembered right, there was a way up onto the bridge and back to the nearest Underground: Nancy's Steps.

A ferocious snarl raised every hair on my body. In the gloom ahead a large dog – almost the size of a Great Dane – appeared as if from nowhere and stood stiff-legged in the middle of the road, barring the way. My pulse leapt in my throat and I nearly skidded to a stop – then, with uncertain relief, I recognised the unwordly glow that emanated from the dog's coat like a silver aurora borealis. The dog was Grianne, the phouka: she *had* got the message from the crap game after all, even though I'd called it wrong. The only problem was, I didn't know if she was on my side or not; things were never straightforward where Grianne was concerned. But hey, it's not everyone that ends up with a faerie dogmother who hates them.

She barked, loud and insistent, a sound that reverberated through the quiet street around me. Humans would only hear the bark; I heard: 'Hurry up, child, the trees are gaining on you.'

Like I really needed her to tell me that! I gritted my teeth and pushed my legs harder.

The phouka snarled again, baring long black fangs that a true dog would never have, then turned, loping towards the steps this side of the bridge, and disappeared. I caught up; the steep flight rose up to the road above. I grabbed the handrail and flung myself after her, half climbing, half leaping. My lungs were starting to burn. Above me the phouka bounded, sharp claws scratching loudly on the stone and the silver glow from her coat casting welcome light back into the dim stairwell.

Second landing. Behind me I heard shouts, then more of the whistling, rustling noise grated against my ears: the ground-eating legs of the tall pale-faced turban guys were taking the steps two at a time. Shit. I swallowed back an edge of panic and, my heart hitting against my ribs, my thigh muscles bunching with effort, I concentrated on getting to the top.

As I reached the last few steps, vicious snarls and growls erupted, quickly followed by horrified yells and human screams, which almost drowned out the growling. I ran onto the pavement to find the phouka crouching over one of the beanie-hatted dryads on the ground, savaging its throat. The other Beanie Hat was screeching in rage. It kicked out, catching the phouka in the stomach. The phouka yelped and went flying, landing in a scrambling, whining heap at the feet of stunned bystanders.

'Hey, you!' I yelled, pleased in some detached part of me that I still had enough breath. 'Leave that poor dog alone!'

The yellow Beanie Hat whipped round, lips curled, face twisted in a snarl that would have done the phouka proud, and sprang at me. I half-crouched, judged my moment, then shifted low and let Beanie Hat's own momentum help me heave her over my back. She crash-landed against the bridge's stone parapet with a noise that sounded like branches snapping in the wind and lay still. The other Beanie lay moaning on the ground, yellow-tinged sap trickling from the wounds on his throat. The onlookers stared, huddled under their umbrellas and muttering, their eyes darting from Beanie to Beanie to me, indecisive.

'Quickly, child,' the phouka said as she trotted to my side, 'tell me where the faeling you've rescued is hidden before these vermin regain their senses.'

'It's not a faeling this time, Grianne.' I looked down at the phouka. 'There's another sidhe in London, and a human has been murdered. I need to know who's opened a gate—'

'Enough, I will attend to this.' The phouka growled, ears flat against her skull. 'Meet me here tomorrow as the sun is cresting.' A wet nose pushed into my hand. 'Now run, child, the other trees are coming. I will detain them.'

For a second, I laid my palm over her rain-wet silky head,
wondering what her help was going to cost me, but— 'I owe
you one, Grianne.' Her eyes blazed yellow and feral as she
dipped her muzzle in acknowledgment, then I turned and
raced towards the Underground.

Chapter Twelve

I hit London Bridge Station still running, slapped my Oyster card over the reader and raced down the escalators into the rush of warm air that signalled a train arriving: Jubilee Line westbound to Waterloo and Stanmore. I tucked myself in by one of the doors, my feet braced, my body swaying with the juddering carriage. My heart slowed and I started to feel uncomfortable, my sweat-and-rain-damp clothes feeling sticky in the hothouse air of the packed Tube train. I wrinkled my nose, hoping I didn't reek too much of exertion and panic, a smell that would be all-too-attractive to any vamps out on the prowl.

I doubted the dryads would follow me underground, but they hadn't looked like they were going to give up their *kidnap the sidhe* idea anytime soon, so just to be sure, I scanned the packed commuters searching for anyone in a hat. My gaze skimmed a big man in a homburg, bushy grey hair poking out round his ears, and automatically dismissed him as human. I passed over a couple with matching camo berets, and a group of Jews in their kippah skull-caps. Why were the dryads chasing me? And why had Cosette warned me about them back at the Clink? Not that I wasn't grateful; if it hadn't been for her, the dryads might have cornered me, but . . .

I swallowed back my frustration at the delay. Still, if nothing else Grianne should have some info for me in the morning.

We reached Waterloo and I jumped off and started running again, speeding through the curved roof tunnels, heading for the Northern Line. I wasn't the only one; half a dozen other commuters raced with me, desperate to catch their own trains. I was just desperate to get somewhere safe, and fast, and I didn't stop until I had flung myself, panting, into the next train. The next stop was Embankment. The doors parted with a clunking sucking sound and I got off, peered up and down the platform and made my way up to the exit. Then I hesitated; I'd been heading back to Tavish almost on autopilot, thinking I'd stay there until it was time to meet Grianne the following morning, but once I was there, doing nothing but hanging around would be a complete waste of time. Not to mention there were a lot of trees to pass between the Underground and the RAF monument.

I leaned against the wall and phoned Tavish . . . No answer. I tried Finn next, and as he picked up I heard voices humming in the background.

'It's me, Finn,' I said. 'I've got a whole copse of trees chasing after me, wanting to take me to their leader! What the hell's going on?'

'Ah yes, I see, that is a problem. Can I ask you to hold for a moment please?' His next words were muted. 'Sorry, I'm going to have to deal with this. I'll try not to take too long.' A door opened, then slammed shut and the background thrum of voices silenced. Finn came back on the phone. 'Just so you know, I'm at Old Scotland Yard,' he said quietly. 'What happened to the party you were supposed to meet?'

'I just told you, the dryads.'

'Where are you now?'

'Embankment Underground. I tried Tavish but there's no answer.'

'Unfortunately my colleague isn't available tonight.' Voices rose in the background again. 'Another matter has come up that needed to be dealt with urgently. I'm not sure I'm going to be able to help you either, not until after midnight. I'm going to be tied up until then.'

Not literally, I hoped.

'Can you get away?' I asked. 'Just to let me into Tavish's? The entrance doesn't work on its own for me.'

'That's not such a good idea,' he said. Someone else laughed: a deep rumble that sounded like a troll. 'That particular course of action could be dangerous.'

'Dangerous! Okay, Finn, stop messing about and get somewhere where you can talk.'

The phone cut off and I stared at it, anxiety churning inside me. *Why dangerous—?* The phone rang.

'Okay, I'm outside now.' He sounded slightly breathless. 'There's too much water at Tavish's; the naiads might try the same thing as the dryads.'

'What the—? Why the hell do *they* want to kidnap me?'

'It's because of the human's murder. They all think you killed him, and they want to take advantage of it.'

'Okay, now you've totally lost me. How can they take advantage of me—?' I stopped, suddenly conscious of the people in the station milling round me. '—of that,' I finished.

'Gen, it's complicated . . .' He hesitated, then said, 'You know about the *droch guidhe* – the curse – don't you?'

'Yeah.' I frowned. 'The local sidhe queen cursed London's fae *to know the grief in her heart* when she lost her son to the vamps. But what's that got to do with anything right now?'

'Well, after the *droch guidhe* first came into being there was a spate of faelings killed by the suckers, and everyone thought that was it.' His voice was flat, almost detached. 'But as time's gone on we've all realised there's more to the *droch guidhe*. Since it was cast, no full-blood child has been born to any of London's lesser fae, only faelings, so not only do we have to watch our children die because they live only a mortal lifespan, but if our magic doesn't procreate, it will start to fade. Once the magic fades it won't be long before we all follow it.'

Fuck. Grianne hadn't told me about that nasty bit of the curse, but— 'So what exactly has this got to do with me?' I asked quietly.

'There've been a lot of things tried to break the *droch guidhe*,' he went on, his voice not sounding quite as detached, 'but so far none have worked. The one thing no one has tried yet, because the queen has refused to allow it . . . is for one of London's fae to have a full-blood child with a sidhe,' he finished quietly.

I blinked as my mind caught up with what he meant.

Grianne had told me the facts of sidhe life when I was fifteen, in more detail than I'd ever wanted to know. Outside of a fertility rite, I'd only ever get pregnant if I wanted to – no morning-after-the-night-before worries for me as Grace had enviously said when I'd told her once – and if I did nothing to influence the pregnancy, then any child I had would inherit only their father's genes.

It's a magical anomaly that always seems 'difficult' for humans to understand. But they'd proved it themselves – back in the eighties, when the witches' right to be called human was challenged. Every DNA test known to man was done, and no matter that their fathers were sidhe, the tests showed nothing other than human genes in a witch's make-up. All a witch's sidhe father contributes – other than life, of course – is an ability with magic. It's why a witch's daughter – born of a witch mother and a non-magical human father – doesn't inherit their mother's power. It's not there to be passed on.

And it was why the sidhe queen's son had been human.

And by the sounds of it, it was why I'd landed on the dryads' and the naiads' Most Wanted list.

'Whoa, wait a minute!' I whispered in shocked disbelief. 'Are you telling me they think they can get me to start popping out babies for them or something? Because it's *so* not going to happen. Even if they kidnap me, they need my freely given consent for that, otherwise the magic doesn't work.'

'Unless the magic has already taken the decision for you, Gen,' he said, an odd edginess to his voice, 'which they think it has. Then your consent isn't needed. It's not even classed as rape under fae tradition.'

'Listen, anyone who tries to have sex with me without my say-so, regardless of magic, or anything else, is in for a whole load of pain,' I muttered furiously, casting furtive glances at the commuters around me. 'And where the fuck do they get such a stupid idea from anyway?'

'The fertility rite ritual.' He sighed. 'Hell's thorns, Gen, I know it sounds stupid, but it's not, not when you think about it from their side. As far as they know, you're not in a relationship, you don't date, not even humans, and you haven't made any *arrangements* with any other fae. Usually the only reason a fae, particularly a sidhe, abstains from sex is when they're preparing to bear a child, so when they hear about what's going on, their first thought is that you've abstained for too long and the magic is making you react to any sexual advance you get, even without a proper fertility rite. They believe their way offers a solution to their reproduction problem, and your own.'

'What,' I snorted, 'so kidnapping me to take part in a fertility rite and get me pregnant is just their way of being practical?'

'Something like that,' he muttered.

'Damn! And I thought it was only humans that got all wound up about the sidhe sex myth thing!'

'Yeah, well, the humans only think about the sex part, and not the reasons behind it. But for them, having children is kind of like falling off a log. For us it's much more difficult, even without a *droch guidhe* to contend with.' The words sounded bitter. 'Anyway, Tavish has gone to talk to them and sort things out, but it might take a while for him to convince them, so you need to be careful. I'm not going to be able to get away from here until after midnight. If you can think of somewhere safe, then I'll meet you there.'

'I don't know . . .' I glanced round and caught sight of a large poster for the HOPE clinic. 'I'll go to HOPE; they're used to dealing with magic and stuff, so if anything happens it's not going to faze them.'

'Okay. Look, I've got to go, Gen. Helen's agreed to let me go with them to speak to the florist's boy. We're going there now. See you later, and *be careful*.'

'Sure,' I agreed, but I was speaking to a dead phone.

I stood staring blindly at the passing crowds, my mind reeling. Crap! Not only were the vamps inviting me to be their nightly pep-me-up and the police playing hide and seek with me, now the fae wanted to chain me to the bedposts and pass me round as their pet broodmare. And why hadn't Grianne filled me in on all the nasty details? She had to know about them . . .

Then a thought hit me like a sucker-punch. If the dryads and the naiads wanted me for a baby-machine, did that mean the satyrs did too? And if they did, what exactly was Finn's role here? Prospective daddy? Was that why he'd gone out on a limb with the witches so I could keep my job? And why he'd kept my secret? Maybe his white knight fixation was motivated by something other than overeager protective instincts and the attraction that jumped between us. In fact— Was there any attraction at all on his side, or was his magic just to ease the way for his herd to hear the patter of tiny cloven hooves?

The questions stabbed into me like sharp knives and I hugged myself against the pain. Was that all I meant to him? I looked at the phone; part of me wanted to call him back and ask, but what if the answer was yes? Bad enough that he kept pushing me away . . . Then I took a deep breath and told myself not to be stupid. Finn *had* been pushing me away; in fact, he'd done nothing but reject me since I'd told him about my parentage, so if he was interested in the role of 'prospective daddy', he was going the wrong way about it. Oddly, the thought soothed the hurt inside me, although why it should I wasn't sure – was being rejected for something I couldn't change better than being wanted, albeit for the wrong reasons? – I shook the confusion off for more practical concerns. At least Finn had told me the details of the curse, which was more than Grianne had . . . or Tavish. But Tavish was one of the wylde fae, not the lesser fae, so where did he fit in with all this? I groaned, part disgust, and part mental overload. Now I had no idea who I could trust.

And did the curse thing have anything to do with Tomas' murder?

But if someone could convince a sidhe to commit murder, wouldn't they be able to convince them to have sex? Although in Tomas' case, they *had* sort of convinced a sidhe to do both at the same time; any sidhe would know that having full-on faerie sex with a human would result in the human's death.

Damn. Never mind anything else – kidnapping dryads and scheming phoukas and tricky kelpies – finding the sidhe murderer was more important. Only other than my morning meetup with the phouka, there wasn't anything else I could think to do just now. I stared at the HOPE poster again. Grace was at HOPE. She really was a friend, and that was what I needed right now. I trusted her.

I slid open the phone and turned it round, taking a picture of the Glamoured blonde bimbo me, then texted Grace to say I was on my way. I dashed back down the escalators and slid onto a train just as the doors were closing.

I checked the carriage carefully, then settled back, scanning new passengers at each station. At Tottenham Court Road a grey baseball cap moving slowly towards me caught my eye, but the red cross embroidered on the cap meant the poodle-perm brunette wasn't anyone to worry about kidnapping-wise. Poodle-perm was a Souler – the Underground is one of their favourite hunting grounds for new recruits; there's nothing like having a captive audience.

A chorus of 'No thanks' preceded the Souler, but her smile stayed in place despite the rebuffs and her shoulders were military-straight under her long grey tabard, which was embroidered with its own large red cross. I looked down, hoping not to catch her eye, and saw my Glamour reflected in a pair of black wraparounds. My pulse sped up. Damn.

A Gatherer goblin.

The goblin's long ski-slope nose twitched like a curious mouse. I looked around for an escape, but it was too late, the goblin had caught the scent of my magic; the Glamour couldn't hide it. He nodded his head, grey pigtails brushing the shoulders of his navy boilersuit, and slid a knobbly finger down his nose in greeting. My stomach tightened into an anxious knot. What if the London Underground goblin workers had been told to look out for me? Would he give me away as soon as I'd acknowledged him?

But I couldn't not return the greeting; it was a mark of respect offered to me as sidhe fae, and not something to be taken lightly. Holding my breath, I slid my own finger down my nose, trying to make it look more like I was scratching an itch.

He stamped his foot, making his trainer flash red. I waited for him to give a howl of discovery, but it didn't come. Instead he snatched up a crumpled paper cup and tucked it carefully away in the pink sequinned beach bag hitched over his shoulder.

I let out my breath, relieved.

He was still following his normal work contract.

'Are you a member of our congregation, miss?' the Souler asked, waving a leaflet in my line of vision.

'What?' I looked up to find her smiling curiously at me.

'It's just Samuel seems to recognise you; he greeted you as one of us.' She waggled her fingers at Samuel, the goblin. He tapped his hand against his own Souler Red Cross badge, pinned next to his London Underground one.

'Although they can't see well,' she carried on, 'they've got very good memories for people, so I wondered if you were an acolyte?' Her smile turned questioning.

'Um, no, I'm not.' I gave her a wary look. 'I was just watching him, thinking about the great job they do clearing up the rubbish.'

'Ah yes, goblins have proven themselves amongst God's creatures: they see no shame in servile tasks, much as our Lord Jesus took it upon himself to wash his disciples' feet.' Her eyes lit up with enthusiasm. 'He is an example to us all, with his help and guidance we can shed our sins, and our souls can be cleansed of the darkness and evil that abounds in our earthly life and we can join Him in all his Glory.'

Inwardly I sighed, resigned. I just had to speak to her, didn't I? Still, ignoring her probably wouldn't have made much difference: all the Soulers were fervent zealots. She'd sensed an opening and was closing in for the kill – sorry, *conversion*.

'Goblins aren't really creatures, you know,' I said, matter-of-fact, trying to put her off. 'They're more a different species.'

'We are all God's creatures,' she jumped in cheerfully. 'All of us, human, goblin, troll, fae and Other. God does not deny any among us his help or discriminate in his care.' I stared at her, bemused. Since when had the Soulers changed their sermon tune? They didn't usually include *everyone* in their salvation message, just humans, trolls and goblins. The rest of us could rot in hell for all they usually cared.

She gave a closed-lip smile to Samuel – at least she knew not to show a goblin her teeth – as he scraped industriously at a glob of chewing gum stuck to the floor, then carried on, 'Samuel, like most of the goblin race, may not enjoy the same legal rights as humans' – she tilted her head to one side, jiggling her poodle-perm – 'but that does not stop God or his acolytes from offering aid where it is needed.'

Okay, now she was really starting to creep me out.

'That's great!' I looked up at the map above the windows.

'Sorry to interrupt, but my stop's coming up . . .' I edged to the side to stress my point.

'No problem.' She took my hand and pressed the leaflet firmly into it. 'Please, do call us.' She smiled again, a knowing look that raised the hairs at the back of my neck. Turning to retrace her steps, she added, 'Remember, when you need us, we can help.'

Was she trying to give me some sort of personal message, or was this just her normal spiel? If so, she was weirder than most of the Soulers I'd come across. Frowning, I skimmed the leaflet; it looked like the usual *come-and-be-saved* stuff. I dismissed it and handed it to the waiting Samuel.

'Ta, miss.' He took it gently between knobbly forefinger and thumb, then, trainers flashing, he clomped along the carriage to give it back to the poodle-perm Souler.

Recycling at its best.

I watched her from the corner of my eye until the train pulled into the next station. The doors hissed open and as I got out a flash made me turn: she had her phone aimed at me and I blinked as it flashed again. She smiled and I watched her with a sense of mounting frustration as the train accelerated away.

Fuck. She *had* twigged who I was, or maybe Samuel had given her the nod when she'd asked. Question was, who was she going to send the photo to – the police? Her boss? Someone else? And what was all that *we want to help* stuff about? Still, there was nothing I could do about it right now, other than maybe ditching the Glamour spell soon – it wasn't much of a disguise if everyone knew what I looked like.

I raced through the streets to HOPE, with the growing feeling I was being followed. I checked behind me a couple of times, expecting to see Cosette again now I'd escaped the dryads. But she didn't put in an appearance, and neither did anyone else, despite my jitters. Nervous adrenalin fuelled me and it wasn't long before I reached the welcome lights of the clinic.

The doors swished open and I rushed in. Hari, the night receptionist, stared out from behind his glass screen and gave me the full force of his trademark *you better not give me any trouble* expression. It almost made my nervousness disappear:

a yellow- and brown-streaked eight-foot-tall troll with fists the size of boulders doesn't have to do much more than frown to cow most patients, but underneath, Hari was a big softie.

'Yes, miss?' he asked in his deep rumble.

Hari wasn't in on the little plan Grace and I had come up with, so I leaned against the chest-high reception counter, still catching my breath, and aiming for desperate, panted, 'I've got to see Dr Hartwell; I've run out of gear.' At least the gasping would give my venom-junkie play-acting an edge of realism. Trouble was, with all the chasing and running and adrenalin speeding my sidhe metabolism, it wasn't going to be play-acting for much longer – like I really needed something else to worry about.

'What's the name?' he rumbled.

'Debby, with a y,' I said, giving the name Grace had told me to use.

'Well, Debby-with-a-y, you just go and sit yourself down in the waiting area. Dr Hartwell is a very busy lady' – he treated me to another deep-fissure frown – 'but I'll let her know you're here.'

I walked past the bank of lifts and the fire-exit stairwell door, trying not to give in to the urge to push through it and run straight up to the fourth floor where the clinic was. Instead I played my part, letting my eyes glaze over while staring at the stippled peach wallpaper, the gold-framed botanical prints and the beige vinyl wipe-clean floor tiles. I wrinkled my nose at the strong smell of pine disinfectant, which didn't quite cover the underlying scent of liquorice and even fainter trace of blood. Two rows of pumpkin-orange chairs lined either side of the waiting area, along with a slightly battered vending machine and the token magazine table with its collection of out-of-date glossies. As I approached, my steps faltered and my heart thudded in my chest. One of the chairs was occupied. Damn. I'd forgotten about him. I thought about turning back, but I couldn't think where else to go – and I wanted to see Grace.

How much trouble could one vamp be anyway?

Chapter Thirteen

Vamps were always trouble, so okay, that was a stupid question. But Bobby, the vamp sitting in HOPE's waiting area next to the soft drinks machine, was just a youngster; he'd only taken the Gift three years ago. And he was supposed to be on his best behaviour.

I stood opposite him, leaning against the wall, hands stuck in my pockets.

He lifted his head and looked me over, his lips quirked in a sulky, sexy way, his grey eyes shadowed and moody. The expression was one he'd perfected for the camera as Mr October, one of London's hot celebrity calendar vamps. The hair in its French plait, the ankle-length leather coat, jeans and silk T-shirt, all of them black, completed the look – a look that had teenage girls and not-so-teenage women swooning with desire and queuing out the door of the Blue Heart Vampire Club in a desperate effort to Get Fanged by the month's star attraction. Of course, his recent arrest for the murder of his human girlfriend and the subsequent, very public clearing of all charges had done nothing to hurt his popularity. If I didn't know better – having been instrumental in the 'clearing' bit – the words Publicity Stunt might have entered my mind.

The silver circlet encrusted with yellow citrines that banded his head and the silver handcuffs that shackled his hands together added a touch of the mediaeval to his über-modern Goth look, and enhanced his bad-boy persona. Luckily neither the media nor the vamp PR machine had yet caught onto that fact, otherwise they'd probably have had him posing for the camera with all that magical hardware.

Not that the cynic in me couldn't see the attraction. Mr October, a.k.a. Bobby, made a very handsome picture. But unlike his devoted fang-fans, he wasn't a picture I wanted hanging on my wall . . . there's nothing sexy about a frightened sixteen-year-old blood-pet on a frozen January dawn in the middle of Sucker Town, which is what Bobby was the first time I'd met him, on one of my rescue missions for Grianne. Of course, that was four years ago, and he'd accepted the Gift since then, which sort of changed things for him. But hey, maybe his chemistry just wasn't right for me.

Although by the way he was giving my Glamour the glad-eye, his own chemistry was thinking something different.

His quirk widened into a smile and his nostrils flared as he sniffed. Then he took a longer, more noticeable sniff and consternation replaced the smile. 'You told Hari your name was Debby,' he said accusingly. 'Debby-with-a-y.'

Vampire hearing, gotta love it. 'Yes, I did.'

'You're her, aren't you?'

'You going to grass me up to Hari?'

He glanced at the glassed-in reception booth, where the troll's bald yellow and brown head was bobbing in time to his iTrod, the overlarge iPod made for trolls. 'No, of course not,' he said, sounding aggrieved, 'not after the way you helped me.'

I nodded as if it was the answer I'd expected, but inside the knot in my stomach loosened.

He made a show of studying the handcuffs round his wrists. 'I'm here to see my dad, y'know,' he said. 'Or I will be as soon as the guard comes to take me up,' he added, resignation dimming his face.

Bobby's dad was a regular human, and was hospitalised in a regular human ward – albeit a private room – in the main part of the hospital, but Bobby being a vamp meant he had to be processed through HOPE before he could visit. The magical silverware was a precaution to stop him using his vampire tricks on any of the other patients, a compromise Bobby's lawyer had won after he'd complained not allowing Bobby to visit his sick father was in breach of Bobby's 'human' rights.

'How is your dad?' I asked. 'Has there been any change recently?'

'There's been the odd brainwave fluctuation.' The cuffs chinked as he clasped his hands, his knuckles turning white with tension. 'But he's not come out of the coma.'

'I'm sorry,' I said, and I was, and not just because I felt sort of responsible for his dad's condition – part of the whole 'clearing Bobby of murder' thing had involved Bobby's dad ending up in the way when a paranoid clairvoyant had tried to kill me. I'd met his dad, and the guy hadn't deserved to end up as another victim.

'Can't Hari tell who you are?' Bobby asked, curious.

'Trolls can't sense magic.'

'So they're not like the goblins then? They can't tell if a vamp is using *mesma*, or putting a mind-lock on someone?'

'They're like goblins in that magic doesn't affect them, but whereas goblins are super-sensitive to any magic, trolls are mostly impervious to it.' I folded my arms. 'But trolls have fantastic eyesight. They can see for miles.'

'But Hari, he can't see through' – he waved his joined hands at my body – 'what is it?'

'A Glamour, it's a spell that changes the surface appearance only.'

'It's a bit . . .' His voice trailed off as he ran his eyes down my body. 'I mean, you look totally hot, but it's the type of figure that's going to get you noticed.'

I sniffed. 'Yeah, well, the look wasn't my choice.' I pointed at his own outfit. 'It's not like you're toning it down yourself, are you?'

'I've got to go to work later. My shift starts at ten and it saves time if I come here dressed. And anyway, it's the only coat I've got.' He gave the leather coat an almost embarrassed look. 'I haven't got the hang of regulating my temperature yet.'

The lift dinged, and I looked up, hoping that it was Grace, or even Bobby's guard come to take him visiting, but it was just a couple leaving. Doing small-talk with a vampire was making me itch, and itching is never a good sign around vampires, not when you've got 3V and it might be the early stages of a venom-flush.

'I mean, I know I should've worked out how to do the temperature thing by now,' Bobby carried on, getting up and staring morosely into the depths of the vending machine. 'All the others had it down pat six months after they accepted the Gift.'

I did the mental maths: he'd accepted the Gift at seventeen, probably one of the last before the Parliamentary Bill changed the age of consent to twenty-one. Whatever vamps look like when they accept the Gift, that's how they stay for the rest of their lives – a prospect that makes all the wannabes head straight to the gym. *Looking too young* had fast become a problem for some of the centuries-old vamps who wanted a slice of the celebrity cake but didn't look old enough to buy a drink, and the market for toyboys, even ones with fangs, isn't all that healthy. I briefly wondered if Bobby regretted taking the Gift when he did, or even taking it at all. Still, not my concern.

'I shouldn't worry,' I said, and tucked my hands back in my pockets to stop myself scratching and stared at the lifts, willing Grace to put in an appearance.

'I'm still working at the Blue Heart,' Bobby said, breaking the silence and I turned to look at him as he carried on, 'Albie, the new boss, lets me come and see Dad before work, then I come back for a couple of hours before dawn, once the club's shut. Albie's not bad; he's not into all the power crap and fucking stupid memory games like He is.'

He was Declan, Bobby's master and head of the Red Shamrock blood family. Declan had a nasty vamp trick of stealing memories, then giving the memories back piecemeal – something he did at random with his vamps for his own sadistic amusement. He'd made Bobby forget his girlfriend was dead at one point, not something that Bobby looked like he was going to be forgiving anytime soon.

Bobby gave me a defiant look. 'I've moved out of the Bloody Shamrock.'

'Oh, right.' I wasn't entirely sure what I was meant to say.

'I couldn't stand being there any more, not after what happened.' He started to pace along the visitors' chairs. 'Not when that bitch Fiona still thinks it's okay to crawl all over me when Declan's not around. It's her fault Dad's in here.'

Fiona was the paranoid clairvoyant who'd tried to kill me; she was also Declan's human 'business manager' a.k.a. daytime flunky and girlfriend all rolled into one.

'I've been thinking about asking to move to another blood family.' He stopped pacing and stood in the middle of the hallway. 'You know, petition the High Table for a different master. What do you think?'

I frowned, puzzled. Why was he asking me? 'I don't know, Bobby. I've heard you can do that, but I'm probably not the best person to ask.'

'I've checked around, on the quiet.' His expression turned anxious. 'I don't want Declan finding out; he'd make sure it never happened. I need to get another master to agree to take me before I petition the High Table – that way, if I'm accepted straight away, Declan can't object – or at least, he can, and then he gets some sort of compensation, but he can't stop me going.'

'Sounds like you need to talk to the other master vamps, then,' I said, checking the lifts again.

'Of course, Albie would be my first choice,' Bobby carried on, 'but he's already told everyone that he's not interested in taking on anyone else's vamps. He's not even going to sponsor anyone for the Gift! He says he's got too much on his plate already with taking over the Blue Heart.'

I suddenly realised I was scratching my neck; I forced myself to stop, wondering how long Grace was going to be. Maybe Hari would find me some G-Zav if I asked nicely . . . or desperately . . .

'Thing is' – Bobby brushed a hand over his hair, fingers hesitating at the silver circlet – 'I never even get a chance to talk to any of the other masters. If I'm not here, I have to be at the Blue Heart. They sell tickets with fifteen-minute time slots, like I'm on a production line or something. I have to bite them one after the other, and the other vamps are all jealous, saying that I should be in vampire heaven or something, but I end up using so much energy making each bite feel great that half the time I don't even get a decent meal and I'm still hungry at the end of the night.'

'Well, don't start looking at me,' I said, feeling vaguely sorry for him, but a little worried that all his chat was the equivalent of him inviting me out to dinner – vampire style.

'I can't, can I?' He moved to stand in front of me and a sullen look settled on his face. 'The bastard ordered me not to, remember?'

Oh yeah, Declan did have his plus points at times. Forbidding all the vamps under his control from sinking their fangs in me was one of them. Of course, that still left Declan and a lot of other suckers out there who had no such inhibitions.

'Good, just so we're clear on that,' I said, my voice calmer than I felt.

'But there is something I wanted to ask you.' His expression turned hopeful. 'I was wondering if you could speak to your master for me, y'know, put in a good word, see if she'd consider having me.'

'I don't have a master,' I said, baffled.

He frowned. 'But everyone's talking about you and Rosa.'

Rosa: the vamp whose body I'd been magically borrowing whenever I used my Disguise spell. Damn. Malik had mentioned something about that; the vamps all considered me her property now. 'Rosa isn't my master,' I said slowly. 'She's something else – and don't ask me to explain, it's way too complicated.'

'Okay,' he agreed, obviously not interested in an explanation anyway. 'But if you could tell her I'll do anything, whatever she wants – I mean, I've heard the sort of things she's into, and I'm fine with whatever.' He lifted his cuffed hands and grinned, flashing fangs as he leaned closer. 'See, I'm getting a bit of practise in already! But seriously, I'd do anything to get away from that bitch Fiona.'

I held my hands up, needing him to back off a bit. 'Look, I can't—'

'No!' He grabbed my hands, lifting them to his mouth. 'Please. I know I can't influence your mind, but whatever you want, whatever you and Rosa want, I'll do.' His lips chilled my knuckles and the handcuffs chinked like heavy chains in my ears. I stared transfixed at where our hands joined.

Around me the peach-coloured waiting area disappeared and in its place was a large square room lit by hundreds of thick creamy church candles, walls hung with rich burgundy drapes and stone-flagged floor sloping down to a grate in one corner, a river of blood streaming . . .

For a stunned moment I wondered where I was, then the memory crashed into me.

. . . I grasped the chain joined to his manacled wrists tighter and jerked my arm back. The force yanked him off his knees and his body crashed onto the hard floor. I pulled the chain, dragging him screaming and spitting across the blood-slicked stone flags until he lay shaking at my feet. I smiled down at him, seeing only the youth of his body, cusped on that edge between adolescence and adulthood, ignoring the centuries that lurked in the darkness of his eyes.

'What did you call me, cara?' I asked, my voice full of silk and seduction.

'Bitch. You're a fucking sadistic bitch,' he sneered up at me, lips curled back, his fangs stained red with my blood.

I threw back my head and laughed, delighted. 'Such sweet words, my lover.' I flicked my wrist and a gun-shot crack sliced through my laughter as the metal-tipped whip flayed another blood-thin line across his naked stomach.

He screamed again, high-pitched, his spine arching with the edge of pleasure the pain brought him. Then grabbing the chain that joined us, he pulled me down, forcing me onto my knees next to him. 'I promise you, on my honour,' he snarled, 'I will break the bones in your body, bitch. And then I will fuck you senseless.'

Eagerness and lust tightened my body, liquid heat flooded between my legs and I touched my tongue to my own fangs, tasting the sweet liquorice of my venom. 'Yes, do all of that, cara,' I breathed, my own excitement mounting as I lowered my mouth to kiss his. 'But first it is my turn to feed.'

'Jesus fucking Christ! What the fuck was that?' Bobby's voice brought me back to the here and now.

I stared into his shocked grey eyes, too shaken to speak.

'It's a memory, isn't it?' Bobby's grey eyes went from shocked to amazed. 'I shared one of your memories – yours and Rosa's.'

Shit, I'd *felt* it, *lived* it, as though it was my own. And I knew the boy, or rather the vampire, I knew his name – Bastien – and I knew he'd taken as much pleasure from the game as Rosa had . . . and I knew he had been true to the promise he had made to her. Bastien was the Autarch; not only that, he had been my betrothed—

Sweat broke out over my body, my stomach lurched with nausea and I pressed my lips together, willing myself not to vomit. Bastien wasn't here. He couldn't hurt me. And it wasn't *my* memory; it hadn't happened to *me*. I swallowed back the taste of bile. The memory belonged to Rosa. So what the fuck was it doing in my mind?

'Look,' Bobby broke into my thoughts, 'seeing that doesn't put me off, okay? I still want you to talk to Rosa—'

'I told you, I can't speak to Rosa for you,' I said, frowning. How could I when I didn't know where she was, or even if she, as opposed to her body, was still alive? I hadn't even used the Disguise spell in the last month—Was that why I'd had the memory? Was something wrong with the spell, or with me?

'Please,' he pleaded, squeezing my hands. 'I don't know what else to do. If there's anything you want—I can't bite you, but I'm good-looking, I'm great in bed, I'll do any type of sex you want, or anything else . . .'

I shook my head, feeling frustrated sympathy at his desperation. 'Bobby—'

'I've got to get away,' he interrupted, 'but if I just put myself out there and none of the other masters want me, then He's got the right to take the Gift back, and then I'd be truly dead and that would leave Dad with no one to look after him. Please. I'm *begging* you.' He jerked my hands up to his lips again—

His fangs caught my knuckle, splitting the skin, and the jagged pain so soon after the full-on sensory memory sent lust and panic spiralling through my body. Without thinking, I tried to pull my hands away.

He groaned, his pupils dilating with need, his hands convulsing around mine. His lips drew back, all four fangs glistening sharp as he licked the blood welling from the cut. The liquorice scent of venom curled around me, heat flushed my skin and I froze. He shoved me back against the wall and raised his head back to strike—

The gems in his silver circlet glowed, the yellow stones shining like cats' eyes in the dark, and Bobby's face crumpled with pain. The jade chips embedded in the silver cuffs flashed green and bright, and his fingers spasmed open, releasing me. He thudded to the floor, whimpering, pink-tinged tears rolling down his cheeks as he curled into a foetal ball.

I gazed at him, wanting to help him, but knowing there was nothing I could do. I let my head fall back against the wall and took a deep breath, feeling guilt and remorse as well as frustration at his plight. Even without the restraints he was wearing, Bobby wouldn't have been able to actually bite me, so I'd never been in any danger. I looked at the bloody scratch on my knuckles, then closed my eyes; it had been stupid to pull my hands away from him. I'd been taught better than that. Matilde, my stepmother, had drummed into me that struggling and running only got a vamp more excited. Of course, freezing wasn't going to stop a vamp biting you if they were lost in bloodlust, but submitting might keep the vamp from killing you. But Bobby hadn't been lost in bloodlust, he was just young, hungry and desperate, even before you threw in the 'memory' we'd just shared. I shuddered and slammed that thought away in a locked corner of my mind. So I should've remembered to stay calm and freeze.

'Ms Taylor, are you all right?' asked a male voice, soft and concerned.

My eyes snapped open and I blinked at the man in the smart grey suit hovering a few feet away, a worried look on his twentysomething face. His well-trimmed Van Dyke and gelled highlighted hair looked familiar. Then I noticed the red Souler cross pinned to his lapel and I came up with a name: Neil Banner.

A Beater goblin, a nearly five-foot monster, was standing next to him.

'Would you like Thaddeus here to assist you with the vampire, Ms Taylor?' he asked.

Thaddeus the goblin hoisted his shiny aluminium baseball bat and bared his black serrated teeth in a warning grin; they glinted red where small cross-shaped rubies had been embedded. His long grey-and-red-streaked hair was bandaged like a horse's tail so it stood a good eight inches straight up from his head, then cascaded down over his massive shoulders. His own red cross was pinned in pride of place above a dozen other badges, right in the centre of his chest. And over the usual *Goblin Guard Security* uniform, his navy-blue boiler-suit, he wore one of the Soulers' grey tabards, again marked with a large red Crusader cross.

'Just say the word, miss,' Thaddeus growled in a voice deep enough to be a troll's, 'and I'll make mincemeat of the sucker.'

I gave Bobby a sympathetic look where he was still curled on the floor. 'I think he'd probably appreciate it more if we left him alone to recover, gentlemen.' I slid my finger down my nose, offering Thaddeus the respectful goblin greeting along with a closed-lip smile; no way did I want him to think I was challenging him. 'But thank you,' I added politely. 'If I ever need to make mincemeat out of a vampire, I'll know who to call.' I wasn't joking either, and not just because Thaddeus stood head and shoulders – literally – over any other Beater goblin I'd seen. The standard-sized ones were ruthless enough; I imagined dealing with a pesky vamp would probably be like swatting an irritating fly for Thaddeus.

'No problem, miss.' Thaddeus' grey wrinkled skin fell into sombre lines as he lowered his bat. He slid his own finger down his nose, returning my greeting.

Neil Banner smiled eagerly. 'Ms Taylor, I wonder if I might have a word?'

I held my hands out, indicating my Glamoured appearance. 'Only if you call me Debby,' I said drily. 'Debby-with-a-y, that is.'

'Oh, of course.' His smile widened. 'I was forgetting you were incognito.' He fished in his jacket pocket and produced a neatly folded handkerchief. He held it out to me. 'Er, you're still bleeding . . .'

I took it from him. 'Thanks.' I dabbed at my hand, frowning. He'd obviously had his Crusaders and their pet Gatherer goblins out looking for me – the poodle-perm Souler who'd taken my picture with her phone on the Underground was evidence of that – but just to be sure, I asked the question anyway. 'I'm curious, how did you recognise me?'

He pulled out his phone, thumbed the keyboard and held it

out to me. The screen showed a picture of my Glamoured self.
'I had a little help.' He smiled sheepishly. 'And I apologise for
the cloak-and-dagger antics, but it's important that I speak
with you, and with the situation as it is, I assumed, rightly as it
turned out, that sooner or later you'd use the Underground, or
come here. And quite possibly be in disguise. And of course,
there's not much magic that can fool a goblin's nose.'

Why was he babbling? 'I take it you're not going to inform
the police of my whereabouts?'

'Er, not at this moment, no.' His smile wilted a bit round
the edges.

Which made whatever he wanted vaguely threatening. 'What
is it you want to talk about that's so important, Mr Banner?'
I said calmly.

'It's rather delicate, Ms—' He clasped his hands together
nervously. 'Um . . . I think you might have something in your
possession that belongs to our Order. As we've met previously, my superiors decided it might be easier if I approached
you instead of a stranger.'

'So what's the item?'

'I'm afraid I'm not at liberty to tell you,' he said apologeti-
cally. 'All I can say is that the item was a bequest to the Order
from someone recently deceased. The solicitor dealing with
the will maintains that it is in your safekeeping.'

I narrowed my eyes at him. 'Why all the mystery, Mr
Banner?'

'The item is important, apparently, so you'll know if you
have it or not.' He was practically wringing his hands. 'But my
superiors don't want any information about the item becom-
ing public knowledge.'

'In other words they don't trust me.'

'I'm sorry,' he rushed on. 'I advocated being straight with
you. I told them that you saved my life at risk of your own
when that vampire attacked me, that you deserved to be told
everything, but—'

'I'm a suspected murderer on the run. Don't worry, I get it.
It hardly makes me trustworthy material, does it?'

His cheeks coloured hot with embarrassment.

'Thought so.' I checked my hand where Bobby's fangs had
caught it. The skin had scabbed over already.

I gave Thaddeus an appraising look. Beater goblins were usually employed in Sucker Town, a private police force paid for out of the vampires' pockets to keep the night-time streets safe for human visitors. It's not such a contradiction as the idea suggests, since goblins are all about the job, right down to the last full stop on the contract. Although the Soulers are the only humans that use Beaters instead of the smaller, more acceptable Monitor goblins for any business dealings involving vampires or magic, since turning up with a baseball-batting bodyguard is *not* the way to engender trustful relations. So Neil Banner searching for me with a monster Beater goblin at his side wasn't that surprising . . . but then he'd mentioned our first meeting. That time he'd only warranted an inexperienced, imported goblin as a minder, even though he'd been mixing with the Earl and a couple of his fang-pals. Either his standing within the Order had gone up in the last month, or his errand was of prime importance. And once I started thinking of the Earl, it didn't take much to put it all together. He was the only one I knew who had died recently and who had given me something of value.

The Fabergé egg.

My bullshit antenna twitched. Why would a vampire leave a religious organisation such a legacy – especially when said organisation believed that vampirism was evil and anyone who accepted the Gift was destined for Hell? And apart from anything else, the Earl had been around for eight hundred-odd years, so I doubt he'd expected to die when he did.

But before I could ask, loud shouting erupted at the clinic's entrance and I heard someone cry, 'Where's the sidhe?'

Chapter Fourteen

'**W**here's the sidhe?' the girl shouted again. She was dressed skimpily in washed-out grey lace and velvet, white hair worn loose down to her emaciated hips. Her outfit labelled her: she was one of the Moths from Sucker Town, so called because they lived – and died – in the unlicensed off-piste blood-houses. Between the scraps of lace and velvet she had so many swollen red bites marking her thin body that she looked like she'd been prepared as a speciality dish for a fang-gang; not to mention she had to be pumped up higher than a kite with the amount of venom and adrenalin fizzing through her blood – not a good thing when she was brandishing a foot-long carving knife like some sort of ghostly warrior princess.

What the hell was she doing here looking for me?

'I gottaseethesidhe,' the girl shouted again. 'GottaseethesidheNOW.' Her words slurred as she banged the knife down on the reception counter.

Hari appeared, his large hands held placatingly out in front of him, his yellow face splitting with cautious concern. 'Now, miss, you want to put that knife down before you hurt yourself.' He moved slowly forward, his big bulky body almost blocking Moth-girl from view.

'*Nooooo!*' She opened her purple-painted mouth wide and screamed, lunging straight for him. Hari dodged out of her way and her forward rush carried her past him into the hallway. She jerked to a stop in front of the lifts and stood, chest heaving, swaying like a sapling in an angry gale.

Beside me, Thaddeus stamped his feet, trainers flashing red, and raised his aluminium bat.

Neil Banner placed a restraining hand on his arm. 'No, my friend, the girl's sick and needs our help, not our judgement,' he said quietly.

Moth-girl looked from our little group then back to Hari, her purple-eyelined eyes in her Pierrot-whitened face blinking like a confused clown's as her brain tried to catch up with her headlong rush.

Junkies off their head weren't that rare at HOPE. The usual plan was to safely distract the junkie, in this case Moth-girl, until security could turn up and defuse the situation, then help her as best we could. Hari knew the drill as well as I did, except I realised he wasn't wearing his stab-vest – what if she spooked? Mountain trolls might be born from rock, they might be tough, they might live a few centuries longer than humans, but their flesh was still flesh, and they could still bleed, even if it was silicate and not actual blood.

Instinctively, I stepped forward, moving as slowly and cautiously as Hari had. 'Hey,' I called, just loud enough for her to hear me.

Her head whipped round, the movement nearly over-balancing her. She peered suspiciously at me, still blinking.

'Why do you want to see the sidhe?' I asked softly. 'Maybe we could help?'

'*Nottellinyou!*' She pointed the knife at me. 'You ain't the sidhe, I seen her picture. Sidhe's got red hair an' those funny eyes, 'n'you're like blonde,' she said accusingly. 'You ain't no sidhe!'

'Miss, I'm sure the sidhe will show herself soon.' Neil Banner smiled at her and kept his voice soothing. 'You'll be able to see her then. I'm here to see her myself. We could wait together?'

I got the message: lose the Glamour so Moth-girl could recognise me. It wasn't a bad idea. Trouble was, never mind anything else – like being wanted by the police, or even why she wanted to see me – the Glamour wasn't that easy to lose. Distracting Moth-girl until security arrived was a much more sensible plan.

'Yes, I'm sure she'll be here as soon as it's possible,' I said agreeably. 'So long as nothing happens to . . . keep . . . distracting . . . her,' I added much more softly, glancing at Neil Banner.

He half frowned, then his face cleared into understanding as he deciphered my return message. He smiled at Moth-girl and said in the same soothing voice, 'We could have a chat while we wait, if you wouldn't mind, miss.' Then he gave a small wave at the orange visitors' chairs and took a couple of cautious steps towards them. 'I'd be glad of the company.'

Moth-girl frowned at Neil Banner, scratching furiously at the arm holding the knife, making the skin there even more red and swollen. 'I got somethin' to give her,' she sniffed.

Hopefully, not the knife!

Neil Banner carried on with his gentle small-talk, trying to keep a hold on Moth-girl's tenuous attention. Behind her, Hari was moving closer. His white uniform shirt was already grimy from the anxious dust puffing from his head ridge. Moth-girl's face scrunched up with pain and she scratched feverishly again, this time at her inner thighs. It wouldn't be long before she suffered a—

'You know she's heading for a blood-flush, don't you?' said Bobby quietly next to my ear.

I only just managed not to jump; I'd been so focused on the girl I hadn't been paying attention to anything else. 'Yeah, I can see that,' I said just as quietly. After my own early morning blood-flush nightmare I knew just how she was feeling: desperate, edgy, driven insane with the venom-fuelled blood burning her up from the inside out. If she didn't lose the knife soon, we wouldn't have to worry about her stabbing anyone; she'd be too busy slicing herself up.

'I could catch her in a mind-lock and hold her still,' Bobby whispered, 'but the minute I try, the headband will shut me down again, unless you can mask the spells or something?'

Yeah, I could *crack* them and blow his head off, or *call* them and knock myself out in the process, or I could spend a couple of careful hours dismantling them. None of which was going to help. I thought for a moment. 'If you can get to Hari without her noticing and explain,' I whispered back, 'he might deactivate the headband. I'll help the Souler keep her occupied.'

Bobby slipped silently away and I turned back to where Neil was extolling the virtues of Thaddeus, who had hunched over. With his bat-like ears turned down, he somehow looked less intimidating than before.

Then behind me came the thud of running feet. Back-up was on its way – except that the thudding sounded like a pack of trolls stampeding towards us, way too threatening a noise; the security guys at HOPE were usually better than that. Moth-girl stopped scratching and froze, her body trembling with sudden fear.

A flash caught my eye and I realised the lights above the lifts were blinking for the fourth floor. Someone was coming – and whoever it was, they were about to walk straight out into the middle of everything.

I started counting down.

The running feet got closer.

Neil Banner's quiet chat notched up in volume as he struggled to regain Moth-girl's attention.

The lift reached the third floor.

Two fully-armoured security guards raced past me.

Moth-girl's eye's widened with terror, the carving knife shaking in her hand.

Second floor.

I starting moving; the beige vinyl tiles seemed to turn to sand, sucking at my feet.

The guards came to a determined stop in front of Moth-girl.

First floor.

She stumbled back, turning to flee.

But Hari loomed in front of her, trapping her.

The lift doors pinged open. Grace, her white doctor's coat flapping open, stepped out, not looking up from the file she was reading.

'Grace,' I yelled, throwing myself at them, knowing I wasn't going to be fast enough, knowing I was going to be too late . . .

... Moth-girl lunged desperately towards the open lift and escape ...

... Grace's head jerked up, her face paling in instant understanding ...

... Moth-girl plunged towards her, the knife, forgotten, held out in front of her ...

... and as Grace crashed to the floor, papers fluttered up and out of her file like a flock of pigeons taking panicked flight ...

I froze in horror as the papers settled.

Bobby stood in the space where Grace had been, his arms wrapped around Moth-girl, his mouth open wide in a snarl, fangs gleaming white and needle-sharp. Moth-girl was pressed against him, crying, her head instinctively flung back to offer her throat because of the vampire's nearness. Bobby lowered his head to strike, and the gems in the silver circlet sparked yellow with magic. He roared in anguish, lurched back and collapsed into a heap in front of the lift doors. Moth-girl gave a grief-stricken wail and raked her nails down her own face and neck, leaving blood-bright furrows. The two guards shouted a warning, then tackled her, pinning her to the ground, where she struggled and screamed beneath them.

I dropped to my knees next to Grace, who was lying on her front, unmoving. I grabbed her shoulder—

—and she whacked my hand away. 'Get your hands off me,' she snarled, glaring up at me, then her eyes widened as she took in my appearance. 'Genny? Is that you?'

'Of course it's me!' I pulled her over onto her back, frantically patting her down for any injuries. 'She didn't get you, did she?'

'I'm fine, Genny, all in one piece.' She pushed me away, back in control. 'Now, let's get this sorted,' she said loudly over Moth-girl's cries as she scrambled up and scanned the hall. 'Right, the rest of the emergency team should be here any second. Genny, you g—'

She stopped speaking, her dark eyes glazing over and her face going blank. Moth-girl's cries cut out a second later as an unnatural stillness descended on all the humans.

Mind-lock.

'Shit,' I muttered, and looked over at Bobby who was slumped unconscious against the lift doors, his silver-cuffed hands clasped over his stomach. Between his fingers protruded the hilt of the carving knife. He didn't look so good: dark blood, a strange red-blue hue, bubbled over his bottom lip and a small puddle of blood pooled on the floor. But Bobby was a vampire and he'd survive almost anything other than having his head lopped off, his heart removed, or being turned into a pile of ashes. And he wasn't the cause of the mass mind-lock.

A sudden tapping noise drew my gaze to Thaddeus, standing protectively in front of Neil Banner, his baseball bat hitting the floor rhythmically. Neil's face was as blank as Grace's, Moth-girl's, and the security guards.

Thaddeus' warning grin stretched wide, showcasing his ruby-encrusted teeth. As he and I stared towards the entrance the question I should've asked myself earlier finally jumped into my head.

Why would a fang-gang attack a venom-junkie like Moth-girl, then send her in to HOPE to look for me? It didn't make sense. The whole thing behind pumping someone up with venom was to get their blood fizzing, so both vamp and Moth would experience the high. Unless they wanted to keep their victim senseless and handy for a sunset snack, there really was no reason not to indulge . . .

Unless she was a distraction?

The doors whispered open and my pulse leapt into my throat. Whoever the fuck it was, and whatever they wanted, it was something to do with me, and I wasn't going to let them hurt anyone else. I started walking towards the entrance.

The doors hissed closed.

But no one had come in . . .

. . . or at least no one that I could see.

Chapter Fifteen

Warmth slipped over me like the summer sun on my skin, heating the bruises that encircled my left wrist and setting my pulse throbbing. I breathed in, concentrating my inner senses, and tasted Turkish delight on my tongue: Malik. Surprise sparked in my mind – he shouldn't be here; he was supposed to be too injured after the explosion. Then wary relief filled me. Malik hadn't set this up; it wasn't his style.

'Malik al-Khan,' I murmured, 'show yourself.'

He appeared as if from nowhere, the nonexistent shadows he'd gathered to him trailing like dark smoke from his body. His enigmatic face was as pale and beautiful as ever, his slanted eyes dangerous black pools that held thoughts I wasn't sure I wanted to know, his hair a fall of black silk that my fingers itched to touch. Anticipation fluttered as a traitorous part of me whispered I could do that and more once I'd made a deal with him. I shut it up.

'Shame you couldn't have turned up ten minutes earlier,' I said, my voice matter-of-fact. At least he didn't appear to be showing any ill-effects from whatever injuries he'd sustained. Of course, I could only see his face and hands; the rest of his body was elegantly hidden by a designer suit in his usual black – even his neck was covered between his hair and the high Nehru collar. 'But as you're here now, and you appear to have taken control, maybe you can help sort it out?'

He stared at me, a fine line creasing between his brows, pinpricks of anger flaring deep in his pupils.

I frowned. What the hell was he angry about?

For a moment I thought he would speak, then the pinpricks in his eyes turned incandescent with flames; he came towards me, his rage sending shockwaves of burning air that lifted my hair and scorched like the desert sun over my skin. Terror slammed inside me and instinct warned me to flee. But this time I remembered my stepmother's words: you don't run, you don't struggle; it gets a vamp too excited. I clenched my fists, forcing myself to stand and face him.

He halted, close enough that the October chill that still clung to his body cooled the heat burning over mine, close enough that the blue veins pulsing under the translucent skin of his throat blurred before my eyes, close enough that the slow, shallow thud of his heart shouted of his need and thirst in my ears.

Not just angry, but hungry too.

Shit. I was neck-deep in trouble here.

I shivered as he smoothed a hand over my head and I felt him twist my ponytail around his fingers. He tugged on my hair, forcing my chin up, leaving my throat vulnerable. My pulse sped faster, jumping under my skin. I stared into his eyes. The flames in his pupils snuffed out, leaving them as opaque as obsidian, a thin film of blood colouring the sclera. Bloodlust. *Fuck*, he was on the edge of bloodlust . . .

My heart hammering with fear, unable to stop the trembling in my body, I placed my palm against his chest, wanting to push him away, knowing I wouldn't, not when the 3V in my blood urged me to give him what he sought. He lowered his head, but instead of my throat, he touched his lips to mine, demanding that I submit. My mouth opened beneath his almost of its own volition and I felt the sharp sting as his fangs pierced my bottom lip. He pulled my lip into his mouth, sucking painfully hard, and as I tasted the honeyed sweetness of my own blood a whimper of terror escaped me. His other hand closed around my throat, almost choking me as he silenced the sound.

A shudder travelled through his body and the pain of his bite dissipated with his *mesma*, twisting fear to warmth and lust, tightening my nipples into aching peaks, coiling desire hot between my legs. His hands stroked down my spine, cupped me and pressed me closer, his own body hard. My knees weakened and I clutched at his arms, sliding my tongue between his fangs, wanting what he was offering.

'*Genevieve.*' His voice sounded rough, somehow desolate, in my mind.

Then he was gone . . .

. . . leaving me trembling, a slice of sorrow lodged like ice beneath my breastbone.

I rubbed at the cold spot, fear, disappointment and need spiralling through me in a whirlwind of conflicted emotions. Malik stood a few feet away, watching me, a considering expression on his face. The blood-kiss, or whatever it was, might never have happened. I touched my fingers to my bottom lip. It felt bruised and tender, and when I took my hand away, a bright bead of blood shivered on my finger. Anger that he'd treated me like a blood-slave, and that I'd let him, pushed the other emotions away. I held my bloody finger out to him.

'What the fuck was that all about?'

His eyes skimmed over my body, the look impersonal. 'You have a penchant for using the bodies of others, Genevieve. I needed to ensure that you were yourself and yourself alone under this new exterior.'

'Ri-ight. You're telling me that little tantrum was my fault? Well, you can think again,' I said flatly, as I tried to calm the rapid beat of my heart. 'I know you can tell who I am just by scent, so using my Glamour as an excuse to have a quick bite has nothing to do with it.'

'Your own scent is strong enough to conceal the scent of another beneath it, so I am unable to distinguish any other within it.' He lifted one shoulder in a graceful shrug. 'But yes, you are right, I am angry. You should not have left.'

I shouldn't have left! Crap, we hadn't even started negotiating and already he was acting like he thought I was going to behave like some fang-hazed blood-pet. And no way was that happening, no matter how pretty he was. I took a deep breath, forcing myself to ignore the fear- and anger-laced adrenalin hyping my emotions.

'I am not your property, Malik,' I said firmly, wanting to get that straight for both of us. 'So don't get any ideas about me hanging around, waiting for you to wake up every night, 'cause it's not going to happen.'

For a moment a bleak expression touched his eyes and a chill skittered down my spine, then I decided I'd imagined it as he said, 'We have the matter of your alibi with the police to take care of.' He gave my Glamour a disparaging look. 'You will need time to make yourself presentable.'

I stared at him suspiciously. Had he really searched me out just to provide me with an alibi? Well, it wasn't like I was going to say no, but—

'Thanks, I appreciate it.' I waved an arm at the mind-locked gathering in the hallway. 'But I'm not going anywhere until I know everyone's okay.'

'This is a *hospital*, Genevieve. The staff are trained, and well-equipped to deal with emergencies such as these.' He smiled, and I nodded at him, agreeing that it sounded reasonable. 'There is nothing to be done here by you, so it is better that we do not impede their efforts.'

As if someone I couldn't hear had shouted 'action', Grace got up. Her determined gaze passed blindly over me and she rushed to where Moth-girl was buried beneath the two guards. The guards leapt out of her way and at her order one of them raced back down the corridor. Grace knelt, started checking Moth-girl's vitals—

'Genevieve.' Malik's calm voice commanded my attention. He was still standing, waiting, his hand now held out to me.

I looked at his proffered hand and thought how good it would be to wrap my fingers round his, to let him lead me away from this place to somewhere safe. Only, that wasn't right, was it? Nowhere was safe, not with him, not with anyone. *Damn.* The annoying vampire was trying to mould my thoughts. Bad enough he kept using his *mesma* on me and playing with my senses without adding that.

'Nice try, Malik.' I gave him an irritated look. 'But the vamp-hypno stuff isn't working so well, so just forget it, okay?'

'My words are true, Genevieve.' He moved to survey the scene behind me. 'There is no one that can be helped here, but if you insist on staying, I must acknowledge our friends.'

I looked over at Grace; she was untying a white ribbon from around Moth-girl's neck. Another doctor – Craig, I thought, judging by his bald patch – was prepping to place a shunt in Moth-girl's throat. Where had he come from? I frowned, uneasy. Had Malik distracted me enough that I'd lost some time? But it wasn't just the lost time that bothered me . . . I turned back to him.

'. . . apologise for disturbing you, troll,' he was saying to Hari, making a gesture that encompassed the hallway, then he inclined his head at the goblin. 'I offer you both my word that I intend no harm to those under your care.'

'Fair enough, guv.' Thaddeus jerked his thumb back at Neil Banner. 'But what about my charge? My contract states I have to oppose any vampire mind-locks with extreme measures.' He tapped his bat, his mouth widening in a ruby-glinting grin. 'So, you gonna let him loose or not?'

'My hold is a precaution only,' Malik said calmly. 'But if you will vouch for your charge, I will have no hesitation in releasing him.'

Thaddeus nodded, his red and grey horse-tail hair fanning over his wide shoulders. 'I've no problem vouching for him, guv.'

Malik inclined his head and Neil Banner blinked, his blank expression changing to anxious concern. Before he could speak, Thaddeus grasped his arm and steered him to the seat furthest away and pushed him down into it. He started talking earnestly, but his voice was too low for me to hear what he was saying.

I turned back to Malik and asked the question that was bothering me. 'What did you mean, there's nothing to be done?'

He stared down at Moth-girl. Her skin was glowing radioactive-red with blood-flush. 'The girl's heart is overstimulated by the venom, and despite her increased level of red blood cells and thus the increased levels of oxygen, the blood is moving too fast for her lungs to cope. They are collapsing, her heart is labouring, and her blood has thickened to the point that the supply to her brain is diminishing.'

A classic case of venom-induced adrenalin-based hypertension, and if unrelieved, it was usually followed by a stroke, then probable cardiac arrest. I knew the symptoms – I'd experienced them myself, but I was sidhe fae. Moth-girl was human. I frowned. Other than the flushed skin she looked quite peaceful, the hint of a smile wreathing her lips.

'Then why isn't she having convulsions,' I said, 'if she's reached that stage?'

'I am limiting her distress.'

'But they're taking blood from her; the shunt will relieve the pressure.'

'Taking blood from the jugular will not suffice,' he said. 'Piercing the carotid artery would improve her chances, but as a medical procedure it is too dangerous. The flow from the heart needs to be controlled.'

I didn't need to ask how. 'Necking' – feeding from the carotid – is a popular, if illegal, entertainment in the less salubrious blood-houses in Sucker Town. Unsurprisingly, the same ones that are usually home to the Moths. One or more vamps stoke a junkie up on venom, then just as the junkie hits the edge, the vamp bites into the carotid, gulping down the blood as if the junkie's a spurting soda fountain. But even in the most unscrupulous houses there's always a failsafe: another vamp able to control the junkie's heart, to stop them bleeding to death and help heal the wound as the vamp 'necking' usually succumbs to overindulgence and falls into a blood-dream. Of course, if the vamp was hungry enough, a blood-dream shouldn't be a problem. I touched my tongue to the small bruise on my lip as an idea formed in my head. 'If you fed on her, could you save her?'

He gave me an impassive look. 'Genevieve, it is not possible for me to feed on her.'

'Why not? Surely you're hungry enough.'

'You are correct. I am hungry, but she is human. If I were to feed in the manner my blood insists, she would not survive,' he said, his voice empty of any emotion. 'I am not able to stop myself from feeding any other way.'

I had a sudden terrifying thought; maybe he'd bitten my lip because he couldn't trust himself not to rip my throat out. Then the recent 'memory' I'd had of Rosa tracing her tongue over her own fangs as she lowered her head to feed came back to me. I knew how I could save Moth-girl.

I shrugged out of my leather jacket and hopped on one foot while I pulled off a trainer.

Malik regarded me with detached interest. 'What are you doing, Genevieve?'

I jerked my head at Moth-girl. 'She needs a vamp to feed on her if she's going to stand any chance of surviving. You won't do it—'

'It would be counterproductive,' he interrupted.

'Whatever.' I pulled off my other trainer and unzipped my jeans. 'So I'm finding a vamp that will.' I tugged the jeans down over my hips, then stopped and looked up at him warily. 'Rosa.'

Pinpricks of rage flickered in the depths of his eyes, then disappeared. 'I do not see how wearing Rosa's body will help the situation.'

I swallowed. 'Rosa—She's—Her body is still a vamp, so when I activate the spell . . . I have the same capabilities as a vamp. That way I can feed on the girl.' I ignored the nervous twist my stomach gave; I'd never fed on blood before as Rosa, only venom. 'You can be my failsafe.' He didn't answer, so I took it as agreement. I let the jeans drop around my ankles and kicked them off, leaving me standing there in my socks and shirt and the magicked-up white bikini bottoms. There was no sign of the spell-tattoo on my left hip; the Glamour of the bikini covered it. I tugged the briefs down, noting absently that Tavish had made me a true blonde, and *looked*, but there was still no spell-tattoo. I traced my fingers over the skin of my hip, concentrating. After a month of not using it, the magic should be jumping eagerly, almost forcing me to activate it. But I could feel nothing. Damn. I wondered again if something was wrong with the spell. Or maybe the Glamour Tavish had tagged me with was interfering with it? Time to get rid of it.

'Scissors,' I muttered to myself and gazed around. I spied a pair on a nearby trolley. When had that appeared? Didn't matter, either I wasn't paying attention, or Malik was still skewing my perceptions. I grabbed the scissors and bent over, flipping the blonde ponytail so it hung down in front of me.

'Miss Taylor.' Neil Banner's diffident voice came from somewhere to the side of me. 'If I might suggest something?'

I peered impatiently up at him. 'What?'

'As I understand it, you and the vampire here think that the only way to save the girl is to feed on her?'

'Yes,' I said. Trust him to pick now to interfere. 'If you've got a problem with that, you'll have to save it for later.'

'Oh no.' He smiled, his eyes lighting with happiness. 'I've no problem, not if it will save her soul.'

I blinked at him in surprise.

'But I think there is a better solution to whatever it is you're planning,' he carried on, pointing at the lifts. 'There is another vampire here, is there not? And one who desperately needs help. Why not let him feed? That way two souls might be saved instead of just one.'

I stood upright and stared at him, trying to get my head round his idea. I looked over at Bobby, slumped in a heap, still clutching the carving knife, surrounded by a wider pool of blood. I'd completely forgotten about him – and by the looks of it so had everyone else. But he was a vampire, he'd survive, except— 'You said he's dying?' I asked Banner. 'How do you know?'

'God has graced me with the ability to see our souls.' He steepled his hands together, pressing them against his lips. 'When our earthly bodies are dying, our auras gradually thin until our souls are released and can travel onwards into the glorious light of God's majesty. It is a wondrous moment to witness' – his face fell into concerned lines – 'unless our souls are too weighed down by earthly sadness and pain to travel upon their journey.'

'Sounds great' – *I think* – 'but what has that got to do with them?'

'Both the young girl's aura and the vampire's are almost nonexistent, Ms Taylor.' He clasped his hands tighter. 'They are dying. Thaddeus and I have been praying for them both, but it might not be enough. I fear that their souls are too heavily laden to reach Our Lord's heaven. The girl's might be

trapped here as a ghost or spirit, and as for the vampire . . .'
He shook his head, despair settling on his face.

I turned to Malik. 'Is he right?'

'I cannot see souls or ghosts, Genevieve,' he said calmly.
'But *he* believes he is right.'

'No, I mean about Bobby dying. He's a vamp, he shouldn't
be dying.'

Malik lifted his chin and inhaled. 'He is young, and if it
has been sometime since his master fed him, he will be weakened. The magic in the restraints that contain him will also
block his bond with his master, so yes, he is possibly suffering
in the same way a human would with that injury.'

'Do it then!'

He stared at me, expressionless. 'Do what?'

'Cut the crap, Malik.' I stuck my hands on my hips. 'You're
playing the master puppeteer, busy pulling everybody's
strings in this show, so tell them to take the girl over to Bobby
and let him feed.'

He stared at me, speculation in his eyes. 'You ask a lot,
Genevieve. My interference in their minds is minimal, just
enough to encourage them to do what the circumstances and
their training are already urging them to. And of course, to
ensure they see us as nothing to be concerned with, since we
do not need their medical help.' He waved a hand in an all-
encompassing gesture. 'To direct their minds in something
alien is a more difficult task.'

'But you can do it?'

'If I wished to.'

'Name it,' I sighed. 'Your price. It's a one-time deal,
though, nothing more.'

He raised an eyebrow. 'Are you offering me a sidhe bargain, Genevieve?'

'It's what you want, isn't it?' I said drily. 'Why else would
you be hanging around, directing the proceedings?'

'Why else, indeed,' he said slowly, then clapped his hands
together, making me jump. 'But it is too great an offer to be
decided on in haste.'

'Three choices then, but I get right of veto, and if I don't
like any of them, then we settle on one offer of blood, okay?'

'Blood in whatever way I choose to enjoy it.' He smiled

slowly, letting me glimpse fang. It wasn't a question, but an obvious statement of his intent.

My heart flip-flopped. Damn. Why did he have to be so beautiful as well as a manipulative bastard? 'So long as no one gets hurt.'

'So long as no one else gets physically hurt,' he amended.

My heart flip-flopped for an entirely different reason. Specifics like that were *so* not good. Was I really going to make a bargain with him? I'd been planning on a mutual business-like deal, not staking my future on a magic-bound bargain. Bargains never work out well for anyone; the magic is too capricious. I looked over at Bobby, huddled on the floor: he'd lost his mother and his girlfriend and his father was in a coma. He might be a hot pin-up for fang-fans, but he was still that scared teenager I'd first met, and never mind he was a vamp, he didn't deserve to die, not if I could help. And neither did the girl, no matter what she was here to see me about. I closed my eyes and said a brief prayer to whatever god might be listening.

'I agree,' I said.

'No.' Malik's pupils flared briefly with bright flames. 'I do not agree.'

My mouth fell open in shock. He was refusing? 'What do you mean, you don't agree?' I demanded.

'I do not wish to make this bargain.'

'But what about them?' I waved my arm at the girl and Bobby.

'They are not part of this concern, Genevieve.' His words slipped over me like a chill shadow on a sun-kissed autumn day and I shivered, goosebumps pricking my skin. Then his gaze turned inwards, his expression almost bordering on pain.

Around us, the hallway erupted into calm but determined action.

The hovering guard strode over to Bobby and, removing his hands from the knife, pulled it out. It came free with a wet ripping sound that had Neil Banner flinching. Bobby groaned with pain as more dark blood gushed from between his fingers. The guard moved him gently so he was lying on his side.

Grace efficiently removed the shunt from Moth-girl's neck and the other doctor, Craig, carried her as carefully as if she were breakable to lay her alongside Bobby. Bobby's eyes fluttered and he raised his head, lips drawing back from his fangs. A yellow gem in his headband sputtered, then fizzed out. Beside me, Malik shifted, a small movement of discomfort. Then Bobby lowered his head and Moth-girl jerked as he struck. The soft noise of sucking whispered through the hallway as Grace and Craig pulled themselves to their feet and moved over to the orange visitors' chairs.

'It is done,' Malik said. He stepped over to where Moth-girl had lain and picked up the bloodstained white ribbon. Bringing it to his nose, he sniffed, then carefully folded it up and stowed it away into his pocket. He walked to reception and started to speak quietly with Hari. As I looked around to locate my discarded jeans and trainers I strained my ears, but couldn't hear what they were saying. I bent to pick up my clothes.

'Ms Taylor.' Neil Banner's voice at my shoulder made me straighten. He smiled hopefully at me, keeping his eyes fixed on my face. 'I wanted to remind you of our earlier conversation and ask whether you know about the matter I mentioned?'

'The delicate matter involving this supposed legacy,' I said, folding the jeans over my arm and holding them in front of me. I'm not shy, but he suddenly seemed to be. 'Before we go any further, I want my solicitor to see the will.' Once I find one, I added, to myself. 'Is that acceptable?'

'Of course,' he said, holding out a card. 'My contact details. Just let me know when you're ready. The sooner the better – tonight even – the head of the Order is keen to get this dealt with.'

Way too keen, I said to myself. I tilted my head, time for a bit of probing. 'How does you being a necromancer fit in with all this religious stuff? Don't most faiths consider you evil?'

'Ah, I wondered if you would understand when I told you about my ability to see souls.' He gave me a half-smile. 'But it is not the gift that is given to us that matters, but what we do with it.'

'Okay, I understand that.' I wanted to ask him to talk to Cosette, but my bullshit antenna was now vibrating like a siren's tuning fork.

'*Genevieve.*' Malik's voice came in my mind. '*It is time for us to go. I have other matters to deal with this night, as well as your problem with the police.*'

I half turned, obeying his command – until I realised what I was doing. I shook my head and made myself stop. Damn annoying vampire, why couldn't he just ask like a normal person? I clamped down on the compulsion to move as I thought about Banner's request and what had bothered me earlier: why would the Earl leave the Fabergé egg to the Soulers?

'The person who left you this legacy,' I said to Banner. 'Do you know why he did?'

Neil Banner smiled his zealot's smile. 'He wants us to pray for his soul.'

The Earl had never struck me as religious, but I hadn't spent more than a couple of hours in his company before I killed him, so who was I to know?

'Fair enough,' I said, taking his card. 'I'll be in touch.'

I looked anxiously over at Bobby and the girl, now being separated by Grace and the security guard. 'Are they both going to live?'

'If God wills it they shall.' He clasped his hands earnestly in front of his chest. 'Both of their auras are brighter, more solid now. Thaddeus and I will continue to pray for them both' – his mouth lifted in a solemn smile – 'and offer them more secular help once they recover.'

'*Come, Genevieve.*' Malik's voice sounded again in my head. '*Leave the doctors to take care of their patients.*'

I wanted to wait until I knew they were both okay. I also needed some answers: what had Moth-girl wanted to give me – and how had she known where to find me? And who had sent her and why? And I wanted to talk to Grace. But the insistent need to go with Malik pulled at me like an overstretched wire, and the stiff set of his shoulders under the black suit jacket and the tense line of his jaw told me his patience wasn't endless. So with my pulse thudding for more than one reason, I followed the beautiful vampire away from HOPE.

Chapter Sixteen

A Gold Goblin taxi waited outside, the sour smell of its methane-fuelled engine hanging like a pall in the damp night air. The Stick goblin jumped out and held the cab door open. His lime-green topknot looked like a hairy tarantula had taken up residence on his head. A gust of chill wind flattened his navy boilersuit against his body and his tall, lanky frame reminded me of the turban-headed dryads who'd chased me earlier. Not surprising really; the goblin queen had cross-cloned tree trolls with indentured sky-born goblins to get workers tall enough and with eyesight good enough to pass their driving tests.

'G'night, miss, g'night, mister.' The goblin slid a triple-jointed finger down his nose and stamped; his trainers flashed green. Another gust whistled past and the leaves in the nearest trees rustled. I wondered if the trees had recognised me and were passing the message on to the dryads, but the goblin didn't react, so maybe it was just the wind.

As I returned the greeting Malik held out a small black velvet pouch to the goblin. 'Any dealings between my companion and I are not to be repeated or conveyed in any shape or form,' he said.

The goblin took the pouch, his spring-green eyes narrowing to a squint as he upended it carefully into his palm. Three black stones the size of misshapen marbles glittered in the interior light from the taxi. The goblin's squirrel-like ears twitched as he brought the stones to his nose and sniffed.

'Are we agreed?' Malik asked.

The Stick goblin rebagged the stones. 'Sure thing, mister.' He patted his wrinkled grey hand over the Gold Goblin crest embroidered on the chest of his blue boilersuit and stamped his foot again.

Malik inclined his head, then ushered me into the cab. 'After you, Genevieve.'

I hesitated for a moment, wondering if we were going to the Metropolitan Police Magic and Murder Squad's headquarters or not. Even as I thought it, Malik said quietly, 'Old Scotland Yard is the correct destination, is it not, Genevieve?'

Reassured, I nodded, and he repeated it to the goblin. I stepped into the taxi and scooted to the far side of the back seat, the plastic cold against my bare thighs. Malik sank down next to me, stretched out his long legs and closed his eyes. The goblin jumped in, crunched the taxi's gears and off we rumbled.

I tugged my jeans back on, struggling to stay on my side of the taxi as it rounded a bend. I glanced at Malik, noticing the map of faint blue veins under the pale skin of his hands and along the fine line of his jaw. He *was* hungry. I'd thought he'd been about to lose it and go into bloodlust back inside HOPE before he'd bitten me. But so far that hadn't happened, so maybe I was working on faulty info from my stepmother, or maybe being a revenant made him different. Of course, he still could go all murderous with bloodlust, and trapped in a taxi with him like this, it wasn't going to be the healthy option. For me anyway.

'I am not so in need of blood that I will put you at risk, Genevieve,' he said softly.

His words answered my unspoken fears, but still they made my pulse hitch.

He opened his eyes, giving me an almost amused look. 'But it would be less difficult if you could calm your heart rate.'

Yay! The monster says he isn't going to eat me. Yet.

I breathed in, aiming for relaxed; and instead a curl of lust twisted inside me as I inhaled his dark spice scent. I banished it with thoughts of Fabergé eggs, necromancers, Moth-girls and Bobby, and finally narrowed them down to the more immediate question of my alibi, or rather, Malik turning up with my alibi at the top of his to-do list – he hadn't even fed properly before coming to find me. So why had he really sought me out? I opened my mouth to ask, then decided not disturbing him might be a better idea for now. The buttoned-up suit made him look distant, unapproachable – then I realised it wasn't just the suit. He'd shut down. He'd stopped his heart from beating, stopped his lungs from drawing breath and dialled his hypersensitive vampire senses back to less than an average human's. It's something most vamps pick up pretty quickly after taking the Gift; it makes it easier to integrate into human society, a way to avoid the siren calls of beating hearts and fang-aching blood scents. Unauthorised nibbling to satisfy those midnight-munchies is a sure-fire route to getting the chop – literally – with a one-way trip to the guillotine. Of course, snacking on a willing victim isn't a problem, so long as it's on licensed premises—

The lens of the taxi's CCTV camera caught my attention and suddenly alarm bells started ringing. I leaned forward and tapped the glass partition. 'We need to go back to the HOPE clinic,' I said to the goblin driver.

He shifted his head slightly and in the rear-view mirror I saw the rear lights of the bus in front reflecting red in his shiny green eyes.

'Keep going,' Malik said quietly.

The goblin gave a sharp nod.

Damn. I turned to face Malik. 'The hospital's got security cameras,' I said, keeping a tight rein on my frustration. 'They'll have caught Bobby feeding, it's not licensed premises, and his being out of it isn't going to make any—'

'The cameras were not focused on that particular part of the incident,' he interrupted. 'The humans will believe it was their efforts that were successful in saving both the vampire and the girl; they will not remember otherwise.'

So he'd adjusted their memories during the mind-lock, which made sense—

'But what about the troll? And the Beater goblin and the Souler, they all know the truth.'

'There have been recent meetings between the Vampire High Table, the Goblin Queen and the Matriarch of London's troll clan.' He pushed the fall of black hair back; the stone piercing his earlobe glinted black against his pale skin. 'We have negotiated several new treaties to ensure the current confidence the humans have in their safety around vampires does not become compromised.'

Surprise winged through me. The vamps and the goblins had always talked, but the trolls were new to the mix. It wasn't just the venom hits I'd missed since I'd given up my regular trips to Sucker Town – as Rosa – but all the gossip too.

'The incident tonight would have been blown up out of proportion by the media,' Malik carried on, 'particularly as it involved Mr October. He has only recently been cleared of murder charges; ally that with the current anti-fae feeling and it is possible that it would incite the humans to turn against anyone Other. It is in the best interest of all to minimise any such incidences.'

Of course, it didn't help that I was in the frame for murder, heating up the simmering anti-fae discrimination almost to boiling point. Still, even if Malik was for minimising any problems, he hadn't appeared too thrilled by the idea back at HOPE.

'If keeping a lid on what happened is for the greater good' – although mostly for the vamps' greater good, a cynical voice in the back of my mind added – 'why were you getting all worked up about sorting things out back there, then?'

'If I had done nothing, Genevieve,' he said, soft-voiced, 'the outcome would ultimately be the same. Mr October would still be a hero, albeit a dead one, and the girl would be just another sad statistic. It was the method used to save their lives, which would have been sensationalised, as you so rightly surmised.'

I ran my hand anxiously over my hair then stopped as my fingers tangled in the Glamour-spelled ponytail. I could just imagine the headlines: VAMP CHOWS DOWN WHILE DOCS WATCH or even, HOSPITAL FOOD JUST GOT BLOODIER. The media would make a five-course meal out of it all. And Grace would lose her job!

'Are you sure the humans won't remember anything?' I asked, worried.

'They may dream.' He touched a finger to the platinum ring that banded his thumb in what seemed a vaguely troubled gesture. 'It is not the ideal way to force human minds as I did, but I had neither the time nor the fortitude to gain their compliance in any other way.'

'Has it done them any harm?'

'No, but the two doctors' minds were difficult.' He lifted one hand, indicating that he'd done what he could. 'If they think about anything too hard, they might recover their memories.'

'Grace is my friend,' I said, frowning, 'she's going to wonder why I left. What did you tell her?'

'You saw she was busy and did not want to disturb her.'

I tapped my thigh; Grace wasn't going to believe that! She'd have expected me to hang around and help. I dug out my phone and texted her to say I'd found my alibi and I'd talk to her later, after I'd been to the police. Then I noticed I'd missed a text from Finn, saying Tavish was home and his place was safe; he'd see me there. I texted back okay and left it at that, not wanting to tell him where I was going, and unsure just how safe Tavish's place really was, thanks to the sidhe queen's curse thing.

'The girl kept saying she had something to give me.' I looked up at Malik. 'Don't suppose you've any ideas?'

'Do you know what this is?' He produced a length of bloodstained white ribbon from his pocket.

'It was tied round the girl's neck,' I said. Something was nagging at my mind about the ribbon, but as I tried to catch the thought it was gone. 'And no, before you ask, I don't know what it means. So perhaps you could hold off on being mysterious for the moment and just tell me what's important about it?'

He smoothed the ribbon between his fingers and I shivered at the sensation as if he'd smoothed the ribbon around my own throat. *Mesma*.

'It is a tradition amongst us that when we wish to court another's favour we will offer a gift,' he said, his expression pensive. 'The colour of the ribbon signifies the giver's intentions. Red is an offering of blood, black is an offering of sex, and white indicates the gift is available to do with as you will, to use for food, or sex, or with the addition of the venom and the knife there is an added option of a different entertainment.'

Watching someone cut them themselves and bleed to death is entertainment? I frowned. But if it was a vamp thing, why had Moth-girl been sent to find me? I looked down at the scraped skin of my knuckles and remembered Bobby pleading for me to talk to Rosa, my supposed master for him.

And then my mind went *click!* 'So, Moth-girl herself was the actual gift.' A bloody box of chocolates, vampire style. 'So some vamp wants something from Rosa' – much like Bobby had – 'but they can't find her, so instead they stoke up Moth-girl and send her to me, presumably thinking I'd know to pass the gift on to Rosa, because they all think Rosa's my "master"?'

'The situation has escalated further than I had imagined,' he agreed.

So now I knew the *what*, and the partial *why*, but I still didn't know the *who* behind Moth-girl, or how they/she'd found me at HOPE. Something still nagged at me.

'It is an issue that needs to be resolved,' he carried on, 'before it spawns any more problems. If one vampire has conceived this idea, no doubt others will.'

Fuck! 'And I thought it was bad enough when all the invitations started turning up,' I muttered, angry that yet another vamp problem had decided to metaphorically bite me. 'But at least they weren't hurting anyone. No way do I want any more *gifts* like poor Moth-girl—'

He captured my wrist, his fingers cold against my skin. 'What invitations?'

I blinked, wanting to pull away, but then a feeling of languor slipped over me; there really was no need. All I had to do was answer his questions, nothing more. Wasn't it more comfortable just to chat? Of course it was. I settled back into my seat, smiling at how pleasant it was to sit here, my hand in his, his thumb gently stroking my sore knuckles . . . Only it was as if the conversation was in another room and I was watching us through a window, not quite able to hear, no matter how hard I tried to listen. Then the glass separating us dissolved . . .

'—and you have had invitations from vampires of all four blood families?'

'Yes—' I frowned, then yanked my hand from his. 'What the hell did you just do to me?'

'Nothing, Genevieve.' His *mesma* soothed over my body with the barest touch. 'It is a small trick to aid the recall of any information that the conscious mind might have dismissed as unimportant. That is all.'

'Fine,' I huffed, slightly pacified. 'Only next time, try asking first, it might make me feel a bit friendlier towards you.'

'You wish us to be friends?' An odd inflection sounded in his voice.

'I'm just saying' – I rubbed the back of my hand, still feeling the gentleness of his touch – 'ask before you pull any more of your tricks on me.'

For a moment I thought I saw disappointment in his eyes, then his mouth curled in a mocking smile. 'My apologies, Genevieve. I will try and remember.'

He turned away to look out of the taxi window. Unsettled, and not entirely sure why, I looked ahead, seeing the Ferriswheel of the London Eye loom bright against the night and recognised the road we were on. We'd be at Old Scotland Yard in another few minutes.

Curiosity edged out the last of the languor in my mind. 'So, what did you find out about the invitations with your little trick?' I asked.

'It is as I suspected,' he said. 'Those vampires who are not yet masters of their own existence might look to Rosa if they are in search for a new master, while those who have reached their autonomy are eager to offer her challenge in an attempt to annex you as their prize. As they have not been able to discover her whereabouts, they have resorted to asking you directly, in the hope that you will accept their invitation to their blood. If you were to change your allegiance this way, then Rosa would become the challenger if she wished to regain you – her property . . . or not, of course, as she wished.'

'It all sounds *so-o-o-o* civilised – well, if you ignore the fact we're talking about annexing *me* as their blood-pet prize,' I said sarcastically.

'The custom of sending invitations is a little-used caveat

among our laws. We may not appropriate another's property, but we can lay down a challenge, or we can offer enticements to the willing, as it were.'

'Right, so that's why no one's clubbed me over the head and carried me off, and of course, they can't find Rosa to challenge her because I haven't used the spell.'

'The situation is one that can be easily resolved,' he said decisively. 'All you need do is tell me where to find Rosa's body and how to release her from whatever magic holds her, then once we have finished establishing your alibi at the police station, I will deal with the matter and it will no longer need concern you.'

I grimaced. 'Sorry, Malik, but that's not going to be possible.'

Pinpricks of anger sparked in the black of his eyes. 'I will not allow—' He stopped. 'Genevieve, you cannot continue to walk in Rosa's skin as you have been doing,' he continued, his voice soft with threat. 'You must see that it has become too dangerous for all concerned.'

Sweat prickled down my spine; he'd once promised to kill Rosa, when he'd first discovered she was no longer *her*, but I'd really thought we'd got past that stage. *Maybe not*, whispered a small voice at the back of my mind.

'It's not that I don't *want* to tell you,' I said, my voice firm, 'It's that I really don't know where Rosa is. I bought what I thought was an expensive Disguise spell, nothing more. All I do is activate it, and then, well, I'm Rosa.'

'From whom did you purchase the spell?' he demanded.

'The Ancient One. She's a black witch or a sorcerer, or maybe both. I guess she must know where Rosa is. She's got a stall in Covent Garden, or at least she used to.' I smoothed my damp hands down my jean-clad thighs. 'I've been trying to find her myself for the last month, but apparently she's been AWOL for a while now.'

'I know of the Ancient One.' His face lost all expression. 'The reason you cannot locate her is because she is dead. The Earl killed her nearly a year ago, over some trifle she refused to give him.'

Damn! And I've been paying her every month for the spell too! Briefly I wondered to whom the money was going, and whether Rosa could be traced that way, but Data Protection and red tape made me dismiss that as the long-winded solution. As Malik had pointed out, with Moth-girl's appearance my problems had indeed multiplied. And with all the rest, like finding Tomas' murderer, the quicker the vamp ones were sorted the better. I gazed at the beautiful vampire now staring out of the taxi window. He was centuries old, he had to have considered all the possible ramifications – like what would have to happen if he couldn't find the real Rosa . . .

I sat back, giving him a quizzical look. 'So that's Plan A out the window.'

He turned to look at me with an enquiring expression.

'C'mon, Malik.' I drummed my fingers lightly on the seat between us. 'Whatever it is you want to happen, you had it all worked out, and all you needed was Rosa. I bet that's why you've been keeping tabs on me, hoping I'd lead you to her, isn't it? Then things got complicated by this murder thing.' And wasn't that an understatement! 'And your little memory trick or whatever it was just now didn't get you anywhere. Shit, you even thought about bargaining for the info back there at HOPE – but then you decided to do the psychological bit and gamble on me being obligated instead.'

Something unreadable flickered in the depths of his eyes. 'And are you feeling obligated?'

Obligated? Yes, but also relieved, now I knew Rosa was the reason he'd been doing the stalker bit, and eager to get on with whatever his plan was if it meant finally ridding myself of all the vamps and their schemes – other than him, of course – which was my aim even before Tomas' murderer had thrown us back together.

'I can make "Rosa" put in an appearance,' I said, the calm words belying the sudden apprehensive thud of my heart.

He regarded me in silence, then finally said, 'This is not how I wished to resolve this matter.'

'It's not really my idea of fun either, but to be honest, not much to do with this business is.'

'One point, Genevieve—' He paused. 'It might be better to settle this issue first, then deal with your alibi later . . .'

'Just in case the police don't believe you and decide to lock me up,' I finished drily.

'It is an unlikely scenario, but it is always a possibility.'

Knowing DI Crane's less-than-positive attitude towards me, it was more like a probability, I thought glumly. Then there was the other reason why a trip to the police right now wasn't as appealing as it might be: my morning meeting with the phouka Grianne and whatever info she might come up with. An alibi was good, but an alibi and evidence, maybe even a name, was way better.

'So what's going to happen next?' I asked.

He leaned forward and knocked on the glass partition. 'The Blue Heart, Leicester Square,' he called to the goblin, who nodded.

Then Malik sat back and gave me a considering look. 'We will need to put on a performance for the others. Are you sure you wish to do this?'

My heart thudded again and I wondered if I should ask what sort of show he meant, then decided maybe it was better not to know until the time came.

'If it will stop that happening again to some other poor human,' I said firmly, 'and get rid of my vampire problems, then yes, of course.'

'It will be dangerous,' he warned.

I laughed, but it wasn't a happy sound. 'So what isn't around vampires?'

Chapter Seventeen

Leicester Square was an assault on the ears and eyes: voices high-pitched with excitement, the slap of shoes on the pavement, the background rumble of late-night traffic and bursts of music from the bars, bright lights reflecting myriad colours in the wind-ripped puddles, damp air chill against my skin. The evening tourists and party-going crowds parted around us as water flows around a boulder in a rushing stream, not even registering we were there – Malik's mind-tricks at work. He closed his eyes, lifted his chin and sniffed the air, checking for vamps.

I'd left my jacket back at HOPE and now I shivered in the cold October wind that rustled through the trees in the central garden. As I stuck my hands in my jean pockets I told myself it was the wind causing my jitters, not the prospect of going in to play games with a nightclub full of suckers. Still, at least I'd be out of reach of the dryads, or any other fae; no fae would be reckless enough to enter a vamp club without some sort of guarantee of safety – and mine was the silent vamp standing next to me. I took a steadying breath and scoped out our destination.

The Blue Heart had started life as a multi-screen cinema

before the vamps turned it into the hot-spot for meeting the fanged A-list celebs. Two-foot high silver letters stood over the entrance, with the 'A' in 'HEART' replaced by the club's blood symbol: a large heart in blue neon that pulsed like it was alive. A huge screen mounted above the letters (a new addition since my last visit) was showing a close-up of Bobby's face set in his trademark Mr October expression, all smoky eyes and sulky, sexy lip-quirk. *Meet Mr October on All Hallows' Eve in the Starlight Lounge* scrolled in blood-red script across his face, followed by *sold out*. The screen switched to a dozen grinning Bella Lugosi lookalikes in full evening attire under a slowly spinning mirrored ball – *Fangs for the Memory presents: The Count's Hallowe'en ball – tickets still available.*

'Doesn't look like the ballroom dancing crowd are too keen,' I said, looking back at Malik.

He was staring at the entrance. There was a stillness about him, almost as if he wasn't there, as if he didn't exist.

'Earth to Malik.' I waved a hand in front of his face.

The slight line between his brows deepened. 'Genevieve, we should go in now.'

'What?' My pulse skittered into my throat. 'No, just wait a minute; I thought you wanted me to change into Rosa.'

'There are private rooms inside the club.' Malik caught the back of my elbow and started guiding me towards the entrance.

I tugged my arm from his. 'Hold up. I'm going to need clothes too – the shirt's okay, but' – I tapped my thighs – 'these jeans are way too small for Rosa.'

'There are any number of costumes inside for you to choose from, Genevieve.'

Costumes? He had to be kidding, didn't he? I shoved the thought away. 'There's the goblins too,' I said. 'Remember they can sense past the Glamour. Do you really want to advertise the fact you're bringing me, *a sidhe*, into the main vamp club?'

'I cannot fool the goblins' minds, but I can mask their small reactions to you.' He gave me a considering look. 'Do you not want to do this, Genevieve?'

'What?' I frowned. 'I told you I would.'

'You are delaying us.'

'No, I'm trying to be practicable . . .' My mind froze as he lifted his hand and traced a gentle line down my cheek, then tipped my chin up.

'I may not like this guise of yours . . .' He reached out and wrapped my blonde ponytail loosely round his hand. The magic reacted to his touch, raising goosebumps over my skin. '. . . but it will make it easier for me to cloud others' thoughts. They will not know you are sidhe. Besides, it is better that Rosa does not make her appearance too soon,' he said softly, then lowered his mouth to mine and kissed me. His lips were cool, a coolness that invaded my mouth, muted the small throbbing pain of his earlier bite and slipped down my throat like numbing ice water on a parched summer's day. He raised his head and smiled at me.

I smiled happily back at him, wanting to kiss him again, to taste him again.

He took my hand and laced his chill fingers with mine. 'Come, we will do this together, Genevieve.'

I blinked at my reflection in the black wraparound glasses of the small Monitor goblin perched behind one of the Blue Heart's ticket booths. His dyed blue hair stuck up in a spiral from his head like a unicorn's horn. 'There you go, miss,' he said cheerfully as he grasped my fingers and stamped the back of my hand with a blue heart the size of a pound coin. 'All ready to party.'

I blinked again. Now I stood with Malik in an empty circle of floor in the middle of the foyer. I looked around with detached interest. It was Saturday night, and the place was heaving. Humans stood in long queues at the semi-circular payment booths, waiting for their own entry stamps, and others waited with bulging baskets at the checkout point in the bat- and pumpkin-decorated gift shop. Yet more gathered at the Blue Artery Bar, where a dark red sludge-like smoothie swirling with toxic orange – enticingly labelled Carotid Cocktail + Scary Shot – appeared to be the hot-ticket item. And opposite the cloakroom was another new addition: a booth where a shorter line of humans waited for *Mr Nash, specialist in dental caps and implants ～ Fangs for the night, or for Eternity ～ Hallowe'en exclusives now available.* Even those who'd paid still had to queue. They snaked between blue velvet ropes, chattering excitedly while they waited to go through the double doors into the club's interior. As I peered through the crowd, I could see more humans having their photos taken with either a bare-chested, fang-flashing vampire hunk or a hissing, diaphanously clad Bride of Dracula.

The fang-fans had to be haemorrhaging money straight into the vamps' bloated bank accounts at this rate. The expense of their new Gold-Plated Coffin campaign was certainly paying them back big-time, and not just in blood.

Malik shifted beside me, reminding me how I'd got in here – or rather, reminding me that I didn't actually *know* how I'd got in here. I glared down at our laced fingers and jerked my hand from his. 'Will you stop siccing me with your mind-melds,' I whispered through gritted teeth. 'I told you, it bugs the hell out of me. And what was that thing about Rosa not appearing yet?'

'Later, Genevieve.' He sounded tired as he looked about him, searching for something, or someone. 'Time is not on our side if we are to achieve both this and deal with your police problem tonight.'

I frowned at him. His face was pale, and the blue veins under his jaw were darker and more pronounced. 'What's the matter with you? You look worse then you did five minutes ago.'

'The humans,' he murmured as an odd, almost panicked expression flickered briefly across his face, 'they are more difficult to ignore than I expected.'

Uneasy, I narrowed my eyes. 'I know you're hungry but you were fine cooped up in the taxi with me.'

'That is not the same, Genevieve.' His eyes darkened. 'You are not food, not as these—'

'Malik al-Khan,' a woman called, her voice sounding right by my ear, 'where is she, Malik? You told me you would produce her tonight. The audience is gathered and they will require some explanation if they are to wait for their entertainment.'

'She?' I asked, narrowing my eyes suspiciously at him. 'Which "she" is she talking about?'

'*Genevieve, please take hold of my hand*,' Malik ordered urgently in my mind. '*Now*,' he insisted. '*Flesh to flesh will make it easier to trick her. You are not who she means*.'

I hesitated, then placed my hand in his outstretched one, his fingers closed over mine in a cold, painful grip, and an icy chill slipped through my veins until it lodged itself like a jagged lump of ice at the base of my throat. I swallowed past the pain and mentally sighed. Figured! As he turned us to face whoever, he pulled me closer to his side, my arm bent up behind my back, our joined hands hidden as if he'd captured me in an embrace – or intended dislocating my shoulder.

A dainty blonde vampire in a twenties-style dress strode towards us, hiding her lower face behind a black lace fan, the jet beads swinging on her dress clicking loudly as she moved. Elizabetta, head of the Golden Blade blood family. Some of the humans, with puzzled, even frightened expressions on their faces, were almost jumping over each other to get out of her way. Others stood and gaped in awe. What the hell was she doing to them?

'*They will see her as Medusa, or maybe a glorious winged angel, or even leading a tiger*,' Malik said. '*Those are her favourites. Elizabetta does not care for humans, but she is an ally, and is willing to assist me this night*.'

'*You heard me?*' I glanced at him as I thought the question.

'*If you think directly at me*' – his voice shivered through me – '*then joined like this, yes, I can hear you*.'

Okay, so at least that was something on the positive side.

Malik squeezed my hand in reply as the dainty vampire halted in front of him. She was small, a few inches under five foot, and she'd been young, maybe sixteen or seventeen, when she'd accepted the Gift, but the disdainful expression in her odd colourless eyes was centuries old, and the power rolling off her made my Glamoured ponytail bristle like a scalded cat. I shook my head to rid myself of the irritating feeling.

'Where is she, Malik?' she demanded, her voice reverberating like an overloud bass speaker through my chest. I flinched, then clenched my free hand to stop from rubbing there. Damn vamp, using her *mesma* on me ... I tried to block her out, but the lump of ice in my throat wouldn't let me. Then I realised her *mesma* wasn't just directed at me;

the humans nearby were rubbing their chests, some were even clutching their heads.

'*She really doesn't like humans, does she?*' I muttered to him in my mind. '*I mean, I heard she was against all this celebrity stuff, but does she want to go back to living in the dark ages or something?*'

'*Try and keep your expression as an adoring human, please, Genevieve, it will make things easier.*' Malik's hand tightened warningly on mine as he said, 'Rosa will be here soon, Elizabetta.'

Ahh. So old Liz was looking for Rosa. Somehow I didn't think it was to have a girly chat.

'I hope she will.' Elizabetta snapped her fan shut. 'I am doing this only as a favour to you. If it was my choice, I'd be the first to sink my fangs in her throat, depraved bitch that she is. Why you want to prolong her existence when she is the cause of so many problems is beyond me.'

Yep, no girly chats for Rosa. I pasted on a smile, only it felt more like a goblin's warning grin.

'Rosa has always been troubled, Elizabetta,' Malik answered her calmly. 'I am sure it was not her intention to cause you any inconvenience.'

'Pah! She has no care for anyone other than herself. She has hunted in all our territories without permission, and she has stolen choice morsels away from our tables. It is not often that fae blood, even diluted with human, comes our way. The bounty should be utilised wisely, not kept for one's own gratification then disposed off.'

'*You have been busy rescuing your faelings, haven't you, Genevieve.*'

'*Damn right I have!*' Then I wondered how he knew.

Elizabetta's next words put that thought from my mind. 'And then this appropriation of the sidhe in secret.' She threw her arms out in disgust, the beads on her dress clacking as they swung. 'Did Rosa think that no one would discover it, that she would be able to stand against the Autarch? We do not need him to turn his attention to us.'

'Rosa will have no dealings with the Autarch, nor will anyone else in London, once you have witnessed her offer of fealty to me, Elizabetta.' His fingers squeezed mine again. 'I will await Rosa's arrival upstairs, and I will have someone inform you when we are ready.'

He inclined his head, then turned to me, gesturing towards the double doors leading to the interior of the club. 'We will go now.'

'Wait!' she commanded, the word digging into me like a hook. 'What is that?' She pointed a lace-gloved finger accusingly at me.

'*My apologies, Genevieve.*' Malik's voice came wearily in my head as he turned back to her. 'It is nothing, Elizabetta.' He gave an elegant shrug. 'I found myself in need of some sustenance.'

Sustenance? Nice! Still, at least he'd said he was sorry in advance.

'Do you not require your usual tithe?'

'Of course, the human is but an appetiser.'

'She's not to your usual taste, Malik.' She stared at my tabloid breasts, curling her mouth in a sneer. 'A tad *obvious*.'

'Her body is strong.' His words were distant. 'Her blood is healthy and she is willing, which is all that matters in a snack.'

Huh! I was a snack now?

'I hope you're not planning on draining her.' Her nostrils flared in disdain. 'Because if so, you should know that the facilities here are not the best for disposal. It would cause difficulties for me.' She gave him an assessing look. 'Difficulties I might not be able to keep from the human authorities.'

'My plans are not your concern.'

'Of course they are! Now the Earl is gone, I am head of London's High Table.'

'That decision is not finalised until after tomorrow's gathering, Elizabetta.'

'Pah! There is no one who can stand in my way. Hearts and Diamonds have none strong enough and while Declan's personal power may be on a par with mine, his Shamrocks are too small in numbers to overcome my Blades. Tomorrow or today makes no odds.' She gave a superior smile, showcasing longer-than-normal needle-sharp fangs. 'So it is now within my jurisdiction to deny you your blood-tithe, Malik. In fact, should I decide that you have succumbed to the curse of your abomination of a bloodline, I am within my rights to demand your death.'

'That doesn't sound good,' I murmured in my head.

He stilled, a line of concern creasing between his eyes. 'Do not pursue this course, Elizabetta.'

'In all the centuries I have known you, Malik, you have never picked up a snack.' She flicked open the fan with a flourish. 'So this one must be of some importance to you.' Her pink tongue slipped out and licked her fangs. 'I'm curious as to what that is.'

'She knows who I am!'

'No, she does not; she would not be talking if she did – she would be trying to tear my head off to get at you.'

'Good to know she's a friend then. I'd hate to meet one of your enemies.'

'Ally, not friend. Elizabetta needed my support to ratify her elevation tomorrow; now, for some reason, she feels she does not.'

'I am here surrounded by humans, and have yet to kill one.' Malik waved a dismissive arm. 'I have evidently not fallen to the curse as you can see, Elizabetta.'

'But you are wrong, I cannot see.' Her odd pupils contracted to nothing, leaving her colourless eyes even more nondescript. 'I think you should show me that you can control your curse.' She touched a finger to her lips in parody as if a thought had just struck her. 'Take your snack now.'

'This is not the place, Elizabetta.' He spoke calmly, but his hand crushed mine. Pain burned in my fingers, then it was gone, frozen by the ice. 'There are too many humans.'

'Pah! I could strike her head off and the humans would see nothing other than what I want them to.' She waved the fan across her face and in an instant a haggard old woman stood in her place. The watching crowd clapped in appreciation. I blinked. Which was the illusion? The girl or the hag? I tried to *look* and nearly choked on the ice in my throat.

'Or do you doubt my power?' Her wrinkled face creased up in an arch smile.

'It is not your power I doubt, Elizabetta' – Malik's voice was hard like steel – 'but your fealty to the Autarch. It will not go well if you cross him.'

'I think it is your fealty that is in question, Malik. I'm not the one who is trying to steal a sidhe from under his nose.' She laughed, a tinkling sound like breaking glass. 'Oh, you didn't think any of us truly believed that Rosa had made a blood-bond with the sidhe without your knowledge did you?' She peered over the edge of her fan, her eyes dull with the clouds of age, the lids drooping with wrinkles. 'It is a nice manipulation of our laws, but then you always were clever. You want the sidhe, but your oath to the Autarch forbids you taking her. But how convenient that Rosa, the only one of your blood to survive the curse, should be the one to tempt her, and how convenient that Rosa then turns feral and is to be put down or corralled – allowing you to force her to eat from your hand again, and hold all her property under your sway.'

'Your perception does me no favours, Elizabetta.'

'Bite her now.' She snapped the fan shut then jabbed it towards me. Malik stepped back, jerking me away.

I frowned, puzzled at his action. '*What was that for?*'

'If I have truly embraced my curse' – Malik indicated the attentive but oblivious audience – 'you would have me start a bloodbath. Even you cannot wish for that.'

'Either you bite her now and prove to me you haven't, or I will kill you both myself and declare your deaths a necessary precaution to protect the humans. There will be no witnesses to say otherwise than mine. Think: where will your precious sidhe be then? Unclaimed property, at the mercy of any vamp who finds her. They are all eager, and stupid enough to try their chances, believing that her sidhe blood will increase their power, believing it will protect them. Then there would be a culling while they fought over her. She cannot even turn to the human authorities, not now they want her for murder. And no doubt her fellow fae will be only too pleased to be rid of her after the nuisance she has caused them.' Her long fangs extended walrus-like over her bottom lip. She tapped the fan against them and the noise was oddly more like metal than plastic. 'Is that what you want, for the sidhe to be used up by the fight? And then the winner gets to claim the patronage of the Autarch by offering him her blood. After all, from what I know of him, he is unlikely to care if the sidhe is not in the peak of health – in truth, he will probably appreciate her being broken in.'

'*Okay, so not going to happen if I have my way,*' I muttered.

'And also, we're wasting time while she's gabbing. Can't you just zap her or something?'

'She is the head of Golden Blade blood, Genevieve. Look sideways at her fan and our audience and see past the illusion.'

I turned my head away, looking towards the entrance and a group of men strolling into the foyer, then checked Elizabetta out in my peripheral vision. Instead of a fan, she was hefting a bronze-coloured broadsword as if it were a feather. The point was inches away from our faces. I took a step back before I could stop myself and she laughed, her face morphing back to the young girl's. The audience applauded again, but now I could see interspersed between the delighted humans were stony-faced vampires, all of them carrying some sort of sword or knife.

'She's got us surrounded!' I glared at her.

'Of course. Elizabetta never goes anywhere without her personal guard.'

Elizabetta regarded me with spite-filled eyes. 'Oh, she is a special one, isn't she? One of your little human friends maybe, else why would you let her see? But then, you always were sentimental about your pets, Malik.' Her expression turned sly and snide. 'Better not let Rosa sink her fangs into this one, not like she did the last.'

'Be careful, Elizabetta,' Malik growled low in his throat, 'that I do not declare you feral and rescind your Gift instead.'

'But of course you won't, Malik, since I am not feral, and it would go against your own code of honour. You see, there are advantages to being less than moral.' She sliced the sword to the side in an easy motion, narrowly missing a couple of wide-eyed tourists. 'Bite her,' she snapped, her canines extending almost to her chin.

Vampires and their fucking games! 'Look, just bite me and get this over with,' I thought at Malik.

'No – she will use it as an excuse to attack.'

'And if you don't bite me, she'll use that as her other excuse,' I snapped. 'It's one of those fucking win-win things for her, and I for one don't fancy being skewered on that monster sword of hers.'

'She is trying to provoke me, Genevieve, it is nothing . . .'

I stopped listening to him as the bizarre sight of a child skipping through the foyer caught my attention. She ran up to the group of men I'd seen strolling in through the entrance, breezing through them as if they weren't there, then turned and smiled at me. Cosette, my ghost. Then she disappeared and I was left staring at the men as they surveyed the crowd. One of them was watching us, curiosity flickering over his face. My memory caught up and meshed with something Elizabetta had said.

'Thanks, Cosette,' I murmured, then smiled at Elizabetta. *'Okay, bitch, here's your missing witnesses.'*

'Hey, Declan,' I shouted, and stuck my arm in the air, waving madly, 'over here, you big Irish totty. Hey, and bring your pals with you!'

Try slicing our heads off now, and see where it gets you.

'What is she doing?' Elizabetta's face twisted in anger as Declan turned and made for us. Her sword snapped back into her black lace fan.

'She is acknowledging a friend.' Malik's voice was calm, but in my head I heard his question.

'Declan is the one who's been supplying me the inside info on all Liz's disappearing faelings. We've agreed a bargain between us.'

I briefly wondered if Malik was surprised that Declan, head of the Red Shamrock Blood family, would bargain to rescue faelings lured into Sucker Town by the fang-gangs. Not that *I* knew why Declan had; oh, I had an inkling that it was because he wasn't strong enough to keep them for himself, so he'd decided to do the dog-in-the-manger thing – of course, Malik wouldn't have any trouble working that one out. No, the real mystery for me was why Declan had never asked for anything much in return for the info he provided – other than the actual rescues.

'Does he know you walk in Rosa's skin?' Malik asked.

'No,' I said.

'Malik al-Khan, Elizabetta. I'll be wishing a good evenin'' to you both.' Declan grinned, flashing fangs; his brief burst of *mesma* made me feel like all the joys of the world had come to visit – that was his speciality. Nearby humans broke out into enthusiastic, happy laughter and his grin widened, but his

eyes were sharp with interest. To either side of him were two
more vampires, his brothers. They looked overwhelmingly
alike, in their tight black leather jeans and collarless white
linen shirts, with fine gold hoops through their earlobes, not
to mention the clichéd tall, dark and handsome Irish good
looks. It was no wonder the Blue Heart's steady stream of
customers had stopped to gape and stare.

Declan turned to me, blue eyes warming with male appreciation as he raked his gaze over me. 'Ah, me darlin', and how
could I be forgettin' you, when beauty such as yours is not
often seen?'

'Debby.' I waggled my fingers at him. 'Debby-with-a-y.' I
heaved a sigh, expanding my generous assets, watching as his
smiling face took on a slightly glazed look. Gotta love any male
that appreciates your looks enough to lose his sensible head.

'Declan.' Malik inclined his head so slightly that the
movement was barely noticeable. 'I see you have your brothers with you. Seamus, and Patrick.' His chin moved down a
millimetre as he acknowledged them both. 'Is the *Tir na n'Og*
closed tonight?'

The *Tir na n'Og* was Declan's Irish bar. The brothers
might not be as well known in the redtop gossip pages as the
current crop of newly minted vamp celebs, but they'd been
around a lot longer – three hundred years longer – and they
had their own fang-fan base. A brief, curious question as to
whether they were jealous of the new kids on the blood-block
popped in my mind.

'Of course it'll not be closed.' Declan blinked, then gave
a satisfied smile. 'Fiona, me darlin' companion, is watchin'
over me business, just as she should be. The three of us'll be
here for your shenanigans with Rosa.' His smile turned cheerful. 'And I'll be hopin' they'll be entertaining.'

Elizabetta snapped open her fan. 'The arrangement was
not for you to be here in person, Declan, just for you to provide a witness of your blood.'

'But of course I'm needin' to be here on such a momentous
occasion, Eliza.' He turned his smile on her. 'Now that the
Earl is gone, I'll not be trustin' any other's decision on any
concerns but me own – especially when it comes to dealing
with Rosa, the nasty wee bitch.'

Surprise winged into me. Declan didn't like Rosa either? It was beginning to look like nobody did. Was this why Malik hadn't wanted me to change earlier? Still, more important, our 'witnesses' were standing there grinning, so . . . time to make our exit.

'Well, all this gum-flapping is fun, but to be honest, it's just holding us up.' I hugged Malik's arm and gave him an inane, adoring look. 'Malik here has promised to take me somewhere special after the business bit of the night is done with. So we'll just toddle off and catch you all later.' I waggled my fingers at them all. 'C'mon, lover boy, let's go.' *Now!* I shouted inside his head, and pulled at his arm. 'This way,' I muttered, heading for the front doors. 'I don't know what you ever did to upset her, but it doesn't seem like a good idea to stick around—'

The world around me went hazy, stuttering horizontally as if bands of interference were scrolling up and down in front of my eyes. The background hum of excited chatter cut out. And I realised Malik was taking us both into his shadows, hiding us from sight and smell and hearing, if not from touch, so we could make our escape. Relief sung through me, then as the nothingness that surrounded us crept into my mind, I stumbled and started falling, Malik's hand my only anchor . . .

. . . and I blinked as my own startled blonde reflection stared back at me from a foxed silver mirror.

Chapter Eighteen

We were in a lift; the foxed mirrored panels lining the sides gleamed with polish. I recognised the lift – I'd spent an uncomfortable twenty minutes in one just like it with the Earl when he'd still been London's head honcho vamp and not the scattered ashes and star of my morphine-induced nightmares that he was now. That lift allowed VIP patrons to bypass the crowds to get to the private bar above the Blue Heart's foyer, so it looked like we were still in the Blue Heart, although I wasn't sure where. I checked the control panel and the small key in the lock and the dimmed lighting confirmed that the lift was shut down. We weren't going anywhere until that key was removed, and until then no one could find us. I looked from my own wide-eyed reflection to Malik's shadowed darkness behind me, both our images reflecting into the distance.

The myth about vamps and mirrors is just that: a myth. Although I had no doubt Malik could hide his reflection as much as he could hide anything else if he wanted to. I turned to face him.

'The idea of a distraction was so we could escape,' I said drily.

He gave me one of his impassive stares. 'Leaving would not help us achieve our objective.' The last of his shadows dissipated, leaving the blue veins standing out in stark relief under his pale skin.

'And staying to get made into shish-kebabs by old Liz out there isn't going to achieve much either.'

'Elizabetta is a setback, but not an insurmountable one if we keep within sight of the other blood-families until matters are settled.'

'You know, I'm really beginning to hate being moved around like some pawn on your own bloody chess board,' I muttered.

'I did not want to involve you in this, Genevieve.' His expression turned pensive. 'I only wished to find Rosa and have her resolve this state of affairs with me. But we both agreed the necessity of bringing this business to a quick close. I did inform you it would be dangerous.'

'Yeah,' I sighed, accepting the rebuke. 'I know, but I didn't think they'd try and kill you, just that there might be the usual vamp grandstanding.'

'But they fight to gain a sidhe' – in other words, *me* – 'as their prize. I am the obstacle to them accomplishing that, so of course they will use any excuse to try and kill me.'

When he said it like that, it sort of made sense. 'But you said no one would go against you?'

'And none would if I were at my full strength and there were no benefit, but while I am depleted like this, they can smell the weakness in me.' As he pushed back the wing of black hair I saw a slight tremor in his hand, 'As Elizabetta said, if I were to die before Rosa bowed to my hand, she would be left vulnerable, and you would be ripe for the picking.'

'I don't understand that.' I frowned, unease slipping down my spine. 'Why does Rosa doing the fealty thing make a difference? I mean, they can still kill you both, or us both afterwards, can't they?'

'Rosa has gained her autonomy. Under our laws, should anyone desire her property, they would have to challenge her and defeat her before witness. If one of us gives up our autonomy, then it is our master who takes up the challenge.'

'Yeah, which brings us back to Square One,' I sighed.

'They'd have to challenge you, and old Liz looks like she's ready to go for it.'

'No, not me,' he said quietly. 'The Autarch.'

'What?' Shock and fear and disbelief sliced through me. 'You mean that if Rosa bows to you, I effectively become the property of that psychotic sadist again?'

'It would seem that way—'

I grabbed handfuls of his jacket. 'I am not going back to him, do you understand me?' I spat out. 'You had your chance at making me and you threw it away. Try it again, and I will kill you, or anyone else who tries, or I will kill myself. I will not become Bastien's property. Not. Ever. Again!'

He covered my hands with his own and my fear receded under his icy touch.

'Genevieve.' His voice was soft, insistent. 'Calm yourself. I said it would *seem* that the Autarch would be the one to challenge over your ownership. It is believed that I still owe him my oath.'

'But you told me once' – when I'd thought he'd come to take me back to the Autarch – 'that you hadn't called him master for the last twenty years,' I said, jerking my hands from his icy hold, rubbing them together to warm them. 'And stop manipulating my reactions like that.'

'I apologise. I wished only to assuage your fears.' He inclined his head. 'It is true that I do not call Bastien master any longer, but publicly it still suits us both that the blood-families think I bow to him. It boosts his status that others think he can force me to his hand, and I do not have to concern myself with challenges from others. And all would think carefully of his displeasure before attempting to assassinate me.'

'Slight problem then! Old Liz doesn't seem too worried about his displeasure just now.'

'She no doubt thinks that if she could court the Autarch's favour by offering you to him, he would take expediency's hand and congratulate her on my removal,' he said calmly. 'Of course, she may believe, like the others, that sidhe blood brings with it enough power that she could survive any challenge, including his.'

'Let me get this crystal-clear.' I narrowed my eyes. 'Once

Rosa is seen to have done this bow, all the other vamps will think I belong to the Autarch except him and you?'

'That is so,' he agreed.

'So if he wants me back, he has to challenge you, or you can give me to him?'

'Yes.'

My gut contracted as I briefly wondered if Malik would fight for me if challenged, or just hand me over if the Autarch came calling. Then I decided it wasn't something I wanted to worry about right now. I had more immediate fears, one of which was getting out the other side of this mess alive. And the vamp leaning tiredly against the side of the lift didn't look like he could swat a kitten, let alone another vampire swinging a five-foot blade, so I wasn't sure how useful he was likely to be.

I pursed my lips and asked the question that was bothering me. 'If you knew Liz or someone might have a go at you because you're weak, why didn't you feed before coming here?'

'None who have already gained their autonomy would offer, and I am unable to feed on those that belong to another blood-family, without their master's permission. Hence the blood-tithe I requested.'

'But there's plenty of free-range junkies wandering around in Sucker Town – I mean, it's not like they all belong to someone, is it?'

'My lineage is that of revenant, Genevieve; you know this. I feed only on other vampires. If I feed directly from humans it could endanger too many lives, either through my own needs, or if I were to inadvertently pass my version of the Gift on to them. That is the curse that Elizabetta hoped to awaken.'

Revenants are consumed only by their need for blood; their lust is never fully sated. Malik's past words came back to me, then I recalled what he'd said to Elizabetta when she was goading him to bite me: *If I have truly embraced my curse, you would have me start a bloodbath.*

'You mean you never bite a human?' I said, stunned.

'Very rarely, and never when I am as depleted as this.'

'So the only way you can feed is if they give you permission?'

His eyes darkened. 'It is the only way. Anything else is not honourable.'

The various ramifications of that barrelled into me like a stampeding hoard of goblins. Was that why he'd only ever sunk fangs into my hand, or my lip, and never my throat? Was that why he hadn't fed from me? What happened if they let him starve? Would he turn back into some sort of bloodthirsty monster and go on a killing spree? Never mind he was dependant on those he knew would kill him if they could? Other questions crowded in but I couldn't even begin to untangle them. Instead something else Elizabetta said raised a tentative thought in my mind.

'She's right about my blood; the magic in it does give a power boost.'

He spread his hands wide. 'It appears so. Without the donation you gave Joseph this morning. I would not have recovered as quickly as I have.'

'But you're still hungry,' I persisted, 'and still weak.'

'Once I have fed again, my strength will return.'

I debated offering my wrist, even half-lifted my arm, but he held up his hand.

'I do not ask for your blood, Genevieve,' he said softly. 'Elizabetta may have refused me the blood-tithe, but the Golden Blade is only one of the four blood-families. All I require here is your assistance as Rosa, as we agreed before.'

Relieved that he'd refused my half-hearted offer, I said, 'Okay, but I'm changing here and now, while no one else can interrupt.'

I waited for him to argue, but instead speculation flickered across his face. 'What about this spell you wear?'

'You need to snap the hair off about halfway down to break the Glamour, then I can use the other spell to change.' I turned so I faced away from him. My blonde reflection was nearly as pale as his.

'Hair is not an easy thing to snap.' He smoothed his hand over my ponytail. The spell leapt to his touch and heat pooled inside me. I frowned, unsure if it was his *mesma*, or the magic itself.

'Well, unless you've got a pair of scissors—'

'I have this.' He held up a thin, sharp-edged knife; the handle was intricately carved from black onyx, the silver blade etched with an overlapping sickle design that shimmered as if drawn in blood. 'Will this do?' His question was low against my ear.

'Yes . . .' My own voice came out scratchy. My mouth was dry, the air around us heavy and tense. Damn, what the hell was the matter with me? I licked my lips and swallowed, then tried again. 'Yes.' The word was firmer this time.

He smiled, and something predatory flickered in his eyes and my stomach dropped into freefall. Then he grasped the length of hair and slowly drew the knife across it. He held his hand out to the side and let the pale strands fall; they drifted like thistledown, slowly dissipating back into the ether before they reached the floor. My image in the silver wall shifted and warped, ballooning out, then shimmering back to tall and stick-thin, as if I stood before a fairground mirror. I gasped as the rest of the magic peeled itself away in one long, relieved sigh, like I'd removed too-tight clothes and only now realised how uncomfortable they'd been. I inhaled, my lungs filling with Malik's dark-spice scent, stretching my spine like a cat as my reflection finally settled back to the true me – or at least the Frankenstein's daughter me, with my short-cropped hair and multi-hued patchwork of healing skin.

'Genevieve.' Warmth slipped over my skin like the last breath of summer. His eyes flared, incandescent with – not anger nor rage, but something else: a slow burn of sorrow. His hands on my shoulders turned me towards him and he traced a cool finger along my jaw.

'Why have you not healed?' he asked with a frown, and pushed aside the collar of my blouse, touching the bruises that marked my chest. 'I gave you my blood, and you have your own magic.'

'I'll heal soon enough.' I shifted away, trying to ignore the tingling from his touch. 'Once everything else is out the way.'

The glow in his eyes snuffed out. 'Yes, you are correct. I will let you continue.' He stepped back and the lift suddenly seemed to have way more space. His lips twitched, almost as if he'd read my mind, and I wondered briefly if he still could, then shrugged the thought away.

I toed off my trainers, unzipped my jeans and started to push them down over my hips, then hesitated; the spell-tattoo was back on my left hip, but the white bikini had disappeared along with the blonde ponytail. Damn, should've asked Tavish for real underwear and not settled for the magical stuff.

'If you are concerned for your modesty' – Malik's voice was amused – 'I can always turn my back.'

'Like that's going to make a difference with all these mirrors,' I huffed. 'Anyway, that's not it. My underwear is gone and the jeans are too small to put back on once I've changed, so I'm not going to be wearing much. I know this is a vamp club, but wandering round in just a short blouse is going to be noticeable for all the wrong reasons!'

'You will have other clothes soon,' he said. 'It will not matter.'

'Not to you, maybe, but it does to me.'

He smiled. 'Then you shall have my jacket, of course.'

I gave it the once-over. It would probably be more of a mini-dress than anything, but it would do. I removed the jeans, lifted the edge of my shirt and ran my fingers over the hard circular ridge of the spell-tattoo, then over the Celtic design knotted at its centre. Its power shuddered through me as if it had been waiting, crouched and ready to pounce like a starving beast.

'This magic—'

Malik's quiet voice startled me, and I jerked my hand from the tattoo.

'What will it do?' he asked

Surprise made me blink. 'It will change me to look like Rosa. You know that.'

'The magic you employed at the bakery knocked you unconscious before its adverse effects caused the explosion.' He gave me an enquiring look. 'Will this affect you in the same way?'

'No nothing like that,' I muttered, restlessness itching down my spine as the tattoo pulsed like a second heart, growling like a ravenous spirit for my attention. It needed blood. 'I need your knife.' I looked up, expectant.

'For what end?'

I shot my left hand out to him. 'Cut it, straight across the lifeline. Make it deep.'

He stared at my hand as if it might bite him.

'Just do it,' I ordered, impatience scraping along my nerves. 'Now!'

He frowned. Around us his myriad mirror images frowned with him, their eyes dark and shadowed, my own images all hard angles and demand, my eyes glowing fever-bright gold, pupils narrowed to vertical slits as the magic gripped me. For a second I saw a third face in amongst all those that stared back at us; Cosette's face – filled with a strange eagerness; then Malik's hand darted out, almost quicker than I could see, and slashed a deep wound across my palm. Nothing – then *pain*, brief and brilliant, forced a cry from my mouth as my blood welled, copper-bright and willing, the honeyed-metallic scent alluring. A shudder vibrated through Malik and his hands clenched into tight fists at his sides, but my mind had no time to care about him. The tattoo screamed out to me, desperate, hungry, and I covered it with my hand, smearing the viscous blood into the spell. My heart slowed until it was beating sluggishly, shallowly. My lungs were burning for lack of air . . .

. . . uneasiness slid into me, something wasn't right; the spell usually worked quicker than this. Desperately I clenched my fist, squeezing more blood from the wound, shoving it into the spell-tattoo. This time the blood ran slick and wet into the twisted design, flooding over its edges and misting red over my body. My skin tightened as if I'd walked into a frigid winter's night.

I tore the blouse off and ran my hands over my borrowed body, revelling in the full lush curves, the hourglass indentation of my waist, the delicate lace of blue veins decorating the pale, almost translucent skin. Long black hair curled halfway down my back and large gentian-blue eyes watched me, arrogant and smug, from my reflection. Rosa was – or at least her body still was – one überbeautiful woman. Was that why Malik had Gifted her?

At that thought I raised my eyes; his were empty, emotionless pools. I could hear his heart now, its beat slow, weak, and I could taste his hunger like sweet copper on my tongue. His rich scent saturated the small confined space, mixing with the tang of honeyed blood, making my head swim with desire, my belly coil with anticipation. I inhaled his hunger, the jagged edge of it grinding like a whetstone against my own thirst. I wanted, *needed* blood. It had been so long since I'd taken it, forcing myself to settle for venom. Then my prey had been human venom-junkies or captured fae, and I'd only ever drunk enough for my needs, or to rid them of their infection.

But Malik wasn't human, and he wasn't fae. I stared at him, listening to the whisper of his blood, knowing that I could take whatever I wanted from him and the certainty that he would let me as he'd always done seeped into my consciousness. He wouldn't – couldn't – deny me; his guilt over what he'd made me wouldn't allow him to. The thoughts swimming like leeches in my mind were both alien and familiar to me and as I traced my fangs with the tip of my tongue, I tried to separate things out, to choose which was *my* thought.

But the hunger wouldn't let me.

It wanted him, *now*.

I smiled, a practised, seductive curve of my lips, and slowly moved closer to him. I raised my hands to the first button on his jacket and released it. His jaw tensed and he looked almost wary, but he did nothing to stop me. I worked my way down, two, three, four, five buttons, then pulled the jacket open and pushed it from his shoulders. As it fell with a soft thud to the lift floor, I grabbed his black silk T-shirt and ripped it, exposing the pale, perfect skin, the lean muscles, the silky triangle of black hair arrowing down to his taut abdomen. I leaned in, pressed my lips to the firm flesh over his heart and, opening my mouth, let my fangs indent his skin. He trembled and I raised my eyes to find him gazing down at me, pinpricks of desire blazing in his pupils. Satisfaction spiralled fast inside me.

I kissed my way down his body, my lips seeking the scar that marked him below his heart, the one I'd given him, the one he hadn't healed, even though he could. Blood bloomed beneath his skin, the scar flushing red like a rose. I struck, quick and hard, the sharp points of my canines piercing his firm flesh, into the heart of the rose, and glorious blood filled my mouth, tasting like spiced nectar and liquorice and sweet Turkish delight as it slipped down my throat, spreading a glittering chill that rushed me towards that edge, almost but not yet tripping me over into mindless, dazzling pleasure. Reluctantly I drew my mouth away and laved at the small wounds, feeling his stomach quivering under my tongue. His blood and hunger hummed inside me like a promise and I straightened, sliding my palms up to run them over his shoulders, my fingers digging into the corded muscles, then I moulded my body to his, crushing my softer breasts against his hard, cold chest. He groaned, and the sound reverberated inside me as his breath spilled along my cheek. I threaded my fingers into his hair and pulled his head back, then rose on the balls of my feet to place my mouth over the slow pulse beating below his jaw. His musky scent teased my nose and I licked his thin skin, long wet strokes, tasting salt and the copper tang of his sweat, as my jaw ached with need. I wanted to fill my mouth with more of the glittering taste of his blood, wanted it so desperately that the torture of holding back was an exquisite pain. He shuddered as his solid, thick length pressed into the softness of my belly. Lust slicked damp and liquid between my thighs, desire swelling my breasts and hardening my nipples into rigid, painful points.

And I wanted more than his blood in my body.

I hooked my leg around his waist, opening myself to him, lifting myself up to rub against the thick length of him, the coarse fabric of his trousers abrading my sensitive, swollen flesh. I sucked at his throat, pulling the soft skin into my mouth, anticipating the moment when my fangs would pierce his skin. A tremor of pleasure echoed through me, and I ground myself against him again, wanting to feel him thrusting inside me, wanting his blood spurting down my throat, wanting his fangs penetrating my body.

I slid one hand down, following the silky arrow of hair until my fingers closed on his belt. I picked urgently at it, freeing the buckle, the throbbing heat between my legs growing ever more frantic—

'No.' Hard fingers manacled my wrist, stilled my hand. 'I do not want this.'

I struggled against his hold, my mouth working, my hips almost jerking with need. *He couldn't say no, I had to have him inside me, had to!*

He yanked my arm behind my back, wrenching it upwards, straining my shoulder, the pain like a lover's pledge. His other hand caught me by my hair, ripping me away from his throat.

He couldn't deny me, I wouldn't let him!

I hit out, catching his chin with the heel of my hand, banging his head back against the lift side, and kicked my heel into the back of his knee, screaming my frustration. He stumbled, falling, his hold on my hair tearing, his hand yanking my arm higher up and popping the shoulder joint. We hit the floor, my body beneath his. Pain exploded like a fire-burst across my back and ricocheted down my spine. I screamed again, lips curling back from my fangs, wanting to tear into his throat, wanting to coat myself in his blood, wanting to fuck him . . .

I wrapped my legs round his thighs, locking my ankles together, bringing him hard against me. He stared down at me, rage lighting his black pupils, his own lips pulled back, all four of his fangs sharp and gleaming. I struggled beneath him, goading him; pain flared in my shoulder, building pleasure between my legs. He growled low and yanked my head to the side, stretching the tendons in my neck, exposing my throat.

Deep inside me a sliver of fear chilled the lust raging through my body.

He twisted my arm higher and pain bloomed hot and razor-sharp in my shoulder. Eagerness replaced the fear.

'Break it and fuck me,' I pleaded, my hips spasming against him with desperate lust even as a distant part of me recoiled in shock at my words.

The fury in his eyes turned to hot flames, flames that licked over my body as if to scorch the flesh from my bones. 'No,' he snarled, 'I will not.'

'Break my arm and fuck me,' I screamed into his face. 'It's what you want, isn't it?'

'Be still,' he ordered, staring down at me, his eyes fixed on my throat, and in the silence I waited, frozen on his command, desperate for him to grant me pain, needing it, knowing that for him to hurt me was the only way he could bring me pleasure.

'Please, Malik, I beg—'

'You will not say it.' The sorrow in his voice twisted like barbed wire round my heart. 'I will not allow it . . . you are not her.' He lowered his mouth to mine, touching my lips briefly with his. 'You. Are. Not. Rosa.'

Then he was gone.

The wire pierced my heart, leaving it bleeding, and I curled in on myself, hugging my knees to my chest, his grief battering against me as if it were a horde of Beater goblins. Tears of shame pricked my eyes that I hadn't pleased him. I struggled to hold them back but they seared down my face, drowning me in hopelessness. Then the feelings were gone, shut off like a tap, replaced by an ice-cold stillness like the depths of frozen water.

I blinked and looked up.

Malik stood there, looking calm and remote. He pointed to his jacket lying in a heap on the floor. 'Get up and put it on,' he said, his voice expressionless.

Silently I grabbed the jacket and scrambled up; contorting so I could pull it on past the distant pain in my shoulder. The silk lining settled over my skin like a soothing caress. Using my good arm, I lifted my hair from where it was trapped by the jacket, feeling bewildered, almost numb as I clumsily buttoned it closed.

What had just happened? Or rather, *why* had it happened? Why had I asked – no, almost begged – him to hurt me? The feelings had felt like mine, but I was pretty sure they'd been Rosa's. Fuck. There really was something wrong with the spell; why else would I experience her memories and her *desires* twice in one night? This was *so* not fucking good.

I wiped the tears from my face with the jacket cuff and shoved the thoughts away. The pain in my shoulder was almost gone as the spell healed it. All I had to do was get through this fealty thing tonight, then I'd never use the spell – never use Rosa's body – again. I'd find some way to cut myself off from it, from her.

'What happens now?' I asked, a part of me still bemused by my own calmness, even though I could feel Malik smoothing over my thoughts.

He turned the key in the lift and it dipped slightly, taking my stomach with it, before the lights flickered on and it started to ascend. 'We shall prepare for the oath, then once that is over we will go to the police station.'

The lift halted, the door gliding open. Blue carpet patterned with small silver hearts stretched down a long, empty corridor lined on one side with steel doors. I gathered the remnants of our clothes as he bade me, then followed him past half a dozen of the doors, my bare feet sinking into the thick carpet, until Malik stopped at one of them. He stilled, then lifted his chin, sniffing the air.

'It appears we have company waiting for us,' he said softly. 'This is not a good sign.'

But before I could ask who, the door slid away into the wall and I had a brief moment of déjà vu. Hannah Ashby, dressed in her vamp-groupie outfit of pumpkin-coloured velvet bustier and black net skirt, stood in the opening.

'Malik al-Khan, and the ever-delightful—Rosa.' She arched one perfectly-drawn-in black brow in a conspiratorial fashion. 'Don't you think it might be better to enter instead of loitering about in the hallway?' She gave a low chuckle, then stood back and ushered us past her.

Chapter Nineteen

My newly changed vampire senses picked up the base notes of patchouli and sandalwood in Hannah's perfume, but for some reason the scent had the same effect as walking into the swamp-dragon's cave. My eyes teared up. I dropped the clothes and clapped my hand over my mouth and nose as I choked on a coughing fit. I felt Malik's hand at the small of my back as he pushed me into the room. I hurried to the far side, putting as much distance between me and the lung-burning scent as possible.

I slapped my hands over my eyes and concentrated, dialling my vamp body's reactions down to nothing, cutting out the toxic smell, the slightly raised *da daum* of Hannah's heartbeat, and the bitter chemical taste of the perfume that made me feel like I'd been sucking on a vamp junkie stoked up on crack as well as venom. After a couple of seconds, I stopped breathing, my heart stopped beating and the perfume was nothing more than a ghost-memory in my mind.

Dropping my hands, I pressed my fingers into my own sternum, where I could still feel the slight burn in my lungs. 'What the hell is that perfume you're wearing?' I asked, glaring at Hannah.

'It's a bespoke perfume created by Roja Dove.' She smiled, looking delighted. 'He's a renowned "nose", trained at the House of Guerlain. He mixes liquid silver into the jus; I wear it as an added precaution when I want to avoid any confrontations with the club's vampires.'

Liquid silver? No wonder my lungs were burning up.

Malik was standing just inside the door, his face almost hidden by shadows. His bare chest gleamed pale in the room's dimmed light, the rose scar under his heart hardly visible, and he looked elegant and composed, despite wearing nothing but his suit trousers. Either Hannah's perfume didn't affect him as much, or he'd known what to expect and cut his senses off before taking a whiff of the noxious stuff.

The room itself didn't manage to live up to Malik's style. It could have been a lounge in any bland hotel suite, decorated in shades of blue with silver-fronted furniture: except for the floor-to-ceiling glass wall behind me. The glass wall gave a god's-eye view of the Blue Heart's dancefloor three floors below, packed with a mass of bodies undulating to a beat that vibrated through the glass, though I couldn't actually hear anything.

Hannah had positioned herself behind one of two sofas, her hands resting on a familiar vamp's broad shoulders – Darius, her personal fang-pet. He sat slumped, staring fixedly at me from half-lidded eyes. He was dressed as the last time I'd seen him, in my flat: naked apart from his diamanté Calvin Klein briefs and calf-high boots. Little beads of blood-tinged sweat shone on his forehead and trickled down his flushed romance-model's chest. He looked like he'd been on a binge-drinking session and wasn't far off collapsing into a blood-dream – the vamp equivalent of being utterly, totally drunk.

'Of course, it doesn't bother too many of the vamps in the club,' Hannah carried on, ruffling Darius' tawny waves. 'Most of them keep themselves offline anyway, unless they're actually feeding. And while there are plenty of willing donors walking around, once I've fed Darius here, I prefer not to worry about anyone else. So the perfume is my way of being safe rather than sorry.'

'What is your reason for being here, Hannah?' Malik's voice was soft, a hint of threat riding along with his question.

I could probably hazard a guess that the answer had something to do with a Fabergé egg, seeing as she knew about my Disguise spell, and no doubt also knew that every other vamp in town was expecting 'Rosa' to turn up tonight with Malik and with me missing for the last couple of days, Hannah being here wasn't really a surprise.

Unfazed, Hannah turned her delighted smile on him. 'I thought I would do you a favour.' She tipped Darius' head back, offering his throat. 'They plan to refuse you your blood-tithe, although I suspect you already know that. So I thought I'd offer you some provisions.' She trailed a finger across Darius' chest, smearing a line in his blood-sweat. 'He has fed well, as you can see' – gorged was more like it – 'and is willing to do whatever you want, aren't you, Darius?' She patted his cheek.

'Yess,' he slurred, eyes still eerily fixed on mine, his head lolling to the side.

Malik didn't move, didn't even blink, but I felt the tension tighten his body. A sudden edge of shared hunger clenched like a fist in my stomach, nearly doubling me over.

'All I ask is you try not to kill him,' Hannah added, leaning down to lick Darius' exposed throat. 'I find him satisfying in so many ways; I would be so disappointed to lose him.'

'Leave us then,' Malik ordered.

She pushed at Darius' shoulder, urging him up. He staggered to his feet and stumbled towards Malik, who opened his arms, catching the taller vampire to his chest, then in one smooth easy movement, hooked an arm under his knees and lifted him, cradling him like a bride about to be carried over a threshold. Darius might have weighed not much more than his Calvin Kleins for all the effort Malik seemed to expend.

'Actually, it's you who's going to leave us, Malik. I still have a favour to do for someone else.' She smiled and lifted a black holdall from behind the sofa and dropped it on the seat. It gave a metallic clank as it landed. 'Elizabetta wants Rosa to dress appropriately for the ceremony.'

Somehow I knew *appropriate* wasn't going to be my kind of thing.

'Use the bedroom.' Hannah waved at the other door. 'Don't worry, we'll both be right here when you finish.'

Malik hesitated, then looked at Darius in his arms, his expression turning predatory, and I swallowed against the constriction in my throat; whether it was fear or envy I wasn't sure.

'*Be careful of this one, Genevieve,*' Malik's voice whispered in my mind. '*She is more than she appears.*' The connecting door opened, apparently of its own accord, and I wondered if he had some sort of kinetic ability too. I filed that question away for later.

When the door had closed behind him and his meal, I turned back to a smugly smiling Hannah. And Malik's warning reminded me that I was in Rosa's body and I had use only of her vamp senses; all my own abilities with magic were gone. It wasn't something that had ever bothered me much in the past, but then, I'd never knowingly sparred with a sorcerer before as 'Rosa'. Now I couldn't *see* the magic, and even my unwanted aptitude for seeing ghosts was gone; after Cosette's recent help, it made me feel oddly vulnerable.

'So, Hannah, what *is* your reason for being here?' I said, echoing Malik's question.

She walked over to me and stood looking at the gyrating dance crowd below. 'They're like chickens in the fox house, aren't they?' she laughed, the sound scornful. 'Totally unaware of the dangerous possibilities that surround them. But we're not like that, are we, Genevieve?' Her fingers toyed with the silver death's head pendant that nestled at the base of her neck. 'We know how unpredictable life can be – unless of course we have a helping hand.' She blew on the glass, misting it with her breath, then waved her palm over the now-opaque window. 'Allow us to *see*,' she murmured.

Within the glass a picture appeared: a room similar to the one we were in. Declan and Elizabetta were standing facing each other and a crystal wine glass – half-full of dark purple-red liquid – sat on a small table between them. Elizabetta held out a thin silver knife – more ornate than Malik's, the blade already bloodied – and smiled up at Declan. Anticipation was written all over her currently young face. Declan's blue eyes crinkled in an answering grin as he took the blade, then he held his arm over the glass and in a movement almost too fast to see, sliced along the vein that bulged blue under his pale

Irish skin. His dark blood dripped down from the cut to merge with that already in the glass.

'They agree to support each other, to spill blood together.' Hannah spoke quietly next to my ear.

Declan offered his still bleeding wrist to Elizabetta as she offered hers to him and together they spoke, lips moving in silent unison. Then with a ritualistic deliberation, they bent their heads to each other's wrists and drank.

'Now they agree to share the spoils,' Hannah said in a throaty whisper.

'Spoils meaning me, the sidhe me, of course,' I said, my matter-of-fact tone belying the apprehension that crept over me. The picture fogged and disappeared. I turned to look at her. 'Neat little show, Hannah, but it's not exactly breaking news or anything, is it?'

'Maybe not, but I think it's always better to know what your enemy is up to, even if all it does is confirm one's own suspicions.' She indicated the bag on the sofa. 'That way, one doesn't fall prey to false promises.'

Ri-ight: Elizabetta's outfit, or whatever it was. I strode over to the bag, which clanked as I unzipped it and pulled it open. I lifted out what was lying on top: a gold neck collar with a long heavyweight gold chain attached to it. The chain looked like it could pull lorries. It ended in a wide gold wrist-cuff. I pursed my lips. 'I *hope* this isn't some sort of muscle-man bondage crap.'

'Look at the rest, Genevieve.'

I pulled it out: an elaborate gold-metal bikini, which could double as a handy chastity belt if the leather thongs that kept it on were replaced with padlocks. Attached to the metal briefs was a fall of red material that was going to end up a tripping hazard, let alone the fact that it did nothing in the modesty stakes. It all looked vaguely familiar . . . As I imagined wearing it all – gold bikini, metal collar and chain – the iconic movie image of the enslaved princess chained to her fat, bloated alien captor clicked into my mind.

'Elizabetta wants me to kill Malik then.' I made it a statement.

Hannah chuckled. 'Her exact message was, "Slaughter the monster, and I will welcome you and yours into my blood with open veins."'

'Open veins,' I mused. 'Interesting choice of words.'

'The movie is one of Elizabetta's favourites, and knowing Rosa's fondness for chains . . .' Hannah shrugged. 'Elizabetta decided the costume was appropriate. You do understand what she means, don't you?'

'Yes. Elizabetta is offering her protection if Rosa kills Malik and swears fealty to her.' I hefted the metal collar; the thing was heavy, even for my enhanced vampire strength. It was some sort of gold-plated steel, maybe. 'And of course, if Rosa took the deal and she was still the vampire that Elizabetta thinks she is, she would bring a sidhe with her.' I lifted my lips in a half-smile. 'The irony is, Rosa is not that vamp, so old Liz is going to be one very disappointed sucker.'

'You're rejecting her offer then?' Hannah asked, sounding only mildly interested.

I gave her my best *do I look stupid?* look. 'C'mon, Hannah, even if I were the actual Rosa, I would have to be suicidal to trust her, wouldn't I?'

'As I said' – she gave me a rueful smile – 'we are both aware of the dangerous possibilities that exist.'

'Which is something I could've worked out on my own.' I narrowed my eyes. 'So if all this info is supposed to make me produce the Fabergé egg in gratitude, it's not working. Why don't you tell me something I don't know . . . like why you really want the egg?'

'The egg is a highly valuable item, Genevieve' – she slyly arched one carefully drawn-in brow – 'surely you Googled it on your computer.'

I smiled, knowing it didn't reach my eyes. 'As I said, it's a neat little trick, spying on people like that.' I waved at the now clear glass. 'But you see, the egg wasn't the only thing I Googled. You don't need that sort of money, do you, Hannah? Not when your net worth is in the same bracket as a small African country.'

She smoothed her hands down her body, giving me a coquettish look from under her lashes. 'One can never be too rich or too thin, isn't that what that American said, the Duchess of Windsor?'

I cast a judicious eye over her well-endowed curves. 'Too thin doesn't appear to be in your remit, so why don't you stop playing games? There's no way you want the egg for its monetary value, and to be honest, if I were going to sell it, I could do that myself.'

She clasped her hands together, then, taking a deep breath – almost popping out of her bustier – she nodded, as if to confirm something. 'Very well, I will explain why it is so important, but first I need to show you something else.' She blew on the glass window again. 'It is a memory, one I find . . . distressing, but— Well, you'll see.'

Chapter Twenty

The mist cleared and another picture formed in the glass. It was like looking the wrong way down a telescope at first, then it rushed closer until two figures, as large as life, were displayed across the plate-glass window. Candles cast flickering lights over the rounded brick ceiling above them and the mural of a barren landscape with its distant, rocky mountain painted on the wall behind them. The figures stood inside a circle marked out in red on the concrete floor, either side of a stone plinth on which was lying a sheet-shrouded body. The material draped close enough to show the body was female. One figure was the Earl, blond hair flopping over his forehead as usual, his arm raised, but motionless, as if frozen in action. His cold azure eyes were assessing as he looked at the other figure. She leaned on her stick, the hood of her cloak pulled back from her fleshless, yellowed skull; the rich purple velvet falling from her shoulders to the floor couldn't hide the twisted hunch of her spine. I recognised her too. She was the Ancient One.

Hannah spoke, a harsh guttural language I didn't understand, and the words raised goosebumps over my flesh and sent a shiver rasping down my spine.

The Earl's arm flowed into movement and he grasped the shroud and peeled it back from the body. The body was Rosa, naked and statue-still, her long black hair curling over her shoulders, her fists clenched in pain or anger, her eyes staring open, lips drawn back from her fangs.

'It is truly astonishing,' the Earl said in his aristocratic voice. 'The body still shows no ill effects after two years of the sidhe using the spell.' He stroked his hand down over Rosa's stomach and dipped his fingers into the bloody wound that marked her left hip. He brought his hand close to his nose, sniffed, and sucked his fingers clean, sighing with obvious enjoyment. 'And the blood tastes even sweeter than the last time.' He smiled benevolent approval at the Ancient One. 'Your magic is exceedingly good, Crone. I really should commend you.'

'My lordship.' The Ancient One bobbed her head. 'But I must warn you, it is not wise to feed as deeply as you have in the past. It could cause an imbalance.'

'I will feed as I personally see fit. You are well paid to control the magic, you and your apprentice here.' He waved a dismissive hand in our direction. 'And indeed, speaking of problems' – he lost his smile – 'the sidhe is now working with the witches; they have offered her their protection.'

'It is not something I could have foreseen, my lordship.' The Ancient One's voice grew querulous.

'Nonetheless, it is a situation that must be dealt with. The prohibition was to end on her twenty-third birthday, but with the witches involved, now she will continue to be out of my reach, unless—' He gazed speculatively down at Rosa, then brushed her hair back and traced the blue veins that ran like cords down her throat. A gold chain nestled in the crease of her neck and he hooked his fingers under it and followed it down to where an oval gold locket rested between her breasts. He slid his hand under the locket, cupped it in his palm as if weighing it, then smiled at the Ancient One. 'You have the sidhe's necklace, Crone, the one that belonged to her stepmother. You shall give it to me, then once she knows I have it, she will come to me of her own accord and the witches' protection will no longer overly concern me.'

The Ancient One's hand tightened on the head of her cane,

her knuckles whitening. 'I can't do that, my lordship. I took it as security only. I have agreed to return it once the debt is repaid.'

'While the sidhe uses the spell, she still owes you, is that not correct?'

'It is, my lordship, but—'

'Then there is still a debt.' He released the gold locket, which slapped hollowly on Rosa's chest, and adjusted his cuffs. 'The necklace will be secure with me, probably more so, so there is nothing to alarm you.'

'No, I will not risk it.' She held a shaking hand up in denial. 'The sidhe is young and unskilled, but it is not wise to cross one of the noble fae—'

'It is not wise to cross *me*, Crone,' he interrupted, leaning forward, menace in his lowered voice. 'Do not think your Black Arts will protect you either. I have lived more than eight centuries, and I have dealt with sorcerers before.' His lips parted on a glimpse of fang. 'And *I* still live,' he hissed, 'and *they* do not – since even a demon-powered carcase such as yours is still mortal, and thus still needs blood and a beating heart to sustain it.' He straightened. 'Now, give me the sidhe's necklace.'

Her stick trembled under her grip. 'As you command, my lordship.' She turned towards us, and for an instant it looked like the empty sockets of her eyes were crawling with fat grey maggots. 'Hannah, fetch the black opal collar from the safe and bring it to me,' she ordered. The large death's head ring on her finger winked its amber eyes in anger. *And Hannah, my lovely, bring me also the powdered dragons' scale. This piece of blood-sucking shite needs to be taught a lesson.*

Next to me, Hannah spoke more words in the hair-raising language.

The picture flickered. Time seemed to jerk from one frame to the next, then the tableau from the past flooded with red and a shower of blood obliterated my view. The blood coated the glass, which cracked and shattered, exploding outwards into hundreds of sharp shards of pain-bright light.

Instinctively I flung my hands up to protect my eyes, imagining that something had hit the plate-glass window and broken it, but I quickly realised it too was an illusion. I leaned my forehead against the cool glass and stared blindly down at the crowded dancefloor below, trying to take in the implications of Hannah's memory.

For three years I'd been using my Alter Vamp spell, thinking I was donning a particularly expensive disguise sold me by the Ancient One. But all those three years I'd been walking round in Rosa's body, and all that time she'd been at the mercy of the Earl, a manipulative, sadistic, *bastard* bloodsucker. Bile rose in my throat. Rosa might have been a vamp herself, and judging by her memories and her reputation she was no Little Miss Goody Two-Shoes – not that many vamps were – but no way would I wish that kind of existence on her, or anyone. And no way did I want it to continue. It wasn't just about not using the spell any more for my own sanity; now I needed to find her body and release her from whatever magical bondage held her.

'The Earl killed her, you know.' Hannah's words brought my attention back to her. She stood there, her hands curling into claws, her face screwing up with hatred. 'When I returned with the necklace, he laughed and ripped her head off in front of me, like he was twisting the head of a chicken. But he was right, she was a sorcerer, and the first thing any sorcerer does is safeguard their soul.' She laughed herself, a harsh sound, like the guttural memory spell. 'There's no point selling it to a demon if you don't get the chance to enjoy the rewards is there?'

She walked over to the silver-faced drinks cabinet and opened it. Lifting what looked like a squat-bellied brandy bottle, she saluted me. 'I loved Gwen.'

I gave her a puzzled look. 'Who's Gwen?'

'My mistress, the Ancient One, of course.' She pulled at the cork stopper and it came out with a muted pop. 'Oh, she wasn't really the stereotypical skeletal crone; that was just a façade. Gwen was vibrant, beautiful, full of life . . .' She trailed off, frowning at the bottle's label as if surprised to see it there.

'So what does this memory have to do with you wanting the Fabergé egg?' I asked flatly.

'What?' She looked back at me, then attempted a smile, but her mouth turned down instead of up. 'The egg's her back-up soul storage. Standard operating procedure, in case there's no available body nearby. It's valuable enough not to be damaged or thrown away, and at the worst she'd end up sitting in a vault or a display case for a while until I could release her – wasted time, of course, but better than turning up in Hell without your demon debt paid.' She shuddered at the thought, then tipped the bottle up and drank straight from it. 'Very unrefined, I know, but . . .'

I narrowed my eyes, still suspicious. 'If the egg was that important to her, how did the Earl get it?'

'My fault,' she admitted. 'The Earl decided to make me his pet sorcerer – after all, Gwen had taught me most of her spells by then. But I didn't have the same protection as she did.' She held up the back of her hand to me and waggled her finger; her death's head ring winked its amber eyes at me. 'It wasn't until he grew tired of using me that I was able to sort things out in my mind and work out what I'd told him – what he'd made me give him.' Her shoulders sagged. 'After a while I managed to retrieve the ring, and then I was able to resist him to a degree, but the 3V infection meant I still had to do his bidding.'

She took another swig, and pointed the bottle at me. 'I tried to get the egg back, but the bastard blood-sucker wasn't stupid; he knew why I wanted it and he wasn't about to allow me to bring Gwen back, not when he'd killed her once. So when he thought I was getting close, he gave it away – to you.' She let out a snort of disgust. 'Ironic really; all he wanted was you and your sidhe blood, and she would have served you up to him on a platter if he'd just been patient, but no, he couldn't wait, and he killed her in a fit of temper.'

It was a good story – and most of it was probably true – but there was something wrong somewhere, and I couldn't quite work it out. Why did Hannah want to bring her mistress back? As far as I could see she had everything sorted: enough money, the Earl gone, a way to manage her 3V – Darius – without being controlled, so other than her professed love . . . One thing was clear, though: if the Earl killed the Ancient One a year ago, that meant Hannah had been caretaking Rosa and my Disguise spell ever since. Which meant she knew where Rosa's body was.

'Okay, Hannah, you've shown me your sad little scene, so what's the deal?'

'I don't do deals, Genevieve,' she remonstrated gently. 'I only do favours.'

'Uh-huh. What sort of favours?'

'Of course,' she said slyly, 'I could show you which body is lying on that slab now, but somehow I think you're smart enough to work that one out.'

Shock sparked through me and I closed my eyes for a moment. *My body* was there, in that room, wherever Rosa's normally was – *stupid!* I'd never considered that my body might be anywhere else other than with me, even after I'd realised the spell didn't just disguise me. Mentally I snorted. At least that explained why I couldn't use magic, or why no one other than Hannah had ever recognised me as a sidhe when I was 'Rosa', not even Malik.

Hannah came over to me with a reassuring smile. 'Oh don't worry, there's no harm can come to you, not now the Earl is gone.' Her fingers tightened round the neck of the bottle. 'He really was disgustingly perverted at times – another reason you should be grateful to me.'

Nausea roiled in my stomach as her words brought images slithering around the edges of my mind. I shoved them away; no way did I want to think about the Earl or what he might have done when my body was lying helpless . . .

'Gratitude isn't what comes to mind when you're holding my body hostage,' I snapped.

'Ah but I'm not – that would go against my ethos of not doing anything that would benefit me directly. It really isn't a good idea to use the power for yourself when a demon has a lien on your soul; they've got this weird profit and loss sin-sheet thing going, so being in the black is just asking for trouble. So I can assure you that you are quite safe, and your own body will revert to you at dawn when the spell shuts down, just as it usually does.' She tilted her head back as she drank, the pulse in her throat flashing like a distracting beacon, then carried on, 'But Elizabetta really does want Rosa to take up her offer, and as I've offered to help her, I've something that might persuade you.' She puckered her lips and blew me a

kiss. The air filled with a spray of fine liquid that expanded
outwards into fat black globules like in a slow-motion movie.
They splattered against my face with the force of boiling tar
and I screamed as my skin bubbled and blistered from the
heat. More boiling fluid ran into my eyes, searing my retinas,
and flooded into my mouth, scalding my tongue. The sulphu-
rous taste of rotten eggs burnt the back of my throat and the
fires of hell scorched down my gullet and bubbled like molten
lava in my belly.

For a moment I was too shocked to think, then my mind
lurched in horror as I realised what she'd done.

She'd impregnated me with demon acid.

Within seconds I could feel the embryo imps crawling
inside me, biting, scratching, digging their miniscule claws
and teeth and barbed tails into my organs, muscles, bones,
brain . . . tiny jagged pains flashed through me like hundreds
of needles. Imps consumed their surrogate – and each other –
in their vicious efforts to be birthed, a true 'survival of the
fittest' competition. At least we weren't talking Rosemary's
Baby here, no nine months of slowly stretching belly to lug
around until the anti-Christ is born; just forty-eight hours
until a newly formed imp entered the world if I – or rather,
Rosa – was lucky.

I stared at her, still too horrified to speak.

'Now don't look at me like that, Genevieve,' she tutted. 'I
know you've probably heard loads of horror stories, but the
imps really are under your control, you know.' She touched
her index finger to my forehead and muttered in the guttural
language; the imps quieted. 'So long as you do as instructed
they should stay reasonably quiescent, then Rosa's body
shouldn't sustain too much damage – and remember, it does
heal extremely quickly. Then tomorrow, when you're back to
your own self, I'd be happy to do you the favour of removing
the imps from Rosa.' She shrugged. 'Or not, your choice – you
could always leave them to follow their natural inclination, in
which case both you and Rosa will be free of the magic that
joins you. After all, if there's no *body* left, there can be no
spell. That is what you want, isn't it?' She looked at me quiz-
zically. 'Although, reassuringly, I've always thought you too
sentimental to take the callous way out of your problems.'

I licked my dry lips, almost heaving at the taste of sulphur that clung to them. 'I take it the egg is in exchange for the imps' removal,' I said, glad my voice came out steady.

'No, of course not; I'd be happy to do it as a favour for you.' She rested her hands on my shoulders. I tried to shrug her off, not wanting her to touch me, then muffled my panic as my body refused to obey. 'But my only worry is that without the egg,' she carried on, smiling sadly, 'and without the possibility of being able to release Gwen's soul before tomorrow night, I might be too upset to work the necessary magics.'

Tomorrow night. All Hallows' Eve.

Debt-collecting night for demons.

And that was what was wrong with her story. She didn't want to release the Ancient One's soul; she wanted to use it as payment.

'You do realise there's a flaw in your plan, don't you?' I said, slightly amazed I could actually think, even if I couldn't move. 'The egg is in a bank vault and there's no way I can walk into the bank and withdraw it, since there's that little matter of being wanted for murder.'

'Oh, silly me! I quite forgot to mention' – she patted my cheek and I gritted my teeth at her touch – 'I've arranged for a solicitor to accompany you to the police tomorrow, at noon, shall we say, to have all the charges dropped. He'll pick you up outside your flat at quarter to twelve.' She chuckled. 'We can call it a bonus favour, for your continued investment in my Hallowe'en Easter Egg hunt.'

Did that mean she knew who the killer was? Or was it just some sort of 'arrangement' thanks to her demon master?

'What about the real murderer?' I asked.

'Now then, let's not worry about that now.' Her fingers moved to toy with the top button on my – *Malik's* – suit jacket and I stifled a shudder of dread, wishing she'd keep her hands to herself. 'Time enough for that tomorrow,' she said. 'Now, I have a few things for you to achieve as Rosa. Elizabetta's requests, not mine, you understand. So long as you actively work towards the requests, the imps shouldn't cause you too much agony.' She slipped the button from its hole, smiling encouragingly as I flinched. 'Elizabetta wants you to wear the costume and kill Malik without giving him your oath – very important, that one – then offer her your fealty. Afterwards, you are to do her bidding until dawn.' She undid the next two buttons, letting the jacket fall open. 'There, see? Not too demanding a list of jobs. Oh, and I know Rosa is the love of Malik's life, so I doubt he'll give you too much trouble, but just in case, I've done you one more favour and evened up the odds.'

My mind short-circuited again. 'What does that mean?'

She tapped the side of her nose. 'You'll find out soon enough. Now, time to get dressed, Genevieve.' She pushed me towards the blue sofa where the golden outfit glittered malevolently. 'And then go and kill Malik.'

I picked up the gold-plated steel collar with one hand and wrapped the heavy chain around my other, staring at it numbly, my mind automatically assessing it. It wasn't exactly a garrotte, but looped round his neck – and there was enough of it to go round the movie-monster's neck, not just Malik's – and with enough pressure exerted – easily done with my superior vampire strength – decapitating him shouldn't take more than a couple of seconds.

Only . . .

. . . only I didn't want to kill Malik.

No, I wanted to kill the evil bitch sorcerer Hannah.

Even as I thought it, pain ripped like wild fire through my body as needle-like teeth bit into my inner flesh. I doubled over, my hand clutching at the steel collar, unable to stop the bloody tears streaming down my face as the world exploded into white-hot torment.

After what felt like an eternity in the centre of the inferno, I managed to work out how to make my mind shape the words the imps wanted.

I'll kill him, okay.

The pain muted in increments to a dull ache. So that was the deal: either I tried to kill Malik, or the imps would eat Rosa's body while I was still inside it.

Catch 22, anyone?

Chapter Twenty-one

The dimly lit bedroom was larger than the lounge, and decorated with so much blood that it looked like an artist's rendition of a murder scene; bright red arcs sprayed up the dusk-blue wall behind the king-sized bed, blotted the white silk sheets and splattered dark trails along the thick blue carpet. Malik and Darius lay spooned together on the bed in a tangle of pale, blood-drenched naked bodies. A cacophony of conflicting emotions – desire, hunger, jealousy, anger and shock – cascaded over me and my dialled-down vampire senses sprang back to life. My heart thudded in my chest as I inhaled the strong tang of copper, saliva pooled in my mouth and my stomach rumbled with emptiness. Listening carefully, I could make out two heartbeats, both slow, but both steady. He hadn't killed Darius. Then the urge to crawl onto the bed and join the two vamps exploded in my mind, not to satisfy my hunger, but to rip their throats out, tear them limb from limb and bathe in their blood, just for the pure gleeful fun of it.

I took a step forward, and another, following the urge, my feet and the chain I was dragging, scuffing over the carpet, then I swayed, dizzy, as I made myself stop. Damn! Looked like the imp-imparted psychosis thing was true, then! The imps don't only consume their host, they infect them with their irresistible enjoyment of chaos and violence.

And fuck, was Malik a messy violent eater or what?

The thought brought an edge of hysteria to the laughter rising in my throat. I strangled it before it could escape – much as the imps wanted me to do to Malik. I looked around the room for anything that might help me: pale wood desk, plasma TV, a laptop, its screen dark, a half-open door to what had to be a bathroom, and the same wall of glass as in the lounge overlooking the dancefloor – but no handy priest or bottle of Holy Water in sight. I was going to have to complain to the Blue Heart's management for their lack of foresight. After all, the nearest church was a five-minute run away . . . an idea almost formed in my head—

The spike-sharp pain in my left kidney prodded my attention back to the bodies on the bed and my allotted task.

'Well, this is cosy, isn't it?' I drawled, my voice calm enough to conceal the horror eating through my body. 'Shame I'm going to have to break up your little blood- and love-fest, Malik, but I've a present here with your name on it.' I snapped a length of the chain between my hands; it made a loud chinking sound. 'And the hell-heated coals I'm dancing on are getting impatient.'

Malik raised his head to look at me over Darius' shoulder, his eyes half-lidded, his expression sleepy . . . but nowhere near soft. He took in my costume. 'Hallowe'en has come early, I see,' he murmured.

'Apparently it's old Liz's favourite film.' I did a twirl.

'The disguised princess chained to the monster.' He quirked his mouth in a mocking smile. 'Subtlety never was Elizabetta's strong point.'

'So. Are you finished here?' I jerked my head at the almost comatose Darius. ''Cos I'm feeling a lot impish and I think we should get on with the killing part of the evening now before it gets too late.'

'Impish?' He frowned, shifting to prop himself up on his bent elbow.

'Yep, that old demon magic thing.' The chain bit into my palms as my hands tightened around it. I eyed Malik's long narrow fingers, which were resting against Darius' impressive bloodstained six-pack; did Malik have to look as if he'd enjoyed himself quite so much? And why was I feeling antagonistic towards someone who was supposed to be no more than a necessary evil in my life? After all, it wasn't like I really wanted *that* sort of relationship with Malik myself . . . or did I? Or was that just Rosa or the imps influencing my desires again? I shelved the questions for later. If there was a later.

'Of course,' I carried on, 'I still have choices and consequences,' and conscious of any listening ears, I spoke the next words in my head, hoping he'd hear them: '*They come down to you or Rosa's body, in fact, because once the sun rises over the horizon, I'm back in my own – body, that is.*' Gnawing pains around my knees accompanied my thoughts and my legs almost buckled. 'So unless you managed to get ordained at some point during your last half dozen centuries – any faith will do, neither the imps nor I are fussy – or can come up with a quick liquid solution, preferably one that's been blessed' – I raised my eyes to the heavens – 'the bell's about to chime for Round One.'

'Time will wait for this, I think,' he said. Blue fire lit his pupils and cast a peaceful glow through the dim room. He brought his inner arm to his mouth and bit into it, then, cradling Darius' head, he offered his bleeding wrist. Darius didn't appear to notice. His eyes were still closed, his face slack and sated, then Malik lowered his lips to the other vamp's cheek, the dark silk of his hair half-covering their faces, and murmured something too low for even my own enhanced vampire hearing to make out. Darius opened his mouth and latched on to Malik's wrist, sucking greedily like a babe at a teat, his body responding with evident pleasure. I watched, mesmerised, the spicy scent of Malik's blood teasing me, the harsher scents of copper and liquorice, and something else, something that my mind was struggling to recognise: a bitter-sweet smell like fermented flowers . . .

A popping sound brought me from my reverie as Malik worked his finger between Darius' lips and disengaged him from his arm, and a vague memory that I'd experienced something like this before brought my brows together in a frown.

'My apologies, Genevieve,' Malik said, his voice sounding regretful in my mind. '*Whilst Elizabetta's plans are not a surprise, if I had realised how Hannah might choose to augment them, I would not have accepted her offer of sustenance.'* He sat, pulling the sheet up over Darius. *'You must make every effort to do as she wishes, and I will attempt to minimise the damage to us both.'*

'Easy enough for you to say,' I muttered, scowling, as I tried to figure out where my uneasiness was coming from, then winced as another jagged pain speared through my solar plexus and wiped the thought from my mind.

Malik slid gracefully off the bed and strolled naked towards the wardrobe. My gaze followed the fine line of his back as it tapered from his sculptured shoulders down to his waist, then on past the taut, hard curve of his butt and down the long muscles in his thighs, watching as they flexed and stretched and the dimples at the back of his knees creased with each silent lift of his elegant feet. The sight had lust coiling tight in my belly, pooling with enough heat to drown out the prickly irritation of the imps scratching inside me. Then I blinked as he stood facing me, the silk triangle of dark hair on his pale chest arrowing down past the rose-burst scar to the low-slung black leather trousers he now wore on his narrow hips.

'Now you may try and kill me,' he said. There was a patient, almost amused edge to his smile, as if he'd been standing there, waiting for some time.

I clenched my fists round the chain. What was going on here? I might be distracted enough by eye-candy to not notice time passing, but the imps, not so much, I'd have thought. Ignoring the shooting pains in my biceps that forced me to lift the chain, I glanced at Darius, then back into the flames that flickered like blue gas jets in Malik's eyes.

'Your eyes usually glow red, not blue,' I said, tilting my head speculatively to one side as I added two and two and got rather more than four. 'Darius is of the Blue Heart blood-family. And the Earl had a habit of stopping time; it was one of his favourite tricks' – except the Earl's eyes hadn't lit up; his skin would just turn blue, like fine porcelain, but hey – 'so I'm guessing you didn't just feed off Darius, you somehow managed to gain some of his bloodline's power?'

Malik's smile widened, letting me glimpse fang. 'Feeding off other vampires has its compensations.'

'Great,' I said through gritted teeth as claws raked along the inside of my hip. 'Any chance you can keep me and the imps suspended until dawn, then let me catch up or something?'

'The effects are not long-lasting, but it would be possible.' He stepped towards me, a smooth, careful motion that wasn't meant to spook me but nonetheless made my heart up its beat. 'But I do not have until dawn, so we must see how this trick can benefit us now.'

'Why don't we have until dawn?'

'Darius' blood was poisoned; half an hour is the most time we have.'

Fermented flowers—Nightshade! 'Fuck, so that's what Hannah meant when she said she'd evened up the odds.' His vamp-healing would eventually clear the poison from his body, but not before the poison knocked him unconscious while it worked its way through his system, which is never a great option when someone is looking to wrap a chain round your neck and use it to decapitate you.

'What about him?' I jerked my head at Darius.

'I have removed enough of the poison that it now only incapacitates him; it will not be fatal.'

Maybe Malik wasn't such a messy eater after all.

'I take it you've got a plan?' I asked, almost doubling up as the imps sent a wave of sharp-teethed pain through my stomach. 'Because I'm not sure I can hold off from trying to kill you for much longer.'

'Of course.' He inclined his head, an amused smile crossing his face. 'We shall give them all what they want: a show.'

'Okay,' I said doubtfully, 'except I'm not sure there's going to be much "show" on my part.'

He spread his hands, his mouth quirking. 'Ladies first.'

I swung the lighter cuff end of the chain, twirling it in short circles around my head, getting its momentum up, then snapped it out with a flick of my wrist, the movements as automatic as if I'd performed them a hundred times before . . . which maybe my body had, just not with me in it. The chain snaked out lasso-like and thudded around Malik's neck—

—or actually, rattled into empty space and thudded on the carpet.

Malik was standing three feet to the left, his arms loose and easy at his sides, his gaze steady.

I yanked the chain back, whipped it low behind me and lashed out again. He shifted and raised his arm, catching the chain and holding it firm while I started to pull, using all my vampire strength. I might have been trying to heave a mountain. He laughed, the sound shivering over me like a teasing spring breeze with just a hint of the heat to come, then let go, and I stumbled back, crashing into the desk, sending the laptop bouncing to the floor. I screamed with rage and the imps inside me jumped with excited glee, egging me on. I hefted the chain, reversing it so I was swinging the collar like a mace. The weight of it felt wrong, lopsided, but I let it fly, aiming for his chest, willing it to keep straight and true. He dodged, but it caught him a glancing blow in the ribs, and the sound of them cracking was as loud as breaking ice. Inside me the imps cheered as he staggered back, nostrils flaring, blue fire blazing in his eyes.

'A lucky hit,' he said softly.

'Maybe not,' I said, just as softly, remembering how he'd opened the bedroom door earlier. *'Isn't Rosa your blood, and don't you have some sort of kinetic powers?'*

'Rosa is of my blood, but she did not inherit all my abilities.'

'Don't bet on it,' I said as I pulled the chain back and swung it round, all in one easy movement, then let it loose again.

Malik moved like a pale blur over the bed, but I was ready, using my will to *guide* the chain, aiming for his head. He dived and rolled, and the collar connected, though it hit his shoulder blade instead of his skull. He rolled again, coming up hard against the window, and I flicked my wrist, the chain snaking out towards the larger target of his torso.

But before it hit he was rolling again, regaining his feet and lunging at me. His shoulder thudded into my stomach, lifting me up and driving me back.

My back hit the wall first, then my head, and the plaster gave way, debris exploding everywhere. I dropped the chain and grabbed for Malik as it clanked to the floor. I screamed, digging my fingers into his back and scoring my nails down his skin.

Hissing in pain, he heaved me up and over his head, throwing me into the glass wall. It cracked with a sound like a thousand gunshots, bowed outwards . . . and gave way, and I stared down into the empty air, feeling the music thumping like a giant's heartbeat in my head as tiny chunks of glass fell like sparkling ice cubes towards the oblivious dancers thirty feet below.

I hung suspended, my toes balanced on the edge, my arms windmilling back, desperately trying not to fall.

It would hurt, a lot, but it wouldn't kill me; Rosa's body would heal the damage.

But the crowd of humans below? Their bodies were way more fragile.

The imps chortled with glee while, panicked, I tried to force myself back—

Then relief washed over me as I realised I was suspended, in time as well as space; I wasn't going to fall.

Malik's arm encircled my waist and the hard edges of the gold-metal bikini dug into my back where he pulled me hard against him. Then the gold collar closed round my neck and his voice shouted in my mind, *'Now we fly, Genevieve!'*

My pulse started speeding, the imps squealed in ecstasy and he stepped out and launched us into the air.

'But vampires can't fly,' I screamed, the sound lost . . .

Chapter Twenty-two

We floated in time and space as the lights strobed around us in a brilliant multi-coloured net of beams, and music, too loud, too harsh and too fleeting for my mind to decipher any recognisable rhythm, bashed against my ears. Salty sweat and clashing scents – perfumes, aftershaves, deodorants and fruity drinks – rose up on a miasma of body heat that visibly shimmered in the criss-crossed strobe lights. And reverberating through it all, like a beacon call to my blood, was the discordant bass-beat of a thousand hearts pulling me under, a tidal wave of pulses drowning me in the metallic tang of hunger and longing and need, until all that existed was prey . . .

An expanse of empty floor opened below us: the hot, glowing bodies of the excited humans were being herded by cooler shadows – vampires, their hearts still and quiet, their faces blank and closed – who were putting themselves between me and my prey.

Not that it would save them.

My bare feet touched down on the wooden floor, the arm around my waist loosened and I straightened, breathing in the scent of recently taken blood. The ache in my jaw intensified and I knew I couldn't be content with a sip this time; the incandescent itch in my veins urged me on. The encircling crowd drew away as I stalked towards the nearest rosy-hued humans, the anxious, high-pitched laughs and frantic pulse-beats almost lost beneath the heavy beat of the body-vibrating music. I reached out with my mind, intent on locking them in place, not bothering with my usual cat-and-mouse; just needing to *devour*. The nearest was young. He grinned nervously at me, his Adam's apple bobbing in his throat. My gaze snagged on the pulse jumping under his jaw and I snarled, lips curling back from my fangs. His eyes widened, pupils dilating in sudden fear, then my mind closed like a steel-trap around his, his face blanked with mind-lock and the connection between us quivered like a plucked string. I reached out and grabbed the minds of a dozen glowing bodies around him, anchoring them to my will, holding them ready: easy prey.

Anticipation tightened my body and my nipples stiffened against the unyielding metal of the bikini and heat slicked between my legs – but this wasn't about sex; sex was being held down, beaten and broken, unable to stop them, no matter how much I begged—

I pushed the intrusive thoughts away and growled low in my throat, a satisfying animal sound. Now it was my turn to rip and tear and damage and offer pain, again and again, and my turn to laugh as they pleaded and cried and screamed as I penetrated their weak, fragile bodies. The visceral desire for blood spiralled through my body. I crouched, preparing to leap, spreading my fingers, watching as my nails elongated and sharpened into skin-slicing claws—

The metal collar choked into my throat, jerked me back, keeping me from my prey. I whirled round, screeching with rage to face him.

'No!' Malik ordered. 'You will not do this.' He yanked the chain up, the links stretched taut between us, then jerked again, pulling me forward until I stumbled and fell to my knees before him. His face expressionless, he held out his hand to me.

I slashed at it, drawing blood, then grabbed at the chain with both hands and tried to wrench it from his hold. He would not stop me, not this time.

His arms and shoulders strained with effort as he held me in place.

I *called* to the humans caught with my mind and heard the collective gasp as they moved up at my back. Then his mind tore into mine and severed them from my hold, locking my rage inside his icy stillness.

The pounding music cut out, leaving silence. Then a rustling murmur started as three spotlights picked us out, pinning us within their overlapping circles. Far away, a voice in my mind – his, mine, *someone's* – muttered, *'Showtime.'*

Elizabetta, wearing her youthful face, appeared at Malik's side, her bronze broadsword resting on her shoulder like a pike-staff. 'You would not believe me when I said she was feral, Malik al-Khan.' Her words amplified outwards as if through a megaphone. 'Now you can witness for yourself that your curse has again manifested in your bloodline.'

'This is due to your meddling, Elizabetta,' Malik responded. 'She is contaminated by a demon – even your carefully nurtured blood would turn feral with such encouragement.'

'Pah!' Her dress shifted, the beads clattering triumphantly, and inwardly I shredded the sneering smile from her face. 'It makes no matter *why* she is like this; she must be dealt with before she causes more disquiet.' She held out her sword and placed the point at the base of my throat. 'Shall I dispose of the bitch myself' – her fangs extended over her bottom lip – 'or would you like to do the honours?'

'No,' Malik said quietly, his eyes flaring blue. He reached out and took the sword from her unresisting hand. 'No, she is mine. It is my responsibility to rescind her Gift.'

I snarled, even though the part of me not wanting to rip his throat out knew he didn't mean it, knew it was some sort of ruse, knew he wouldn't kill me – the Rosa me – because then we would both die . . . wouldn't we? Looking up into his face, seeing his implacable expression, I wasn't quite so certain. But I was still locked by his will; I couldn't move, couldn't fight.

Inside me, the imps boiled and burned, impatient, intolerant of their inability to force me to violence.

'But first, she will bow to my hand.' He let the chain drop from his grasp and it fell to the floor in a rattle of links.

'Nooo!' Elizabetta lifted her foot and lowered it slowly back to the floor, a stamp made slow by his hold on time. 'I will . . . not . . . allow . . . it.'

'The choice is not yours, but belongs to Rosa.' He knelt on one knee before me, blood-tinged sweat beading on his forehead. '*Genevieve,*' I heard, the command gentle, '*you must repeat these words: I offer you my oath, accept only you as my liege and drink of your blood.*'

I repeated his words, my voice harsh as if rusty with disuse, my mouth struggling to form the syllables past the scorching pain constricting my throat.

He touched my cheek and ice spread through my veins, freezing the imps into calmness. He held out his wrist. '*Now feed, Genevieve.*'

I kept my eyes on his, drew my lips back and struck, sinking my fangs into his skin, sucking hard, desperately.

'*Be ready to run, Genevieve, at my command.*'

He stood in one smooth motion, breaking my hold on his flesh as he drew me up with him. Then he looked up, and I saw through his eyes Hannah watching us from the broken window, her face contorted by magic. She lifted her arm and traced a glyph through the air. It glowed brightly before streaking down to slam into my chest, freeing the imps and sending them screaming in triumph through my veins.

Malik turned back to me, eyes dark and shadowed and drew back the sword . . .

Disbelief and outrage filled me. He couldn't, he wouldn't dare—

. . . and plunged it into my body.

The blade sliced into me—

—and I stared down at the hilt where it pressed up in my stomach, feeling the sharpness of the blade cutting through my heart, and the hard length that protruded from between my shoulders. '*Whatever happened to running?*' I screamed in my mind. Then pain shattered through me, spinning me out in a tornado of golden dust, and I spiralled into the red-dark depths of memory.

My fourteenth birthday.

My wedding day.

I stood, tall and straight as I'd been taught, in the centre of the great hall. The high mullioned windows were open to

the faint moonlight and the distant bark of a fox was the only
noise other than the soft sound of my breaths. The guests – all
vampires, not a human or fae amongst them – surrounded me.
A handful I knew, those of my father's blood, but the rest were
strangers, here to see their liege lord take his sidhe bride.

I stood, shock numbing my mind, ignoring them all, pretending to ignore the still-warm blood that drenched the hem
of my gold-brocade dress and soaked into the thin fabric of
my shoes. Blood that smelt like sweet ripe pears.

Sally's blood.

Sally had been given to me as a present on my twelfth
birthday: my very own lady's maid and companion. We were
supposed to be inseparable, two young girls growing up
together, but Sally was three years older than me, and she
wasn't interested in being friends, not with me, anyway. Not
that I minded; she was pretty, with her pale blue skin and long
blue-white hair, and part fae – her great-grandmother was a
Cailleac Bhuer, one of the Blue Hags – so I'd been happy just
to follow her around.

My prince – my betrothed – Bastien, the Autarch, the
monster – came towards me. He let the sword fall from his
hand and it clattered to the ground. His bare feet soaked up
the blood, leaving unbloodied footprints on the flagstone
floor. The wet ends of his hair dripped down his shoulders.
The splatters on his face looked like teenage freckles. Not
even his height – he was close on six feet tall – could make
him look much older than the fifteen he'd been when he'd
accepted the Gift.

The shadows followed behind him, always present, never
breached, never mentioned, and never revealed—

Only now I knew what the shadows hid: Malik al-Khan,
the Autarch's . . . what? The question rose like an accusation
out of my memory then sank slowly back into the darkness.

'You are looking very beautiful, my sidhe princess.' The
monster's handsome young face smiled, a joyous, open grin
that didn't hide his fangs, nor the gleam of lust for pain in his
eyes.

'Thank you, my prince,' I whispered, unable to stop my
legs trembling the closer he came.

The monster executed a low, elegant bow and held out his

hand to me. Sally's thin plait of blue-white hair lay limp in his palm. 'To the victor the spoils, is that not right, my bride?'

I curled my shaking fingers into the heavy material of my dress. I didn't want to be the victor; I'd never wanted to be the victor – I hadn't even realised there was a contest until it was waged and lost. I'd always known he would have others as well as me, for my father had educated me well. In my future there had been no winners or losers, just fairy tales of happily ever after with my prince. But Sally hadn't known the rules; she'd set out to win, unaware her battle was a barely noticed skirmish until she'd staked her victory flag where all could see it.

'Do you not want my gift, my lovely sidhe?' He wiped the plait across his bloody chest and presented it again. 'Is this not what you wanted?'

'Take it, Genevieve.' The order came into my mind and my hand reached out and snatched the plait from his palm before fear or conscious thought could stop me.

'I hoped my present would please you,' the monster said softly, and waved around, an expansive gesture, 'but I have another gift for you to mark our wedding day.' He held out his hand once again and the necklace sparkled in the flickering candlelight, the diamonds like pink stars as they dripped blood from his fingers. 'Turn around, my princess. I will fasten it for you.'

'Do as he says,' said the voice in my mind.

I curtseyed slowly and dipped my head in acquiescence, then I turned as he bade me, my heart thudding shallow in my chest, fear cramping my stomach. I stared at my father's aristocratic face, the proud lift of his chin not quite disguising his own fear, then at the frightened expression of Matilde, my stepmother. Her fingers fluttered up to touch the black opals that encircled her own neck, her lips parting with a glimpse of fang, as if to speak, as if maybe to stop him . . .

Then she pressed her lips together and her sapphire-blue eyes dropped down to the spreading lake of blood on the floor.

It was the last time I would ever see her look at me.

'Be ready to run, Genevieve. At my command.'

The diamonds settled around my throat, the stones heavy against my chilled skin. 'A gift fit for a queen, *my* sidhe queen,' said Bastien, the monster, drawing the necklace tight, making it dig into my flesh with a spiteful twist of his fingers. He touched his lips to the curve of my neck; they felt like a brand. His sharp inhalation of my scent sent panicked shivers down my spine.

'Sidhe blood, as sweet and rich as fear-spiced honey,' he said, his voice a mixture of anticipation and satisfaction. 'Sidhe – and virgin too; is that not so, Andrei? On your honour, none has tasted your daughter's blood or body? I have your assurance that she is ready and willing to be broken on my sword?'

Terror fractured the last edge of numbness inside me and piss trickled down my leg to mingle with the blood beneath my feet.

'As you wished, my liege.' Anguish flickered in my father's eyes, then was gone.

'*Run. Now.*'

I ran, out through the heavy oak doors and into the night, the ground slippery beneath my feet, the heavy brocade dress tangling my legs, my lungs gasping for air, my belly taut with terror, knowing I had to escape, knowing I couldn't outrun the shadows . . .

He caught me from behind and then there was nothing but pain and terror as he held me down, his hand tight in my hair, my smaller body crushed beneath his, and the sudden sharp sting of his fangs piercing the curve of my neck as I pleaded with him and screamed for him to stop . . .

. . . and his lips touched mine in a kiss as cold as death.

Red-blackness pressed against me as insistent hands tried to prise and pinch and pull me apart. Rich spice scented the air and copper sweetness filled my mouth, and in the far distance a haze of gold circled me like an aurora. I'd been here once before, tethered by the same black silken cord that wound around and through me and tied me to the red-blackness, keeping the determined hands from scattering me like dancing motes into the golden haze.

'*Genevieve.*' Malik's voice came from above and below, confusing and indistinct, and the black cord tugged at me from both directions, as if it wanted to tear me in two.

'It has been too long, vampire.' A snort of unease edged

the deep, burred tone. 'Her soul should have returned to her body by now.'

'My connection with her is still there, kelpie, although there is more resistance to my call now than the first time her soul was severed.'

'*Genevieve.*' The call came from below me this time, stronger, more urgent. I flowed down towards it.

'*Genevieve.*' An echo stretched faintly above me, making me hesitate.

'T'would have been better to let the spell take its natural course and let the bodies reassert themselves at dawn as they were meant to, instead of forcing the magic to revert early.'

'That would have left Genevieve's body at the mercy of the sorcerer.' There was a note of forced calm in his voice. 'It would have been too much of a risk.'

'Aye, but what if it has been too long since you bonded with her, what if the bond breaks?' The words sounded harsh. 'Her soul could wander, become lost – maybe even *fade.*'

'*Genevieve.*' Pain slid like brittle ice along the silken cord, snapping it and flinging me back . . .

I came to, naked and alone, lying in the dried-up lake of blood, the scent of sour pears gagging in my throat. Like the first time, the noonday sun streamed through the high mullioned windows, cutting oblongs of light and shade into the stone floor. Ignoring the pain in my body I pushed up onto my hands and knees, then stood, straight and tall. The gold-brocade wedding dress lay torn and crumpled near the heavy oak doors, the plait of blue-white hair abandoned near it, and as I looked at where Sally had been butchered, the sunshine caught and flashed in my eyes. I walked over to where the sword lay discarded from the night before and stared down at it, my hands clenched into fists.

This time I wasn't a child.

This time I wouldn't run.

This time I would make him pay.

Then a hand, colder than my own, took hold of mine and slowly I turned to stare into the dark, cautious eyes of Cosette, the child-ghost.

'This is no longer your time, Genevieve.' Her voice was soft. 'You must not stay here any more, it is too perilous.' She tugged me, anxiety flitting across her face. 'Come, they are both waiting for you, and there are the others . . .'

Others?

I turned and followed Cosette as she led me back into the red-blackness . . .

I came awake again with a start, pulse thundering in my ears; my eyes snapped open and I looked up into Malik's face as he straddled me. His hands were pressed to the cold skin over my heart. I could see stars scattered like pieces of silver across the night sky above him, and the ground shifted sand-soft beneath me.

'Genevieve—' His voice was rough, as if he'd been calling for some time.

'It was you that night.' I licked my lips. My voice sounded thready, scared. 'You bit me that night.'

'Of course.' A fine line creased between his brows. 'Who did you think it was?'

'Him. I always thought it was him . . .'

'He would not chase you down himself, not when he had me as his tool.'

Fear exploded into anger. I clenched my fists. 'You bastard! You left me for dead!'

An odd expression crossed his face. 'I did not leave you for dead.'

'Bullshit.'

'I killed you. As I did tonight. Your heart was still, your blood had settled in your body, your lungs no longer drew breath and your skin was cold and lifeless to the touch. If you had not been sidhe, I doubt you would have revived.'

I stared at him, my mind reaching for something I couldn't quite grasp—

'I don't understand.'

His frown deepened. 'Would you have preferred me to have given you back to the Autarch alive?'

No! my fourteen-year-old voice screamed in my mind.

He touched a hand to my forehead. 'Sleep now.'

Chapter Twenty-three

I awakened for the third time to the quiet burble of water, the scent of clean air, and silk sheets caressing my skin. I huddled tense and wary, listening, but a feeling of calm enveloped me, finally convincing me that I was on my own, and safe — even if I wasn't entirely sure where I was.

I squinted out from under my lashes. Everything in the room was round: the bed on which I was lying, and the dais beneath it; the skylight in the domed ceiling that framed the stars piercing the night sky; the porthole windows, behind which darted shoals of tiny fish in neon-bright blues and oranges and yellows. Even the pillows on the bed, the huge vault-style door, and the dive hole set in the thick green-glass floor leading down into the water were round. If I didn't know better I'd have guessed I was on some sort of movie set instead of Tavish's bedroom.

The calm feelings persisted, dampening down my surprise at being here, and a vague notion made me *look*. A barely discernible net of cool green magic covered the walls and ceiling, shifting softly as if pulled by a peaceful sea. I wondered if it was some sort of Containment spell, but when I reached down to where it gathered by the bed it rippled away, then re-formed as I removed my hand. Some sort of Wellbeing or Tranquillity spell, or even a Healing spell, maybe?

Just what I needed after being skewered with a five-foot-long bronze sword.

Still, the sword-in-the-chest incident might have been an abrupt ending to our dramatic fealty performance, but one thing was clear: even in the haze of imp-engendered bloodlust I – or rather, Rosa – had given Malik my oath. And that effectively shut the door on any vamp in London – or anywhere else – contacting me. Relief overwhelmed me. No more invitations, no more worrying about paranoid witches demanding I be evicted, no more visits from poor stoked-up Moth-girls. Now they'd have to go through Malik – although hopefully not as literally as Elizabetta had tried to do – and all I needed to worry about now was the pretty vampire himself.

I shivered; did that mean my life was better or worse?

The thought brought on the unwanted image of my torn wedding dress; nausea roiled in my stomach and I jerked up, clamping my hands against my mouth to keep from vomiting. *The past was gone.* It had been a nightmare, nothing more; my mind had equated one trauma involving a sword with another and coupled it with Elizabetta's talk about the Autarch. That's all it was, nothing more. Malik wasn't Bastien, the monster, and I wasn't marrying him – I wasn't doing anything with him. And Malik had had more than one opportunity to do me harm, and he hadn't taken it . . .

A huff of almost hysterical laughter escaped me: that was if I discounted the recent sword-in-the-chest episode, of course. I took a deep breath and let the green magic calm me as I rubbed the cold spot just below my heart where the sword had entered. Nervous, I pulled the sheet down to check my body. It looked normal – and uninjured. I ran my fingers under the base of my sternum, pressing and prodding: nope, definitely no sword holes, not even a pink patch of new skin or a left-over yellowing bruise. I looked as good as new. But then, Malik held the true Gift, and he'd healed me before.

He'd also killed me before.

Betrayal sliced through me with as much pain as the sword had. I hugged my knees tight and dropped my head onto them, tears pricking my eyes, aching in my throat. *The voice had told me to run that night.* I swallowed the tears back. I was *not* going to cry. *But you don't* run *from vampires.* I'd trusted the voice in my head, trusted *Malik's* voice, *trusted it meant escape* . . .

But Malik had hunted me down like an animal.

Malik had sunk his fangs in me.

Malik had infected me with 3V.

Not the Autarch, as I'd always believed.

Rage filled me like a tidal wave, surging up and out of me in one long, furious scream. Why the fuck had he? Why hadn't he just killed me, instead of condemning me to an eternity of needing him, or some other vamp? I punched the bed, ripped at it with my hands, grabbed the pillows and threw them, one after the other until they were all gone, wanting to smash something, wanting to break something, wanting all of it to never have happened. I screamed again; screamed until the tears spilled hot and scalding, and until I slept again, limp and exhausted and numb with grief.

I lay quiet amongst the shredded sheets and stared up at the fading stars in the pre-dawn sky.

You don't run, *you don't* struggle; *it gets a vamp too excited.*

Maybe Malik hadn't meant to infect me; maybe he'd just lost control . . .

He *had* saved me from the Autarch.

Like some beautiful but deadly guardian angel.

Gratitude washed over me, muting my anger and soothing my grief, and bringing a curl of need to the confusion swirling inside me. I wasn't sure if I wanted to offer him my throat, my body or even my heart . . .

Or if I never wanted to see the beautiful vampire again.

Then, as if my thoughts had conjured it, Malik's not-quite-English voice came faintly through the open doorway: '—only way to destroy the imps before one or more could hatch was to kill their host, kelpie.'

Slowly, I sat up and hugged my knees, and listened for an answer. But none came. The silence stretched, thinning out until the soft slap of the water and the background hum of the magic disappeared and there was nothing but the waiting thud of my pulse. And I finally admitted to myself that 'not seeing him again' wasn't what I wanted. But as for the rest, right now the only thing I was offering him was . . .

'Thank you,' I murmured, knowing he would hear me. 'Although, next time you decide to kill me,' I added, a touch more caustically, 'perhaps you could try a less violent option.'

'*I do not intend there to be a next time, Genevieve.*' His words slipped with sorrow and regret into my mind.

I lay back and returned to contemplating the fading stars above me. The net of calming green magic crept up and when I didn't rebuff it, gently tucked itself around me like a soft, warm blanket.

'Aye, but killing the host body 'twas a chancy thing tae do, vampire.' Tavish's burr sounded disapproving. 'Especially as Genevieve's soul took its own sweet time coming back.'

I sighed; at least I'd survived. But had Rosa's body? She was a vamp, so it was likely, but . . . I sent a prayer to whatever god was listening that it/she had, and reminded myself that she was on my problems-to-deal-with list. Still, Malik's drastic sword-option had solved the *Rosa's body being consumed by imps* part of the whole 'Rosa' problem.

'Even if the body Genevieve occupied had survived the imps' physical onslaught,' Malik said, tension in his voice, 'it was always possible her mind would have been destroyed. Genevieve was already influenced by Rosa's persona, and Rosa's mind was unstable long before the sorcerer's manipulations.'

Gotta give Hannah her due, her *favours* were to die for.

And thinking of favours, I realised I knew how to solve the Rosa problem. All I had to do was give Malik the info he'd been following me for. I quietly said, 'Hannah Ashby knows where Rosa's body is. She's the one who's been controlling the spell since the Ancient One died.'

'*Thank you, Genevieve,*' Malik's voice came again in my mind. '*I will arrange to deal with both the sorcerer and Rosa.*'

Great, two solutions for the price of one. I crossed them off my list and added the Fabergé egg – with a mental footnote that flagged Neil Banner's dubious interest – though quite what I could do about the Ancient One's soul the egg contained, I wasn't yet sure.

'I've told you, our *bean sidhe's* nae weakling.' Tavish's voice held equal measures of pride and concern. 'You hae only tae look at what she did when the bastard Earl had a go at her and the satyr last month.'

I frowned: the vampire and the kelpie were chatting together like old friends, or at least old acquaintances. It made for a curious, surprising situation. And they were discussing me as if they'd done it all before, and more than once at that.

Their voices faded as I chased the thoughts darting back and forth in my mind like the shoals of tiny fish. Tomas' murder and finding the sidhe responsible slipped through my mental fingers, and the one I caught was Hannah's big-screen memory of the Earl talking to the Ancient One just before he killed her.

The prohibition was to end on her twenty-third birthday, but with the witches involved, now she will still be out of my reach.

I hadn't paid much attention to the words at the time, but some sort of 'prohibition' explained why London's vamps *hadn't* pursued a vulnerable teenage sidhe when the opportunity presented herself on their doorstep. And whilst I'd spent the last ten years being übercareful, all it would have taken was a couple of weeks' captivity and the venom cravings would've been so bad I'd have been begging the nearest vamp to sink his or her fangs in me . . .

Then of course, I'd got the job at Spellcrackers.com just over a year ago, a few days before my twenty-third birthday. I'd been as happy as a blinged-up goblin; not only did the job involve magic, but because it was a witch company, the job came with the witches' protection. No wonder the Earl had been angry. The prohibition might have ended, but I was *still out of his reach.*

And there weren't many vamps powerful enough to force the Earl – and the rest of London's blood-families – into a prohibition in the first place, so it wasn't such a leap that Malik was involved – but why would Malik do such a deal? Especially when he'd told me himself he'd coveted my blood since I was four years old? Why hadn't he just come after me and snatched me up? I was infected and he'd obviously known where I was all this time.

I opened my mouth to ask him—then my thoughts snagged on the sidhe queen's *droch guidhe* and the fae's *need* of a baby-making machine, and I got my answer. London's fae – presumably through Tavish – had somehow stopped him. But if they had, the surprise of it was that the dryads or some other fae hadn't decided to kidnap and impregnate me before now.

A fourteen-year-old sidhe is much easier to control than a twenty-four-year-old.

But Tavish was one of only four fae I'd spoken to in all the time I'd been in London, and I'd been so concerned about keeping my part-vamp parentage a secret that it had never really struck me as odd. Now, as I thought about it, it was nearly as odd as spending ten years relatively unmolested by vampires.

Until you added in a flipside to the prohibition.

With the sidhe queen's curse hanging over their heads, what, or who, could make London's fae agree to stay away from me?

Had to be the queen, of course, since she was ultimately the one calling the shots.

Suspicion crept on black-tipped claws into my mind. And who was her ambassador? Grianne, my not-so-friendly faerie dogmother—

I looked up at the dawn-streaked sky.

—who I was due to meet as the sun was cresting.

Early birds catching worms, or in this case *answers to prohibitions, curses and murders*, came to mind.

I sat up and looked round the room, hoping to find some clothes . . .

Only I wasn't the only one looking around.

My pulse jumped and I stilled.

Someone was watching me from the dive-hole in the glass floor. He – my eyes flicked downwards, yes definitely a he – had his top half in the room, pale-grey scaly forearms flat on the floor, webbed, clawed hands clasped together, while his blue-grey legs and long, whip-like tail floated in the water below. His wide lipless mouth yawned in a grin, showcasing rows of tiny, sharp green teeth, and the opaque membrane covering his eyes slipped up, leaving gleaming black orbs reflecting back the room's soft green light.

I lifted the tattered sheet and tucked it under my arms,

blinking at him in amazement. What the hell was a naiad doing in Tavish's bedroom? And even as I asked myself, the answer popped up, pretty much as quickly as the naiad had: the sidhe queen's stupid curse. I did a quick check through the glass floor of the room to see if there were any more of the naiad's pals lurking outside in the water, but he seemed to be on his own.

He nodded at me, the thick fluted fins on either side of his head flaring outwards, then he put his webbed claws flat on the floor and started to push himself up and out of the dive-hole.

I shot out my hand and said firmly, 'Hold it right there, fishface. No way do you get to come in unannounced and uninvited.'

The naiad's elbows locked and he stopped. 'Fishface, luv?' His lipless mouth appeared to have no problem forming the words. 'What sort of half-assed greeting is that?'

'The only sort you're going to get when you pop up naked and unwanted in my bedroom,' I snapped.

'Your bedroom?' His spiny headcrest lifted up in what looked like surprise. 'This is the kelpie's bedroom.'

'Ever heard of possession?' I said. 'The kelpie's not here and I am, therefore it's currently mine.' I waved my hand in a 'get lost' motion at him. 'You want to see him, you can go round the front way.'

'There's a bloody big sand-dune out there, luv. It looks like he's imported half the bleeding Sahara, and I'm a naiad, not a bleeding camel-toed horse.' He made a high clicking noise and I realised he was laughing.

'Fine, I'll remember to tell him that after you've made yourself scarce.'

'S'okay, it's you I've come to see anyway.' He hauled himself out and stood dripping, legs apart, headcrest brushing against the curve of the ceiling, his tail trailing back into the dive-hole. 'Word has it you're in the market for a *firionnach*, *bean sidhe*, so us naiads had a little game of poker and, lucky for you, luv' – he thumped his chest with a closed claw – 'Ricou here plays a mean game of five-card stud.'

'You won me in a poker game?' I blurted out in affronted disbelief.

'Yep. Bleeding great, ain't it?' His mouth did the grin-yawn thing again. 'So, before all the official rigmarole with the Lady Meriel, I thought I'd swim over and let you have a look at my credentials.' He looked down and carefully took hold of himself, one webbed claw around each of his overly excited credentials. 'There you go, double your money's worth, luv.' His fluted face-fins flared proudly. 'Just to prove I'm full-blood naiad and not some halfling pup.'

Two! Okay, so I'd heard the rumours, but—I stared, I couldn't help myself, it was that whole car-crash thing . . .

'Oh and just in case you're wondering,' he went on, the membrane slipping down over his left eye in a wink, 'they're always like this. We naiads ain't got the same shrinkage problems as everyone else.' He did a little flip and his non-shrinking credentials somehow managed to stick out at right angles. 'So, luv, whenever you're ready for a bit of slippy-slippy, I'm up for it.'

I did an astonished double-take, then got my mind back on track.

'Tavish,' I yelled, glaring at the open vault door, 'get in here, now!'

Tavish strolled in almost immediately, silver beads spar-kling at the ends of his dreads, black harem pants gathered at his ankles and the green-black skin of his chest gleaming like watered silk. He smiled, and my mouth lifted to smile back at him before I could stop myself. I pressed my lips together and dragged my eyes away before I ended up staring like a charm-struck human again.

'What the hell is he doing here?' I pointed at Ricou.

'If the naiad's nae tae your liking, doll' – he gave me a bland look – 'just say the word; I'm sure the Lady Meriel will let you choose from the rest o' them.'

'But that's not bleeding fair, kelpie,' Ricou cried. 'I've just told the *bean sidhe*—'

'Hey, fishface' – I waved my hand at him – 'shut up, before you make me do something you'll regret.'

'Like what, luv?' The clicking laugh came again. 'I mean, the way I heard it, you ain't got any bleeding magic to speak of.'

'Yeah?' I gave him a just-you-try-it look. 'So who do you think built the sand-dune out there?'

His headcrest slowly subsided.

'Of course, doll, if there's nae one o' the naiads takes your fancy,' Tavish said coolly, his delicate black-lace gills shifting slightly at his throat, 't'would be an easy thing for me tae tell the Lady Meriel that we're courting and save you the bother o' disturbances like this one.'

Save me the bother? 'C'mon, Tavish,' I snorted, 'this is your own private aquarium. The only way fishface could get in here is if you let him, so whoever you think you're fooling, it's not me.'

'Ach, doll, I'm only showing you your alternatives.' He smiled, his silver eyes sparkling like the full moon on the sea. 'Far be it from me tae stop you having a litter o' naiad pups, or maybe half a dozen saplings.'

And as for that idea—No way was I being manipulated into something as important as having a child, so the whole lot of them could hold fire until I knew more about it.

'Unless there was something else you were wanting?' Tavish added.

Behind him, Malik appeared in the vault doorway, an edge of shadowed darkness slipping from him. He'd found a black T-shirt from somewhere and the plain cotton moulded itself to his lean, muscular chest, leaving a tantalising glimpse of pale skin at the low-slung waistband of his leather trousers. His black eyes fixed on mine with a half-lidded, almost lazy expression, a hint of a smile twitching one corner of his mouth, a suggestion of a promise weaving like smoke through my mind.

Crap. Talk about a double-act of annoying eye-candy! The pair of them were in it together. It almost made me want to take them up on their offer, whatever it entailed, just to see how far they would go . . . *Okay, crazy thought* – and one I had a suspicion wasn't mine. I glared at the pretty vamp. No doubt they'd go way further than I could imagine.

Damn, the whole curse thing needed sorting out, and while I could empathise with its awful consequences, I was getting more than a little pissed off with being either chased by dryads, hit on by fishface, or having a scheming kelpie try to trick me into whatever. Hadn't any of them heard about sitting down and talking? Not that I had time for it right now, not until after my meeting with Grianne—

That was it, wasn't it? Same as yesterday: they didn't want me to meet the phouka, the queen's ambassador.

'Prohibition,' I said softly. Neither of them made the slightest movement, which was telling enough in itself. 'Or, to give it another name, everyone controlling, manipulating and deciding my fate. And you two are still doing it now.' I waved at the naiad. 'Trying to distract me with fishface here, threats of saplings and promises of whatever! Well, thanks for the offer, but I've got more important things to do. Like getting information that might solve a friend's murder. So I'm not staying here in Tavish's bed, however *attractive* the inducement, and just in case neither of you can recognise it, *that* was sarcasm.'

Tavish grinned, displaying his sharp-pointed white teeth. 'I could always make the inducement less attractive, doll.'

Frustration filled me until I felt I might explode. Still, if he wanted to play tough . . . Stun spells sounded like a handy idea, except of course even in *Between* I couldn't cast spells. But the magic seemed to like me just fine, so . . .

'Yeah, well how about this?' I lifted my hands and *called* the magic net. It bundled itself into my palms until I felt like I was holding two balls of soft green cotton. I threw one out towards Tavish, willing the net to trap him. I was taking a chance, not certain the magic would heed me – it might just leave me with metaphorical egg on my face – but my frustration seemed to fuel the spell, just as it did before, and the net swirled out and landed over his head, tangling in his dreads. His silver eyes flashed with surprise as his fingers pulled at the net, trying to deny the magic—

I *cracked* the spell, exploding the net – and his silver beads – into tiny motes that glowed briefly before dissipating into the ether. He grabbed hold of the shredded ends of his hair, snorting in dismay as he examined them.

Okay, childish I know, but also satisfying pay-back for the blonde-bimbo Glamour he'd sicced on me.

I turned towards Ricou, who was staring at Tavish in

wide-eyed amazement – at least I think that was what his gaping mouth and bolt-upright headcrest meant.

'Hey, fishface,' I called to get his attention, 'unless you want me to do the same to your *credentials*' – I tossed the other ball of magic in the air and caught it – 'you'll go back to the rest of your poker-playing pals and tell them that *if* I'm ever up for it – and believe me, I'm not talking about sex here – then I'll be the one that comes visiting, got it?'

'Got it in one, luv.' His face-gills slapped back against his head and he did the grin-yawn thing again. 'And just in case you do fancy a bit of slippy-slippy, luv' – he thumped his fisted claw on his chest and winked at me again – 'drop a bit of blood in the water and give Ricou a shout, okay?' Then he leapt and twisted, diving into the hole, and sped away like a dark streak through the water.

Yeah, I'd give him a shout – like when the Thames froze over again . . .

'Next time, Tavish' – I held up the green ball of magic and blew on it until it exploded into tiny filaments that coated the glass floor like iron filings on a magnet – 'it'll be your aquarium here.' I raised my eyebrows. 'How's that for a less attractive inducement?'

Tavish snorted. 'Neat bit o' magic, doll, I dinnae ken you could do that.'

'I've been practising,' I said. Getting the equivalent of 'knocked out' every time I *absorbed* a spell was *so* not fun. Trouble was, I could only *call* the smaller, more benign magics so far. Still, nice to know that Finn wasn't reporting my every move back to Tavish . . . and now it was time to put a stop to Tavish having any more crazy ideas.

'I think it's time for some ground rules,' I said, in my most reasonable voice. 'I know about the nasty effects of the curse; Finn's told me – something *you* should have done ages ago.' I looked pointedly at Tavish.

'Aye, doll' – he nodded – 'that's as maebe, but it's nae the sort o' thing one jumps intae when one's courting. Better tae test the water first.'

Okay, so telling a girl on the first date you wanted her to play 'mummy' to your 'daddy' might be coming on a bit strong, but when it comes to pregnancy, by the time you get round to testing the water it's usually too late.

'And I get that the pair of you have been watching out for me with this prohibition,' I carried on in the same reasonable tone. 'And don't think I don't appreciate it, or that I'm not grateful' – *or that I don't know you've both got your own reasons for doing it* – 'but the longer you keep me in the dark, the more everything seems to get screwed up around me. So I'm going to meet the phouka, get whatever info she's found out about the murdering sidhe' – *and ask her some pertinent questions about the prohibition* – 'then we can all have a chat about what to do next, okay?' I glanced up at the paler circle of the skylight, although not 'all' of us would still be awake.

Tavish looked at Malik as if to say 'up to you'.

Malik was still watching me from half-lidded eyes, but all the amusement and seduction was gone. 'Genevieve—'

'I know the phouka's dangerous, Malik,' I said, firmly. 'I don't need convincing of that.' *And she's not the only one*, I thought, looking from one to the other, hoping they weren't going to make this a fight . . . one I'd probably lose . . .

'Have a care.' He inclined his head in what I took for acceptance, as opposed to something more irritating, like consent.

'Great, glad we've got that sorted' – I stood, pulling the sheet with me – 'so any chance of some clothes?' I smiled at them both. 'Naked's *so* not the best way to walk around London unnoticed.'

And the sun would be rising soon and the phouka would be waiting for me.

Chapter Twenty-four

Tavish's magic beachfront door expelled me under London Bridge this time. I walked out of an open doorway near the entrance of the London Bridge Experience, the very one where I'd spent an uncomfortable time surveying ghosts with Finn a few days past – right now it felt like a particularly long lifetime ago. The green and blue lights twinkled in the pavement, and a couple of the exhibition actors – two women in ankle-length woollen robes made up to look like mediaeval plague victims – were organising the visitors waiting to go in. It might be Sunday morning, but scary tourist shows were definitely the in-thing for Hallowe'en.

I headed past the chattering queue, many of them stamping their feet and breathing into their hands against the cold wind that whistled off the nearby Thames. As I reached the bottom of Nancy's Steps, I stopped and looked up, recalling my escape up them the previous night from the turban-headed dryads. The phouka, in her doggy guise, a faint silver sheen to her silky short-haired coat, gazed sphinx-like from the top. She angled her head to one side, ears pricking forward, then, giving me a tongue-lolling smile, she bounded down to meet me.

'Hello, Grianne,' I said drily as she shook herself, casually

scattering raindrops over me, and just as casually *casting*
an Unseen spell. The magic settled round us like a cocoon,
blocking out the noise of the excited tourists and the traffic
rumbling across the bridge above.

'How's my faerie dogmother this morning?' I asked. 'Did
you get enough exercise chasing sticks last night?'

'Please do not refer to me by that ridiculous mortal name,
child,' the dog snapped; any human listening would hear just
a low growl. 'I am a phouka. And the dryads caused me no
more problems after you had departed.'

'Great to hear it.' I shoved my hands into my jacket pockets
and started along the street. After some discussion – during
which Malik had disappeared to wherever – Tavish had
finally come up with some clothes – the jacket, trainers, jeans
and T-shirt all thankfully real – in exchange for me heading
straight back after meeting the phouka, something I'd been
planning to do anyway.

'So,' I said, as the phouka fell in beside me, 'have you
managed to find any info on the sidhe who's decided to visit
London yet?'

'None in the Fair Lands has opened any of the three gates.'
Her black-tipped claws clicked sharply on the pavement.
'Clíona, my queen, has forbidden any from doing so.'

'Because of the *droch guidhe*.' I bent down and looked the
phouka in her pale grey eyes. 'Of which there is a detail you
forgot to mention to me: like, the lesser fae who can't have
full-blood children?'

Her ears flattened against her head. 'It was not your
concern.'

I straightened and gave the phouka a 'don't bullshit me'
look. '*Of course* it's my concern, Grianne! I'm running round
Sucker Town on *your* rescue missions, picking up any stray
faelings that end up trapped there because you keep telling
me *your* queen can't break the curse and feels guilty about
them. Now I find out not only is there an additional problem
with the curse, but that she's been refusing to speak to any of
the fae here about it. I take it you *do* know what their solution
is, don't you?'

'Enough, child.' She growled at me for real this time,
baring long black fangs. 'I am aware of the situation. But

regardless of what I might have wished, I was, like all others, constrained by the prohibition.'

'Which is another thing.' I tilted my head to look at her. 'Everyone else was "prohibited" from coming near me, but you just got told to keep the secret. What makes you so different?'

'The curse does not afflict me' – the hairs along her spine rose in a stiff ridge – 'nor am I a vampire who wishes to enslave you.' She padded a couple of steps forward and the air blurred around her. Grianne stood before me in her more human form, her usual haughty expression on her long, narrow face. A swathe of fine silver fabric was caught in a clasp at one shoulder and fell to pool around her feet, clinging like silk to her tall, slender body. It gave her an oddly ethereal air that belied her strength. Her ash-grey hair was feathered against her scalp, parting around the pointed tips of her ears, and her skin shone the same faint silver-grey as the dog's. Anyone seeing her would know her at once for a fae – not that anyone would see her with her magic hiding us.

'Fair enough.' I stopped, giving her a wary look. 'But they're not the only reasons, are they?'

'Of course not, child.' She smiled, her teeth as black and sharp as the dog's. 'As I have told you before, I abhor what you are; even were you not infected with *salaich siol* you have your father's taint in your blood, and I intended to end your life at first.' She might have been discussing the weather for all the emotion in her voice. 'But you proved yourself to be resourceful, courageous and stubborn that night, and I owed you a debt.'

Yeah, it wasn't me the vamp sunk his fangs in, was it? I said to myself. The stupid sucker had been so excited at catching a phouka that he completely missed the fourteen-year-old sidhe right under his nose. Not that I'd missed him. And Grianne's feelings for me were nothing new. But it was nice to know I'd impressed her; at least that was something.

'So I agreed to the prohibition,' she carried on calmly. 'I would not attempt to remove you from London, either by death or any other means, so long as you were no hindrance to my queen.' Her mouth turned down. 'Although at the time I was not aware that the vampires were part of the same agreement.'

In other words, someone had tricked her and she really *had* expected me to end up as vamp chow. And what she was telling me confirmed my suspicions about why the fae – as well as the vamps – had agreed to leave me alone for the last ten years. If they hadn't, Grianne *would* have killed me, and deprived all of them of their sidhe prize.

Mentally I thanked Malik and Tavish, whatever their motives. I might have despatched the vamp that attacked Grianne that night, but I'd been hurt, so if she had decided to kill me, I'd have been easy dogmeat. I shuddered; Death by Phouka is *so* not a pleasant thought.

'I suppose the question, Grianne,' I said slowly, 'is why you decided *not* to kill me on my twenty-third birthday, once the prohibition came to an end.'

'You are more valuable alive, child.' She walked on, her dress trailing behind her. 'My queen agreed that I should stay my hand.'

'Thanks,' *I think*. I wondered what 'valuable' meant, and how much longer 'valuable' would last, but I pushed those thoughts away to examine later and got my mind back on the real reason for my meeting with Grianne: information on the sidhe who murdered Tomas.

'So, "None in the Fair Lands has opened any of the three gates".' I half-smiled, as I repeated her words. 'That's very specific information; care to tell me what you're not saying?'

'First, I have a proposition for you.' The wind ruffled her sleek hair. 'My queen is willing to testify to the human authorities on your behalf about this crime.'

'Why?'

'You have succeeded far better than I ever did at rescuing those fae entrapped by the vampires, for which my queen is grateful.' She pointed a black sharp-tipped fingernail at me. 'You know how to think like the humans, you have contacts within the witches and vampires' circles, and amongst the Others, the trolls and the goblins. Your knowledge of London is invaluable.'

'Why, Grianne, I didn't know you cared so much,' I said, then held up a hand at her look of displeasure. 'It's okay, I get the message. There *is* another *bean sidhe* wandering round London, and she's somehow managed to bypass the gates without your queen's knowledge, and now your queen wants me to find her. In exchange she'll get me off the hook. I take it she also wants the sidhe repatriated, rather than being handed over to the authorities?'

'This is so.' She held our her hand. A smooth pebble of gleaming haematite lay in her palm. 'All you need do is find the sidhe and give her this. It will return her to her home in an instant.'

Magic, gotta love it.

I took the pebble; it tingled like electricity against my fingers. I dropped it into my pocket. 'I'm going to need whatever information you've got. All of it, no keeping things back this time, Grianne.'

'So you agree to do this?' She angled her head to look down at me, her eyes gleaming oddly yellow for a moment.

'Isn't that what I just said?' I raised my brows, then sighed at her expectant silence. 'Yes, I agree.'

She smiled, satisfied.

'Good,' I said. 'Now that you're happy, please start talking.'

'Very well, child. The three London gates have not been opened, but another has been recently conjured by a mortal in this part of the world. As yet, my queen has not succeeded in locating the gate's anchor, either here on in her own territory.'

I frowned. 'When you say "anchor", what do you mean?'

'Gates are traditionally opened at specific landmarks, anchored by a combination of earth, air and water magic, which makes them easy to locate and to guard.' The pointed tips of her ears seemed to flatten. 'This gate is anchored by blood magic.'

'Which means?'

'The gate can be opened anywhere, here or in the Fair Lands, by whomsoever controls the blood.'

'So the anchor is the person and not a place?'

'Almost correct, child. The anchor is two persons, the two halves of the gate. It will be a mortal on this side, one who shares a close blood-connection with someone in my queen's court.'

'What sort of blood-connection?' I asked.

'A parent on this side whose child is in the Fair Lands.'

'A mortal parent this side,' I said, putting the pieces together in my mind. 'So you're talking about, what, a stolen child on your side?'

Grianne paled in shock. 'My queen would *never* sanction a stolen child at her court! That would be to break the bargain the human monarch Victoria brokered with all the queens of the Fair Lands on the birth of her first child.'

I wasn't quite sure how many queens of the Fair Lands there were; I'd asked Grianne once and finally got out of her '*more than twenty*' along with '*as many as the magic desires*' when I'd pressed the matter. Both were typical answers when she either didn't know, or didn't want to tell me something.

'Queen Victoria died more than a century ago,' I said, matter-of-fact.

Her shock turned to puzzlement. 'There is still a queen on the throne of England, not a king, is there not?'

'Yes, Queen Elizabeth. The Second.'

'Then the bargain will have been renegotiated on the birth of the current queen's first child.' She waved dismissively. 'The tradition goes back to Boadicea.'

'Okay, so if the child isn't stolen, what is it?'

'A treasured gift given to my queen,' she said softly, 'at a time of great sorrow.'

Ri-ight. I wondered briefly who actually suffered this great sorrow, the queen, or the poor human who was persuaded to give up her child as a gift? Still, there couldn't be many who'd done so, whatever the reason, which would narrow the search. 'So who's the parent?' I asked.

She placed a hand on my arm. 'There is a complication, child.'

Figured! 'Go on.'

'The gate has not been used by either the child or the parent, but by someone unrelated to either of them.'

I frowned. 'But you said the gate needed their blood to make the connection.'

She nodded. 'This is true.'

'So whoever has opened the gate has access to their blood,' I mused. 'Which means they have to be close to the parent, so finding the parent should lead me to the gate-conjurer and then to the sidhe.'

'This quest would be of benefit both to my queen and to

you yourself.' Grianne guided us around a large oil-slicked puddle. 'When you find the anchor, my queen will intercede on your behalf with the human authorities to confirm that you are not responsible for the human's death.'

'Fair enough.'

'There is one more thing you should be aware of.' She hesitated for a moment, then said, 'The *bean sidhe* is not in her right mind.'

'I'd kind of got that by the fact she's murdered someone,' I said drily.

'She may not realise she has done so.' The tips of Grianne's ears twitched. 'It is important you take care that she is not harmed.'

'Fine. The information, Grianne.'

'It is in your pocket, child.' She turned, the air wavered about her, she dropped to all four doggy paws and bounded off, nails clicking sharply along the street.

'Make an exit, why don't you?' I muttered, pulling out a folded sheet of parchment from my jacket pocket. Opening it, I glanced at the name—

—and sighed. Helen Crane, a.k.a Detective Inspector Helen Crane, Head of the Metropolitan Magic Murder Squad, the person in charge of hunting me down for a murder I didn't commit.

Crap. Could my day get any worse?

Chapter Twenty-five

Helen Crane's blood had been used to open a gate between London and the Fair Lands, a gate that led to her child – a child she'd given to the sidhe. A changeling, then. What was I supposed to do, ring her up and say, 'Hi, Helen, I know we're not best buddies or anything, but hey, just heard you've got a long-lost kid, one that's off in the Fair Lands, and guess what? Someone's using your blood connection to let the murderer come through – any ideas who that might be?'

And I could just imagine the superior look on her beautiful, patrician face as she replied, 'Well, that's very interesting, Ms Taylor, but isn't this the murder we suspect you're responsible for? The one I'm investigating? And not that it's relevant, but don't you think I'd know if someone had used my blood?'

Damn. Whichever way I looked at this, it didn't get any better.

Helen liked me even less than Grianne did, and she had even less incentive to listen to me, thanks to our butting heads over Finn – her ex . . . and if anyone would know about DI Helen Crane's long-lost child, her ex should. Okay, so they'd only had a broom marriage, but even so, seven years and seven days isn't exactly ships passing. Asking Finn what he knew about it was a way better option that trying to beard a powerful witch in her police den at Old Scotland Yard. Not to mention I'd been planning on seeing him as soon as anyway.

'*Genevieve!*'

I jerked my head up at the sound of my name and scanned my surroundings. The street was empty, other than the three costumed actors outside the London Bridge Experience. Beyond them, thirty-odd feet away, was Tavish's doorway, still propped open for my return, but Tavish hadn't appeared there, and no one else was near it. I did a quick circle, checking out the steps leading up to the bridge above, and squinting at the bridge parapet—

'*Genevieve,*' the voice came again—

—from the direction of the actors. I frowned at them. The two women were engrossed in their gossiping, but the man was standing off to one side. As I looked, he started shuffling towards me, dragging his feet over the ground. I froze like the proverbial rabbit, pulse jumping in my throat, staring at the sunken eye sockets, the nose eaten away by a sore, the deep cut marring his left cheek . . . and as he got closer, I caught the rotten smell of putrefying flesh. The hairs at the nape of my neck lifted in shock. He wasn't staff; he wasn't an actor playing the part of a plague victim, but the real thing: Scarface, the ghost who'd kept bumping into Finn's magic circle.

Adrenalin finally broke through my fear and I started sprinting for Tavish's doorway on the other side of the bridge.

Scarface jerked and shuffled faster, changing his course to cut me off.

The world narrowed to the gap between ghost and wall.

The women looked up in surprise.

The gap got smaller.

An arm stretched out for me—

A scream lodged in my throat—

—and then I was past him, my lungs burning, nearly there—

—and my foot caught the kerb, sending me sprawling. Sharp grit cut into my palms and my jeans-clad knees. Skeletal fingers snapped at my ankles. I cried out and kicked back, my foot sinking into something soft and fleshy, then I struggled to my feet and, staggering, started running again, crouched over,

not daring to look behind me, desperate to reach the doorway
and safety. I hit the opening at full pelt and felt the magic
resisting me like sticky syrup as bony fingers raked down my
back. I screamed again, threw myself forward, not caring for
anything except getting away, grabbing for something, anything, to stop him dragging me back . . .

I smashed into a hard body and familiar arms wrapped
around me, pulling me through, leaving the clawing fingers
behind. I huddled against him, hiccoughing and trembling
with adrenalin and fear.

'Sssh,' he murmured, his breath a soothing warmth over
the top of my head as his familiar berry scent curled into me
and his reassuring hands stroked my back. 'It's okay, Gen,
I've got you,' and I felt his lips touch my hair.

I pressed closer to him, instinctively seeking the comfort
he was offering, and slipped my arms around his waist, tucking my face into the warm hollow of his neck. He tensed, a
brief moment of wariness, then it was gone and I felt his heart
beating calm and steady next to my own more frantic *thump-
thump*. His heat seeped into me, calming my trembling. Part
of me thought about moving out of his embrace, but I wanted
to be there, wanted him to hold me, wanted to be held because
I was me, not because I was sidhe, not because of my blood,
not because I might break a curse, not because of anything.

A tear rolled down my cheek and I blinked, then before I
could stop it another followed it, and another. I started to pull
away, squeezing my eyes tight, my cheeks burning with the
hot prickle of shame at giving into my stupid, unreasonable
fear, but his arms tightened even more.

'No, Gen,' Finn said quietly, 'let me hold you.'

I stayed, letting him hold me, letting the tears fall and listening to the steady beat of his heart while his hands gentled
my back and his scent surrounded me. Gradually the tears
stopped, and this time when I pulled away he let me, his hands
sliding up to rest on my shoulders.

I rubbed my eyes and face and gave him a rueful smile as I
briefly touched his damp shirt where it lay open at his throat.
'Sorry, I didn't mean to leak all over you.'

'Hey, I'm happy to be leaked on.' He lifted my hands and

turned them over, frowning at the almost healed cuts and grazes on both my palms. 'Want to tell me what's the matter?'

'It's nothing,' I said, slowly pulling my hands from his. 'A ghost spooked me and—Well, you know . . . that's all.'

'Don't, Gen,' he said, moss-green eyes dark and serious. 'Don't brush off what just happened. Talk to me.'

Talk to him? Okay, that was what I'd told Grace I'd do, wasn't it? And while I'd talked to him at Tavish's, it had been about what had happened to me, and not about whatever our relationship was or wasn't . . . only knowing about the curse sort of changed things on the *relationship* front . . . I looked around to see where I was. Pale wood and chrome furniture, sand-coloured carpet, a view out of the window over the cobbled expanse of Covent Garden between the Apple Market and St Paul's Church: Finn's office at Spellcrackers.com.

'I'm not sure what to say,' I said finally, crossing my arms. 'Other than I'm tired. I had a hell of a night, on top of all this murder business there's the *droch guidhe*, then this ghost jumps me and instead of behaving like a rational person, I do the frightened idiot act and run.'

'Straight to me,' he said softly.

Oh—*Oh, that didn't sound good.* Not that I hadn't enjoyed being held, or that I didn't want him, but surely he couldn't think that now the curse was out in the open – or rather, hanging around like an eager invisible matchmaker – that that one little embrace meant I was going to choose him, could he? Didn't he realise that right now I was even less sure about where I stood with him than I'd ever been before? That I needed time to sort things out in my head?

'Of course, straight to you.' I kept my voice even. 'I was planning to talk to you about visiting the florist's lad last night when the ghost did his scary jumping-out-at-me thing.' And what a nicely ironic decision on the magic's part, to bring me straight here so it could throw me into Finn's arms. 'That's what happens when you use a' – *much too* – 'helpful magic door instead of the Underground.'

'The magic didn't bring you here just because it was convenient.' Finn caught my hands within his. 'Gods, Gen, can't you feel the magic, can't you feel how it's changed?

As he said it, I realised I could. The magic was humming quietly in the background, not sparking or urging, as it had between us before, but purring like a self-satisfied cat.

'It's not pushing us together any more' – he raised our joined hands up and kissed my knuckles – 'because it doesn't need to. It knows there's something between us. I told you before, it doesn't happen like this with every fae. Why won't you believe me?'

'Why won't I—?' I took a calming breath; anger wasn't going to help. 'Finn, you've spent the last month keeping your distance when all you did before was keep asking me out. And you wouldn't talk to me, and okay, I admit I wasn't talking to you either, but . . . it makes for a lot of confusion,' *and disappointment*, I added silently, stepping back out of his hold. 'Then there's all this stuff about the curse, and how every male fae in London thinks I'm hot to produce the next generation of . . . whatever. And now I've found out about the prohibition that ended on my twenty-third birthday. From where I'm standing it looks like Tavish was first in line, and then when that didn't work out, it was your turn.' Crap, it sounded so depressingly calculated. 'So you know, telling me that the magic isn't like this for everyone doesn't really make me feel very special, not when you take everything else into consideration.'

'Hell's thorns, Gen, it's not like that—'

'Then what is it like, Finn?' I asked quietly.

'Okay, yes' – he pushed his hand agitatedly through his hair and rubbed his left horn – 'I'll admit the *droch guidhe* was part of the reason the herd put the money up for Spell-crackers and why I was the one to take over the franchise. I'm one of the youngest in the herd, Gen, and I've spent more time among humans than the rest, so when Tavish didn't announce he was courting you after the allotted time, the elders picked me – but, Gen, that doesn't mean I didn't *want* to do this—'

'So I'm right,' I said, trying to ignore the spike of hurt. 'You were second in line.'

'Gen, someone from the herd always was,' he said softly. 'Among the lesser fae, the satyrs are stronger than the dryads or the naiads, always have been. I was just lucky it happened to be me.' He held his hands out. 'Then, okay, you didn't seem quite as keen on the idea, but your magic kept calling to me, so I thought things would work out sooner or later – but then everything else started to happen and things got messed up.'

'Messed up like you discovered I've got 3V and my father's a vampire,' I stated, hating the accusation in my voice, but still feeling rejected by how he'd withdrawn when I'd told him my secret, despite everything else.

'No, messed up because I discovered you weren't in control of the magic,' he said, his own voice firm, 'and between the magic encouraging you and the *salaich sìol*, and you not having dated recently, well, it probably meant you weren't thinking straight.'

In other words, because I hadn't had sex recently, I was supposed to be gagging for it and anyone would do. Fucking sidhe sex myth; it was the stupid reason behind most of my current problems.

'And I didn't want to take advantage,' he finished quietly.

So Grace was sort of right about why he'd backed off; not that his 'not wanting to take advantage' made me feel any better, not now.

'I admit the *salaich sìol* and your parentage came as a surprise,' he carried on. 'The elders didn't tell me about either, and I haven't asked them if they even know. But as you said yourself, it's not really relevant: you're sidhe, and your child will have whatever genetics you want it to. It's a choice the sidhe have always made when they breed with Others.' A muscle twitched along his jaw. 'All I was supposed to do was get your agreement to the child being satyr – which was okay when I thought you understood what was going on, but then I realised you didn't, so I backed off.'

A hollow, empty feeling settled beneath my breastbone. I didn't know if I wanted a Happy Ever After with Finn – or anyone else – right now, but I had wanted a chance at Happy for Now with him. But the whole curse solution thing turned all that upside down; Happy for Now didn't work when it was my child-bearing ability he wanted and not just me. Not to mention it all sounded even more depressingly premeditated now – particularly the fact that the whole set-up with Finn and Spellcrackers had been organised by his herd so he'd be in with a shot at getting me pregnant. I stared out of the window, looking at the heavy, grey rain clouds darkening the October sky, locked the hurt and disappointment away and tried to look at it logically. Okay, with the curse hanging over their heads, I could understand why – hell, if breaking the curse involved just me, then I wouldn't even have to think about it – but it would mean bringing a child into the world for something other than its natural purpose. The magic is capricious and fickle at the best of times; throw in a curse and who knew what grief the child would have to bear.

And none of it the child's own choosing.

It wasn't a decision to be taken lightly.

Or by a committee.

And yeah, the whole philosophising bit still didn't stop me being as pissed off as hell about the broodmare part I was supposed to play. Or the fact that Finn had agreed to it all before he'd even met me—

'Fuck, Finn.' I curled my hands into fists. 'Doesn't it bother you that they pimped you out as a stud?'

'I'm a *satyr*, Gen!' he said, exasperated. 'We're fertility fae, it's what we do! We court whoever the herd elders decide – that's the way it is. But if I hadn't wanted to do this, either before or after I met you, I could've said no; it's not like I'm the only satyr in London.' His face hardened. 'And I'm not the only fae in London either.'

Yeah, and didn't I know it, what with dryads chasing me, and the early morning wake-up call from Randy Ricou.

'So what you're telling me,' I said slowly, 'is that I have to choose.'

'Yes.'

That didn't leave any wiggle-room for doubt, did it?

'Look, I want you to choose me, Gen.' He clasped my shoulders, hope sparking in his eyes. 'But I saw the way you looked at Tavish, so' – his eyes turned flat and bleak – 'anyway, whoever you choose, you need to do it soon, otherwise the dryads will try and make the choice for you.'

'That's not a choice, Finn, that's a *fait accompli*.'

'Exactly. That's what I'm saying.' His hands tightened almost painfully on my shoulders. 'Once you've made your choice and it's official, then the dryad problem will go away.'

'No, you don't understand; it's not the dryads doing the

kidnapping and whatever that's the *fait accompli*, it's the whole thing. Having a child should be *my* choice, *mine and the father's*, not a group decision taken by people I've never even met who want me to pick out a magical sperm donor from a line-up. But none of you will give me that choice, will you?'

'No,' he said, quietly, desolation echoing in his voice. 'Not when it means we die out.'

I pulled away from him and sat down, rubbing my hands over my face, a sick, frightened feeling in my stomach. I didn't want this, didn't want the responsibility. Why couldn't it be someone else's? Why me? But of course the answer was easy; it was only me because I happened to be handy, no other reason.

'Gen,' Finn said sadly, crouching down in front of me, 'even if all of London's fae did give you that choice, I'm not sure the magic would.'

'What?' I looked up, startled.

'Why do you think it keeps pushing us together like this?' He took hold of my hands and the magic hummed as if in agreement. 'So far it's just being . . . helpful, but it could change, you know that. The magic wants to survive as much as any of us, and it's not just the magic dying that's killing us; if we *fade*, so will the magic.'

My mother had *faded*.

My father found my mother at a fertility rite, got her pregnant, and then after I was born, she'd lost so much blood, he couldn't stop her from *fading*. Or so the story goes. I'd believed it as a child, but now I realised no sidhe would willingly agree to have a vampire's child – *got her pregnant* was just a pleasant euphemism. And I was the result. And while I might be my father's daughter, I was still the valuable commodity he'd been determined to produce when he'd raped my mother – still the valuable commodity he'd traded to a psychotic vampire.

It's not a story that dreams of happy families are made from.

Or one that had ever made me want to have my own children, even without a curse to contend with. But if the magic decided to *encourage* me . . . Even if London's fae left me alone, I might not be able to trust myself to make the right choice, a prospect that terrified me even more than everything else.

I looked down at where he clasped my hands. 'What about the child?' I said softly.

'It'll be a child, Gen. It'll be loved and cared for, whoever its father is. You'll see to that.' His expression turned hopeful again. 'Can we at least talk about it, maybe try and work out where we go from here?'

Part of me wanted to, but another part knew Finn's 'where do we go from here' was him asking for a decision about him. And I wasn't yet ready to make that decision – not to mention the real question hanging over me: what would happen if the curse attached itself to the child? That wasn't one Finn – or, I suspected anyone else, for that matter – could or would answer. And magic aside, while they'd all got it into their heads that a sidhe-born child would break the curse, I wasn't convinced . . . But no matter where that left me, Finn or any of them, it wasn't going to be resolved here and now.

Now, I was here to ask about another child: Helen's changeling child, in the hope that the answer would help me find the sidhe who'd murdered Tomas.

I pulled my hands from Finn's and straightened in the chair. 'What happened when you and Helen went to see the florist's lad last night?'

'Hell's thorns, Gen! Why won't you talk to me?'

'Because I'm not ready to.' I pressed my hands flat on my knees, focusing on the snags in my jeans where I'd fallen over, keeping everything else – fear, hurt, anger and frustration – all bottled up. 'And because right now,' I carried on, 'we have other things to worry about, like finding the sidhe who's already killed once. What happened with the boy last night?'

'Okay,' he said, almost to himself, 'okay, if you're not ready, we can do this later.' His brows drew together into a thoughtful frown. 'The florist's boy, yes . . . we went to see him, only he wasn't there. His dad said he was off to some concert or other with a mate. Helen's got someone checking into it.'

Damn. The boy was a dead end. Now for the other question. I kept my gaze on my hands, not wanting to see his face.

'I've just seen the phouka,' I said, my voice neutral. 'Helen gave a child to the sidhe. A changeling.'

He inhaled sharply, then he rose and retreated to sit behind his desk.

I looked up at him. His face was closed, all expression banished, leaving just a handsome mask. As I had expected. A dull pain twisted inside me, then I had a sudden – horrible – thought: was it his child?

But his next words denied it. 'That is not for me to discuss.' His voice was as blank as his face.

'Well, you're going to have to discuss it, Finn,' I said, determined. 'Someone's used her blood and her connection to the child to open a gate between here and the Fair Lands. That same someone has let another sidhe into London.'

'She wouldn't do that.' A line creased between his brows. 'In fact, I'm not even sure she'd know how to.'

'I'm not saying she would, but it's her blood, Finn. Who else would have access to it?'

He grabbed his phone, pressed a button and clamped it to his ear. After a few seconds, he asked, 'Helen, when was the last time you used blood in a spell?'

I pressed my lips together; nice to see his ex was on speed-dial, and that she answered him almost faster than the speed of light.

'No, I need the answer first, then I'll tell you.' He snagged a pen and pulled his pad towards him. 'That was the Seek-Out spell you did at Old Scotland Yard, wasn't it? And before that?' He listened. 'More than a month ago, right. And what about the Witches' Council Blood Bank?'

I raised my eyebrows. The council kept a Blood Bank for spells?

'Okay.' His face turned thoughtful. 'Who would have access to it?' He scribbled a couple of names on the pad in front of him. 'Yes.' He met my gaze briefly and admitted, 'She's with me.'

Damn, he just had to tell her, didn't he? On the other hand, he couldn't lie outright, and if he'd been evasive she'd have twigged.

'No, I will not – and neither will you, not until after I ring you back, okay?' His knuckles whitened as he gripped his pen. 'Helen, it's to do with what happened in the past, with the changeling.' Another longer pause, then, 'Five minutes, no more, and I'll phone you back.'

He thumbed the phone off and looked at me, his eyes unreadable. 'She says there's no blood stored at the police station; they use it too infrequently. They call in a police doctor as and when they need it. So there's no possibility of anyone stealing it from there.'

'And the witches' Blood Bank?'

'The council takes donations from all working witches for use in the more complicated spells; it's easier than trying to get them all together at casting time. Helen gives once a month.'

I could see the benefits. Most Witches' Council spells took a whole coven – thirteen witches – which was why they were so damned expensive. 'When did she last donate?' I asked.

He tapped his pen. 'A week ago yesterday.'

Yes! Now we were getting somewhere. I jerked my head towards the scribbles in front of him. 'Who's got access?'

He flipped the pad round to face me. 'These three are the administrators.'

I didn't recognise the first two, but the third— 'Sandra Wilcox is one of my neighbours.'

'I know, and she's also a highly respected member of the Witches' Council, and not only that, she's over eighty years old. Somehow I can't see her stealing blood and persuading a sidhe to kill someone.'

'She's also a paranoid old witch who's been campaigning like mad for the last month to get me evicted. Can Helen check and see if her blood's still there?'

'It won't be. Blood is destroyed if it's not used within five days. It loses its potency.'

'Destroyed by the administrators, no doubt,' I said drily. 'So the old witch could've used it and no one would be any the wiser.' I stood. 'I'm going over there to find out what she knows.'

'Gen, I'm really not sure that's a good idea. Let me fill Helen in and she can arrange to talk to her.'

'C'mon, Finn,' I sighed, 'no way am I going to let my fate hang on two witches, not when both of them are fully-paid-up members of the Get Rid of the Sidhe Club. And Helen's got every reason to keep this under wraps, 'cause she's hardly likely to want giving up her child to the sidhe to become public knowledge, is she?'

'Helen will do her job—'

'Phone her then, Finn, if that's what you want. I know you have faith in her. But I don't, so I'm going over there now, and if that means a whole division of police turn up, so much the better. That way there'll be no sweeping things under the carpet.'

I turned on my heel and left.

Chapter Twenty-six

Five days isn't a long time to be away from home, but I'd missed it. Shoving that less-than-cheerful thought aside, I looked, and *looked*, around the communal hallway and up the stairs, checking for any new spells that might be lying in wait. Nothing. I pushed the main door shut without activating the Ward; the police needed to get in, after all. Taking a deep breath, I inhaled beeswax and faint musty earth – the scents of the goblin cleaner and Mr Travers, my landlord – almost buried beneath the less pleasant reek of Witch Wilcox's garlic and bleach-laced Back-off spell: garlic for vamps, bleach for fae, so Tavish had told me.

The spell was going to be a problem. How was I supposed to knock on the old witch's door if I couldn't get near it? Still, determination had to count for something. And if the sidhe was with her, better I got her back to Grianne before the police turned up, even if it meant I'd probably spend the next few days sitting in a cell waiting for Grianne's queen to sort it all.

I ran quietly up the stairs and stopped a couple of steps shy of the third-floor landing and *looked* again.

Sure enough, the anemone spell's violet-coloured tentacles undulated over the landing. As I studied it, the dark gaping mouth in the centre of the anemone thing puckered up to a small round hole and then expanded, blowing me something that looked disturbingly like a kiss. Damn! The spell had been hanging around long enough to develop a sense of humour! I really hated it when the magic did that – I usually ended up being the butt of its jokes.

'Well, if it isn't the little sex-deprived *bean sidhe*,' a rough voice drawled. 'We've been waiting for you to turn up. Got ourselves a nice little party all planned.'

Adrenalin flooded my body as I looked up towards the voice. A male, a purple bandana tied round his clipped head, was leaning over the banister; he was the dryad who'd chased me from outside The Clink museum: Bandana. He grinned, revealing teeth stained brown from bark-chews, his eyes glinting the anaemic yellow of dying autumn leaves.

I went for the important question, keeping my voice light and slightly bored. 'Who's invited to this party then?'

'A couple of close friends.' He rubbed his jaw, leaving streaks of pale green where he'd scratched away his surface skin. Then he leaned further out, looking down through the narrow gap that separated the stairs from the landing. 'I think you might have met them in passing.'

I looked down quickly. The lanky turban-headed dryad was making his way up towards me, his red turban bobbing with each long stride, and following him was a straw Panama above a pair of wide pinstripe-suited shoulders. Yep, friends all right; though not mine, obviously. Panama stopped to catch his breath, then squinted up.

'Hi.' He gave me a fat-fingered wave. 'Nowhere for you to run to now, *bean sidhe*,' he said, much too happily. 'I liked the blonde bimbo look better, but then, this isn't about looks, is it?'

'Not where you're concerned, Shorty,' I said sweetly.

His face screwed up in anger and he started thudding up the stairs again. Red Turban hooked a long arm round Shorty's stocky neck and yanked him to a halt. 'Cool it,' he said in a surprisingly high voice. 'The *bean sidhe* is not to be damaged, remember.'

Good to know they planned to pull their punches. Shame for them I had no intention of reciprocating the go-easy policy.

Red Turban released Shorty and looked up at me, his expression cold. Then he patted Shorty on the back and said, 'I can show you plenty of other ways to get maximum enjoyment out of her body, whatever it looks like.'

Not if I can help it, you won't! I thought, determined. Red Turban's twin popped his blue-turbaned head over the banister above me and gave me an equally cold stare. Ambushed! How lucky was I? Then another dryad – this one in a yellow beanie hat – sneered as he hung over the banister next to Blue Turban and Bandana. So, five of them in total.

A low rustle, like leaves shifting in the wind, filled the stairwell. Crap, now they were talking together – not that I needed to understand what they were saying to work out their objective, not when they'd got me cornered and outnumbered.

This was *so* not good.

My gut twisted with nervous tension as I tried to come up with some sort of plan. The police would be here soon, and hopefully Finn. If I could hold the dryads off until they arrived . . . I had two options – up or down – and neither looked promising, not when *up* meant getting past the witch's anemone spell—

I turned to face the two below me and the rustling rose in volume. Red Turban tapped Shorty on his Panama hat again and up they came, Red Turban's long legs eating the stairs two at a time, Shorty puffing red-faced behind him.

A creaking noise above had me itching to look up, but I ignored it, concentrating on the two below. I was only going to get one chance at this; either it worked, or I was in serious trouble. I grabbed the banister and braced myself. Time stretched as I took a calming breath.

Red Turban was seven steps away . . .

A double thud like the *duhm duhm* of a heavy heartbeat sounded behind me. I pricked up my ears, hoping for a third, but it didn't come. Shit. I'd hoped all three of them would jump or run down together, but it looked like the good luck wasn't all on my side.

Five steps . . . Red Turban paused, a puzzled look in his maple-red eyes, no doubt wondering why I was ignoring the two at my back.

I swallowed. He'd find out any second—

Right on cue the screaming started: a high-pitched noise like storm winds shrieking through winter trees.

Two dryads down, three to go.

Red Turban's eyes flicked to the scene behind me. His momentary distraction was what I'd been waiting for and I jumped down two steps and used the banister to propel me up. As I leapt I kicked out and jammed my feet into his chest, and it made a satisfying crack like branches breaking. One good thing about dryads: hit them with enough force and their bones splinter like brittle wood. Air puffed like dust between Red Turban's surprised lips and he fell backwards, long fingers grabbing for the banister – but he missed and, arms flailing, knocked into Shorty like a tall, lanky domino, sending the smaller dryad barrelling back down the stairs where he crumpled in a heap on the landing below. I landed back on my own feet with a thump that jarred my whole body and tightened my grip on the banisters.

Three down, two to go.

Red Turban shook his head and started to pull himself up; I kicked out again, swinging my foot into his temple. Another gunshot-loud crack reverberated above the screeching dryads behind me and Red Turban collapsed. This time he stayed down, limp and still. Then the screeching cut out, leaving behind only silence.

Only one dryad left now.

Then my good luck ran out.

A disturbance in the air behind me warned me, but too late as thick muscled arms clamped like a steel trap around my torso and lifted me from my feet. 'I'm impressed, *bean sidhe*,' Bandana said in his rough drawl, his breath hot and moist against my skin. 'I like a girl with a bit of fight in her. It makes the sex more interesting.' He shoved his hips forward, pushing his erection against my butt. 'And you're a fucking feisty one.'

I'll give you fucking feisty, I thought, jerking my head forward then ramming it back as hard as I could. It connected with a gratifying crunch as my skull shattered his nose. He let out a gurgled roar and staggered back, falling, still hugging me to him like I was his favourite blow-up doll. He landed on his back and the fall vibrated through me, stealing what little breath I had left. We slithered and bumped our way down the stairs, coming to an abrupt stop as we crashed into Red Turban's unconscious body.

I struggled, clawing at his arms, kicking my heels into his knees and shins. He scissored his legs over my thighs, locking my body against his. I reached back and grabbed his ears and jerked my head back again and there was another loud crack as his cheekbone splintered. He grunted, increasing the pressure round my chest, squeezing out what little breath I had left. I had to stop him before he broke something or I passed out. I slid my hands round his head, searching for his eyes, and jammed my thumbs hard into the soft sockets, praying that would be enough to make him let me go. He yelled furiously and his arms tightened even more around my chest and I felt something break inside me. A sharp pain pierced my right side as whiplike cords snaked round my wrists and yanked my hands away, up and back above our heads. More thin branches banded my neck, constricting and choking my throat. I bucked against him, panic battering in my mind, as his branches hardened and trapped me immobile against him.

'Keed stihl, you studid ditch,' he growled, his words almost unintelligible. 'Dode wad you stragglin' yoursel' jus' yet.' He jerked his arm and the vicious hot pain spiked in my side again. I screamed, but the corded branches round my throat snapped tighter, choking me, and the edges of my vision started dimming . . .

. . . then the ceiling blurred back into focus and the pain in my side spiked with each intake of breath. I lay there trembling with the effort of keeping the panic away.

'You fuckin' droke my dose,' he said. Out the corner of my eye I saw him tentatively touch his face. 'You'll pay for dat.'

'Should . . . be an . . . improvement,' I gasped. Whatever happened to not damaging me?

'Ditch,' he shouted and jerked his arm around my chest again.

I panted through the pain until it dialled back to an agonising throb, telling myself it was stupid to antagonise him while he had the upper hand. He sniffed and snuffled against my cheek and I could feel his magic brushing against my skin; he was trying to speed up his healing. Crap – yet more magic I couldn't do. As we lay there, other smaller discomforts started to make themselves felt: the roughness of the bark around my wrists and throat, the ache in my shoulders from where my arms were pulled awkwardly above my head, the prickly sisal carpet on the backs of my hands. At least he was underneath me; the stairs had to be way more uncomfortable for him to lie on, and if he wanted to try anything else, he was going to have to release either my legs or the hold his branches had on me. I stared blindly up at the ceiling. Of course, he wasn't the only one on his back, and he could hold me still with just one arm . . .

The panic threatened to boil over again . . .

I gritted my teeth, told my mind not to go there.

A rustling whisper echoed through the hallway, and I realised he was talking . . . or calling for reinforcements, maybe?

And speaking of back-up, where were the police, and Finn, or even my neighbours? Helen and her crew had had enough time to get here twice over by now. And it wasn't like the dryads had been the quietest of attackers: right now I'd have happily welcomed the most unfriendly of witches with open arms.

'So, we're going to stay here like this until one of my neighbours comes home, or what?' I said, aiming for unconcern, but the tremor in my voice meant I didn't quite make it.

'Dode worry, do one's gedding in, *bean sidhe*,' he said, and patted my cheek. 'Dot wid de Tank spell we pud on the building.'

I swallowed, trying to ignore the branches digging into my neck. A Tank spell – whatever the hell that was – presumably stamped out the possibility that someone – *anyone* – had noticed something and might be coming to rescue me.

'Bud while we're waiding for more of by frieds' – his hand fumbled at the waistband of my jeans; my gut twisted with dread – 'you can keed still and waid with me.' His arm round my ribs squeezed, shooting sharp, hot pain through my chest. 'Or I'll dock you out agaid, okay?'

There was no way I wanted to be unconscious again, not even for a fraction of a second. I forced myself to stay still, to think. He had to be a willow; they were the only ones whose branches grew fast and long like whips. But those branches couldn't be all real: they had to have some magic in them, didn't they?

'We mide as well use de time well.' His legs clamped harder around my thighs as he struggled to pull the zipper on my tight jeans. 'Now, remember, *bean sidhe*, keep still.'

I *looked*, and saw the magic flowing around me in multi-coloured currents, swirling and eddying like different strands of paint mixed into a jar of murky water: lacklustre greens and feral yellows merged into dull oranges, deep reds faded into sickly violets and brackish purple, and through it all sparkled tiny motes of gold. Crap, even I was leaking magic. I couldn't see where his magic started and mine or the witch's anemone's ended. What would happen if I tried *cracking* it? No, that was a really stupid, mind-blowing idea . . . Wasn't it?

'I always wanded to be a daddy.' He flattened his hand over my bare stomach, rubbing it. 'I'm going to plant my seed in here and watch it grow.' I didn't bother telling him he needed my willing consent if he wanted me pregnant. I just prayed he'd stay *thinking* about his future fatherhood and wouldn't try and do anything about it yet. At least in this position it wouldn't be possible; he'd have to let me up, which would give me a chance—

—a whiplike branch scratched across my stomach, pushing and slithering down the front of my jeans.

'Shame we can'd make new shoots the fun way,' he murmured against my cheek. 'But dis way works just as good.'

The thin branch poked into my briefs.

No fucking way!

Anger rose like a golden tide inside me . . . and I reached out, *focused* on the magic, pushed all my will into it, and *cracked* it—

—and the world exploded.

Chapter Twenty-seven

An angel smiled down at me out of a cool silver-gilt mist that twinkled with rainbow lights blurring in and out of focus. A silver halo hovered above the long curls of her pale-gold hair, and a bridal confection of silk, satin and lace wrapped her slender form. The air smelled of cinnamon, and oranges and sweetened vanilla. She held a star-tipped wand in one small hand, and offered her other hand to me. I stared at it, oddly bemused. Her fingernails were painted different colours: blue, green, yellow, red and black. They didn't go with the rest of Angel. Was I dreaming, or hallucinating? Maybe I'd died and heaven really was just like the Christmas cards. I squeezed my eyes shut. But when I opened them she was still there, still smiling, still holding out her hand. I peered through the mist, trying to discern if the filmy image at her back was actually wings or not. Her delicate face creased in a frown as she turned and looked behind her.

'Am I dead?' I asked, my voice croaking like a strangled frog's.

She turned back to me, bewilderment making her look even younger. 'I don't know,' she whispered. The rainbow lights slowly stopped blinking and faded away. 'Do you feel dead?'

I thought about it. It felt like my hands had been ripped off. I held them up in front of my face, vaguely concerned. Nope, still attached, though as scratched and bloody as if I'd fought my way out of a thorn thicket. If I squinted, I still had the right number of fingers. My throat felt like I'd swallowed a cactus, and when I touched it, my fingers came away sticky with blood and bits of green flaky stuff, while my head felt like a bad-tempered troll had stomped on it and turned it into squashed mush. But compared to the spiky pain in my ribs, all that was a minor torment. I decided if I was dead, I hurt too much for this to be heaven; so it was more likely the other place.

'But they don't have angels in hell, do they?' I murmured, or rather, croaked again.

Her expression turned mutinous and she wrinkled her nose. 'Angels bite you if you misbehave.'

I blinked. Not quite the answer I was expecting.

She bent at the waist and ran a strand of my hair through her fingers. 'Your hair looks like dragon's breath, all pretty golds and coppers. Can you spin it into smoke?'

Her eyes came into focus, beautiful pale-gold eyes with vertical cat-like pupils, and I realised she wasn't an angel, but something I'd never seen before – at least, not without a mirror.

She was sidhe.

The mush in my mind started to rearrange itself into something more lucid.

Was this *the* sidhe? Tomas' murderer? She had to be; there couldn't be two of them in London, that would be too much of a coincidence. Only the eyes I stared into were as wide and guileless as a child's – but she was sidhe fae, and while she might look to be in her late teens, she could be anything from that to – well, *centuries* old.

But not only were her eyes blank; her mind wasn't at home behind them either.

'No, I can't spin it into smoke,' I said slowly.

She pursed her lips in disappointment as she straightened. 'Cecily can, and she can make pictures in the smoke, like the moon and the sun and the stars and even mountains and castles.' She formed the shapes with her hands as she spoke.

I struggled to my feet, my hand clamped to my right side. 'What's your name?' I asked.

'*No names, no shame, us dames are all the same,*' she trilled in a high falsetto, and grasping the long silk skirts of her dress she curtseyed before dancing away through the mist.

'Fine,' I muttered, pinching the bridge of my nose, trying to banish my headache. What had Grianne said? Something about being careful with her when I found her . . .

I sighed; I was beginning to see what she meant. I lifted my head and looked around, trying to work out where I'd ended up.

The silver mist was dissipating, leaving only a fine haze in the air, and I realised I hadn't gone anywhere; I was still on the third floor of my building, only now I was standing in the middle of the landing, my jeans half round my hips and my stomach covered with bloody scratches like my hands. I winced at the pain in my side as I zipped up my jeans. The landing looked the same as before I'd *cracked* the magic – well, almost, if you ignored the jagged opening that now replaced the doorway leading into Witch Wilcox's flat. And the wood shavings that blanketed the landing and stairs.

There were a couple of mounds under the sawdust, which I took to be the dryads laid out by the purple anemone Back-off spell. I looked down the stairs: yep, two more mounds, a.k.a. Bandana and Red Turban, and at the bottom of the stairs I could just make out the top of Shorty's Panama, covered with its own sprinkling of wood shavings.

It was a lot of sawdust: more than one wooden door and frame could account for, so I guessed some of it had come from the dryads themselves. But *cracking* the magic – which had to be why I looked like I'd been pulled through a thorn-hedge backwards *and* frontwards – didn't look like it had killed them, for their bodies hadn't *faded* away to nothing. But I didn't plan on playing Florence Nightingale; Bandana had been calling for reinforcements and I wanted Angel out of here before they or the police arrived. Any injuries the dryads had, they fucking well deserved.

I turned back to Angel, who was giggling with excitement as she lifted handfuls of the shavings and threw them into the air and pointed her wand at them; they didn't fall to the

ground, just spun around her in dizzying circles, like bees
round a honey pot.

Time for her to go home. I wiped my scratched hands on
my T-shirt, cleaning off the blood, then, careful of my ribs,
I unzipped my jacket pocket and pulled out the smooth haematite stone Grianne had given me. It hummed as I held it in
my palm, and I felt the faint noise vibrating down my spine.
I waved to Angel, trying to catch her attention, and she lifted
her voluminous skirts and skipped over to me, kicking up
shavings to add to those already flying through the air.

I gave her a coaxing smile, the same one I'd offer a child.
'Would you like to go and see Cecily?' I asked, reasonably
sure that Cecily must be some sort of carer, or keeper.

'Yes!' she cried, clapping her hands together, a big beam of
a smile on her face, then, just as I was congratulating myself
on an easy success, she dashed past me back into Witch Wilcox's flat.

I sighed and followed her through the jagged opening into
a short, windowless corridor. The metallic scent of old blood
hit me, pricking goosebumps over my skin, and I hurried past
two closed doors and stumbled into a living room.

Except the 'living' part was now a misnomer.

Daylight filtered around the half-drawn curtains. All the
furniture was pushed back against the walls and a multitude
of dirty-white candles had burnt down to misshapen blobs of
wax. The air in the room was thick and heavy, as if something
unseen lurked there. A shudder crawled down my spine. In
the centre of the room was a large expanse of blue plastic with
a circle marked out in red sand. Inside the circle lay a naked
body, diminished by old age.

I took a careful step forward and then another until the
toes of my trainers were just short of the red sand. The stench
of blood mixed with the sour smell of sulphur and death-
expelled bodily excretions hit the back of my throat, making
me gag. A gaping wound ran from just under the breastbone to
the crotch. I wasn't going to check, but I was betting the heart
and other internal organs had been removed.

Witch Wilcox wasn't going to be campaigning to get me
evicted any more.

I clenched my fists; the black pebble buzzed anxiously

against my palm. I might not have liked the old woman or her obsessive paranoia, but all of me wished she was still around to complain. At least then she wouldn't be dead.

'Can we go and see Cecily now?' Angel appeared from a door on the other side of the room and skipped around the outside of the circle. Her dress pulled itself in and away, even though she didn't seem to notice anything odd – but then, she'd seen it before. She stopped in front of me and smiled happily. 'I want to show her my new books.' She held up half a dozen children's comics: Cinderella smiled merrily at me from the cover of her *Christmas Spectacular*, complete with rainbow twinkling lights, meringue bride's dress, and silver halo. Now I knew where Angel's outfit came from.

I opened my mouth to ask something, but stopped as Angel looked over my shoulder, her pale-gold eyes widening, her pupils dilating in fear, her bottom lip quivering.

'Genevieve.' The woman's dulcet voice made me flinch as I recognised it. 'I had hoped you two wouldn't meet until much later, but *que sera, sera*.'

Fuck, she was just who I didn't need right now!

I grabbed Angel's hand, dropped Grianne's shiny pebble into her palm and closed her fingers round it. 'Travel safe,' I murmured as she disappeared in a bright blinding blaze of silver-grey light.

Typical Grianne: flashy and efficient as ever.

And no doubt Angel was safely back in the Fair Lands before I'd even had time to blink.

I turned, still a little blinded by the dazzle, and said calmly, 'Hello, Hannah.' Obviously Malik hadn't had time to deal with her yet – that whole 'vamps don't do daylight' thing has its disadvantages – and just as obviously, Hannah had replaced the vamp-groupie look with a Chanel-inspired navy and white suit. She was also standing in the doorway, blocking my escape route. But though she might be a sorcerer, physically, she was still only human. A human I could take. Her magic? I wasn't so sure about that.

'Figured you'd turn up sooner or later after seeing your sorcerer's handiwork here,' I said drily.

'I'm impressed, Genevieve.' Her perfectly outlined lips smiled, but the expression in her coffee-brown eyes was more about smiting me on the spot. 'I wasn't aware you were capable of Transportation spells.'

I shrugged. 'You learn something new every day.'

'Ah. Well, it must be time for your next lesson then.' She stepped aside. 'Joseph?'

Malik's doctor friend stepped into the room, his owl-like eyes blinking rapidly. He lifted his arm and aimed a gun straight at me . . .

Oh shit.

. . . and a sharp pain pricked my chest. I looked down to see a steel dart embedded in the swell of my left breast, then there were three darts, then too many to count as the world fractured around me into tiny unrecognisable pieces and I felt myself falling . . .

Chapter Twenty-eight

'Is she dead, Doctor?' I heard Hannah demand.

I opened my eyes and found myself looking into the masked face of Doctor Joseph Wainwright, a.k.a. the bastard who had just shot me with a tranq gun. I glared at him, but he didn't appear to notice, just carried on shining a bright pencil light into my pupils. I squeezed my lids tight shut, then opened them again, struggling to see beyond the blinding spot of light into the candlelit darkness that closed in behind his head. I could make out a brick roof arching overhead. On one side there was a high bricked-up archway with an open wooden door at one end, on the other a mural of some sort. I squinted, and a painting of a barren landscape with a distant, rocky mountain came into focus.

I frowned as I recognised the place from Hannah's big-screen memory of Rosa lying in agonised state while the Earl killed the Ancient One. I was in the sorcerer's lair, wherever that was, and no doubt the stone slab I was lying on was her proverbial sacrificial altar.

How lucky could I get?

Of course, I'd be even luckier if I could figure a way off the table, preferably before the sacrifice bit happened.

I slowly winked at the doctor.

He ignored me.

I stuck my tongue out at him.

Still nothing.

I realised he really couldn't see me; I was having some out-of-body experience. Panic started bubbling and I pushed it down. Panicking wasn't going to help.

'Doctor?' Hannah's imperious question came again. 'Is Genevieve dead?'

'No, not quite.' He adjusted his mask and looked at something next to him. 'There's still some brain activity.'

I followed his gaze. He'd got me hooked up to his machines again. One showed a faint green line winging across its screen, the other, the heart monitor maybe – I checked; yep, more electrodes stuck to my chest – wasn't flashing up any numbers.

Damn. My heart wasn't beating. And nothing hurt any more.

Not a good sign.

It was beginning to look like Doctor Joseph's diagnosis was wrong. Mentally, I cheered him on. I might not be sure if he was a goodie or baddie, but if he was saving my life, he had my vote – even if he was only trying to revive me so Hannah could reverse the situation at her leisure. At least that way, I had a chance.

'Hurry it along, Doctor, we're on a tight schedule here,' Hannah said impatiently.

I turned towards her and she didn't notice; apparently seeing ghosts or spirits wasn't one of her sorcerous powers. She stood almost within touching distance, dressed in a floor-sweeping black velvet robe, heavily embroidered in red with symbols I didn't recognise and tied at the throat with matching red cord that ended in foot-long tassels. The outfit had to be her sorcerer's robe, but it looked more like she'd dressed herself up in a pair of recycled curtains.

'I'm going as quickly as I can,' Joseph said, his voice filled with nervous tension. 'Her metabolism is faster and more resistant than a human's. And I have to balance out the morphine with the tranquilliser, they're working against—'

'Oh, do shut up and get on with it,' she snapped. 'Time is of the essence here.'

'Why don't you just stab the sidhe? It would be quicker,' said another voice from somewhere near my feet.

Stab me? Wasn't the doctor trying to save me?

I sat bolt upright, staring at the plump, curly-haired woman who was standing there. She popped a liquorice torpedo into her mouth from the white bag she was holding. Her robe was identical to Hannah's, but where Hannah looked almost regal, she just looked dowdy; something not helped by the sullen expression on her fat face. Ex-Police Constable Janet Sims: my favourite security guard in Covent Garden. No wonder she wanted to stab me.

Only I didn't think she needed to. With a sort of horrified inevitability I looked down at myself. I might be sitting up, but my body wasn't sitting up with me. It was laying stockstill, eyes closed, naked except for the electrodes and a funnylooking cap with a thicket of wires trailing from it back to the first machine. My face, neck, arms, chest and stomach were covered in scratches from my run-in with the dryads.

Okay, looked like the out-of-body experience had escalated to worse. I was dead – and not only that, I was a ghost too.

Fuck. I clenched my fists and built the wall higher against my panic.

My body was still there, and that meant I wasn't truly gone, just separated.

So all I needed to do was to work out how to pull myself together again.

'I told you, Janet' – Hannah's tone was long-suffering – 'she might be sidhe fae, and she might heal quickly, but I can't wait for that. I need to use the body straight away to get the Fabergé egg out of the bank.'

Use my body?

'It's bad enough I'm going to be walking round flatchested' – Hannah grimaced – 'and looking like I've been attacked by a litter of angry cats without being incapacitated by a knife-wound in the heart. Although if this so-called doctor doesn't hurry up, it'll be his heart with a knife in it. Are you listening, Doctor?'

'Yes.' He pushed his glasses back up his nose, his finger trembling.

My mind clicked into place: so Hannah was planning on using the equivalent of my Disguise spell – except *I* was the one being evicted from my body, and *she* was gong to be the one walking round in my skin.

Fuck.

Janet walked up to Hannah and looked down at my prone self. 'But I should be able to heal you now I've got Granny's powers,' she pouted. 'Granny was always good at healing things.' She rubbed her hands together eagerly. 'That way I get to stab the sidhe slut here. I've always wanted to do that.'

No way was I going to let this happen – only I couldn't see how to stop it.

'Genny.'

I jerked towards the whisper, but couldn't see anything.

'Janet, dear,' Hannah sniffed, 'you've had Granny's magic for a week now. So far, you've managed, what?' She ticked them off on her fingers. 'An invisibility shield that reflects in shop windows, an exploding flour-storm, and whatever that disgusting smelly spell was that you attached to Granny's door – a spell which, incidentally, did nothing at all to stop dear Genevieve from getting into Granny's flat while you were out buying children's comics and nail polish.'

Her words registered in the part of my mind not panicking: *Dumpy Janet* was Witch Wilcox's granddaughter? The one who was staying with her?

'Fairycakes kept on whingeing and crying. It was bugging me.' Janet's mouth turned down. 'And it's not my fault the dryads were waiting for the sidhe slut.'

'Of course it was,' Hannah said briskly. 'The only reason they were chasing her was because you couldn't stop that addle-brained sidhe from killing your baker boyfriend. All you had to do was get her to bespell him, just enough to put pressure on Genevieve, but oh no, you decide to have your own little orgy, Genevieve ends up wanted for murder, London's fae think she's ready to break their curse and you put all my plans at risk.'

'Genny,' came the whisper again, closer this time, and a small, cold hand crept into mine and tugged. I looked down

into the big dark eyes of Cosette, the ghost, and felt a shiver of fright crawl up my spine. *'You need to come with me, Genny,'* she whispered.

Did I? She'd helped me twice before, and sitting here wasn't getting me anywhere, was it? I slid off the stone slab and followed her – stepping over a line of red sand that marked the edge of a circle – towards a dark corner.

'Do you know how many strings I've had to pull to sort that murder charge out?' Hannah carried on. 'And how many promises I've had to make? If you hadn't made such an almighty mess of things, we'd have had this spell done days ago, instead of having to rush things at the last minute.'

'I didn't mean to,' came Janet's sulky reply. 'It all just got a bit out of hand.'

We reached the corner and stopped. It was just a corner. I was a little taken aback that it wasn't some sort of help, or an escape route. I frowned down at Cosette. 'What happens now?'

'Now we watch,' she said, amusement lighting her eyes. 'Oh, and Genny, think some clothes on, please.'

Huh? I looked down and as I did, my missing jeans and T-shirt materialised around me.

Cosette patted my hand. 'That's a good girl.' She didn't sound like an eight-year-old, even one born a hundred years ago.

'Start using your brain instead of worrying about who to let into your knickers,' Hannah snapped at Janet. 'If it wasn't for the fact that you're my little sister, I'd have offered your soul up to the demon long ago. And stop eating those bloody sweets; you don't need them now. Granny's magic is powerful enough without you adding sugar to it. You need to lose some of that fat you're carrying round with you. Do that and you could have your pick of boyfriends instead of having to moon about after those ugly trolls all the time.'

'Trolls are not ugly,' Janet huffed.

Ugly! Pieces of the jigsaw started slotting together in my head.

'You're the Ancient One, aren't you?' I said to Cosette, looking down at her. 'So what happened to the old crone look?'

'You have a phobia about ghosts, Genny.' Cosette gave me a knowing smile; it sat oddly on her little girl's face. 'I thought this would be a more acceptable manifestation with which to approach you.'

I shuddered. She was right; the chest wounds had been bad enough – if I'd met her ghost with its yellowed skull and maggot-filled eyes . . .

'I will explain,' she continued, 'but first we must watch the proceedings.'

'Well, each to their own,' Hannah was saying, drawing my attention back to the squabbling women, 'but I'll tell you what, after we've finished you can have a look at Darius, my pet vamp. I'm not going to need him any more after tonight, so you might as well have him.'

'I don't want your cast-offs,' Janet pouted.

'Sure you do,' Hannah said firmly. 'Darius is almost as big as a troll anyway, so he'll be right up your street.' She arched a perfectly drawn brow at Joseph. 'Now, Doctor, are we done yet?'

'She's dead,' Joseph said quietly, turning away to fiddle with a medical trolley next to his machines.

'Right, now stay out the way, but *don't* leave the circle, and remember what I told you. Make sure you do it, otherwise come midnight yours will be one of the souls going to the demon.'

Joseph crossed himself, his face pale.

It looked like he might be a goodie, which begged the question how in hell had Hannah got her claws in him?

Hannah loosened her robe and let it fall to the ground, leaving her wearing nothing but a gold locket on a chain around her neck. She stepped up to the altar and used a small step-stool to climb up and onto me, swinging a leg over until she was straddling my thighs. She stared down for a minute then cupped her own full breasts and sighed. 'I'm going to miss my curves' – she gave my own smaller breasts a prod – 'but thank goodness for silicone.'

Shock slammed into me as I realised she wasn't just going to be *borrowing* my body. She was taking it over.

Permanently.

Hannah lifted her arms and removed the gold locket,

opened it and placed it on my stomach, where it sat like a frozen butterfly. She waved at Janet, who hurried over, holding out a black embroidered cushion like a tray. 'Your athame, Mistress.'

'It's not an athame, Janet,' Hannah rebuked her, 'It's a very special knife, forged by the northern dwarves from cold iron and silver.' She picked it up and ran a finger carefully along the thin blade. 'It was tempered in dragon's breath. The handle is carved from a unicorn's horn, and this' – she smiled as she stroked the oval of clear amber set in its handle – 'this is a dragon's tear.'

'A Bonder of Souls,' whispered Cosette in awe. 'Wherever did she discover that?'

I narrowed my eyes. The last time I'd seen the knife, other than in my dreams, I'd been four years old. 'She stole it,' I said flatly. 'From Malik al-Khan.'

'Ah, of course – that is how he tied your soul to his when you were a child. I was curious about how he'd done so.'

I eyed her with suspicion. 'How do you know about that?'

'Any knowledge is available if you're prepared to pay the price,' she murmured, her gaze fixed on Hannah.

Ri-ght, the demon information service. Figured!

Hannah held up the knife and started chanting in the same guttural language I'd heard her use before. Then she leaned forward and carved three interconnecting crescent moons in the centre of my chest.

I recognised them at once. Cosette had the same marks on her own small chest – only now I was beginning to suspect she might have put them there herself, and not, as I'd always thought, had them inflicted on her.

I watched, tense and powerless, as blood, glinting like wet rubies in the flickering candlelight, seeped into the marks carved on my chest. Hannah offered the knife to my blood and it rushed up the silver blade, turning it crimson. Then she held the knife over the locket and I watched as the blood drained down and pooled inside its open wings.

'Your soul to gold, Genevieve,' she chanted, kissing the knife and leaving a smear of blood on her lips, 'my soul to your flesh,' as she bent and touched her bloody lips to my mouth, 'your flesh and my soul to join.' Then she gripped the knife in both hands, held it out in front of her and reversed the blade. She took a deep breath and plunged it into her body, under her ribs and up into her heart.

Screaming, she threw her head back as if in ecstasy, hands still clutching the knife as blood dripped down between her fingers, then, after a moment, she wrenched the knife from her chest and let it drop as she half-fell, half-lowered herself onto me to press her mouth to mine, her body twitching in its death throes.

Joseph turned away, his face pale.

Janet stared avidly, her mouth parted, her bag of sweets clutched in her fist, forgotten.

Beside me, Cosette watched just as avidly. 'She always was a good student, that one,' she said, her dark eyes lit with something almost like pride.

Anger flooded into me, washing away the shock and panic. I bent down to look her in the eyes. 'Right, now that your erstwhile pupil is happily stealing my body, want to tell me what I'm supposed to do to stop her?'

'You can't stop her, Genny,' Cosette said, holding up a hand to silence me, 'but you might be able to reclaim your body.'

'How?' I demanded.

'You'll need to expel her soul and rebond your own into your body.'

'And somehow I just know that's going to be easier said than done. Any hints?'

'Use your connections.'

'Short, sweet and cryptic doesn't do it for me,' I said. 'Want to tell me how in more practical terms?'

'Let me show you something first.' She gripped my hand again and even though I knew what she was – *who* she was – I couldn't bring myself to yank my hand from hers. She led me past the wall with its painted mural to a small, dark alcove. Inside was another waist-high stone slab, on which was lying a woman's body, half-shrouded in a white sheet. Her long dark hair curled around her shoulders and her mouth was drawn back in a rictus, showing her sharp white fangs. Another gold locket nestled between her full breasts. Rosa. Thankfully, the only wound she had was the one on her left hip, the one that corresponded with the spell tattoo on my own left hip. She'd obviously healed any damage done by having a five-foot sword run through her.

'You're not suggesting I use Rosa's body, are you?' I asked guardedly.

'Sadly, that is no longer a possibility,' Cosette told me, squeezing my hand. 'The vampire's body is bonded to yours through flesh and magic, not by soul or spirit. But I have more to show you.' She put a finger to her lips and tugged. 'Come on, we must be quiet. It is better if they do not see you.' She led me to the open doorway in the bricked-up archway and motioned for me to look. 'Stand here at the side,' she murmured.

I peered around the door and into a big, dark, arched-roof space. I frowned as a feeling of déjà vu snagged in my mind, then the thought vanished as I saw the people – thirty or so of them, men, women and a few children, sitting in rows or standing in silent groups . . . no, not living people, but souls, ghosts, shades.

I turned back to Cosette and whispered, 'What are they all doing here?'

'Hannah has gathered them to pay her demon debt; she has been collecting ghosts from all over the city.' She pointed to the far side where a ghostly teenager was curled on his side, tears streaking down his face. Another ghost, a woman carrying a posy of wilted flowers, bent and ruffled his hair consolingly. The boy flinched and his head jerked up. He looked around, wide-eyed and scared. 'Who's there?' he whispered, then sucked in the silver hoop piercing his bottom lip and huddled up again, more tears squeezing from his eyes.

Shock sparked in me as I recognised him: the florist's lad. Then I realised something else and I turned back to Cosette. 'He's not dead, is he?'

'The demon always likes a virgin sacrifice.' Her thin little shoulders shrugged. 'He qualifies. He's also a witness they need to be rid of. With him and all the souls she's collected, that's an abundant offering. She's hoping this will free her totally.'

'But if she does that, she won't be a sorcerer any more.' I was missing something.

'No, she will be sidhe fae – or at least her body will. And she will control its magic – just as you controlled the vampire's magic when your soul inhabited that body.'

That made ambitious sense; I could see the advantage in upgrading to a body with its own magical power source, instead of owing a demon for every spell you cast. Didn't mean I had to like it, or let it happen. Or that I was stupid.

I crouched down next to Cosette. 'Okay, you've been haunting me for long enough, you've shown me a sacrificial virgin and a load of ghosts that need rescuing from the fiery pits of hell, so now you can tell me what you get out of all this.' I smiled, knowing it didn't reach my eyes, ghostly or otherwise. 'And don't try telling me you're suffering from an attack of remorse or sudden altruism, because I won't believe you.'

'Of course not, Genny.' She patted her chest. 'I want you to save my soul from the demon too, but I appreciate you might not feel as charitable towards me as some of the innocents in there – look on them as an added incentive. Oh, and just to make it perfectly clear, Hannah intends giving your soul to the demon as well, in return for making her soul in your body a permanent transfer.'

'Of course she does,' I muttered. 'So tell me about these connections.'

She waved her small arm at me. 'Look and you will see.'

Great. More cryptic clues—

But as I looked, I realised I could still *look*, that I could still *see* the magic, and both my own body and Cosette's were as transparent as a heat shimmer. Queasiness roiled in my stomach. I closed my eyes briefly, regaining my equilibrium, then *looked* again. This time I could see two ethereal threads attached to my ghostly form; the first was the black silken rope which dangled from my left arm, the rope I'd seen before, when Malik's sword-trick at the Blue Heart had thrown me back into the nightmare of my memories. The other was a fine red thread joined to the knuckles of my left hand.

'How do they—?'

A loud buzzing shattered the quiet as one of Doctor Joseph's machines leapt to life.

'Yes, it worked,' Janet yelled loudly, and slapped Joseph

on the arm. 'C'mon, help me get it off her. You take the legs.'
She yanked at Hannah's old body, jumping out of the way as
it rolled and hit the floor with a loud smack, sounding like
nothing so much as a side of meat. Joseph froze, his eyes
wide above his face-mask, staring down at the blood-covered
corpse.

Janet walked round and gave him a little shove. 'C'mon,
Doc, get on and do your stuff,' she ordered.

Hands shaking, he trundled the small trolley nearer and
reached for a swab. He cleaned the blood off my body's left
breast, then lifted what looked like an elephant-sized hypodermic. He held it up and pushed the syringe plunger until a
bead of clear liquid appeared, then tapped the syringe until,
finally appearing satisfied with his preparations, he felt along
my ribs, and positioned the needle. He hesitated, and I could
see his eyes blinking behind his glasses, then he pushed down
hard until the needle was up to the hilt in my flesh. Then he
injected the liquid.

'Do you think that's going to be enough?' Janet hovered
over him.

'I've given her enough adrenalin to get a horse started; it's
almost three times what she needs for the body weight,' he
said quietly as he withdrew the needle and swabbed again.
'It's the equivalent of a massive build-up of venom, which is
what I think brought her – it – *the body* round last time.'

We all stood and watched my body.

'Give her another—'

My body's spine arched and my arms and legs started spasming as if plugged into a live electrical socket. The machine
beeped into life and numbers flashed red and began rising
fast, and faster. My body opened its eyes; my mouth formed a
wide, overjoyed grin and jerked upright.

'Oh my goodness,' my mouth yelled delightedly, 'it worked,
it really worked!' My body lifted its hand and muttered and a
ball of light glowed like the sun in its palm; my body threw it
up and blew it a kiss. The light shattered into rainbow colours
that rained down like a spring shower. 'Oh, the power! It's like
driving a Ferrari instead of a cranky old rustbucket!'

Fuck. And I didn't even know how to ride a bike.

I rubbed my hands over my face. I needed to work out how to get out of this, and I needed to get my own body back – before the demon appeared to claim all those poor souls, and mine—I clamped down on the terror that thinking of the demon brought and shoved it away. I looked up as my body threw another spell in the air and it showered me/it/Hannah with coloured light; and filled me with freaky confusion.

Okay, now I needed to think of *my* body as Hannah's.

'Get this stuff off me,' Hannah said, flicking at the electrodes stuck to her chest. Doctor Joseph worked quickly, removing both the electrodes and the cap of wires that hatted her head. As soon as he was done, she fastened the gold locket around her neck.

'Wow!' she said, smiling at Janet. 'You know what? I feel wonderful' – she held out her hand; it was shaking – 'if a bit quivery.' She swung her legs off the altar and slid to the ground, reaching out to grab hold of Janet's arm as she wobbled. 'Time waits for no woman, or in my case, no sidhe fae. Shower first, then tidy up that mess you left at Granny's. After that I'll pay a visit to the bank. I still need to get the Fabergé egg.'

'What's the Fabergé egg for?' I asked Cosette.

'The egg's a soul trap. Without it she can't collect all those souls she's gathered and hand them safely over to the demon, and that means the demon will take her own soul instead as payment.'

Ri-ight. So pretty much as Hannah had explained, except without the oh-so-relevant specifics.

'What do you mean, tidy up round at Granny's?' Janet asked, her voice petulant. She popped another liquorice torpedo into her mouth.

Hannah gave her a disbelieving look. 'Well, there's Granny's body for one, and that wood shaving mess in the hallway. The police will have found it all by now, won't they.'

'I s'pose so – but won't the sidhe slut get the blame?'

'Janet, little sister, I *am* the sidhe now – and if you ever call me a slut again—' Hannah gave her a warning look. 'And unfortunately, my stool-pigeon has flown the nest, thanks to you.' She waved an imperious hand at Joseph. 'Doctor, please shoot her and put her out of her misery.'

'Shoot me?' Janet's mouth fell open as Joseph turned round, picked up his tranq gun and, without hesitating, aimed, then shot Janet in her ample chest—

She looked down, her eyes round with surprise. 'But—?' She dropped her sweeties.

'Damage limitation, little sister dear,' Hannah said briskly. 'Someone's got to get the police off my back, and since you're actually guilty, you might as well take the blame for the baker's, the boy's and Granny's deaths.'

Janet's eyes fluttered, then she did a tree-topple and thudded to the floor.

'Is Janet really her sister?' I asked Cosette, stunned.

Cosette nodded.

Talk about dysfunctional families.

Hannah prodded the unconscious woman with her foot. 'Don't worry, if all goes well, I'll try and get you out before they burn you at the stake.' She looked up at Joseph. 'Don't just stand there; tie her up or something. You should enjoy that; after all, isn't that what you like to do at that little club you go to?'

He pushed his glasses up his nose, lifted the tranq gun and pointed it at her.

'Don't be silly, Doctor,' she sighed. 'Just put it down, otherwise that DVD of you cavorting about in all that tacky leather and chains could still accidentally find its way onto the internet . . .'

He did as he was told, his hand trembling.

'You should be glad, you're going to be labelled a hero for rescuing me from the dangerous sorcerer's clutches.' She smiled. 'Which is much better than being labelled a pervert, isn't it?'

His cheeks flushed with either anger or embarrassment and I remembered all the 'clothes' in his mirrored wardrobes – the ones he'd said belonged to a friend!

'Compulsion spell tied to a nice bit of blackmail,' Cosette muttered as Joseph pulled out the cord from Hannah's discarded robe and started to tie Janet up. 'She always was rather good at that.'

'I see you started without me.' A man strolled out of the gloom, his sun-streaked, gelled hair and well-trimmed Van

Dyke glinting blond in the candlelight, a red Souler cross pinned to the lapel of his smart grey suit. Neil Banner. Not totally surprising considering their supposedly separate but similar quests for the Fabergé egg. I wondered whether they were an established item, or if the egg had only recently made them soul-stealing mates. Not that it made any difference.

Cosette gave a small gasp and whispered, 'That one is the necromancer who has been collecting the souls for her. I did not think he would be back so soon.'

'Neil!' Hannah held her arms wide and my body did a shimmy. 'Look, it worked. Do you want a feel?'

His face twisted in disgust. 'Not when you're all covered in blood, Hannah.'

'Genny,' she snapped, 'you must call me Genny, nothing else.'

He waved her anger away. 'I will; it's just that I still see your soul, not hers.' He frowned, looking around. 'Where is her soul, anyway?'

She patted the gold locket. 'In here, of course.'

'No, it's not.'

She clutched at the locket in panic. 'It has to be! I did the ritual perfectly.'

'Don't worry,' Neil said calmly, 'she can't have gone far; she's probably still disorientated from being cast out.'

'You don't understand—' Hannah grabbed his arm. 'I have to wear her soul close until tonight. What if it dissipates? Then this body will fade away and I'll be left with nothing—'

'Hannah, it's you that doesn't understand.' He extricated himself, then with a self-satisfied smile he pulled out a blood-stained hanky from his pocket. 'The sidhe's hand was bleeding last night when I met her at HOPE. I managed to get a hook into her soul then.' He touched the hanky to his nose, muttering as he turned a slow circle. 'She's not going anywhere.'

I clenched my fists. Bastard.

'You must go, now!' Cosette grabbed my left hand, in as much panic as Hannah, and touched the thin red thread there – it was stretching out towards Neil Banner.

Crap.

I tried to break it, but it was like pulling at elastic; it just kept stretching. 'Go where?' I demanded.

'There.' Neil pointed straight at me. 'She's hiding in the corner with that stupid child. Open the locket and I'll call her to it.' Hannah fumbled with the catch as he resumed muttering.

Cosette pushed at me frantically. 'Go!' She indicated the ethereal black silken rope that wrapped around my left arm and dangled down around my feet. 'Follow it, and pray that the necromancer is not strong enough to call you back.'

Neil's muttering rose to a crescendo and the red thread yanked at my hand, dragging me towards him. I stumbled, almost falling, but my fingers closed round the black silk rope—

—the rope slipped through my fingers as if it was slick with blood, and I fell, spinning out in the red-blackness . . .

Chapter Twenty-nine

The red-blackness was as before: empty, silent, scentless . . . nothingness. This time the mist that circled the blackness was no longer pale and far away, but pressed close, and shot through with hot golds and coppers and reds, like the rays of the sun that backlight the dark side of the moon. I didn't want to think what that might mean. The black silk cord tailed down and away below me.

Hand grasped tightly round the blood-slick silk, I continued to fall . . .

Where was I, some sort of limbo place for the soul?

And how was this supposed to get me my body back, let alone save virgins and kidnapped ghosts? Use my connections, Cosette had said, which was fine, except she'd hadn't told me how, thanks to Neil the necro turning up.

What I needed was help – but how, when the only 'people' I could talk to were other ghosts, or my local not-so-friendly neighbourhood necro? Of course, if I could make my way to a graveyard, I could talk to anyone living – whoever happened to be around at midnight. I could even touch them, since I'd be corporeal again for the hour between one day and the next – except that midnight on All Hallows' Eve is traditionally when demons made their house calls, so midnight was going to be way too late.

But I was falling the same way I had after Malik skewered me with the sword – only then I'd tumbled back to my wedding night. No way did I want to relive that memory; one return visit was around a hundred times too many for my liking. I shuddered in the darkness as I kept on sliding down. Malik had called to me the last time, as if from above and below, but still I'd kept dropping, until I'd come round in the hallway the morning after – so did that mean *down* was the past? But in the past, when I'd been fourteen, I'd never picked up the Autarch's sword, I'd never decided to go hunting, hadn't even met Cosette, so it had been less like a memory and more as if my adult self had travelled back to that time. Could I do that again? Could I pick a time where I could step into my own body and change things?

But when?

My descent slowed, as if the silken cord wanted to give me a chance to think.

The last time I'd revived seemed to be the most obvious point, when Malik had called my soul back to my body and I'd awakened to the realisation it was Malik who had chased me on my wedding night, Malik who had sunk his fangs into me, not the Autarch. I felt my hand slip, almost as if the black silken cord was reacting to my thought, and I dropped faster again, the air rushing past me as if heralding an approaching train—

—and the black silk cord frayed to nothing within seconds.

Stunned, I hung in the red-blackness spinning slowly, clutching the thin red thread that was hooked through the knuckles of my left hand. Frustration sliced into me, sharp and painful, like the bronze sword of my memory. *Damn*. Whatever bond Malik had tied my soul with was broken – so now what? Did I hang around waiting to see if Necro Neil was strong enough to haul me back so I could be part of Hannah's demon debt? Or . . .

I looked at the red thread dangling below me. Necro Neil said he had hooked into my soul at HOPE—

I took a deep breath – not that there seemed to be any air to breathe – and loosened my tight hold on the thread . . .

* * *

... and beige vinyl floor tiles rushed up to meet me. Blurry peach-coloured walls and bright orange chairs jarred in my vision and in the distance I saw myself talking to Necro Neil. Thaddeus, the monster Beater goblin, was standing next to him, his high horse's tail of red and grey hair fanning over his shoulders—

I slammed into something solid and cold, something I couldn't see. I stared into Necro Neil's blank, mind-locked face, and our tiny shared past stretched out behind him like a stack of freeze-frame photos, right up to the point where he handed me his handkerchief and I pressed it to my bleeding hand.

That had to be when he'd hooked me.

'I bin lookin' for you, sidhe,' a girl's shrill voice broke in. 'I got sumfing to give you.'

I turned towards the voice and the girl pointed her foot-long carving knife at me. Her hip-length white hair floated in a nonexistent wind and scraps of washed-out grey lace, satin and velvet fluttered like hundreds of wings against her anorexic body. The faint scent of liquorice and blood clung to her like day-old smoke.

The fact that Moth-girl could see me didn't bode well for either of us.

I looked behind her.

Bobby, a.k.a. Mr October, huddled against the lift door, hands clutched to his stomach, a dark pool of blood beneath him. Malik, a fine line creasing between his black brows, watched the Glamoured blonde-bimbo me as I stared down at Grace, who was kneeling, checking for a pulse on Moth-girl's unconscious – or more likely dead body, judging by the girl standing next to me. The two security guards hovered nearby.

It looked like I'd arrived in the middle of Malik's mass mind-lock – was that why I couldn't go any further?

The red thread in my hand gave a slight tug.

'Hey, I'm talkin' to you, sidhe,' Moth-girl shouted in my ear. 'Can you 'ear me?'

'Yes, I can,' I said, flinching as I turned back to her.

'Good, I've got sumfing to give you.' She waved her

carving knife at me, then plucked at the white ribbon tied round her throat. 'D'you know wot this is?'

'Yes.' I pursed my lips. 'You're supposed to be a *gift*, from one vamp to another.'

Her own purple-painted lips grinned. 'That's right; well, see, my Daryl, you knows 'im as Darius, 'e said to tell you—'

'Darius?' I interrupted. 'The vamp that's shacked up with the sorcerer?'

'Yeah, that's 'im. 'E did 'is dance for you.' She gave a little wiggle of her hips. 'Well, 'e's my Daryl, 'as bin since we was kids togevver at school.' Her fingers toyed with the ribbon again. 'And 'e said, if I come an' show you this, then it means 'e can ask for your 'elp.'

I held my hand up to stop her. 'Wait a minute, *Darius* sent you as a gift, not some other vamp?'

''Course 'e did! Anyways, Daryl said as 'ow you'd understan', an' you'd get 'im away from the old devil-witch, seein' as you've got that spell-fing on your hip for the ovver vamp, Rosa's 'er name. Daryl says the devil-witch were on the blower to sumone an' they tole 'er you'd be 'ere tonite.' Her grin widened and she waved the knife again. 'So 'ere I am, all wrapped up an' ready.'

It sort of made sense. Darius had been there in my flat, listening and watching whilst Hannah had been talking to me about Rosa and the Disguise spell. He must've decided that having a sorcerer for a master wasn't for him – not that I blamed him – and as Hannah and Neil were in it together, Neil was probably the one who'd told her I was at HOPE. Darius, no doubt doing his impression of Big Ears, had overheard, so he'd followed vamp tradition and tied a ribbon around Moth-girl's neck and sent her to me/Rosa with his 'request'.

But once Moth-girl had got to HOPE, not only could she *not* find me – because I'd been wearing the blonde-bimbo Glamour – but it looked like she'd died even before we tried to save her and Bobby. And sad as I was that Moth-girl hadn't made it, I needed someone who could communicate with the living world, not with the dead. Right now another ghost was about as much use to me as—

'Oy!' She jabbed the knife at me. 'You needs to pay attention 'ere.'

. . . well, the ghostly knife Moth-girl was jabbing at me. Not that it didn't stop me jumping out of its way. Someone points a knife at you, even a ghost one, and instinct takes over.

'Okay, you've got my attention,' I said, indicating the knife.

'Sorry,' she said unrepentantly, 'but you gotta listen. Don't fink I got much time, the stupid twit pumped me up wiv too much vamp-juice again, fink he might of nearly killed me this time, so I ain't wantin' to be out too long.' She looked at Grace administering to her body and gave a disdainful sniff. ''Ope that doc knows what 'er's doin'.'

I frowned, surprised. 'You're not dead?'

'Not yet.' Her Pierrot-whitened face glared down at her prone body. 'Not s'long as the doc does 'er stuff right.'

An idea started to form in my mind. 'So you'll be able to wake up again and talk to people?' I looked down as the sharp pull of the thread across my knuckles caused an anxious flutter inside me.

'Hope so! It's what we Mofs do all the time; gettin' necked on 'urts like a blinder if yer don't make yerself step away from the pain.'

I blinked. 'You mean you leave your body like this all the time?'

''Course – ain't that wot I just said?' She jabbed the knife at me again and it nicked my palm.

'Ouch!' I jerked my hand back and peered at the bead of blood. I was a ghost, and so was the knife. Why was I bleeding? I shook my head. 'Look,' I said, 'I want you to do something for me—'

'No, you look, sidhe.' She pointed to my hand where she'd nicked it with the knife. 'See, I can still 'urt you as a ghost, and if you don't listen, I'm gonna come an' haunt you an' make your life a bleedin' hell. So, you gonna help my Daryl or not?'

'Depends if I can . . .' I paused as an idea struck me. 'Do you know where the devil-witch lives?'

She nodded. 'Yeah, Lunnon Bridge way, underneef it, I fink.'

The arched-roof tunnels of the bridge's foundations! Of course – where I'd done the ghost survey with Finn; no wonder the place looked familiar.

'Okay,' I said, 'if you want me to help Darius, then you have to help me.' I turned her round and pointed at Malik. 'See that vamp?' I said. 'His name's Malik al-Khan. When you wake up, or whatever it is you do, you get Darius to tell him what you've told me, and tell him he's got to come to the devil-witch's place before midnight tomorrow night, Hallowe'en, and he's got to kill me.' I squeezed her arm; her bone felt as thin as a bird's beneath my hand.

I decided that I needed more than one basket if I was going to have a chance at saving the souls destined for the egg and the demon. I pointed at Bobby. 'Tell him the same thing; tell him if he does this, Rosa will be his master.' Then I pointed at Grace. 'And tell the doctor everything too – then tell her to go to the police. Got it?'

'Yeah, gottit: you wants 'em all to come an' kill yer tomorrow – but ain't you already dead?'

'Yeah, I think so, but my body isn't,' I said, trying to sound matter-of-fact. 'The devil-witch is in it.'

'Ah, now I got you.' She nodded sagely.

The red thread yanked my hand high into the air.

I pulled it down, then turned back to the blonde-me again. *I* could see ghosts – but the blue eyes of my Glamoured self were still staring fixedly at Grace kneeling next to Moth-girl's body; I didn't appear to notice the ghostly me at all. I tried tugging the blonde ponytail, then pinching my cheek, but my fingers touched nothing, felt nothing. Could I take over my body, as I'd done when I'd picked up the Autarch's sword?

'You'll give 'er nightmares like that,' Moth-girl sniffed. ''Er spirit'll know sumfing's wrong, even if it don't know what.'

I pursed my lips, then walked round the back of the blonde me and stepped forward, merging myself with . . . myself. Still nothing. I stood and looked out of my eyes and tried to lift my hand; my ghostly hand moved, but the blonde-me hand didn't.

'How do you know about the nightmares?' I asked, sticking my head out of blonde-me's face to talk to her.

'I 'ad it done it to meself once.' She gave a little shiver. 'Couldn't sleep for a week, an' I know it was me pal as done it, seeing as I asked 'er to. Awful it was.'

'Were they like picture nightmares, as if someone was telling you a scary story?'

'Nah.' She shook her head. 'I just kept fallin' into this big black 'ole all the time.'

Disappointment settled like an iron ball in my stomach. So much for getting inside the blonde-me and trying to communicate, by dreams or otherwise.

The thread jerked me out of blonde-me and slammed me back into the cold, invisible barrier, and back to staring into Necro Neil's blank, mind-locked face.

Damn. He was getting impatient.

'Oy!' Moth-girl ran over to me. 'Yer gonna save my Daryl, ain't yer?'

'I'll do my best,' I said, not wanting to promise something that might be impossible.

'Okay.' She chewed her lip, then held out the knife. ''Ere, take it. You ain't gonna 'urt no one livin' wiv it, but it can hurt the dead all right.'

'Thanks.' I grasped the knife – for a ghost blade it felt warm and heavy and very real in my palm.

She sauntered back to where her body was lying. 'Watch out for my Daryl, won't yer?'

'Yeah, I will. Oh—' I realised I didn't know Moth-girl's name, but the thread jerked again, and the next second I was airborne. 'Don't speak to him' – I pointed down at Necro Neil – 'or let him see you out of your body. He's a necromancer, and he's in league with the devil-witch.'

Her lip curled with disdain as she looked at Neil. 'Gotcha: 'e's a fuckin' ghost-grabber.' And with that she fell apart into hundreds of tiny moths that disappeared into the patchwork of lace and satin and velvet her body was wearing.

I looked anxiously up at the tiled ceiling; it was only a foot away. I slashed the knife against the thread – maybe I could break his bond – but the knife slipped through it as if it didn't exist. Then the thread yanked again and the wind rushed past me as I streamed through the red-blackness of wherever.

Chapter Thirty

The stench of putrefying flesh invaded my nose as skeletal fingers squeezed my throat, choking me, and a heaviness compressed my chest. Pain and blackness were eating at the light in my mind. A brief thought flickered in the encroaching darkness: being dead wasn't much different to being alive; there were still some who could hurt you if they wanted to badly enough.

'Have you managed to get her into the locket yet?' A woman's voice, far away.

'I told you I'd let you know, Hannah.' Anger and frustration, and something fervent in the male's voice.

'Hurry it up,' the woman said, 'there's less than an hour to midnight.'

A tug on my hand. 'Into the locket, Ms Taylor. Now!' The command came again.

'*No*—' I whispered, the same answer I'd given him before. The fingers squeezed my throat tighter, squeezing out the light.

'We wouldn't be having this problem if you'd waited for me in the first place, Hannah,' the voice said curtly.

'Why don't you put her in the Fabergé egg with all the others?' the woman asked.

'Because if I open the egg to put her in, I'll let the rest of them out again.' The voice was scathing this time. 'You stick to your spells, Hannah, and leave me to worry about the shades and souls.'

'I would do, if you could handle your side of things efficiently.' She was closer, sounding suspicious. 'You've been trying to persuade her for so long that I'm beginning to wonder if you're not enjoying this a little too much.'

The light narrowed to a pinhole and panic fluttered in my mind like a terrified flock of garden fairies. The skeletal hands weren't going to—

'Stop.' I heard the command and the pressure on my throat eased up.

Relief flooded through me, pushing back the darkness, letting the light in, and though the weight on my chest still pressed me down, I drifted like a feather, the voices rising and falling around me, indistinct and unimportant.

Gradually I settled back into myself.

I kept my eyes closed. There was no point opening them, not when it would only encourage fucking Necro Neil to get his tame ghost torturer to have another go – and if I didn't open my eyes, I didn't have to look at my torturer's plague-eaten face – its missing nose and rotten black stumps of teeth were still freaking me out. I lay there, trying to ignore Scarface the ghost sitting on my chest, pretending to be more dead than I was, thankful that at least the ghost's pain-inflicting skills were limited to strangling and suffocating me; he hadn't enough personality left to implement Necro Neil's more inventive – and considerably less wholesome – ideas.

Never mind giving myself nightmares from trying to possess my own body, as Moth-girl had predicted: if I got out of this I would have more than enough of them to last until I hit my third century.

Of course, that was if I got to see another dawn.

And that was looking less likely every time Scarface's bony fingers closed round my throat.

'Well, Ms Taylor' – Necro Neil's eager voice was accompanied with a tug on my hand – 'you look like you've recovered enough for me to ask you again: will you go into the locket?'

'No,' I croaked in a whisper, not entirely sure why he couldn't force me.

The ghost shifted his position on top of me and I braced myself ready for the next attack.

'That's our guest,' Hannah said, excitement colouring her voice. 'Come on, leave her for now. She can't escape again, not with the added Containment spell I've put on the place.'

'I thought you said you could handle him on your own.' Necro Neil's words carried a sullen edge.

'I can – but better to be safe than sorry. We don't want anything going wrong at this late stage, do we?'

'No,' he said, and their voices faded into nothing.

I felt carefully around for the ghost knife. It had still been in my hand when Scarface and half a dozen other ghosts had jumped me when the red thread deposited me back at Necro Neil's shiny black shoes. No one had tried to take it away from me – but then, no one had needed to, not when there were ghosts enough to sit on every limb . . . but now only Scarface was left, perching on my chest like some malevolent spirit.

A bony finger poked me in the cheek and I flinched, but kept my eyes closed. The reek of rot made my stomach give a dry heave. A voice rasped next to my ear, 'Grab . . . go.'

Grab go. The words didn't make sense.

'Wake,' the voice rasped again. 'Ghos . . . grab . . . go.'

Ghost-grabber? Was he saying Necro Neil was gone? Why? Warily, I opened one eye and squinted up at Scarface. 'What?' I whispered.

His lipless mouth opened wide, the scar on his cheek splitting like a second pair of lips to reveal the glistening bone. 'Up.'

Was he telling me to get up? 'Can't,' I croaked, 'you're sitting on me.'

One dried eyeball rolled in its socket. 'Sor . . . ry,' he rasped, and shuffled off me.

Relieved, I lifted my arm and rubbed my throat; being

strangled had hurt at the time, but it didn't appear to have left any lasting injuries to my ghostly form.

'Up . . . help.' Scarface was crouched beside me now. A bony finger poked urgently at my shoulder. 'Grab . . . back . . . soon.'

Mystified at being let go, but not enough to question it, I rolled over and pushed myself up onto my hands and knees. The knife was still there. I picked it up. The handle felt warm and solid, almost comforting, even if it only worked against other ghosts. I scrambled to my feet and looked around. Scarface was shuffling away into the distance, just the same way he had when I'd watched him during the ghost survey . . .

And it was in the same arched tunnel – the same tunnel where all the ghosts had been gathered . . . Only the place was brightly lit now, and the ghosts were gone; all that remained was the Fabergé egg, which sat in solitary splendour in the middle of a large circle marked out in red sand. Curled up next to the egg was the florist's lad, still tied hand and foot, a fresh black eye decorating his tear-stained face.

It looked like the demon welcome mat was laid out, all ready to go.

I headed over to the circle and stopped at its edge. The boy's chest rose and fell; he was either unconscious or asleep. I was betting on the former. I stuck out my hand, but my palm flexed against an invisible wall and when I looked down, there were flecks of green and chunks of grey dotted with rusty stains mixed in with the red sand: yew, to stop the dead from passing, and consecrated bone splashed with sanctified blood to contain the demon.

Not a circle I could pass in my ghostly form. I'd have to find some way to come back for the boy before midnight.

Who was the guest? Maybe whoever it was could help, or at least provide a distraction. I headed for the breeze-block wall at the end of the tunnel, keeping close to the side and carefully skirting round the pile of cordoned-off old bones, I eased through the open doorway and peered into the room beyond. It was the one with the wall painting of the barren landscape, where Hannah had performed her seppuku ritual and taken over my body. There were people inside, live ones, and I ducked back, then mentally snorted at my stupidity. I was a ghost, and Necro Neil was the only one who could see me – and without his ghostly minions he couldn't touch me, not until midnight. I crept inside, then stopped, keeping my eye out for him.

Hannah was walking towards me, sweeping the long train of a ballgown in burnt-orange and black – her Hallowe'en fetish was still showing – with her hair piled up in some sort of beehive style that sported a coronet-thing sparkling with amber and diamonds. For a second I almost didn't recognise my body under the dress, new hairdo and make-up. At least she hadn't managed to give me a boob job in the last few hours. When I finally dragged my eyes away from my own body, I realised who was walking with her.

Malik al-Khan.

My ghostly heart thudded: why was he looking at her with his usual impassive expression on his perfect, pretty face? Didn't he realise that it wasn't me in my body but Hannah? And why wasn't he killing her? I clenched my fists. I wanted to shout at him to get on with it, but knew he couldn't hear me. Then my heart thudded for a different reason. What if Moth-girl hadn't woken up? What if she hadn't managed to find him, or pass on my messages?

Damn. Plan A wasn't working; time to find another one.

I scanned the room, but I couldn't see Necro Neil anywhere. I looked back at Hannah, wearing my body. She had her hand tucked into Malik's arm. They made a striking couple, her in her ballgown, him in what had to be a hand-tailored evening suit and shirt, both black, the only relief the triangle of smooth, pale skin at his throat where he'd dispensed with the bowtie.

'Here she is.' Hannah stopped in front of an alcove – Rosa's alcove.

I moved forward until I was standing near enough to watch both them and the vampire lying in soulless state on her altar of stone. Candles lit the interior of the alcove, casting wavering shadows over the white shroud that covered Rosa's body.

Malik drew back the sheet with the hand not claimed by Hannah and stared down at the grimacing, fangs-drawn vampire, his eyes as unemotional and opaque as black glass. 'You are certain you will be able to restore her soul to her body?' he asked.

Hannah smiled and patted his arm. 'Of course, Malik. I told you, with the soul-bonder knife you gave me, all I need is a small spell. It takes a matter of seconds.'

Malik had *given* her the knife? She hadn't stolen it? And he *knew* 'I' wasn't me! What the hell was going on here?

'And Joseph is correct? She has not been harmed?' he asked, still with no change of expression.

'There is no wound other than where her flesh was taken for the original spell.' Hannah lifted the sheet to show the bloody circle on Rosa's hip. 'But that will heal once she is herself again.' She let the fabric fall.

'Once her soul is returned, her body will become her own again, will it not?' He turned to her. 'There will be no tie between her and this body you now wear.'

Anger warred with confusion and I felt the sharp edge of betrayal slice inside me.

'None at all,' Hannah assured him.

'Good.' Satisfaction flickered so quickly across his face that I thought I might have imagined it. He stroked a finger along her jaw. 'What of the sidhe's soul? What has become of that?'

'There's no need to worry.' She took his hand and cupped his palm to her cheek. 'After tonight, her soul will be gone. Then this body and the power in its blood will be fully mine.' She lifted her chin and pressed his palm to her throat. 'And it will be my pleasure to share it with you, in any and every way that you desire.'

He smiled, wide enough to show a glimpse of fang. 'Then I fear you are wearing too many clothes,' he said softly, trailing a line down to her cleavage. 'Shall I tear this from you, or would you prefer to remove it yourself?'

A hopeful suspicion started to edge out the anger and confusion inside me.

She laughed, a low, husky sound. 'Soon, Malik.' She stilled his hand. 'Have patience; it will be better if we wait until after midnight. We will have more time then.'

'No, I have waited long enough for this body.' His eyes gleamed, predatory. 'And now the prize is within my grasp,

I do not wish to play second fiddle to your demon.' He threaded his hand into her hair, tugged her head back and melded his lips to hers. She made a low moan of appreciation, her hands rising to grasp his shoulders, her body visibly shuddering. His hand tightened on the silk dress, then he ripped it down to her waist, the sound violent in the quiet alcove. He placed his palm between her breasts, over her heart, and she trembled, her fingers clutching desperately at his arms, and whimpered.

An answering shudder rippled through him.

I watched, gripping the ghost knife, as a long-ago memory surfaced and cut away the last of my confusion.

The forgotten memory told me he was killing my body, his cold kiss searing like fast-freezing ice through my veins, stealing my breath, stopping my blood from flowing and my heart from beating.

It was how he'd killed me when I was fourteen, how he'd managed to give my lifeless body back to the Autarch all those years ago . . .

. . . while his bond with my soul had kept me from *fading*.

I took a breath, releasing the tension in my gut.

He *was* doing what I wanted him to.

Hannah's body stilled. Her hands dropped away and her knees sagged until Malik's mouth on hers and his hand on the nape of her neck and over her heart were the only things keeping her from falling. A shimmer moved under her skin, her head turned – only it wasn't her head, but a transparent shade – and pulled away from his kiss, pushing at his shoulders, trying to break his hold.

Slowly he raised his head and I saw his eyes, incandescent with flame.

Now I needed to do my part.

Gripping the ghost knife, I plunged it into my body's back—

—and a screech of rage shattered the quiet. Hannah's ghost stumbled backwards, then swung round to face me. I stabbed her again, under the ribs and up into her heart, as she'd stabbed herself when she'd stolen my body. I used the knife and my hand to push her back until she was wedged between me and the stone altar behind her. She clawed at my face and yanked at my hair as I thrust the knife higher, then buried my face in her neck, biting and tearing at her throat, going for the carotid. She might not be living flesh, but neither was I, and Moth-girl and Scarface had taught me that while ghosts couldn't touch the living, they had no problem killing those already dead. Hot blood spurted over me, blinding my sight, filling my mouth with its salt-copper taste, and I fed, mindless, desperate, insatiable, drinking it down, as some instinct told me I had to take it all and let not one drop remain in her body, not if I wanted her truly dead.

The blood slowed and thinned, turning as liquid as water, and her flesh dissolved under my hands until the taste was faint, almost insubstantial, and I held nothing more than wisps of air. And still I reached out, to trap each fleeing wisp and shred it with my fingers, until even the scent of her vanished into the darkness.

I slid down and huddled against the side of the stone altar, feeling sated, bloated with power that writhed around my bones, like snakes slithering in ecstasy through my body.

It was not an easy feeling, and yet it was seductive, and with a promise of more, if I would just let it in—

'Genevieve?'

My murmured name intruded on my languor and slowly I raised my head. Tavish was frowning down at me, his delicate black gills flaring at his throat.

'I am calling her back to her shell, kelpie, but I no longer sense her presence.' Malik's voice attracted my attention: he was kneeling over my limp body, his hands pressed to my bare chest. 'Is her soul still here?'

'Aye, she's here, vampire,' Tavish said softly, crouching down in front of me. His eyes shone dark pewter in the candlelight, the same colour as the beads on his green-black dreads. Apprehension and concern crossed on his face. 'But the sorcerer's darkness has tarnished her brilliance; it weighs her down, it swims like polluted eels in her consciousness, and still it tries to lure her away with it.'

The snakes flicked out their tongues and slithered down my arm, eager to taste. I reached out my hand and pushed it deep into his chest and he jerked back, snorting, his nostrils flaring and a rim of white fear showing round the edge of his dark silver eyes. And I tasted him: oranges, cut tart with terror and sweetened with yearning.

I smiled, and the snakes twined with lazy satisfaction as Tavish straightened and backed away.

'What if I give the body an injection of adrenalin?' a new voice said hesitantly. Joseph, his brown eyes blinking owl-like behind his glasses, stood in the doorway, hugging his black medical bag to his chest. 'It's what worked last time.'

Malik looked up and said, 'Joseph, my friend, I thought we agreed that you would wait outside until this matter was settled.'

'I couldn't.' He looked nervously round and moved towards Malik. 'I want to help, after what that—what that *woman* made me do.' He stopped, gazing down at my body. 'I have to try and help.' He crouched down, put his bag on the floor and pushed his glasses up his nose. 'I feel so awful about it all, as if it was my fault.'

The snakes hissed in unease and I tilted my head, puzzled; something was not right about the doctor.

'You are not responsible for what the sorcerer made you do,' Malik said quietly, sorrow lacing his words. 'It was a spell she laid on you. The guilt is all hers.'

Joseph nodded, quick, anxious bobs of his head. 'I understand that in my mind, but—' He opened his bag. 'At least let me try.'

I shifted anxiously and started to crawl towards him.

'It canna hurt any, vampire,' Tavish said, still wary as he followed me.

Malik removed his hand from where it rested on my body's chest and leaned back. 'Then please try, Joseph.'

Joseph gave him a quick smile, but the shape his mouth made was wrong, triumphant, instead of pleased-to-help. He dipped his hand inside his bag and pulled something out, pointing it at Malik. There was a *snick!* and a quivering dart lodged at the base of Malik's throat. Then Joseph turned and shot Tavish, the dart going straight into his chest.

I jumped up, the snakes writhing in alarm, leaping for him—

'Stop,' Joseph said almost casually as he looked up. 'Don't move.'

—and I stopped, held in place like a fly trapped in amber.
What the hell had he done to me?

Cosette flew into the centre of the room, her long dark hair
whipping about her head, her small hands held out towards
me. A wind blew from her hands and threw me back until I
crash-landed at the base of Rosa's stone altar.

'Nicely done, Joseph.' Cosette's child-face split in an approv-
ing grin, then she came and stood over me. 'Genny, I think
you and Joseph have already met.' She beckoned him over.
'But I don't think you've been *properly* introduced.' She held
out her hand and somehow managed to take hold of his.

'Genny, this is Joseph. My son.'

'Your son?' Stunned, I scrambled up to my feet.

'Yes. He's a fine figure of a man, isn't he?' She smiled
up at him, pride in her eyes. 'And a true necromancer, not
like that piffling weakling Hannah managed to dig up from
somewhere.'

'Sit down, Genny,' Joseph said, using that same quiet casual
tone, fixing his owl-like gaze on me.

I was sitting on the floor, legs crossed Indian-style, before
he'd even finished speaking my name. Fear and fury coursed
through me in equal parts, and the snakes retreated uneasily,
hiding under my skin. Cosette was right: Necro Neil might've
managed to push me around a bit, but his commands had been
nothing compared to Joseph's effortless control.

She puffed up with even more pride. 'And if things had
been different, I would have liked to see what sort of grand-
child you two would have given me – but that's not going to
happen now – while I might trade with a demon, I still draw
the line at incest.' She patted Joseph's hand. 'After all, Hannah's idea of usurping your body for herself is really too great
an opportunity to be missed.'

Fuck. Out of one sorcerer's frying pan and straight into the
other one's fire.

What the hell was I going to do now?

Chapter Thirty-one

'Come on, Mum, time to get you sorted,' Joseph said. He walked over to my limp body and picked it up, grunting with effort as he lifted it – being a necro obviously didn't give him any perks in the physical world. He laid my body gently on the sacrificial altar and started cutting away the remnants of the orange dress. 'You don't want to be still in spirit form when the demon turns up, do you?'

'Of course not,' she said. She smiled up at him as she climbed up on the altar and sat herself down so she was half in and half out of my body. 'Although the demon should be happy enough with the sidhe's soul.'

'Glad someone's going to be happy,' I muttered.

Joseph rummaged inside his black bag, laying things out on the trolley next to his machines. I briefly wondered if he'd had some sort of practise run, playing around with my soul and my body while I'd been out of it after the explosion at the bakery, when he'd supposedly been taking care of me. I shoved that deeply disturbing thought away. It was more important to figure out how to get my own body back before Cosette took up residence in it. Then I had to stop the demon gobbling up all the other ghosts, never mind the virgin sacrifice – because something told me that just because the sorcerer directing operations had changed, the treats on offer for the demon's Hallowe'en visit hadn't.

And now Malik's and Tavish's heroic rescue attempt had ended in disaster, Cosette probably intended adding them to her bag of demon treats too. I banged my head back against the stone altar in frustration and anger. With friends like Joseph, Malik really didn't need any enemies.

'So if I'm to be a demon snack' – I raised my voice, waving at the unconscious bodies – 'what's going to happen to the two of them?'

'Um.' Cosette considered Tavish. 'The soul-taster is a problem; he's not dead, so I'm not sure the demon will take him, but we'll see. But as for the vampire, he's going to come in useful for Joseph here, much as Rosa was for you these last three years.' She smiled up at him as he inserted a shunt into my body's arm. I really wanted to wipe that saccharine look off her little girl's face. Later, I promised myself.

'Now I've perfected the Body Transference spell,' she went on, 'it seems wasteful not to use it again, doesn't it, Son?'

'Yes.' He glanced over at me, then inserted a hypodermic needle into a clear glass vial and filled the syringe. 'I understand it can be an interesting experience.'

So Joseph was going to walk around in Malik's body, just as I had in Rosa's. My heart lurched: I might have done the same thing myself, but it was unwittingly, and I'd never had Rosa do anything I wouldn't have done myself. Somehow I didn't think Joseph would take the same care of Malik's body. Not that Rosa had taken that much care of her own body, if her memories were anything to go by. I looked up at her a little speculatively. Was there any way I could use her to get out of this? Cosette had said it wasn't possible earlier, but she had her own agenda, and it wasn't like sorcerers were known for telling the truth. I looked at my two captors, but they were deep in discussion about whatever evil nastiness they were planning now.

Slowly I got up, relieved that Joseph's 'sit down' command must've negated his earlier 'don't move' one. Holding my breath, trying not to catch his attention, I climbed onto the stone altar, wincing as my hands and knees sank inside Rosa's body. I lay down, positioning myself so I merged inside her.

Nothing.

I stared up at the brick-arched ceiling, fists clenched like Rosa's, willing it to work.

Still nothing happened. Damn. I'd really needed Cosette to be wrong on this one. Maybe if I concentrated, tried to think like Rosa, I could spark her into life. I closed my eyes and imagined Joseph tied up in chains. It was a great image; it fed my anger and frustration, but nothing else. Joseph was pleasant-looking – even if his intentions were anything but – but he wasn't exactly eye-candy. Maybe what Rosa needed was for me to think of someone more—

'Psst, I tole you, that don't work, sidhe.' The sharp whisper made me flinch. 'All you gonna do is give 'er nightmares.'

My heart thudding with disbelief, and the tiniest touch of hope, I looked towards the voice.

Moth-girl's white face grinned at me. 'We've come t'rescue you,' she whispered happily. 'Great, innit?'

I rolled out of Rosa's body and off the slab and crouched down next to Moth-girl, hoping that Joseph couldn't see ghosts through stone. 'Who's "we"?'

'Me, Daryl, an' that ovver vamp I stuck wiv the knife, oh, an' yer doctor pal.'

Anxiety spiked through me. Crap, what the hell was Grace doing here?

'I couldn't find that ovver vamp you wanted me to tell, y'know, the Asian-lookin' one,' she went on.

'Doesn't matter,' I said. 'He turned up anyway. What about the police? Did you tell them?'

'Oh yeah, them's coming too,' she sniffed, adding, 'well, maybe.' The grey patchwork of her clothes fluttered with disdain. 'That bitch-witch in charge weren't too impressed wiv my story; 'er and yer doctor pal had a right set-to 'bout it all. So the coppers ain't 'ere yet.'

Damn – did that mean the police would get here before the demon or not? Detective Inspector Helen Crane had to know that midnight was demon dinner time, didn't she? Of course she did, the cynic in me agreed, but wouldn't a delay suit her if it meant I wasn't around to cause her any more problems?

'Hey, don't look like tha'.' Moth-girl's eyes sparkled with excitement. 'We don't need no bleedin' coppers, not when we got ghosts and shades. ''Ere, 'ave a butcher's.' She peeked over the top of the slab, then rose up and rested her chin on her hands, grinning.

I joined her. Scarface shuffled silently in through the doorway. A woman carrying a bunch of withered flowers ambled behind him, then another man limped in; his head wrapped in a dirty bandage. The reek of putrefying flesh filled the air, but this time it was almost welcome. Then there were more ghosts, men and women, all moving silently: a boy with a flat cap leading a small tan and white dog on a string; two dark-haired little girls, about six years old, clutching each others' hands and skipping in their charred frilly dresses; a soldier, his khaki-coloured uniform ripped and bloodstained, using his rifle as a crutch . . . they kept coming.

I watched, bemused. 'Where did they all come from?'

''Mazin', innit?' she whispered gleefully. 'Yer doctor pal just picked up th'Easter egg fing an' opened it, an' whoosh, out they all come. I told 'em to come in 'ere an' disrup' fings.'

I spotted the ghost knife lying at the side of Rosa's stone altar; if I could reach Cosette before Joseph noticed—

'C'mon, then.' I snatched up the knife and rushed round the altar. 'Let's see how much disruption we—'

'Stop.' Joseph's voice reverberated through me, pinning me in place. 'Turn around and go back to the other tunnel.' I watched hopelessly as the ghosts turned as one and started shambling away.

Joseph's brown eyes were blinking fast above his face-mask. He held up the hypodermic in one hand and pushed back his glasses with the back of his wrist as he watched them leave. I stared at Moth-girl's retreating back. I wanted to tell her it was a good try, that no way could she have known Joseph was a necro, or how powerful he was, but I couldn't move. Joseph's command to go back to the other tunnel evidently hadn't applied to me.

He looked over at me, frowning. 'I don't know how you did that, Genny, but—' He stopped and looked around. 'Someone else is here, aren't they?'

I stared up at him from my frozen, half-bent stance, fingers inches away from the knife. He'd asked me a question. I discovered I didn't have to answer.

'Tell me,' he commanded.

'Friends,' my mouth blurted.

'The police? Tell me.'

'No.'

'Who then—?'

A dark blur dropped from the roof as if gliding on black-leather wings and landed on the sacrificial altar, crouching in front of him. Joseph jumped, a startled, high-pitched cry issuing from his mouth. He stabbed at the black blur with his needle, embedding it in the blur's chest. The blur shook itself, snarled and leapt at Joseph, ploughing them both into the machines – which crashed in a crescendo of noise, sparks showering upwards in bright tracer-like arcs. Amidst the chaos, the blur hunched over Joseph and buried its head in his throat and a short, pain-filled scream resounded through the tunnel. Then the scream cut off as a fountain of blood cascaded over the hunched figure, leaving only an echo in its wake.

Had the demon come early?

I launched myself towards the blur, knife still in my hand then stopped to stare down at a blood-drenched but vaguely familiar tawny head of hair. The owner was now gnawing its way through Joseph's throat. The sounds of tearing flesh and muscle and the quick snap of bone and the metallic scent of blood made my stomach roil, and brought the snakes hissing and slithering in agitation over my skin.

'My Daryl got 'im!' Moth-girl fluttered to my side, punched her arm in the air and whooped, 'My Daryl got that fucker ghost-grabber!'

Darius the lap-dancing vampire lifted his head and gave her a gore-covered grin. 'Your plan worked great, didn't it, Shaz?' he said, pushing himself up on all fours and rising to his feet in an oddly inhuman move.

He unzipped his black leather coat and slipped out of it; underneath he wore just his sequinned Calvin Kleins – not even any boots. Didn't he have any other clothes? He shook the coat, and blood and other heavier bits splattered to the concrete floor, then he shrugged it back on, zipped it back up and licked his lips. 'Real great.' He grinned again.

I looked down.

Joseph was lying there, his glasses askew on his mangled head, the white of his spine glistening in the bright red abstract of his neck, his legs at an odd angle. I was still puzzled by Joseph. He'd seemed . . . well, nice, and strangely naïve when I'd first met him. But evil doesn't always show its face as ugliness, or fangs, or strangeness. That would be much too easy.

And yeah, Moth-girl's plan had worked real great! It might not have been pretty, but Joseph was gone, and I couldn't feel anything other than satisfaction.

But now there was the rest of it to finish.

I looked over at my body, still lying on the sacrificial altar, wondering why Cosette hadn't put in an appearance. Then I saw the reason for her absence: sticking out of my body's chest was the handle of the soul-bonder knife, the oval amber of the dragon's tear winking in the candlelight. Darius must've have attacked Joseph mid-ritual, so Cosette was trapped—

'Genny,' an anxious voice called from behind me, 'is that you?'

I clutched anxiously at the ghost knife as I turned. Grace peered at me as she hurried through the archway, her pink-check jacket flapping over her blue doctor's scrubs, her frizz of black curls flattened and tangled with cobwebs on one side, dust streaking the dark skin of her left cheek like a half-finished war stripe. She carried the open Fabergé egg in one hand and led the tearful florist's lad with her other, her backpack slung over her shoulder. Heartfelt relief flooded into me. They were both still alive.

Bobby stalked behind Grace like some sort of übergoth warrior in his all-black Mr October outfit, his hair neatly pulled back in his trademark French plait. He carried Moth-girl's body in his arms. 'Hey, Sharon,' he called, 'are you getting back in here, or do you want me to keep carrying you around?'

Grace dropped the lad's hand and rushed up to me – the ghost me – and flung her arm round me in a tight hug. 'Thank the Goddess you're okay, Genny. I've been so worried about you.' The snakes flared, then settled, but she didn't appear to notice them. She also appeared to find me very solid, and that meant it was close to midnight, when the dead could converse – and more, if they wanted – with the living.

I hugged her back just as hard, keeping the ghost knife safely pressed to my thigh, breathing in her comforting floral perfume with its faint underlay of antiseptic. 'Thanks for coming to the rescue, Grace,' I murmured, totally inadequately, 'and I'm fine now – but what on earth happened to you?'

She trembled slightly, then sniffed and gave a nervous laugh. 'That Souler chap, Neil, jumped out at me when I went to help the lad here. Stupid really, I should've checked for someone guarding him first.' She gave another hiccoughing laugh and hitched up her backpack. 'I don't think I'm cut out for this action-rescue business. Although I did bring spells.' She pulled away and looked back at Bobby, a slightly scared expression on her face. 'But Bobby took care of him.'

Bobby had laid Moth-girl's body down on a clear patch of floor and was now staring at Rosa where she lay on her stone slab.

'Took care of him, how?' I asked, frowning.

'Oh, he didn't bite him.' Grace blinked, her pupils nearly eclipsing the dark brown of her irises. 'He just threw him against the wall.' She did that hiccoughing laugh-thing again and I realised she was suffering from mild shock . . . but then, treating victims in a nice bright clinic like HOPE, even the violent ones, took a different type of courage to venturing underground with a couple of vamps and a sometimes ghost girl. 'He's dead – broken neck. I checked,' Grace added with another blink.

Good riddance, he'd certainly got what was coming to him. But Grace didn't need to hear that right now. I hugged her again and murmured, 'Hey, it's okay, you're doing brilliantly, and the lad's safe now, thanks to you.' I looked at the boy in question, who was standing there shivering, hunched over—

Then a thought hit me like a sucker-punch to my stomach.

Grace had broken the circle to get the florist's boy and the Fabergé egg out.

And that meant there would be no magic to contain the demon when it turned up. And without even the tenuous boundaries of a graveyard to hold it, it would be free to roam *anywhere*! *And it would be free to take anyone – not just the dead!*

I had to get everyone out.

And I had to get the circle closed again.

'You need to get out of here, Grace,' I cried, letting her go, 'and take the lad with you. MOVE! Now!'

A rumble shivered the ground.

Grace froze, her eyes wide with shock and fright.

I pushed urgently at her, yelling, 'You need to get out, all of you, get out now—!'

The rumble came again; this time dust and bits of brick fell from the ceiling and muted explosions like a hundred-gun salute reverberated through the tunnel.

'What the bleedin' 'ell is that?' Moth-girl squealed.

'Fireworks,' Bobby shouted, looking warily up at the arched roof. 'The trolls are having one of their Hallowe'en parties up on London Bridge.'

'Run,' I shouted again. 'It's midnight.'

Chapter Thirty-two

Midnight.

All Hallows' Eve.

It's the time of year when the veil between the living and the dead dissipates . . .

. . . and demons come trick-or-treating.

This particular demon had dressed up for the occasion in a navy lounge suit, his pale blue shirt open at the throat and fastened at the cuffs with links of heart-shaped sapphires the size of thumbnails. His top pocket sported a silk handkerchief the same colour as his shirt. He exuded 'relaxed man-about-town' charisma, but as he surveyed the room, the azure of his eyes shone colder and sharper than the sapphires at his wrists. The demon had dressed up as the Earl, London's ex-head big-cheese vamp, the vamp I'd killed, and the star of my nightmare after the bakery explosion.

I tried to see the irony in that, except my mind was still short-circuiting with fear.

'Genevieve, my dear, how nice to see you again.' The demon gave me the Earl's charming smile. Centuries of practice meant he showed no hint of his fangs. 'Well now, this is all terribly interesting.'

Interesting wasn't quite the word I'd have chosen. Everyone apart from Moth-girl and me was frozen in place; she hovered next to Darius, scared, but with a defiant expression on her white-painted face. I frowned as my mind finally came up with a question. Demons aren't usually the chatty sort, more the fast-food type. He was loose, there was no circle to contain him, and we were in an unconsecrated graveyard. Why hadn't the demon just gobbled us all up?

Or maybe he really was the Earl, and all this demon stuff was new to him.

'So did you turn into a demon when you died, or what?' I asked, surprised my voice came out steady.

'Oh no, my dear, this is just a guise – I found his soul wondering unclaimed in the pit and decided I liked the look of it.' He adjusted his handkerchief. 'I thought you might appreciate its appearance, as you are somewhat acquainted with each other.' He grimaced slightly. 'Although I have found his personality is a bit ingrained after all his time in the mortal world – I do keep getting this urge to talk at length about certain things, like the ongoing rights of vampires. It is mildly irritating.'

'Feel free to go back to hell and change,' I said offhandedly, keeping the ghost knife close to my thigh. A vague plan started to form in my mind; the tunnels were on the south side of the Thames, so the river had to be to the north. 'Don't let us keep you,' I added.

'Ah, but our time is so short, a mere hour, so it appears I will need to continue with him for now. So, onto our evening's purpose.' He rubbed his hands briskly. 'I see there is a good collection of souls, spirits and shades on offer next door. Some are a little the worse for wear, but nonetheless acceptable.' He walked over to study the florist's lad. 'And I do approve of the virgin.' He sniffed at the boy's neck. 'It's been a few years since I've been presented with one. They appear to be rather hard to find nowadays.'

'To be honest, virgin sacrifices rather went out with the Dark Ages,' I said flatly, cautiously unhooking Grace's backpack from her unresisting arm. The painting of the barren landscape at the end of the tunnel room showed the sun setting. Whatever the painting's use was, no sorcerer would have anything that depicted the world incorrectly; it would screw with their magic. I looked along past the painting, so north had to be . . . there.

'Actually it was *after* the Dark Ages,' the Earl said pedantically. 'But that is a discussion for another time. What are you doing, my dear?'

I carefully tucked the ghost knife under my arm, then unzipped the bag and stuck my hand in. 'Seeing if my friend bought any Holy or Blessed Water with her.'

'She didn't,' he said, sounding pleased. 'Most remiss of her.'

I rummaged around. He was right, she hadn't; but I was looking for other things too. My fingers closed round a paper bag of small lumps of a putty-like substance and what felt like a large squishy pack of cotton-wool balls – the spells Grace had brought with her. Other than a bottle of water and some medical stuff, there was nothing else, so they would have to do.

The Earl prodded Malik's tranqed body with his navy loafer and nodded to himself, then strolled up to Darius. He looked him up and down as if contemplating buying, then reached a hand out to the zipper on his black leather coat.

'Oy, leave 'im alone,' Moth-girl snarled at him.

The Earl snarled back, his mouth yawning wide, plunging us into a deep, dark abyss, so deep you knew there was no end, that you'd be forever falling, forever screaming, forever terrified, forever burning, with the darkness and the flames eating you up, over and over again—

Then we were back in the tunnel room, the candles flickering over the roof, sweat beading my forehead and the hot trickle of piss wetting my jeans, and Grace's floral perfume chasing away the reek of brimstone and sulphur.

Moth-girl had collapsed to her hands and knees and was retching violently.

For a moment I thought I would join her as my fingers convulsed around the squishy cotton-wool spells and I swallowed painfully, my throat as raw as if I really had been screaming for aeons . . .

The Earl went back to unzipping Darius' coat. He took a long look, then walked towards Bobby, who was still standing next to Rosa's body. He ran his hand over Bobby's head, taking the French braid and weighing it in one hand. He leaned down to place a kiss on Rosa's slightly parted lips and as he straightened, he reached out and tapped a fingernail almost thoughtfully against the gold locket that lay between her breasts.

I grabbed the mass of cotton-wool balls – *Security Stingers ~ the Ultimate Intruder Deterrent* – and threw them at him, willing them through the air. *Please let this work*, I prayed, as the spells zoomed towards him like a swarm of bees. The majority crashed or stuck to the wall behind him, but some whizzed and buzzed around his head, trailing streams of fine sticky threads that drifted like fibre-glass in the air. He gave a casual wave of his hand, as if batting them away, and they crashed with all the others against the wall.

He turned to give me an amused, slightly puzzled look.

My heart sped in my chest as my hand closed round the lumps of putty: Sticky-Sleep spells. I pulled them out, dropping the backpack and the knife, and started lobbing them at him. A couple hit the stone altar, splattering like chewing gum; one caught Bobby on the cheek and burst into a blaze of white powder. I winced; that was going to knock him out for a good eight hours – if he was still around to be knocked out, of course – but the rest slammed harmlessly to the wall behind the Earl.

'Genevieve, did you really think those paltry little magics would affect me?' He gave a long-suffering sigh and looked behind him at the wall. 'And to be honest, my dear, your aim is not what it might be.'

I dropped my shoulders in defeat.

He was right; they were cheap little spells, nothing more than anyone could buy at the witches' market. But I couldn't think of anything else. And at least if my plan worked, it might save some of them. It was better than just giving in.

Moth-girl sat back on her heels and wiped the back of her hand over her mouth. She gave me a scared, tremulous smile, then cautiously sneered at the Earl.

He walked over to my body, laid out on the waist-high stone altar. He took careful hold of the soul-bonder knife with his thumb and forefinger and pulled it out, then placed it next to my body's hip. I clenched my fists as an even more desperate idea came to me. If I could get to the knife . . .

Then he shoved his hand inside my body's chest and yanked out a struggling Cosette and held her up, dangling her by her neck.

'Hello, Gwen, my dear,' he said, this time flashing fangs as he smiled. 'I am so delighted to meet up with you again. I was devastated after we missed each other last year – as I am sure that you must have been. It has been such an age since we last conversed, has it not?' He snapped his fingers and Joseph's ghost appeared, his owl-like eyes blinking behind his glasses. 'And here is your charming son, Joseph. You have kept him out of the limelight, but I must say, I am overjoyed to make his acquaintance at last.'

Then he opened his mouth . . .

I blinked—

. . . and they were both gone.

The Earl was now looking down at Tavish. The tranqed kelpie slept on peacefully, his gills flaring with each breath he took, one hand outstretched as if pointing towards Bobby and Rosa. I'd seen him sleep like that, nestled into the mud and sand of the riverbed.

'A soul-taster, no less.' The Earl smiled merrily at me. 'My, my, there really is an abundance of riches here, is there not, my dear? The gathering of shades and souls out there—' he waved a limp hand towards the open doorway— 'four vampires, three tasty little humans, two necromancers, a soul-taster, and a long-lost sorcerer.' He almost sang the list, making it sound like a cheerful little Christmas carol.

Suddenly he was standing next to me.

I swallowed again, my mouth dry as dust, my throat still painful.

'Then of course, there is you,' he said softly. 'But I fear we are still missing someone.' He circled behind me, trailing a fingertip across the back of my neck. I froze, my heart stuttering in sudden terror. The snakes woke up, slithering and shivering under my skin. 'My, you have been enterprising,' he went on, still speaking softly. 'It has been a long time since a sidhe has fully consumed a soul, and I do not believe one has ever consumed a soul belonging to a sorcerer – a soul that has already been marked as mine.'

'What do you want?' I asked, my voice harsh.

'What do I want?' As he leaned in to whisper in my ear a musty sulphur stench seared along my cheek. 'I want an avatar, my dear, someone to do my business in this mortal world, someone whose body is more resilient than a human's, someone whose body will not grow old . . . Someone who will always be here for me.'

'I am not that someone,' I said, clenching my hands to stop from screaming.

'No?' He sounded thoughtful. 'Then choose one, Genevieve.'

'Choose one what?'

'A soul, of course.' He stepped back and spread his arms wide. 'There are more than enough on offer.'

'No.'

'Well then, I shall take them all.'

'W—ait a b—leedin' minute 'ere,' stuttered Moth-girl, stumbling to her feet, her dress fluttering like frightened wings. 'If she ain't gonna choose, then I get to. You c'n take me.'

'Shut up, Moth—Sharon,' I snapped.

'No, I knows 'ow this works,' she hissed. 'If I'm willin' to sacrifice, then he don't get t'take any of 'em ovvers. Only fing is—' Her voice cracked and she stopped for a moment, then went on, 'You've gotta promise to look after my Daryl – 'e's a smart enuff, but 'e's a bit soft, see.'

'All terribly commendable, I must say.' The Earl gave her an amused, patronising smile. He leaned down to her and whispered, 'So you're willing to spend eternity suffering in the fiery pits of Hell to save your friends, are you?'

She gulped. 'It ain't a real pit, is it?' she whispered back. 'Me Gran allays said as 'ow it's jus' the vicar's make-believe so's we'd be good.'

'Hell is what you make it,' he said solemnly, then as he straightened, he chuckled. 'Or maybe Hell is what *I* make it. But unfortunately, my dear' – he touched her forehead with his finger – 'your basic information is wrong. You see, the willing sacrifice only works when you are dealing with gods, and I, luckily, am not a god, but a demon, and that whole righteous, holier-than-thou martyrdom that the willing have just takes all the profit out of the job. And thus that particular rule does not apply to me.'

'Bleedin' 'ell,' Moth-girl cried, 'so what's the point in 'er choosin'?'

'Trick or treat, Sharon,' I murmured, bending down to pick up the ghost knife, then walking slowly to stand next to my body, still going over the flimsy plan in my head. Nerves twisted in my stomach; I kept expecting him to stop me – then I decided he was probably arrogant enough to let me try whatever it was I was going to do, since I couldn't possibly win against him.

I really hoped he was wrong.

'He wants me to think that I can save the rest by choosing just one,' I carried on. 'That's the treat – but the trick is: it's actually the other way round. Only the one I choose will live, so long as I do what he wants, of course. Isn't that right, demon?'

'It appears the joke is against me, my dear,' the Earl sighed. 'I was so looking forward to that part of the proceedings. So now I believe I will rescind my offer of a boon.'

''E can't do that, can 'e?' Moth-girl cried, frantic.

I *looked* at the wall behind Rosa and Bobby. The spells caught there glowed like pinholes of light against the dark stone, their magics small and insubstantial. Was it going to be enough? Not that it made much difference; it was the only option I had. It either worked or it didn't.

'I'm a demon, my dear.' He shot his cuffs and smoothed the lapels of his jacket. 'There is no blessed blood and bone to curtail me, it is All Hallows' Eve, and so, I am delighted to say, I can take any soul not already claimed by another.'

'Wot, even them's not dead yet?'

I *focused* on the heart of all those tiny spells, concentrating my will.

'Well, perhaps not technically,' he said, smiling, flashing fang, 'but life – human life particularly – is such a transient part of our existence.' He stood in front of Grace and brushed his knuckles gently down her cheek, then hooked his finger into her scrubs. 'This one is the only soul here barred to me.' He pulled out a gold chain; a small pentacle glinted on the end of it. 'But then again' – he smiled cheerfully – 'I can still have fun dismembering her along with all the rest of you.'

I *cracked* the magic.

The wall exploded inwards, throwing brick and rubble across the room, and a torrent of murky water gushed through a hole the size of a drain cover, sweeping all before it.

The Thames had come to join us.

Tavish and the vamps would be okay; they could survive under water, and so could the souls and shades, since they were already dead. It was the three humans I feared for most; I prayed Grace, Moth-girl and the florist's lad could all swim better than me.

Within seconds the water was swirling around my knees, then it was up to my thighs. I turned to face the Earl, my heart pounding with fear and hope.

He stood in the gushing torrent, the faintly amused smile still on his face, as if the water was nothing more than a childish trick I'd played on him.

Fuck, this *so* had to work.

'Demon,' I shouted over the thundering waves, 'under River Lore, all souls here belong to the kelpie, and so I claim.'

His face *shifted*, his eyes blazing into burning red holes, his mouth stretching into the blackness of the abyss, the water bubbling and boiling into steam around him as he advanced towards me. I grabbed the soul-bonder knife in my other hand and, praying to whatever gods might be listening, waited until he was close enough, then stabbed both blades up and into his chest.

The River Thames closed over my head.

Epilogue

I woke to a sky that glittered and twinkled with rainbow-coloured lights, only this time it wasn't an angel that peered down at me out of the mist, but something else, something oddly smooth and unformed, as though it had yet to be sculpted into something finished. I blinked, and the face above me resolved itself into something more normal; the rainbow lights reflected wetly in the highly polished skin, the mouth split in a wide smile revealing worn stumps of brown-coloured teeth, and I recognised Mr Travers, my landlord.

'Hello, Genny,' he rumbled loudly above the bangs and shrieks of the fireworks. A drop of water collected on the end of his shiny nose and fell to splatter on my chin. 'Good to see you back in the land of the living.' More fireworks exploded into a cacophony of multi-coloured stars above his head.

My stomach rebelled and I rolled over, retching and coughing, the rank taste of sulphur and the river souring my mouth.

'That's it, better out than in.' A large hand thumped my back. 'Your insides will thank you for it . . .'

*   *   *

Now I stand in the gardens of St Paul's Church in Covent Garden. It's quiet here, the traffic a muted rumble as if far away. The sun is shining, but the November wind is cold, a harbinger of the winter to come. The grass is crisp with frost beneath my feet and my breath steams into the air. A memory of water boiling and bubbling around me tries to intrude and I push it back, shut it in the box in my mind and turn the key. The demon is gone. For now. The snakes lie quiet beneath my skin and Mr Travers smiles, a sad, careful smile, as he offers me a pink paper candle holder on a stem. I wrap my numb fingers around it and hold it up in front of me like a torch of hope.

All Souls' Day.

We are here to pray for the dead.

Mr Travers holds a taper to the small tea-light I clutch, and I watch as the wick flares with a tiny bright flame. My hand trembles and his face creases into deep, concerned lines. Anxious dust puffs above his head ridge and he glances around as if seeking help. But then his soft beige eyes come back to mine and he smiles his slow, careful smile and pats my shoulder.

The service starts, the words rising and falling around me like the ebb and flow of a distant sea.

The trolls came to our rescue that night, jumping from their Hallowe'en party on the bridge, straight down into the murky river. Mr Travers has refused to leave my side since he pulled me out from under the bridge's foundations. He tells me that us fae are all heroes now, you only have to look at the papers. One tabloid shouted: **ALL HALLOWS' FRIGHT NIGHT: SIDHE v. DEMON**. Another ran with **NAIADS AID WITCHES IN THEIR MIDNIGHT HOUR OF NEED** . . . *working together to cast a circle through earth and water and air to prevent the demon escaping to terrorise London.* Of course, not all the reports were as positive: **LONDON BRIDGE IS FALLING DOWN** . . . **AGAIN** – *Bridge closed for foreseeable future while structural repairs are carried out. The cost to the taxpayer* . . .

The florist's lad – his name is Colin – is recovering at HOPE from a combination of shock and minor cuts and bruises.

They're also monitoring him for any less-than-healthy effects of his October swim in the River Thames.

Bobby and Rosa are both still missing. The general consensus is that their bodies were taken by the current, and since neither was aware at the time – Rosa because her soul is bonded to her locket, Bobby thanks to the Sticky-Sleep spell I'd accidentally tagged him with – they would have been at the mercy of the river. The naiads have searched in all the usual places, but so far their bodies haven't been found. Of course, it's possible that Rosa could endure an extended period underwater; she's at least two centuries old, but Bobby's chances are less optimistic. A group of his fang-fans are holding a candlelit vigil from sunset tonight until tomorrow's dawn.

Sharon, my Moth-girl, didn't make it. The naiads found her body under the rubble that exploded out of the wall. So far her ghost hasn't surfaced among the shades and spirits the naiads say are again haunting the tunnels in the bridge's foundations. Darius – her Daryl – is holed up at the bloodhouse in Sucker Town where she lived with the other Moths. I never actually made the promise to look out for him, but I'll be keeping it anyway. Soon.

Ex-Police Constable Janet Sims has been charged with the murder of Tomas, her baker boyfriend – the redtops are calling it a crime of passion – and the murder of Witch Wilcox, her maternal grandmother. Mr Travers tells me they are debating whether she is to be burnt at the stake or not. Technically she's not a witch, just a witch's daughter, but now she has her granny's power, she's too dangerous to leave mouldering in a jail cell, however magically protected it might be.

The Fabergé egg has not been found.

Movement around me draws my attention back to this cold, bright, November day.

The witches are noticeable by their absence.

My gaze slips past the assembled trolls towards the side of the church, where London's fae are gathered. A sleek silver-coated dog sits to attention at the front, her pointed ears pricked forward, her grey eyes watchful and quiet. Lady Meriel is next, her waterfall of hair almost translucent in the daylight; half a dozen of her naiads, dressed in sharp sharkskin suits and human Glamours, are fanned out behind her.

Then there is Lady Isabella, a black pill box hat perched high on her forehead, the clipped skin of her head gleaming pale green like the first weak shoots of spring. She leans on the arm of a tall dryad, his black Stetson hanging down his back, a stubble of twigs dotting his own forest-green skull. The dryads who attacked me have survived, but only through her personal intervention. They have returned to their trees to finish their healing.

Off to one side is Finn, flanked by two of his brothers; they are all standing solemn and tall in their tailored black suits, their horns barely noticeable above the dark blond waves of their hair. Mr Travers tells me Finn spent All Hallows' Eve in the cells at Old Scotland Yard; Detective Inspector Helen Crane arrested him for obstructing the police in their duty. She's since dropped all charges. I haven't spoken to him. Not yet. But I know he waits for my answer to his suit, much as the *droch guidhe* waits in my mind for my own decision.

Tavish stands alone, his green-black dreads beaded with black, wraparound shades hiding the silver of his eyes, his long black greatcoat shifting restlessly in the wind.

He tells me Malik is fine.

Then, between one breath and the next, the world is silenced.

And the phouka, Grianne, stands before me in her human form, the ash-grey tips of her ankle-length fur coat quivering in the stillness.

'Clíona, my queen, wishes me to convey her deep appreciation for the safe return of her lady.' Grianne's voice is low, her own gratitude echoing through it. 'She would offer you this as a reward.' She holds out her hand and a gold apple materialises on her palm; the faint scent of liquorice catches my senses.

I stare at it blankly.

'You are not the first fae to suffer *salaich sìol*, child,' she continues gently, 'and the purge does not always remove the vampire's taint. But if the apple is not to your taste' – she clicks her teeth together and silver-painted blackberries appear in the apple's place – 'I have these.' Their juice stains her palm with the darkness of a vampire's blood. 'Try one,' she urges softly.

In the far reaches of my mind, a quiet warning whispers about fairy tales, temptation and poison. I hesitate.

'I would not waste your death on poisoned fruit, child.' She smiles, black fangs sharp, an eerie yellow glow lighting her pale grey eyes and the wind brings me a whiff of her butcher's shop scent. 'My word: there is no harm.'

Her word is more than her honour; the magic sees to that. Not that the numb part of me truly cares. I pick up one of the berries. My mouth waters as I inhale its warm fragrance and I place it between my lips. Ripe juice flavoured with liquorice bursts on my tongue and I close my eyes as it trickles like sweet blood down my throat. A haze of well-being, stronger than I expect from one small fruit, shivers through my body.

'See child, no harm,' Grianne murmurs as her black-tipped nails place another berry in my mouth. 'My queen would also offer you sanctuary.' She has raised her voice. 'Her offer is extended for a year and a day; as long as you refuse to bear a child.'

A ripple of emotion runs through the gathered fae.

The phouka's promise and threat is clear to all.

The queen has given me her *protection*. She has also, intentionally or not, given me a year and a day to find a way to break the *droch guidhe*, other than the fae's current solution . . . but then I will need to make my choice.

Sanctuary or death.

When I sleep, I dream.

Once again I stab the knives into the demon.

Once again his mouth opens and the abyss yawns deep and dark below me.

Once again I start to fall . . .

And Grace wraps her hands around mine and pulls, and the knives slide from his chest, black blood pumping into the water like swirling ink. She pushes me down onto the altar, presses me back into my body and leans over me, smiling. Her curls float like a dark halo around her head. Her eyes are resolute, unwavering, determined; her hands are confident but gentle as she fastens the pentacle around my throat. Above and behind her the darkness of the abyss rears up, reaching . . .

* * *

Now I stand in the gardens of St Paul's Church. I look up at the cloudless blue sky above and watch as a lone black crow glides through all that emptiness. The same emptiness that fills my every thought, my every cell, and all my soul.

All Souls' Day.

I am here to pray for the dead.

I am here to pray for Grace.

Acknowledgements

My heartfelt thanks go to those who have helped this book on its way.

To Fiona MacKenzie for her endless enthusiasm, pep talks and splashes of red; Alison Aquilina for the 'feelings'; Malcolm Angel for the 'action'; Judy Monckton for those all-important questions; Doreen Cory for those 'bon mots'! And Paul Knight for finding Tavish's perfect 'home'.

To the Gollancz crew for their dedication, to John Jarrold for his belief and support, and especially to Jo Fletcher for all her fantastic work in continuing to make my books so much better.

To Norman for being the wonderful, patient person he is and for making this, my second book, truly possible.

And last, but not least, to all those readers who have told me how much they enjoyed *The Sweet Scent of Blood*, a huge, huge thank-you; it means more than you can ever know.

Continue Genny's story in

THE BITTER SEED OF MAGIC

Coming January 2012 from Ace Books

Explore the outer reaches
of imagination—don't miss these authors
of dark fantasy and urban noir who take you
to the edge and beyond . . .

Patricia Briggs	Anne Bishop
Simon R. Green	Marjorie M. Liu
Jim Butcher	Jeanne C. Stein
Kat Richardson	Christopher Golden
Karen Chance	Ilona Andrews
Rachel Caine	Anton Strout

penguin.com/scififantasy